Better Believe It

Fern Ronay

Better Believe It
Red Adept Publishing, LLC
104 Bugenfield Court
Garner, NC 27529
http://RedAdeptPublishing.com/

First Print Edition: December 2019

Cover Art by Streetlight Graphics

For my mother

Prologue

The first time I got my heart broken, I was five years old. It happened in the kitchen. My sister, Orly, was a toddler, still in diapers, waddling around and babbling. I was sitting at the kitchen table, perfecting my writing of the alphabet on red construction paper. Using a freshly sharpened black crayon, I swung out the curve of my *u* too wide when I heard the bang. Orly had bumped into the cabinet as she turned the corner from the dining room and fell back on her head.

"Wahhhh," she wailed.

My mother whipped around, dish towel swung over her shoulder, and bent to pick up my sister. She spoke in the syrupy voice she only used when speaking to Orly. "What happened? Where are you hurt?"

"She bumped into the cabinet and fell," I said as I formed the second leg of my letter *v*.

"Oh, my little chickpea." My mother sang the words to Orly.

I had asked her once, "If Orly is your little chickpea, what am I?"

"I don't know, Jada. You're my..." She paused to light a cigarette. "You're my kidney bean."

"Do you like kidney beans?"

"They give me *agida*." She blew smoke in the other direction, a stream flowing from her lips, which a few hours earlier had been lined with red lip liner and filled in with matching red lipstick. *Red. Always red.* "Fix your barrette. Did ya have it like that all day in school? Ya have to know how to fix your own barrette." She had pointed at the side of my head. "Get those side hairs. Over here. The side ones. Do ya want to look like a ragamuffin?"

Now, as I continued alphabet writing at the kitchen table, my mother rocked her whimpering chickpea.

Is she singing? I stopped mid *w*. *What is this song? I like it. She never sang it to me before. She's not a singing mom. She doesn't sing.*

"Hush, little baby." She swayed back and forth by the kitchen window.

I would like a mockingbird and a diamond ring.

She stopped once Orly was calm and distracted by the paper towel roll in her hands.

I finished the alphabet and held up my construction paper. "I did it! And on red paper, your favorite color." I brought it over to my mother so she could get a better look.

"Nice," she said as she stretched her neck past Orly's resting head and Orly's left hand, which bopped me on the head with the paper towel roll.

"Hold on." I walked around to the other side, so she didn't have to strain her head. "See?"

"I see, Jada. Very good."

I made her hold it.

"Uh-huh, good. Is that supposed to be an H? It curves in. Looks like a capital A."

She was right. It wasn't perfect. *What was I thinking? That H does look like an A. That H is horrible. That H is disgusting.* I ripped it up.

"What did ya do that for?" my mother screamed. "Pick those pieces up. Why would ya do that?"

"It wasn't perfect," I hollered back, flipping through the construction paper for a fresh, new sheet. "Hold on."

I started over, and by the time I finished and checked every letter, I was confident in my redo. I held it up to double-check. *Yup, perfect.*

By then, Orly was napping, and my mother was smoking a cigarette on the porch.

I carried the new masterpiece with my fingertips toward the porch. "Look now."

She blew smoke out the enclosed porch's window as she reviewed my letters. "Good."

"Why don't you ever sing to me?"

"Huh? Oh, Jada, for Christ's sake." She took a long drag while I waited for an answer. "Because you're the big sister. That's why. Go clear the crayons off the kitchen table. We're going to have dinner soon."

"I like songs. I liked that song a lot." I swayed from one foot to another, willing her to sing to me now.

"Jada, please! Go clear the table before your father gets home."

I threw the crayons in the box instead of placing them neatly in rainbow order like I normally did. *Little sisters are smaller and cuter and get sung to.* I snapped the plastic container shut. *But I go to school. Yeah, I'm smarter than a stupid little baby.* I carried the construction paper and crayons up to my room and slammed the door behind me. *I hate being a big sister.*

Chapter 1

I hate my husband.

Mark was a hard-working, successful intellectual-property attorney and a good father to our three-year-old son, Ethan. But every time he opened his mouth, I cringed.

I watched him push Ethan on the swing as I sat on a bench a few yards away. Every time he pulled the swing back, he would say in a high pitch, "Up, up, up." And when he let go, he would say in a low baritone, "Down, down, downnntown."

I surveyed my surroundings. All I had access to at the moment was a large, heavy stroller piled high with a bag of supplies, most of which were never used, like the first aid kit, emergency change of clothes, emergency change of underwear, and boxes of juice.

Can I stab myself in the neck with a juice straw? Will it kill me? Will it end this misery?

I assumed I felt that way because I was wasn't grateful enough. I had only myself to blame. I had to get better at gratitude. My friend Veronica Buccino Blackman was always rattling off all the things she was grateful for, and I could only ever come up with "I'm grateful for chocolate." *Dark. At least 70 percent cacao. The higher, the better.* And I was grateful for quiet people on the train. People who talked on their cell phones on the train—or worse, people who tried to make conversation on the train—were the worst people in the world. Quiet people were so underappreciated.

The sun was directly overhead, pulsing hot rays through my skull. I scanned the park for another bench in the shade, but the one to my left was occupied by the mom of twin girls around Ethan's age and their schnauzer, Popcorn. Popcorn was a park regular. He was cute but a notorious toe licker. *Disgusting.* My sandaled toes curled in repulsion. The bench to my right was empty, but it didn't provide all that much shade. Still, I reached for Ethan's stroller, and as I struggled to move it, his *Buddy the Bulldozer* remote control fell. *Ugh.* We were already on our third replacement. Luckily, Ethan didn't see that as he was going "downnnntown." I recoiled.

As I pushed the stroller toward the other bench, still in sight line with Mark's broad shoulders pulling back the swing, he called for me. "Hey, Jada. Jay. Jay!"

I shielded my eyes from the sun. "What?"

"Can you bring over a juice?"

I stepped down on the stroller brake, popped a straw in a juice box, and walked over to the swings.

Ethan took one sip and declared, "No. I want applesauce."

I walked back to the stroller, retrieved an applesauce, twisted off the cap, and walked back over to the swings.

Ethan took one mouthful and declared, "No. I want to get pushed."

So I went back to my bench, but not before I got them to smile for a picture. I posted it with the caption, "Another perfect day in the park with my boys!" and a heart emoji. I plopped down on the bench and wondered what wrong turn I'd taken in life to get to this point.

Is this it? Is this happiness? Sitting in a park on a Saturday in the summer, watching kids drip their snot all over the slides and monkey bars? Serving up juice and applesauce? Hating your husband?

"Popcorn!" The frantic scream came from behind me. Popcorn ran as fast as he could right toward me. I wondered what he was gunning so hard for all of a sudden. *The nearly full juicebox?* Then he ran right past me. *The exit?*

I stood, stretching my neck toward the wrought iron gates of the park so my eyes could follow Popcorn's path. *Run, Popcorn! Run!* I found myself cheering inside. *Go, Popcorn! Go! Freedom awaits!*

"Potty time." I hadn't noticed Mark's approach. He and Ethan were red-faced and smiling after their marathon session on the swings.

"I need the potty!" Ethan said.

"Okay." I glanced around for the closest trash can to throw away the virtually untouched juice and applesauce now baking in my hands. *Ick.* I let go above the garbage can.

"I want applesauce!" Ethan announced a nanosecond after it hit the bottom of the metal trash can.

Of course. I rifled through the diaper bag for more pouches, but I was fresh out. "At home. There are more at home. Let's go."

"I want appa sauce!" he wailed. All of the swing glow was replaced with pure rage just like that, like flipping a switch.

"Did you have fun on the swings with Daddy?" I asked in a sugary tone that felt as fake as it sounded.

"I want appa sauce!" He'd started throwing in some stiff arm and leg movements.

Mark was unfazed, thoroughly going over each of the fingers on his right hand with an antibacterial wipe.

I bit my top lip. "All right. To the car. Now. Come on."

Ethan was a wailing, flailing animal, and I was his captor. I finally succeeded at strapping him into the stroller and sustained only one punch to the nose.

Mark was going over his left hand with the antibacterial wipe, one finger at a time.

I started pushing the stroller toward the car. "Can you push this so I can find my keys?"

"Wait." Mark looked up from his hand cleansing. "He has to use the potty."

"We don't use the bathrooms here since they found a syringe in the sink two months ago."

"Oh." Mark leaned into the stroller. "Hey, buddy, we'll be home soon, and we'll get you on the potty, and then maybe we'll play in the backyard. We'll play cops and robbers or Batman and Robin."

"Batman!" Ethan shouted all the way to the car.

I unstrapped Ethan and hoisted him into his car seat.

"All right, buddy. Batman it is." Mark reached behind me to high-five Ethan.

After Ethan was buckled in, I whispered to Mark, "Hey, after you play with him for a little bit outside, can you put him down for his nap? I have to set the table and straighten up the TV room."

I didn't want Ethan to hear his least favorite word: nap.

"Sure thing," Mark said.

Sure thing? How did I end up married to Mr. Rogers?

Mark pulled the plastic bag of celery sticks out of the diaper bag and started munching in his usual manner. *Chomp. Chomp, chomp, chomp. Chomp.*

I turned up the sound on the radio. *Save me, Bruce Springsteen.* As we pulled away from the park, I glanced out the side window.

That was when I spotted Popcorn. His owner had him clutched tightly under the forelegs. His ears, her ponytail, and the blond bobs of the twins all bounced in unison as they marched toward their car.

I'm sorry, Popcorn. At least you tried.

• • ❧ • •

RALPH LAUREN PLATE. Ralph Lauren fork. Ralph Lauren knife. Ralph Lauren spoon. Polo napkins.

While Ethan was still napping—*Hallelujah!*—and Mark was reading in the living room, I finished setting the table for my mother, father, sister, brother-in-law, and two nieces, plus myself, Mark, and Ethan. We were celebrating my parents' anniversary that night.

Ralph Lauren salad bowl. Ralph Lauren bread plate.

"I thought this was clothes," Orly had said when I, for some reason, took her with me to Saks Fifth Avenue to register for my bridal shower a few years ago. She couldn't understand my choice in Ralph Lauren dinnerware.

"Yeah, they make clothes, but they also have a dinnerware line. It's tasteful."

"That's weird," she said.

"Is it?" I tried to sound unbothered when what I really wanted to ask her was why anything that didn't match her or my mother's taste—they were one and the same—was considered "weird." Maybe if she had ever left Queens, anything new and different might not be so "weird," like a brand that licensed their name for dinnerware.

I was in the middle of being annoyed by the memory when I heard, "Mommyyy!"

"Can you get him?" I called to Mark, who was reading on the couch.

"Mommyyy!"

"Mark! Get him! I want to finish setting the table, and they'll be here soon."

"Huh? Oh, yeah." He tapped his iPad a few times before getting up.

Where was I? Oh yeah, Ralph Lauren. Nine place settings. Mom, Dad, Me, Mark, Ethan, Orly, Paul, Isabella, Arianna.

One set of parents. One family of four. One family of three. That thought made me wonder if my mother would ask me tonight when we were going to "make our family complete." I guessed, in her eyes, Ethan was only pulling half his weight. *Better hurry up and give him a sibling to make us whole.* At least, that was my mother's view. *Better not hold your breath.* That was my view.

• • ❧ • •

"YOU SHOULD COME TO Lavalette for the Fourth of July weekend," Orly said while she cut her filet mignon.

"I don't know. It's so far," I said. "I don't really want to spend four hours stuck in traffic to spend three nights in a motel on the boardwalk. Plus, I hate the beach. I have a pool in my backyard. No need to get sandy."

"It's not that far," Orly replied. "The Garden State Parkway southbound is good because you don't have to pay tolls unless you're going northbound." As she explained, she flicked her hands around, her long, fake hot-pink nails accosting the air in my cream-colored dining room.

"That doesn't really cut it down. It's still at least three hours by the time we get off Long Island." I shook my head. "I think we're just going to relax here."

Orly shrugged as if in surrender, as if to say, "I'll never understand you." And the feeling was mutual. We were so different. While I had been away at college in Pennsylvania, she'd stayed home and commuted to a local college in Queens. She now worked part-time at a medical supply company. While I had been in law school in New York, she'd gotten married. While I had been single and living in the city, she'd had my nieces. She had basically followed my mother's lead—married with two girls, all by the age of twenty-six.

"How many Fourth of July holidays will the kids have to spend together?" my mother chimed in.

Here we go.

"If ya think about it, I mean really, they grow up so fast. One day, you're brushing the sand off their legs, puttin' on the suntan oil. The next thing, they're teenagers, and they don't wanna be botha'd." Now she was swatting the air with her bright-red nails, half disgusted, half resigned at the thought of teenagers who didn't want to spend time with their parents. She meant me. Orly and my mother had always done things together, even when my sister was a teenager.

"Mommy's right." Orly renewed the fight. "We have to create 'cousin memories' now while they're still young."

"We're creating memories right now. Let's live in the moment. Isn't that what all those memes you post say?"

"We could go down the night before, on the third, and leave on the fifth," Mark said. "Two nights might be worth the drive."

I gave him a look that I hoped said, "Would you shut the hell up, please?" I doubted he wanted to go, but I knew what he was doing. He loved to take my family's side. It was like a playful "gang up on Jada," but it never felt playful to me. I stabbed my steak with my fork and cut.

"We could get really cute pics of them watching the fireworks." Orly sat up in her chair. "I need a good candid shot of the three of them in my living room."

Candid shot? Her house, which was two blocks from my parents' house in Queens, looked like a JCPenney portrait studio that used the same dark-haired family in all their displays. There were posed wedding shots on the mantle, posed kid shots on the walls, and posed family portraits on the corner tables.

"We can get some candid shots of them playing after dinner tonight." I gulped my wine. "We'll throw them in the pool and tell them to act like they're having fun."

"You are a piece of work, Jada," my mother said. Mark laughed the loudest at that. *Piece of work.* That was his and my mother's favorite nickname for me.

"Well, this piece of work has a peaceful backyard and huge pool," I said, defending myself. "And I hate traffic, so—"

"Is there any ketchup for my baked potato?" my brother-in-law, Paul, asked.

Thank God for my lug of a brother-in-law for interrupting this ludicrous conversation. I started to get up, but Mark beat me to it.

"Ketchup on a baked potato?" my mother asked for the thousandth time in a decade.

Paul shrugged. "It makes it taste like french fries."

That was what Paul did with his baked potatoes. I'd forgotten to put the ketchup out. If I remembered that little detail about Paul, my mother certainly should have. Still, my mother asked the same question time and again. *Ketchup on a baked potato? Who does that?* Oddly enough, I liked when other people did things that baffled her. It made me feel better. I wasn't the only one she couldn't understand.

"Well, that was the most delicious steak I have ever eaten." My father beamed, his shock of white hair and the gold cross around his neck catching the light as he lifted his wine glass to me. "What a cut. Perfect. Thank you, Jada and Mark."

As long as the food was good, my father was happy. "You're very welcome." I smiled back. "Well, I have good news." I held up my wine glass.

"You're pregnant!" my mother said.

I said it was good news. "Yes, and drinking red wine," I chided. "No. I got a promotion."

My mother's shoulders slumped.

"Congratulations," my father and brother-in-law said at the same time.

"So, what does that mean?" my sister asked. "A lot more hours? You already work so much."

"Uh, well." I rubbed my pointer finger along the stem of my wine glass. *How about a congratulations?* "No. Not more hours." I smiled. "More money, though."

"Well, congratulations," my father repeated, holding his glass up in a toast. We all clinked.

Mark kept his glass in the air. "And now for the reason we're here. Happy anniversary to JoAnn and Dominic."

"Happy anniversary," the table toasted.

"So tell us." Mark rested his elbows on the table. "What's the secret to a long and happy marriage?"

Oh, for the love of God.

"Communication," my mother announced.

Ha! By that, she meant she did all the talking. My father barely spoke, and my mother barely noticed. That was what kept them going. *Although, what if you both barely speak to each other, and only one of you seems to notice, like Mark and me?*

"You're a role model to the rest of us," Mark said.

If we weren't on the first floor, I would jump out the window.

Mark's nauseating rapport with my mother was in stark contrast to how I acted with his mother. False flattery wasn't my style, for one, plus we barely saw her. His parents lived in Albany, and so did his sister, her husband, and their kids. When we did get together with them, they talked about things I had zero interest in like knitting, something called cross-stitching, and baking different kinds of bread. But they were like Mark—polite, reserved, and well-mannered. Sometimes, when our families were in the same room, I wondered if my in-laws were horrified by my mother—her accent, her nails, her word choices, her intrusive questions. I imagined them regaling their knitting group with stories about her or maybe even doing an imitation of her.

It was time to end this night but not before getting in a photo. "Mark, take a picture of Orly and me and my parents." I handed him my phone.

I then posted the photo with the caption, "Great night celebrating my parents' anniversary and my promotion at work!" with three champagne emojis.

After Orly got ten shots of every combination of both of our families posed on the couch, she and my mother started to clear the table.

I downed my last sip of wine before joining them.

They couldn't leave soon enough. Ethan couldn't take his bath and drift off soon enough. Mark couldn't be engrossed in reading *Planetarium Magazine* soon enough.

• • ❧ • •

AS ETHAN SPLASHED AROUND in the bathtub, I sat on the floor and scrolled through my phone. Veronica had just sent me another article about JFK and Fidel Castro's mutual mistress. We shared an obsession with that time period.

"Where do rubber ducks come from?" Ethan asked.

I didn't glance up from my phone. "The toy company."

"They make them at the toy company?"

"They probably have a factory. A rubber duck factory."

"And they make rubber ducks? And other stuff?"

"They might make other things."

"What other things?"

"Probably rubber things like, I don't know, rubber boots." I paused halfway through the article I was reading to search "rubber duck factory," but before I could pull up an image, Ethan moved on to water.

"Where does water come from?"

Who the hell knows? "Um, the reservoir," I said.

"The water factory?"

"No. I guess before the reservoir, it comes from rain."

"Where does rain come from?"

"The sky." I took the rubber ducky out of his hand, gave him a once-over with the sponge, and hoisted him out.

"So it goes from the sky to the bathtub?"

"Yes," I said as I toweled him off. "Ultimately."

"What goes from the sky to the bathtub?" Mark appeared and leaned against the doorframe.

"Water," Ethan said.

"There's a reservoir in between, remember?" I dried each of his little legs. "Now it's bedtime."

"The water factory," Ethan said proudly.

Mark kneeled. "Actually, how it works is the hydrologic cycle."

Shoot me in the fucking head.

"You boys talk about the hydrological cycle." I stood up. "And then you can put him to bed."

"Hold on." Mark checked his phone. "I can't. I have a conference call with the Shanghai office in ten minutes."

Another wife might ask why he had a call on a Saturday night, but I was also a lawyer at a large firm, so it didn't faze me. I carried a damp, naked Ethan to his bedroom.

I got him into his *Buddy the Bulldozer* pajamas with only one more question.

"Where do pajamas come from?"

"Louise Pajamas. She's an old lady who makes pajamas for the whole world."

"Her name is Pajamas?"

"Yup! Get in bed."

Ethan lay down, and I lay next to him. He lifted his right foot.

"This toe is Mac." I squeezed his big toe. "And these are his brothers, Zak, Jack, Dak, and Lawrence."

"Now do this one!" Ethan lifted his left foot. This was our nightly routine. I named his toes. They got different names each night, and they kept the monsters away, along with his nightlight. *Kids will believe anything.*

"Covers time." I pulled his bedspread up.

"I'm thirsty," he said.

Here we go. After bath, pajamas, teeth brushing, naming the toes, and attempting to induce sleep, what inevitably followed was a sudden declaration of hunger or thirst. We would rinse, repeat, lose patience, sometimes cry—both of us—then succumb to exhaustion—also both of us.

Not tonight. Please. I can't ask Mark for help. He's on a call with Asia.

"Let's play a game. Can you name all seven of Snow White's dwarves?"

"Sneezy. Happy."

I pet the bottoms of his feet. "Who else?"

"Sss...sss...uh...Sleepy. Dah, ah..." *Yawn.* "Doc."

It worked, and faster than usual. *Success!* Although Ethan was in a sort of twisted position, I left him like that and snuck out.

Finish up in the kitchen, wash face, floss, brush teeth, moisturize, and then it's me and my phone. I cannot wait.

Mark was still working in the office when I went to bed. I peeked in to see him staring at the computer. He was pinching his eyebrow, something he did when he was deep in thought. It always made him seem even dorkier to me. Despite his handsome face, broad shoulders, and thick brown hair, the eyebrow pinch was such a nerdy nervous tick.

I crawled under the sheets, which felt refreshingly icy from the central air, and savored the quiet of our bedroom. Finally. Alone. *What's everyone else up to?* I opened Frontbook on my phone.

There's Veronica with her arm around her husband, Syd, on his sister's boat, looking tanned and relaxed. Her kids are getting so big. Who would have thought I would see them so infrequently that it would ever strike me how much they've grown since I last saw them? But that's how it is.

I flicked my thumb, scanning my feed for the real reason I was always checking in on Frontbook. *Jessica Carlin posted three new photos of her kids. The kids eating ice cream by the pool. The kids eating pineapple by the pool. The kids in the pool. Same photos all summer.*

Then I found exactly what I was hoping for—Todd Carlin pouring a drink at their outdoor bar. His hair still got so blond in the summer. *Is he making a martini, extra dirty, with large Spanish olives?* He got that from me. *Does that mean he misses me? Okay, I'm pathetic. But that liquid he's pouring looks extra dirty.*

Chapter 2

"I want a divorce," I said. I stuck a fork in my chicken parmigiana. The mozzarella cheese atop the red marinara sauce slid to the right.

"We know," Grandpa Tony said.

"You can read my mind?"

"Your heart," he replied.

"How could we read your mind and know that?" my grandmother asked. "You haven't admitted it to yourself yet."

We were seated at our favorite restaurant in Little Italy. I looked around, remembering another time we were there a few years ago. I had been confiding in them about Mark and wondering what to make of my friend Veronica's assessment that I was only back together with him because I was afraid to be single.

Now, Grandpa Tony snapped his fingers to the music coming from the band in the other room, his glasses sliding down his hooknose. They were playing "Only the Lonely." Grandma Rose sat next to him, swaying back and forth to the beat. Her tight, dark curls were perfectly set, and her cat-eye glasses hung from a chain around her neck.

I leaned forward and raised my voice. "Every time he pinches the outer corner of his eyebrow, I cringe. There's something about that gesture that makes me feel in my gut like 'How did I end up with this one?' We are not a match. It was a mistake."

"No such thing," Grandma said, her eyes now closed. "La, la, la, di, da, da."

"And what do you mean I haven't admitted it to myself? I've been Googling 'Is my marriage beyond repair?' for three years now. Three years! My social media feed is full of ads for marriage counselors." I waved my hands in front of my swaying grandparents, trying to get them to focus. "Hello?"

"Sorry, dear," Grandpa said. "Isn't that a beautiful tune?"

"I'm not really listening to it."

"Remember the last time we were here?" Grandma Rose swirled the red wine in her glass.

"Uh, yeah, I do. I was contemplating my relationship with Mark, after our breakup, before we were married. You couldn't have stopped me then?"

"Doesn't work like that," Grandpa said, tucking the red cloth napkin into his collar.

"We don't tell you what to do," Grandma Rose said. "We guide you toward the path that will, ya know, be the right path for you, the one where you'll learn the most."

Marrying Mark was the right path?

Grandma Rose and Grandpa Tony guided me then as they guided me now, as they had guided me all my life. They were my mom's parents, and they had both died before I was born. I was so comfortable there, with them, even though I had never actually known them in life.

That was how it worked. My grandparents had explained it to me on several occasions. "When you're awake, alive, going about your life with your guard up, you can't see or hear or feel us. But when you're asleep, on another plane, you can see, speak, be with your loved ones on the other side—us and all of the ones who've gone before ya, even if we've never met on earth. You work it all out with your spirit guides even if you don't remember, which you usually don't. You may not believe in such things while you're awake, but when you're asleep, you are in a meeting. There's a reason things always seem better in the morning."

"Jada, we know you're lonely, dear," Grandma Rose said as she twirled her linguini. "We can see it."

"Well, if you see things, you would know I'm not living in some basement, playing dominos by myself every night. Lonely? I would love to be left the hell alone most of the time."

"Just because you're not alone, doesn't mean you're not lonely."

I would have described my current state as miserable, depressed, unhappy, or stuck. It had never occurred to me that I was lonely. I had so many people in my life: Mark, Ethan, my parents, my sister, my brother-in-law, my nieces, my in-laws, my coworkers, my mommy friends.

"Well, okay, call it what you want," I said. "But something has to change. I want a divorce."

Grandpa Tony lifted his head from his bowl of linguini as he twirled the noodles with a fork and spoon into perfect spiraled bites. "Big talker."

"I mean it."

"Oh yeah?" Grandma Rose asked. "Something has to change? Tomorrow, you're going to talk to Mark about this? Oh, Jada Ann, how you talk like you are so brave. But your mouth is bigger than your actions. Always has been."

"Gee, thanks. Well, don't we meet here so you can help me? That's what I need help with."

They smirked at each other.

"Please. Don't you see my life? Don't you know what I'm feeling?"

"Listen, sweetheart, we love you. But right now, we need a little extra help," Grandpa Tony explained as he lay down his fork and spoon and leaned forward. "We gotta call in the big guns. Ya know what I mean? A different energy, as they'd say. We got no choice, especially with what's coming next—"

"Tony!" My grandmother cut him off.

"What's coming next?" Panic rose in my chest. "What does that mean?"

"We're able to see things like a fly on the wall. That's how we explain it," Grandma Rose said. "We're able to see what's coming down the pike, what's happening that you can't see. But you will know soon enough. Ya know, like where you're going to be at a certain time and place and who else will be there."

"Huh? Who? Where? What are you talking about?"

"So with that being said," my grandfather continued as if he hadn't heard my pleas for more information, "we think ya'd do better with a different energy."

"A big gun, like Grandpa said."

"Who? What? God?" I asked.

"No. Not that big."

"Who?" I pressed.

"Gina Rose," my grandfather said.

My mouth went dry. I reached for my wine. My cousin. She was Gina to me. The only person who'd ever called her Gina Rose was her mom, Aunt Fran, my mother's sister.

The car accident had happened twelve weeks before my wedding. I'd woken up in the middle of the night to my mother screaming into the phone and being held up by my father in the kitchen while she was still on the line with my uncle Eddie, Gina's father. I had stayed at my parents that night because we were supposed to go to my sister's maid-of-honor dress fitting the next day.

I'd visited with Gina on the other side in these dream visits before. She always seemed happy and had the same relaxed glow my grandparents had, which I guessed came simply with being there. But she wasn't a regular. When I did see her there, it wasn't easy. It wasn't like meeting with my grandparents, who looked like they did in old family photos. Although they'd died in their thirties, they still carried the aura of being old and wise. Maybe it was their old-fashioned glasses, hairstyles, and clothes. It was different with Gina. It was hard to see someone who looked so young and "present-day" on the other side.

"Gina's stopping by?" I asked.

"We'll check in here and there," Grandma Rose said as she inched to the edge of her chair to stand up.

"You're going to leave me with her?"

"Speak of the devil," Grandpa Tony said, waving his hand toward something behind me.

There she was, all spiky black hair and Converse sneakers. Her tiny diamond nose ring flickered as she stood there with her hands in her front pockets. "Hey." She shrugged as if we'd just seen each other.

I stood and hugged her hard and tight. She was so tiny. I choked back a tear as her bony shoulder jabbed my throat.

"Jada, what the fuck?"

Still Gina. "Sorry. I guess it feels like..." *Like you shouldn't be here, and it's tragic.*

"Like what?" she asked. *Was she going to force me to say that?*

"Nothing." I swallowed.

She peered over my shoulder. "Hi, Gram. Hey, Gramps."

They said, "Hi, sweetheart," and "Hi, Gi," at the same time, like they'd just spent time with her yesterday, which they probably had. But time seemed to work differently there. It was not a three-dimensional world. There were no time, space, or other constraints, like calories, Grandma Rose often pointed out.

"How have you been?"

She put her hand on my shoulder. "Good. I'm happy Grandma and Grandpa want me to help. We'll figure this shit out."

"What shit?"

She tilted her head. She looked exactly as I remembered her—five feet tall, barely a hundred pounds. She wore a white T-shirt with a drawing of a dragonfly surrounded by stars and planets.

We'd always had similar personalities but different styles and interests. While I had been taking the LSAT and pursuing law, she'd been taking drugs and pursuing music. She'd left Queens, too, and had lived in Manhattan the same time I had. But she'd hung out downtown, going to live concerts in art-collective lofts, while I'd drunk martinis and flirted with investment bankers. I often regretted not making more of an effort to hang out with her, especially considering we'd lived only a couple of miles apart.

"Didn't you tell Grandma and Grandpa you want a divorce?"

"Oh. Yeah." I lowered my gaze for a second. "You can help with that?" I followed her eyes toward our grandparents.

"Jada and Gina, together again," Grandpa Tony sang as he stood behind us with his arms open wide. "We used to watch you from the other side and say, 'We have two little rascals to look after.' And here ya are."

"All right, let's get going, Tone. Vincent Bianchi died. Big welcome party. Shrimp the size of your hand, I hear. Come on." Grandma Rose scooted him toward the door.

"You just ate," I said.

"Yeah, and? What's your point?" Grandma asked.

Grandpa Tony blew kisses. "We love you. We'll see you soon." Then he turned to Gina. "God help ya," he said under his breath.

"I heard that," I called to him.

He held up a hand and waved without turning around as we watched them walk out of the restaurant.

"How are you?" I asked Gina. "Are you happy? I like that T-shirt. Have you seen your mom and sister? Aren't the girls cute?" I assumed she must see a lot of her nieces.

"Yes." She waved to a server to order a black coffee and a piece of rum cake. "They're so cute."

"I should try to see Andrea more. I know they see Orly and her girls a lot."

"Don't worry about that kind of stuff. You're busy. It's okay. Let's talk about you."

"Do we have to?"

"That's why I'm here."

"So how are you going to do any better?" I asked. "How are you going to help me? No offense, but what do you know?"

"Ha. Well, even though we never met Grandma and Grandpa while they were alive, they're still our grandparents, and maybe some things are easier to talk about with your cousin than your grandparents." Her rum cake arrived, and she forked a huge bite into her mouth.

"What? Like sex?"

"Like a lot of things. You'll see."

"See what? You're all freaking me out this visit." I reached for my temples.

"Okay. Let's not talk about you. What do you want to talk about?" She scraped up every last bit of rum cake.

"Cori's getting married. It's so unfair, isn't it? She's there, getting married, and you're here."

Cori was Gina's best friend. She had been driving the night of the accident. I couldn't understand why she would ever send me a connection request on social media, but I'd accepted, and now I saw her doing all of the things Gina should have been doing—vacations, new jobs, new relationships, milestones. *It's so unfair.* I knew I should have hidden her from my newsfeed, but I was too curious.

Now it was Gina's turn to not want to talk about something. She flipped it back and got right to the point. "Why haven't you ever said the words 'I want a divorce' to yourself? Like in your waking moments, not just here."

"I don't know. It feels too big, too final, and too overwhelming, I guess."

"I want to help you." She reached into her back pocket and pulled out a pack of cigarettes. "Want?"

I shook my head. "You still smoke?"

She lit one, inhaled, and exhaled slowly. "God, I love smoking. Sure you don't want one? We're here, not there. It doesn't count, like calories."

"I'm good, thanks."

"Isn't it great? You go to bed, meet with your dead relatives, they talk you off the ledge, you eat junk food, smoke cigarettes—if you want—and wake up with a whole new perspective? A whole new life plan if you so desire." She winked as she held the cigarette between her teeth.

"Ah, yes, I've heard that's how it works."

She took another seemingly satisfying drag. It was amazing to see her still being so very Gina. She'd never been prim and proper. She was born carefree, and it appeared she would stay that way. I guessed that was how it worked. *You are who you are.*

We'd both been willful children. According to family lore, when we were around six years old, Gina and I had fought over a Barbie doll at Orly's birthday party. It was mine—Executive Barbie with a pink suit and pink briefcase—and Gina wanted to play with it, but I didn't want her to play with *that* one. I had five other Barbies she could play with. That *one* was not to be played with by anyone but me. Still, she insisted. By the time our mothers tore us apart, Executive Barbie was missing a head and a left arm.

When Gina left that day, I repaired Barbie's limb and put her head back on. We never did find the briefcase, but I substituted a beach bag from Malibu Barbie, and she was back in business. I'd hidden her under my parents' bed every time Gina had come over after that. I told Gina I'd thrown her away because she'd ripped Barbie's head off and that she should feel very sorry. Now, as she sat before me, I would give her a truckload of Barbies and more if it could reverse time.

"The feisty ones are the most fun to watch over," Gina said. "Remember Barbie? Her briefcase ended up flung into a ball of wrapping paper from Orly's presents. It got thrown away. I know that now."

"Huh, so that's what happened to it." I cocked my head. "What else do you know?"

"You'll see." She exhaled a trail of smoke and smashed her cigarette out in the cake plate. "Buckle up." She snickered.

"Will you people stop it, please, with these ominous statements? I'm going to wake up with a pit in my stomach. Thanks a lot."

"Sometimes that happens."

"Do you see us? Mark and me?"

"Two ships."

"Passing in the night? Not really. More like two ships that came upon each other, tied their anchors together, and just float there. One of them has a water slide and a bar, and the other one has the PBS radio hour blaring from the speakers."

"Which one are you?"

"Water slide, of course."

"I don't know if you see each other the way you really are, Jada. You're not exactly a party girl."

"Not anymore. I have a job, a kid, a commute."

"You weren't even when you were single. I mean, you had fun in college and law school with your friends Veronica and Lauren, but you weren't a crazy girl."

"Maybe not like you, but we have different styles." I tipped my head and smiled, hoping that expressed what I didn't want to say.

She read my mind. "I didn't do that many drugs. The point is maybe Mark doesn't think you're all that much fun either."

"Does he wish I'd steal his *Planetarium Magazine* and he would have to tickle me to get it out of my hands?"

"Maybe when he's explaining the hydrologic cycle, he could be thinking, 'Nothing, Jada? Not even a little curious?'"

"He thought that? Well, no, not curious. Not interesting to me. Sorry."

"It doesn't matter. I'm just saying maybe you're two ships with different ideas of fun."

"Agreed. So how the hell did we end up together? I know—he was perfect on paper. But what a mistake."

"There are no mistakes, only lessons."

"Oh, please! What have you turned into?"

"I'm still me." She reached for another cigarette. "But I'm here now, and I can see things differently. And I can help you see things from where you are." She held her fingers in a V formation over her mouth while she savored the first drag. "I see what you're going through, though. I do. You created a life that looks good from the outside but doesn't feel good."

I nodded. "Another one I've seen on a meme with an ocean background. They all have ocean backgrounds."

"It's still true, isn't it?" She offered me a puff.

I accepted it this time and, like Gina, tried to savor the moment. My lips squeezed it slightly, and I inhaled. "It's good to see you," I said as I exhaled.

She toasted me with her coffee cup. "You too."

"Gina Rose, you've been so missed."

"Well, I'm here now. And you can't get rid of me." She smashed her cigarette into her dessert plate. "You can't avoid me like you avoid Mark and the state of your marriage."

"I don't avoid him."

She cocked her head to the side as she studied my face.

"Well, he avoids me too."

She pointed her finger at me as if to say, "Bingo!"

I pushed her finger to the side. "It's rude to point."

"You have to do something for me. An assignment. Well, not for me. For you."

"What?"

"Don't sound so excited. I'm here to help you. Remember?"

"Will I remember this?"

"In your gut. You'll see."

"Like 'Trust your gut. It'll never steer you wrong'? Please stop talking in memes."

"No. I mean 'in your gut' like I'm warning you to buy adult diapers."

"Oh."

"I'm kidding! Yes, trust your gut. It's a message from us, over here." She waved her hand above her head. "Some memes happen to be true. So listen to it."

"Okay, what do you want me to do? Now I'm just relieved I'm not going to shit my pants." I adjusted in my seat and rested my elbows on the table.

"Good. You have been Googling how to improve your marriage but doing nothing about it. What you actually know to be true is that you and Mark have gone as far as you can. What you want is a divorce, but you can't admit it to yourself. You admit it here, but over there, you would rather suffer through this life and daydream about running away rather than admit 'defeat.' You are ashamed to have made a mistake. But there are no mistakes."

"No mistakes. Yes, you mentioned that."

She smirked.

"So what do you want me to do?"

"Two things. First, you have to admit to yourself what you truly want."

"I know what I want," I said.

"Oh, really? To improve your marriage? You and Mark should go to counseling, then?"

"No."

"Why not?"

"Because that's not what I really want."

"Exactly. You've never made the leap to admitting you want a divorce because you equate it with admitting defeat. You'd rather suffer as long as your life looks good on social media. You have to finally admit to yourself what you know deep down."

"How?"

"Get quiet. Get off your phone. Get out of your head. Listen to what's around you. Really listen. The answer will come."

I blinked for a long second to stifle an eye roll.

"Roll your eyes all you want."

"What's the other thing?" I asked.

"Talk to Mark."

"I was afraid you were going to say that."

"Talk to him. Get his thoughts on the state of your marriage. See what he says. And do it before you go to San Francisco."

"San Francisco? I'm moving?"

"No, traveling. You'll see. Just listen to me. You and Mark need to speak directly and honestly, face-to-face, no distractions."

"Like a date night? We haven't had a date night since before Ethan was born."

"I know. You don't actually have to go out. I know you don't trust a babysitter, your nanny works all day, and your parents and sister live in Queens. I know. I see it all. Put Ethan to bed, have a glass of wine, and talk."

"About what?"

"About why he likes his eggs sunny-side up."

"He likes to dip the bread in the runny part."

"About the state of your marriage, you idiot! This kinda involves him, so you have to actually have a conversation that's more than surface level."

I bit my lip. "That's kind of the problem. I can't remember our last deep conversation, if ever. How is that possible?"

"I know. Just give it a try." Gina leaned in. "I'll know if you don't."

I leaned forward and met her gaze. "That's creepy."

We laughed. "Not really," she said. "I promise." She reached for her cigarettes and pulled out two. She lit one and handed it to me.

"Another one?"

"When in Rome. Or heaven."

I took it and inhaled. "I've got a tough guardian angel."

She lit her own cigarette and leaned back. "The best kind."

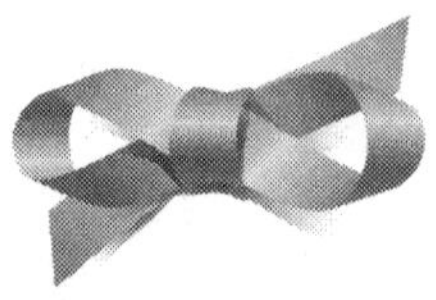

Chapter 3

With one eye open, I checked Ethan's baby monitor. *Still asleep.* I grabbed my phone and saw the time was 5:05 a.m. *Figures. Why should my body let me sleep late on the weekend? It can't seem to tell the difference.*

Mark did not have the same problem. His breathing was steady as he slept. I propped myself up on my pillow, ready to check email, social media, and the news, all with one eye open.

But I didn't. I put my phone down and listened. I heard nothing but the sound of Mark's white-noise machine.

"We have to talk." Does that sound too foreboding? What about "Let's talk later" or "Can we talk later?" I inhaled deeply just to hear something besides the noise machine. I let it out, concentrating on the sound that left my nostrils.

What do you want, Mark? Is this enough for you? What do I want?

I listened to Mark breathing.

Divorce.

My heart flipped.

This is stupid. I grabbed my phone. *Oh, look at that. Cori is registering for her wedding. Ralph Lauren dinnerware is too preppy for her, I'm sure.*

• • ∾ • •

"LANGSTON, NO!" MELODY hollered. "Langston, let go of him now! I will call your father in three, two..."

Langston was Ethan's age, and as he spun around while holding hands with a smaller boy, it was only a matter of time before they both fell down. I was grateful we were at Long Island at Play, where everything was padded.

Long Island at Play was a large, refinished warehouse. The main feature was a monstrous plastic-cushion-covered jungle gym right in the middle. The routine was the same each time. Moms walked in, checked in, tried to get their kids to eat something—anything, usually a hot dog or chicken fingers from the snack bar—then released them into the wild where they ran around like maniacs while the moms sat with their lattes and talked at the tables along the wall. They didn't serve booze, but the coffee was decent. It was an opportunity for Ethan to run like he couldn't run in our house, where nothing was padded, and it also wore him out. He was always easier to get to sleep after a day at LI at Play.

That was where I'd met Danielle, Melody, and Jessica.

We were all moms to at least one boy around three years old. Danielle had four children—Triston, Trevor, Trace, and Trent. I called them the Tree kids. They were all tall for their age with shiny blond ringlets like their mom's.

Melody, with the neat honey-colored pixie cut and pearls, had Langston. Melody-of-Many-Questions. *Do you like your street? Who was your realtor? Was the pool already there? Why don't they let you work from home one day a week? Why wouldn't you want to? Do you have to be a certain level of associate for that? Why are you putting your head down? Do you have another headache?*

Then there was Jessica, Todd's wife. *That Todd. My Todd. My ex, Todd.* He was the reason I was constantly checking Frontbook, always hoping to get a glimpse into his world via Jessica. Admitting it sounded creepy, but it was the truth. When we had first joined LI at Play and I discovered her last name, I'd almost choked on my latte when I realized who she was. I hadn't said, "I know your husband," or "I used to date your husband," or "Your husband is such a jerk and not just because he ripped my heart to shreds." Instead, I'd stayed quiet and then became a serious social media stalker.

I was always afraid I would say something that would reveal too much. I could imagine Jessica saying something like, "I'd get my husband a gift certificate for a massage for Father's Day, but he says he hates massages. I mean, who hates massages?" And I would blurt out, "Well, it's because he's so ticklish!" *God forbid.*

So whenever I found myself in a conversation with Jessica, I tried to steer it away from talk about our husbands, or even homes and kids, to safe territories like movies, books, and news.

"So my husband is going away on business next week," Jessica said, pushing her long brown hair off her shoulder and sipping her coffee. "I hate those weeks. It's so nice when he comes home from work, and I can finally clean up the kitchen, eat something, and watch TV while he bathes the kids. You know when it's finally that moment in the day that you get to yourself? But when he's away, I don't get that. It's just *constant.*" She sighed.

We all nodded.

"And I really miss him."

My heart fell. She obviously was not Googling "Is my marriage beyond repair?"

"I like your hair color," I said. "Who does it?"

"Thanks. My mom, actually."

"She does hair?"

"No, but she's been dying her own for years, so she does mine too."

"Oh! It's like from a bottle? From the drugstore?"

Jessica nodded and shrugged while I cringed at my stupidity. *Good going, Jada.* In my attempt to steer the conversation away from her husband, I'd inadvertently been rude. I tried to make up for it. "It's really pretty."

I was saved when one of the Tree kids came barreling over. It was Tristan. "Ethan is crying."

"Why? Where?" I walked toward where Tristan was pointing. In a corner stacked with padded blocks, Ethan was wiping his eyes and staring at another boy in a tiny blue hockey jersey sitting on a red block. "What happened?"

"He scared me," Ethan said.

"Who? Him?" I pointed at the boy in the jersey, who pivoted and ran.

Ethan nodded.

"What happened? Let's go over here and talk. Or maybe we should leave. You must be tired now." *I am.*

"No!"

"Okay, okay. Why don't you play by the balls? Or over there. Those rings are fun. You like those."

Ethan meandered toward the rings, and I resumed my seat with the moms, but I kept my eye on him.

Melody fiddled with her pearls. "Jada, where do you work in the city?"

"On the west side. Not far from Times Square. It's a shit show. Did you work in the city?"

Melody's voice chirped in the background as she went through her entire work history.

Jessica, apparently as bored as I was, checked her phone quickly before dropping it back in her bag.

Still, I was pleased to be off the subject of hair dye and traveling husbands. My biggest fear was that Jessica would ask where I'd gone to college. I couldn't lie, and when I said Lafayette, she would say, "Oh, do you know my husband's sister, Michelle?" I couldn't lie about that either. Michelle had been my good friend, which was how I'd met Todd. After Todd and my brief courtship, years later in the city, Michelle and I had lost touch. I'd searched for her on social media, of course, but she wasn't on.

"I never worked in the city," Jessica chimed in. "My first job out of college was on Long Island, but I'd go in on the weekends and hang out. That's how I met my husband."

I glanced away as I swallowed that one, and that was when I spotted Ethan being strangled by the boy in the blue jersey. I bolted toward them. "No, no, no, no!" I screamed as I ran, my heart quickening.

Blue Jersey Boy didn't hear me. His hands were around Ethan's neck as Ethan croaked out, "You're scaring me."

"Stop that! Where is your mother?" I yanked the boy's elbow, startling him. "Where is your mother?" I repeated.

He pointed toward a tall, slender woman with a pin-straight ponytail, wearing black yoga pants and a puffy vest in the middle of summer. She was engaged in conversation with other slender women in black yoga pants, curious puffy vests, and straight ponytails.

I marched up to her. "Is the kid in the blue jersey yours?"

Her friend butted in. "What happened? I saw you touch him."

"He was choking my son. He was scaring him. I'm sure he's a sweet kid, but—"

"He's only four years old." Blue Jersey Boy's mom shrugged.

"Exactly. We have to teach our four-year-olds to keep their hands off each other. I thought you should know—"

"It's going to happen." She shrugged again. "Is he your only boy? I've got two. This is what they do."

I wanted to grab her ponytail and strangle her with it like her son had been strangling Ethan. "Does your son have all his teeth?" I asked.

"What?"

"No one's knocked them out yet?"

She blinked dramatically as if she couldn't believe what she was hearing.

"You know, in self-defense. It's going to happen." I shrugged like she had. "Better teach him to keep his hands to himself." I shrugged once more for effect.

She rolled her eyes.

Before I could sit back down, one of our little ones ran past me to announce he did "doo-doo" in his pants. It was Logan. Jessica took him to the bathroom, so I was stuck with Melody because Danielle was rallying the Tree kids to head to their cousin's birthday party. Maybe I was too hard on Melody. Maybe I shouldn't constantly think about how annoying she was. I sat back down. Maybe she wasn't so bad.

"So, where do you get your hair done?" Melody asked.

"Cut or dyed?"

"Dyed, I guess. You want your hair that dark on purpose, right?"

Okay, she's the fucking pits.

Before I could answer then wait while she asked me nine million more questions, including how much I tipped, I pretended to see Ethan getting strangled again. "Oh my God." I beelined toward nothing in particular, got lost in the crowd of jumping kids, and found Ethan. "Are you ready?"

"No!"

We'd been there long enough. If we stayed seven hours, he still would not be ready to go. That was one downside of Long Island at Play. It was a kicking, screaming, crying fiasco anytime anyone had to leave.

I knelt to Ethan's eye level. "Listen, we have to go home because we have important things to do. Okay? We have to swim in our pool. Then we have to eat chicken fingers. Then we have to eat ice pops and watch *Buddy*. So come on."

"No!"

I picked him up and, karma being what it was, almost got my teeth knocked out.

"Ugh," I said to Melody as I tried to hold onto a wailing Ethan. "We've gotta go. We have a million things to do at home."

She nodded like she completely understood. *Doesn't every mother have a million things to do?* We bumped into the Tree kids as we left. One of the Tree's forgot his backpack full of army men. God forbid that ended up in the wrong hands. But I could tell he'd been crying. *Poor thing.*

"I'm glad you said something to one of the ponytail moms. Her son strangles everybody's kid, and she's too busy running her fingers through her ponytail to ever notice," Danielle said, lifting her sunglasses to the top of her head.

"Ha. Not sure how effective I was. She just shrugged and rolled her eyes."

"She did? What a—" She glanced at her boys. "Well, at least we found each other. Finding other nice, normal moms shouldn't be so hard, but it is. It's like middle school all over again."

I laughed. "Seriously." I liked being described as a nice, normal mom. And I liked Danielle. Meaningful connections were so rare for me lately. I took whatever I could get.

• • ❧ • •

I WOKE UP BEFORE MY alarm went off. I hadn't had an uninterrupted night of sleep since Ethan was born. Even if he didn't wake up at some point in the night, I did. I usually woke up to use the bathroom around two a.m. then held the baby monitor to my ear to make sure Ethan was breathing before I went back to sleep.

Sometimes, if I couldn't fall back to sleep, I would text my friend Veronica. In our most recent exchange, she'd texted her words of wisdom.

Veronica: *Try hard to fall back. I'm reading this book about how we meet with our loved ones and spirit guides while we sleep. We need sleep not just for our bodies but our souls too.*

Jada: *I don't believe in that shit.*

Veronica: *Ha. Then count sheep. I'll get you started.*

That text had ended with ten sheep emojis.

Now I leaned over to hear Mark still sleeping soundly. The old-fashioned alarm clock on his nightstand read 3:43.

Get quiet. Get out of your head. I listened to Mark's white-noise machine. *Divorce.*

I placed my hand over my heart in a feeble attempt to slow it or calm it or comfort it. *Enough of this.*

I lifted myself onto my elbows, perched the pillow behind me, and adjusted my eyes to the bright light of my phone before opening Frontbook.

Oh, look, Kelly from law school bought a pink bicycle with fringe hanging from the handlebars that she plans to ride in Central Park. She was always a dipshit. And so are every one of these friends of hers replying, "How cute!" and "Riding in style!"

By the time I'd scrolled through my news feed, it was 4:05. Mark's and my morning routine was the typical commuter nightmare. He set his alarm for 4:10. I set mine for 4:15. He snoozed until 4:18 then got in the shower. I snoozed until 4:29, and as he was getting out of the shower, I got in. If Ethan was already awake by that point—his waking hour was unpredictable at this stage—then the one of us who wasn't showering would hang out with him in our bed and play YouTube videos of *Buddy the Bulldozer* on one of our devices. Hearing the "Vroom, vroom, boom, boom" theme music of *Buddy* before five a.m. could make anyone wish a bulldozer would suddenly appear and run over their ears.

Our nanny, Joyce, arrived every day, Monday through Friday, at six on the dot. Then Mark and I left for the Long Island Railroad by

6:15 and not a second later. If Ethan was awake, we would start saying our goodbyes at 5:55 because he would cry and hug our legs and tell us he was going to miss us. It was awful. We'd recently started to tell him we were going "down the street to the neighbor's house where we worked" and then snuck out while Joyce distracted him. It had worked like a charm at least twice and might become part of our repertoire.

We then each drove to the station for the 6:36 from Long Island to Manhattan, which got us to our respective offices by about 7:25. We didn't commute home together because we both left at different times each night, never able to predict when one of us would have to work late.

"Mark." I gently nudged him. "Mark." I put my hand on his shoulder. "Mark?"

He jolted up. "Huh? Oh. Huh? Jada?"

"I got up early. Want me to shower first?"

He rubbed his eyes. "Uh. Yeah."

I fell back asleep in the shower, still upright. My eyes were closed until I was jolted awake by Mark's voice.

"We're out of milk. I just used the last drop for my coffee," Mark said, standing in the bathroom.

"Hold on. I have some in here," I said, proud of my ability to joke even in my groggy state.

"Huh?"

"Never mind."

"I'll pick some up after work," he said and walked out.

Are you kidding me? You have to tell me, while I'm showering, that we're out of milk? Like I can do anything about it? Or even better, like it's that interesting? If you're going to pick some up after work, then leave me alone while I'm showering. And sleeping.

Joyce arrived at six. Ethan was still asleep, and we were out the door, parked at the train station, and from one island to another by 7:25 a.m.

I savored the first quiet hour of work before my boss, Dan, and fellow law associate Karen arrived. I would flip the lights on in my office and, depending on the time of year, adjust the blinds to let the sun shine in. I would sip my coffee, lean back in my leather chair, check up on social media again, and read the entertainment websites online. In recent years, since Veronica had gotten me into JFK assassination conspiracies, we always sent each other articles we would find.

I was typing, "Have you ever heard of this? Oswald's visit to Cuba?" when I heard, "How was your weekend?"

I lifted my head to see my boss, Dan, leaning in my doorway.

"Like every other weekend. Same shit. Completely exhausting. How was yours?"

"Good. We went out east. Just laid around. Cooked. Swam. Took my new Lexus convertible for a spin. Got it washed. It was beautiful weather all weekend."

Dan and his wife, Susan, had a house in the Hamptons, an apartment in the city, two dogs, and no kids. Their life seemed so calm and thoroughly enjoyable. It really pissed me off sometimes. *Note to self: Unfollow Dan on Frontbook.*

"For some reason, I couldn't sleep on Friday night, though," he went on. He shifted his feet, readjusting all of his five-two frame to the other side of the doorway. "If I don't get my solid eight hours of sleep a night, I'm a grumpy old man. So on Saturday, I just napped all day by the pool. Think I got burnt." He rubbed his arm.

"I hate you. Eight hours? You took *a nap*?"

He laughed. "All right, I'm in meetings all morning, but let's meet in my office after lunch. Say, two? It's going to be a busy week."

"Cool," I replied as I opened my email. *Okay, let's work. It distracts me from social media.*

• • ❧ • •

"JUST LIKE OLD TIMES," Veronica said.

And it was. We sat on our old "usual" bench in Bryant Park, eating our salads. We were wearing the same shoes—black heels with ankle straps—and virtually the same outfit—black pants and gray tops. It didn't help that we looked alike too. We were both five foot three with long, dark hair.

"Do you think people are wondering if we planned this?" I asked.

"Let's hold up a sign that says, 'We're not that corny!'"

But it wasn't just like old times. Veronica had a different job, so she didn't work nearby anymore. And we both had husbands and kids. On the bench next to us were her coworkers from NewYork3News—the cameraman, Ken, the driver, and Lou, the guy who taped wires to the floor. At least they were a bench away and we were able to talk freely.

"What are the kids up to?" I asked.

"Well, we're going on that cruise next week with Syd's parents, sister, cousins, everyone, and we just got the kids' passports yesterday. I was freaking out. I was going to start badgering the mailman. Like, 'um, are you sure there's not something else in that mailbag, sir?' We couldn't go without the passports. They don't accept birth certificates anymore."

A pang struck me as she spoke. *Jealousy?* I had no desire to go on a cruise—ever—and definitely not with Mark's family or mine. But I guessed that was it. She seemed to want to be with those people. If I were in that situation, I would say, "Oops. Ethan's passport never arrived. Bon Voyage," and feel relieved.

But not Veronica. She had her people like we all had our people. But she actually liked her people. She didn't seem hungry for a meaningful connection lately, or ever, like me.

"You're going to have a lot of fun," I said.

"Yeah. I'm excited. What's going on with you?"

I want a divorce. I cleared my throat.

"Nothing. Same shit." I wanted to confide in her, but I'd only recently allowed myself to even think it and then only for a few brief moments. I was nowhere near ready to say it out loud. Plus, it was hard to confess my unhappiness to someone who seemed so happy. It made me feel like a failure. And on top of all of that, she might think—or even say—"I told you so." Back then, she had told me I was making a mistake getting back together with Mark after being stung by Todd. She'd thought I should be single for a while. That was a few years ago, but I still couldn't admit any of this to her.

"Is Todd's wife still in that mommy group?"

Pang of the century. I felt like my chest was going to explode right there in Bryant Park, all over my salad. I had confided that tidbit to her a while ago. She was the only one, in fact, who knew. "Yeah." I shoved a forkful of salad into my mouth to hopefully disguise the deep breath I had to take. I sucked in through my nose while I chewed. I couldn't ever reveal how much I still thought about Todd. It was too embarrassing, and she wouldn't understand.

"Such a small world." Veronica shook her head. "Ah, well, who cares anyway? You're happily married now."

I nodded. Before I was so "happily married," Veronica knew what had happened with Todd. She'd lived through it all with me.

"Todd. That all seems so long ago now," she said. "That fucking turd. Todd the Turd."

I feigned a laugh. "Hey, did you read that article I sent you about Oswald?"

"Yes! I thought I wrote you back. Insane."

We talked about Lee Harvey Oswald for the rest of our short lunch. There we were, two dorks in the same outfit, giddily discussing history. I hadn't always been obsessed. As a matter of fact, I actually used to make fun of Veronica. Any conspiracy theory sounded so outlandish to me. I used to tell her I was going to make her a tinfoil hat because she sounded like a crazy person with a survival kit and an underground bunker in her yard.

But then I saw a book on Todd's shelf one day, and in a pathetic attempt to get closer to him, I asked to borrow it. It was fiction but told from the perspective of one of the secret service staff. I read it, and I was in. *Hooked.* That was pretty much all I'd gotten from our short time together. No venereal diseases, thankfully. Just a crushed heart and a history obsession. At least it was something that bonded my old friend and me.

• • ❧ • •

"ALL RIGHT, I'D LIKE both of you to go over the contract one last time, take out all of the stuff related to section five-eighty, compare to the prior version, and send to Diane. Sound good?" Dan asked.

Karen, my fellow associate at the firm, and I looked up from our yellow legal pads and nodded. We were in the guest chairs in front of Dan's desk.

Dan mindlessly tapped his Mont Blanc pen on his mahogany desk as he reviewed his notes. "I'll let Diane know it's getting done, and if that peon from Lynch calls me, I'll have to tell him where to shove it. We did everything he asked for and more. He better love it."

"Love it or shove it," I said.

Dan pointed his finger as he continued to read his notes. "I like that."

Karen laughed. "You should put it on a bumper sticker."

"On his precious Lexus? Never," I pointed out.

"Maybe you can put it on a wine glass for my birthday," Dan suggested.

Karen giggled loudly now. "Jada knows where to order those."

For Veronica's bachelorette party, I'd ordered one hundred stemless wine glasses that read "#VeronicaSydYes" and had them delivered to the office. I had just moved to Long Island at the time, but her party was in the city, so I hadn't wanted to have them delivered to my house and then have to lug them with me into the city from Long Island.

There had only been twenty people invited to Veronica's bachelorette party, but it was cheaper to buy a hundred. So the law firm of Perl & Brown had #VeronicaSydYes wine glasses floating around that people actually used to drink water or the free soda the firm stocked to keep everyone awake.

"All right, so that's the Morgan matter. Now, about the Frankel matter, who wants to go to San Francisco next Monday for a week?" Dan folded his hands as he waited for an answer.

"Me!" I said. I hadn't been on a plane since my honeymoon. It was too hard to travel with a child.

"It's okay. I'll go," Karen said. "Jada has Ethan."

Karen and her husband were also one of those child-free and carefree couples, like Dan and his wife. It was funny to think that I used to call her "the one who lost her broomstick."

On my first day at the firm, Dan had brought me to her office and said, "Meet our new associate." Karen was in the middle of something, frantically grabbing a file from her cabinet, and said, "I'll meet you in a minute," before running out the door.

How fucking rude! I hated her instantly. And in my infinite wisdom and maturity, I'd hated her for a solid two years. I had even gotten my friends to call her Broomstick for short, and they still did out of habit. But once I had removed the stick up my own ass, I'd gained a little perspective, enough to see that Karen was one of the most considerate people I knew. She just got frazzled easily. But she would bend over backward for anyone, and I was glad I finally saw it. It would have been a very awkward decade around the office if I'd held on to my stubborn grudge from such a silly, perceived slight.

"Karen, why do you have to be so fucking nice?" I asked. "You went to Houston last time. Remember? It's only fair. Honestly, I'm happy to go. And Ethan will be fine. He has another parent. This guy named Mark. And I can ask Joyce to stay over for the week. Joyce might like to stay in the guest bedroom and not commute. It could be a vacation for her too."

"Are you sure?" Dan asked. "It might make more sense for you to go because you prepared the motion, so you're a little bit closer to it than Karen at this point, but—"

"You're right. It should be me."

"Okay. Can you send an email to Lionel and let him know you'll be the one in San Francisco?"

Ugh. Lionel will be there. That's the only piss on my parade.

Lionel O'Shea was the general counsel of our main client, Fortified Warehousing and Storage, a company that owned thousands of warehouses and storage facilities that leased space to businesses. Dan always used to say, "Lionel is an interesting character."

I had always replied, "Is 'interesting character' your term for asshole?"

Dan would beg, "Jada, please."

And Karen would giggle.

The first time I'd met Lionel, I was in my second year at the firm. He had come to our offices for a meeting about documents we would be handing over to opposing counsel the next day for their review only, meaning they couldn't leave with them. As a junior associate, I was tasked with "babysitting" the documents while this occurred. That was what they called it.

"Here's our babysitter," Dan said, introducing me as I stood in the door of the conference room. Lionel had the roundest head I'd ever seen—it was a perfect circle—and he sweat constantly, no matter the temperature in the room. His dark eyes moved from my face to my feet and back up again. I tried to make eye contact before he grunted and turned back to the document in front of him. On the whole, that first meeting with Lionel pretty much summed him up.

As we sat in Dan's office now, my thoughts switched from the awfulness of Lionel to the splendorous visions of a quiet hotel suite. Room service would knock on my door to wheel in my multi-course dinner covered in silver domes while I relaxed in a fluffy white robe.

But I was jolted from my daydream at Dan's next comment. "And, Jada, let's keep our cool no matter how Lionel responds today, okay?"

"I'm always cool with people who are cool to me."

"Jada, please. Let's not push it."

"Dan, I am a professional and an adult." I circled a note on my pad—the one about asking my assistant to book my trip with a window seat—in a big, sweeping swirl that I carried off the pad and into the air.

Dan shook his head. We wrapped up and retreated to our respective offices. I shut my door and sauntered to my desk, waving my notepad in the air. *Yes, I'll have to deal with Lionel for a week, but it'll be worth it.* I leaned back in my chair. *Jada Marlone, pack your bags. You've won an all-inclusive five-day, four-night trip to San Francisco. That's right. You'll be staying at the Fairmount Hotel and Resort in downtown San Francisco, complete with a restaurant and bar frequented exclusively by adults. You heard that right: No kids! There will be room service. There will be fluffy white bathrobes. There will be adult beverages. And best of all, a flat-screen television where you can watch anything that is not animated, or beeping, or squeaking. All of this, you will relish without being interrupted with cries for juice, a cookie, or the potty. A dream vacation beyond your wildest dreams! Congratulations!*

I texted Mark immediately: *Ugh. I have to go to San Francisco next week. All week.*

He replied right away: *Monday through Friday?*

Jada: *Unfortunately.*

Mark: *Do you think we can get Joyce to stay over? In case I have to work late? She can do bath and bed.*

Jada: *I don't know. I'll ask her. But she's always talking about her mother and how she has to check on her at night a lot. Can you give work a heads-up that you will have some family issues to attend to next week?*

Mark: *No. You know how it works. Either take time off or be committed around the clock here.*

I had a death grip on my phone. I wanted to write, "Come on! I'm planning a vacation here! Well, a work trip actually, but still."

Jada: *Okay, I'll ask Joyce tonight.*

Mark: *Where did you get your hair cut in the city? Alana is looking for a new place.*

Alana was Mark's work wife, as I called her. I'd met her a few times, at a work dinner on one occasion, and another time when I had to drop something off at Mark's office. She was a tall, pretty, freckly redhead—bubbly and sweet. Alana was the complete opposite of me, so there was no concern Mark would ever be interested in her. She was not at all his type.

Jada: *DiGiorgio Salon on E 53rd. Jack for color. Ray for cut.*

Mark: *Do you have the number?*

Jada: *Did Alana's Google break?*

I immediately felt bad. "That was harsh," I mumbled.

A minute later, I texted again: *Give me a second.*

Mark: *Okay. Thanks.*

I suddenly felt an overwhelming desire to rest my head in my hands for a moment, to get quiet. I tried to listen to the sounds around me. I heard my secretary's printer and a phone ring.

This is not sustainable. We need to talk. Sooner rather than later.

I lifted my head and searched for the number of my salon.

• • ❧ • •

THAT NIGHT AS JOYCE was leaving, I had to ask her something I'd never asked her before. "Would you be able to stay overnight next Monday through Thursday?"

Joyce pointed downward. "Sleep here?"

"Well, not right here on the floor, like in a sleeping bag in the foyer." We laughed. "But yes, overnight in the guest room. We'll pay you, of course! Twice the day rate. Is that fair?"

"I'll have to check with my husband, but I think he'd like the extra money. And my sister can help out for a change and check on my mother."

"Great!" My upcoming work trip was starting to cost me. "I know Mark will appreciate it. You know how unpredictable our jobs can be. He wasn't home until after ten two nights last week."

"I think it would be fine, and I'll be out of my husband's hair for a few days. That'll make him happy."

"Ha!" Maybe Mark and I had a marriage like everyone else after all. Actually, no, we weren't in each other's hair. We were quite out of each other's hair. Too far out.

I knew Joyce had been married to her husband for over thirty years. They had two sons in college, and she wanted her mother to move from Queens to Long Island to be closer to her and her family. But her mother had lived in the same rent-controlled apartment for forty years, so she wasn't going anywhere. And that was pretty much the extent of what I knew about Joyce, other than that she took great care of Ethan. He loved her, and she had a valid driver's license. She had been my neighbor's nanny for ten years, which was how we'd come to hire her. But we never really had much time to chat. In the mornings, I was usually rushing to get out the door, and in the evenings, she was rushing to get home. Ethan was fed, hydrated, and arts and crafted out at the end of every day. We hadn't seen our refrigerator in two years because it was covered in Ethan's "work."

"Hey, you know, can I ask you something about my mother?" Joyce asked.

"Ask *me* something about *your* mother?" I was so surprised by the question, I was afraid I'd sounded rude. "Sure. Of course. Yes. What's up?"

"You see, her landlord, he doesn't respond, and she's having issues with her air-conditioning. Some days, it won't turn on at all, and she has to spend the day at the community center down the street. Last week, she spent the night at my house because it was just too hot in her apartment. He says he'll send someone, and then a couple days later, same problem."

"It just keeps turning off?"

"Yes. Just stops working." She fished through her large zebra-print bag. "I have her lease here. I hate to ask you to do this, but is there anything legal that can be done? We don't know what her rights are, and we don't know who to ask."

I watched her pull out a wad of folded papers. "I have to tell you, Joyce, I handle warehouse leases for large corporations. Our firm doesn't represent individuals."

"Oh." She pulled the papers back to her chest. "Okay. I just thought I'd ask because she can't afford a lawyer. And she can't afford to pay for someone to fix it herself. Neither can we. I was just wondering if it says anything in here that we can go back to him and say, 'Listen, you have to fix this now.' Ya know? He's the owner of a rent-controlled building with a lot of people who've been there a long time, and I think he's doing this stuff on purpose to get them to move."

"That's horrible! I'll look at it. I mean, I don't know how I can help, but I'll look." I took the papers.

For dependable, capable, animal-print-loving Joyce, who I may not know well except that she makes my family's life easier, it's the least I can do.

"If you could just look. Thank you," she said. "Is your flight early next Monday morning? Maybe I should sleep over Sunday night."

The idea of Joyce entertaining Ethan while I packed elated me.

"Yes! It's very, very early. I think. I don't know, but either way, that would be great." I held up the lease, smiling. "And I'll look at this tonight."

• • ❧ • •

WHEN MARK CAME HOME, he gave Ethan his bath and put him to bed. As Mark went to the office to continue working, I cleaned up the kitchen. Then I carried two wine glasses and a bottle of Chardonnay to the office, where Mark was reading something on the desktop as he pinched his eyebrow.

He seemed startled to see me. "What are you doing?"

I rested the wine bottle on the desk. *Alcohol will make this easier for both of us.*

"Well, Ethan's asleep, and I thought we'd talk." I sat on the leather couch in the office, holding the wine glasses.

"About what?"

This marriage is not sustainable! This is not normal! No. Too harsh. Baby steps. "I don't know. Want a glass of wine?"

"I don't drink."

"You drink wine occasionally."

"With dinner."

I held up the glasses. "Well, I'll drink for the both of us."

He shook his head, confused, and went back to reviewing whatever was on his desktop. Then he started typing.

"Can I ask you something?"

"What?" he asked, annoyed.

"Are you working?"

"Yes. Is that your question?"

"Do you think this is normal?"

"Drinking?"

"No. This." I motioned to the space between us. "When was the last time we had a real conversation? I mean, I know we don't have date nights but... I don't know, the way we exist. Do you think this is normal?"

He glanced up, confused. "Do you feel okay?"

"I feel fine," I said defensively. "I know. I'm a piece of work, right?"

"What are you doing?"

"Trying to talk." *About our marriage.*

"You only ever talk to me when Ethan or your family's around ."

"That's exactly how I feel about you."

He shrugged. "I guess that's just how we are."

"And you're okay with that?"

"It's just how we are, Jada. I have work to do." His eyes went back to the screen as he dragged his mouse.

I want a divorce. Say it. Right now.

I stood up.

"Is Joyce able to stay over next week?" he asked, his eyes still on his screen.

"Yes. She can do it."

"Were you going to tell me?"

"I forgot. I just asked her before she left, and then we had to do bath and bed, and I had to clean the kitchen." I grabbed the wine bottle and glasses.

"I did bath and bed."

"And I cleaned the kitchen," I said, enunciating each word. He continued to type, his eyes focused on the email I assumed he was composing.

"Don't forget to make sure the guest room is cleared out for Joyce," he said. "You've had those boxes with Christmas decorations on the bed for months now."

I squared my shoulders. The wine bottle and glasses dropped to my side, clinking lightly. "I want..." *Say it.*

His eyes found me. "Want what?"

Say it.

"To go through the decorations and *accidentally*, on purpose, throw out the stupid ones from my mother and sister, the ones that read 'Ain't No Christmas Like an Italian Christmas.'" I opened the door with my free hand. "I know—I'm a piece of work."

He didn't respond. I made my way back to the kitchen and put the wine and glasses away. Then I opened the freezer, stuck my head in, and got quiet. I listened to the humming of the air. *This is stupid.* I found the vodka, opened it, and threw back a swill. Then I washed it down with a piece of extra-dark chocolate.

• • ❧ • •

LATER, IN BED, I TRIED to read Joyce's mother's lease, even though I knew there would probably be nothing in there out of the ordinary and that she should just call some local agency that fought landlords who didn't provide basic necessities. Still, I made a promise. Yet no matter how hard I tried to focus, I kept daydreaming about being alone in San Francisco. I researched spa treatments I could book before or after work. *Mmm. The deep-tissue shiatsu fusion massage looks divine.*

Then I checked in on social media. Cori was describing her wedding as goth meets chic. *Vomit. Gina would have been in the wedding, in a frilly dress and combat boots, I bet.*

After I shut off the light, I tossed and turned for a long while. My mind swirled with several thoughts—what a coward I was for not being able to tell my husband what I was truly feeling, Gina and Cori, the logistics of being away from Ethan for a week, and my feelings about being away from Mark.

I can't wait.

Though when it came to Ethan, I had a feeling that after one day, I would be wishing I was home. *Will he wonder where I am?* I was going to want to know what he ate, what he talked about in his bath, and if he was scared before going to bed. I would have to add "Explain toe naming to Mark and Joyce" to my to-do list.

As I was finally drifting off, I felt a hand on my forehead and then a poke in my left eye.

"What the—" I shot up. "What are you doing?"

"Sorry," Mark said. "You turned over. I thought you might be awake."

"So you put your hand on my forehead?"

"I was feeling if your eyes were open. I thought I was doing it gently."

"So if they were, you were going to poke me in the eye?"

"No." He leaned in. "I was going to ask you if you ever let Orly know whether we're going to the shore with her for Fourth of July. Not that I want to go either. I just want to make sure you gave her our answer."

I plunked my head back on my pillow and exhaled, my hand over my eye. This marriage is like a ping-pong game, taking turns baffling and annoying one another. "Yes. You were there. Remember? I said no. I would rather get stung on the ass by fourteen jellyfish and not be able to sit for four weeks than spend four hours at the Jersey Shore with my sister."

"Just checking," he said. "I know you have a lot on your mind, and you forget to tell people things."

"I didn't forget. I told her no. That's what you wanted to ask me?"

"Yeah. I don't want to go either. It just came to my mind. 'Kay. Good night."

As he rolled over, I placed my hand over my now tearing eye and tried to get quiet. Mark's white noise machine hummed.

Lonely. I'm lonely. I'm lonely in my marriage, in motherhood, in my life.

Theoretically, the more people a person was around, the less lonely she should feel. But in my case, being with my parents, my sister, her family, or Mark—individually or all together—made me feel lonelier than being alone. It defied logic, but it was true. I couldn't say that to Mark or anyone else, but it was true.

God, that is so depressing.

And now I had something else to think about as I struggled to fall asleep. Both eyes started to tear, and I needed to blow my nose. I crept to the bathroom because Mark was now sleeping.

I grabbed a tissue and leaned over the sink. I put my head in my hands and listened to the quiet space of my cavernous bathroom.

Something needs to change. Something will change. I will make this happen.

I lifted my head and started singing to myself. "Only the Lonely." I assumed I must have heard it on the oldies station at some point recently.

Chapter 4

My Uber driver on the way to the airport was my favorite kind of Uber driver: silent. Unfortunately, that peace was short-lived because my sister called.

I answered the phone, assuming the worst since she was calling me so early. "What happened?"

"Nothing. I woke up really early, and I know you're on the way to the airport."

"So everything is okay?"

"Yeah. Everything is fine. I don't know why I can't fall back to sleep. It's awful. I can't believe you get up at this hour to commute every day."

"Is that why you're calling? To talk about my daily schedule?" I did not hide my annoyance.

Orly seemed unfazed. "Did Mommy tell you she's going to the doctor on Tuesday? In the city?"

"No." *Of course not. You know I don't talk to our mother every day, let alone multiple times a day like you.* "For what? Her annual appointment?"

My mother left Queens for Manhattan twice a year—to see the *Nutcracker* with Orly and my nieces every December, and to see her gynecologist, who'd moved to the city twenty years ago.

"Um, yeah. I thought we would go to lunch after, but then I remembered you have to travel for work."

"I *get* to travel for work. I'm excited. So yeah, I won't be able to meet you for lunch."

My Uber pulled up to the curb.

"Have fun in California," Orly said. "Will you get to go to Disneyland?"

"I'm going to San Francisco, nowhere near Disney, and I'm going for work."

"That's too bad."

I hung up with her as my driver slammed the trunk shut and hoisted my bag onto the sidewalk. After I checked my bags and made my way through security, I headed toward the gate, with my water bottle and gum in tow. I caught a glimpse of the sun starting to rise. When I'd left the house, it was still dark out. I had told Mark and Joyce not to wake up. They'd listened. I reviewed the lists I'd left for them on the kitchen table, detailing Ethan's schedule and routine, before realizing they knew all of that information, except for the toe-naming monster deterrent trick. Ethan slept soundly as I quietly snapped a photo and posted it with the caption, "Going to miss this little guy while I'm traveling for work this week."

I felt a tug in my gut as a thought struck me. *What if I had written the whole truth?* The caption definitely would have been different: Of course, I'm going to miss my child, every bit of him—from his curly hair to his cute toes—but hallelujah, Mama gets a break! Later, kiddo.

As I boarded, I prayed for a seatmate as antisocial as me. When I got to my window seat, I pulled out my magazines, put my water bottle in the backseat pocket and reclined. Two seconds later, I felt a presence.

The woman was about my age but tall, lean, and fit in her skinny black pants. She popped her probably perfectly packed luggage into the overhead compartment and smiled at me as she slid into her seat. "Hopefully, we take off on time," she said.

I smiled. "Hopefully." *Do not say another word. Please.* I inserted my headphones solely for the purpose of appearing as though I were listening to something and shouldn't be bothered.

The woman didn't trouble me the rest of the flight, not overtly. But she did manage to make me feel like shit.

First, she pulled out her stack of magazines, which were all parenting related. *Oh, come on.* I subscribed to two of them. But they either had articles that scared the crap out of me: "This mom didn't notice the rash on her son's elbow until it was too late." Or they had articles that made me wonder who the hell had time for this crap: "Make a tree house with your child out of paper towel rolls."

Then she FaceTimed right before we took off with what appeared to be her son and daughter, and they couldn't stop gushing over each other.

"I'm going to miss you, Mommy!" one of the children said.

"I'm going to miss you. Don't forget to draw me a picture every day."

"We won't forget!"

I couldn't picture Ethan saying he was going to miss me. He would sometimes tell Mark and me he would miss us when we left for work in the morning, but it was directed at both of us. He didn't gush over me like other kids seemed to gush over their mommies. I supposed I wasn't a gusher either. I hadn't been raised that way. JoAnn was not the gushy type, not with me at least. I tried to protect Ethan and make him feel safe. Gushy, though, I was not.

The woman next to me didn't care how loud she was. "I love you more than the earth and the moon and the stars."

"We love you more than the earth and the moon and the stars!" one of her kids declared back.

What if I call my mother right now and scream into the phone, "I love you more than the earth and the moon and the stars"? I think she would have me committed.

"Please turn off all electronic devices," the flight attendant said as she walked up the aisle.

Thank God.

My neighbor didn't make a peep the rest of the flight. She read her parenting magazines cover to cover and folded over some of the pages. I read my non-parenting magazines and savored my corn muffin and coffee refills. I didn't even miss checking my phone every ten minutes. The free Wi-Fi wasn't working, but I was engrossed in my magazines and also getting out of my head and listening to the sound of the air and the engine.

Something has to change. But I don't have to think about it for five days. I'm going to use this time to rest, relax, recharge—oh, and work. Then when I get back home, I'll do what needs to be done.

I was feeling calm until it was time to interact with another human—a line cutter.

"Excuse me," she hissed as I stuck my foot in front of her rolling bag.

"Were you in this row? Row four?" I asked the honey-haired line cutter, who was in row five and trying to exit out of turn.

She rolled her eyes. "Go. Go ahead."

"Row four is exiting now." I slowly strung my strap over my shoulder. I would have taken more time, but I had nothing in the overhead compartment. "Four comes before five." I straightened the strap on my bag.

"Yeah, I know," she said.

I smirked and walked out.

As I waited at baggage claim, I checked on Ethan and Joyce and posted on social media, "Landed in Cali!" Then I got a cab to our local counsel's office, where, within the first half hour of being there, it became apparent that these lawyers had it covered. I wondered what I was even doing there, which was fine with me. I sat down in the comfortable leather chair of the conference room—or "war room" as they referred to it—and pulled up the hotel spa menu again.

A text from Dan popped up: *How's it going?*

Jada: *Good. We had a good strategy session. I think we're up to speed now that I'm here.*

I hoped my reply read as "Jada is needed in faraway locales. Jada is needed on whatever cases require long flights and quiet hotel rooms."

My main contact was a gorgeous black woman with green eyes named Kaya, who, upon greeting me at the elevator, immediately apologized for not being able to take me to dinner that night because she had to go to her son's karate ceremony.

"No problem!" I replied. "I have a three-year-old, almost four. So I'm looking forward to going back to the hotel and not having to feed or bathe anyone but myself. By the way, is Lionel getting here tonight or tomorrow?"

"His flight was rerouted! An issue with the landing gear. But luckily, they were able to land in Chicago."

"What a shame. I was so looking forward to seeing him." I snapped my finger across my chest in an *oh darn* gesture.

Kaya failed to suppress her smile. "He'll grace us with his presence soon enough."

"Gird your loins."

The rest of the day was simple—a lot of reviewing deposition questions, strategy, and changes to questions. The conference room had the pièce de résistance—the ultimate Frontbook snap—a stunning view of the Golden Gate Bridge. I posted a picture with the caption, "Room with a view!"

As I packed up to head to the hotel, I could practically feel the terry-cloth robe brushing against my skin. After a quick ride across town, I let the bellhop carry my bag, and then I tore off my heels as soon as I got to my room. Plopping down on the bed, I grabbed the room service menu. There were no oysters. There was nothing, actually, that looked appetizing to me. *This isn't the menu I saw online.*

I called the front desk. It rang while my hunger intensified. By what felt like the hundredth ring, I was annoyed and ravenous: a lethal combination.

I hung up and popped open my suitcase to grab my flip-flops. *Crap*. I could have sworn I packed them, but I didn't. I wrangled my toe-crunching stilettos back on and headed down to find food.

My heels clicked and clacked on the marble of the lobby floor. It wasn't hard to find the fine-dining steakhouse to the left of the concierge desk. It was dark and a little chilly from the air-conditioning. I really wished I'd brought my suit jacket, but I was getting hungrier by the second.

I slid onto a sturdy leather barstool. "Do you happen to have extra-large Spanish olives?"

"We do."

"I love you."

The bartender opened his arms wide. "And I love you. What can I get you?"

"I'll have a vodka martini, extra dirty, with extra-large Spanish olives. And the oysters."

And Mama will want an entrée after her oysters. Let's see, filet mignon or lamb chops or...

While it was quiet at the bar, the ambient noise of a raucous business dinner of about ten men trickled over.

Or lobster or veal or...

"Fuck yeah!" someone shouted.

The wild dinner party just got rowdier. It warranted a death stare.

As I whipped around to burn them with my eyes, I noticed one of the men was signing the bill.

Thank God. Get out of here. I turned back around. *Lamb chops. Definitely the lamb chops.*

"No way!"

Fucking fraternity boys. Leave already.

I pierced them with another glare as they all stood up and walked through the bar to leave. I noticed the last one in the pack, walking quietly with his hands in his pockets.

It was Todd.

Chapter 5

"Todd!" I called. If I'd actually had a moment to absorb the fact that a guy I thought about on a daily basis was on the same coast, in the same city, and in the same restaurant as me, I would have had the presence of mind to identify it as an extraordinary coincidence, but not one I should act on. I would have hovered over the bar and hidden my head in the cocktail menu, and maybe texted Veronica. "Guess who just walked by in SF of all places. TTT—Todd the Turd."

But I'd reacted.

He looked up, and it was too late.

"Jada?" His face was full of shocked delight. It had only been six years, and I'd seen on social media that he hadn't changed much. Maybe he had a few more forehead wrinkles like we all did, but he was the same. Same light hair. Same broad shoulders. Same blue eyes.

I rose from my barstool to do... I wasn't sure what. *Kiss him on the cheek? Hug him? Offer a handshake?*

I decided on a hug. It was long and warm, followed by excited and awkward simultaneous exchanges of "What are you doing here?" and "on business," "me too," "you look great," and "you too."

"Wow, Jada," he said. "In San Francisco, of all places."

"All the way across the country." I shook my head. "Crazy."

"What have you been up to? Did I hear you got married?"

I noticed his coworkers waiting for him in the lobby. "You're not going with them?"

"Nah. I see them all the time. Hold on." He walked to the doorway. I heard him tell someone to text him the name of the bar where they ended up, and he would meet them there. I was elated for a moment, in spite of myself, that I would get more time with him.

He came back and pulled out a seat. He ordered a vodka and tonic for himself. "Martini, extra dirty, with extra-large Spanish olives?" He remembered.

My legs threatened to quit on me as I settled back on my barstool. "I already ordered one."

"So, wow. You got married, right?" he asked again.

"I did." I displayed my left hand. "Had a kid too. A boy. Ethan. Almost four years old now. He's great. Not planning on another one soon, though. We're taking our time."

"Nice. I'm married too. We didn't take our time. Got pregnant just before the wedding. Shhh." He smirked. "So, where are you and your husband living?"

"On Long Island." That was my attempt to be vague, hoping he wouldn't ask what town. "We decided we wanted Ethan to have a suburban childhood. Even though we love the city, I think Mark—my husband—and I just felt like it would be easier to raise kids in the suburbs."

"Us too. Me and Jessica, my wife. Same thing. We're on Long Island too. Never thought that'd happen, but at least I don't drive a minivan."

"Ha! Me neither." Our drinks arrived at the same time.

"Let's drink to that."

We lifted our glasses and clinked just as our knees brushed.

"Where on Long Island?" he asked.

I had to concentrate on swallowing and backing myself up on the barstool to avoid another knee brush. "Empire Hills."

"No way. We're in Roseland. Wow. We live in neighboring towns and had to fly all the way to San Francisco to run into each other. Another toast," he declared. "To San Fran and old friends."

"To San Fran and old friends."

We sipped. I concentrated. *Swallow. Back up again. Little more. Not too obvious.*

I scooched back and said, "This is pretty crazy. You know—"

But I couldn't finish because he reached for the small of my back, leaned in close to my neck, and said, "You look amazing."

I cleared my throat. *Say something.* "Thanks."

We chatted more about houses and home improvements and work and kids and family.

"So..." He moved back as if to get a better look at me. "Are you happy?"

Despite my internet search history, I had only recently confessed to myself the undeniable truth about my marriage. I still hadn't said it out loud to anyone.

"No," I replied before I could stop myself. *Well, the truth is out.*

After a few more martinis and vodka and tonics, he knew too much and so did I.

He and Jessica had had problems from day one. They may have rushed into it with unrealistic expectations. She wanted several children. She wanted a bigger house. She wanted a nicer car. She wanted it all. And when he wanted to end a fight—or start one—he would just tell her she lived in a dream world and had better start living in reality.

"There are good times," he said. "We laugh over the kids, and we have our good moments, but overall it's, well, it's not what I expected."

They appeared so happy in their photos on social media, but if anyone could understand what a façade that was, it was me.

When it was my turn again, I let another truth leave my lips for the first time that I hadn't realized was just beneath the surface. "I've found motherhood to be unfulfilling." I quickly explained that I loved my son with every fiber of my being, but motherhood was harder than I'd ever imagined.

What is in these martinis?

He nodded as he put his arm on the back of my chair. "That's what they should tell women in that book about expecting. 'Don't expect what you expect.'"

"Yes!" I shouted, spilling a bit of my martini.

"But what can you do about it now, right?"

That doesn't sound so good. I half-nodded. My throat clenched, partially from the guilt of admitting it all and partially from the relief of finally feeling understood for the first time in as long as I could remember. I was afraid I might cry, so I changed the subject.

"Did you read the latest news about Lee Harvey Oswald's trip to Cuba?"

His shoulders lifted a little as he laughed and sipped his drink. "Yes. You did?"

"Yeah. Remember my friend Veronica? She has an obsession with true crime and history too. I used to be completely disinterested, and then I saw a book on your shelf once, and I borrowed it."

"*Agent X*? So that's where it went."

"You gave me permission, by the way. Must have slipped your mind that I still had it when, you know, we went our separate ways. Anyway, remind me, what got you interested?"

"The movie from the nineties. *JFK*. I saw it on TV once and read a bunch of books after that. I remember Veronica. How is she?"

"Good. Happy."

"How do you know she's happy?"

"I can tell. And I'm happy for her."

"Are you really?" he teased.

"Ha. Yes." I said pointedly. After a moment, I added, "But sometimes, it feels like, I don't know, kind of like her happiness is a sort of personal affront to me. Does that make sense?"

"No. You're jealous."

"No," I pleaded. "It's almost like her happiness magnifies my unhappiness. Do you have any friends like that?"

"I know what you mean."

I touched the stem of my drink. "This has turned into a real confessional."

"We'll both say three Our Fathers when it's over."

I couldn't be sure if my lifted mood, and what I confessed next, was due to the drinks, the relief I felt after confessing the truth about my marriage and motherhood, or the thrill of seeing Todd.

"Well, while we're still at it, I have another confession to make." I adjusted myself on the barstool and licked my lips. My mouth started to feel puckered and dry. "I know your wife. Our kids play together at Long Island at Play."

"Say that again?" He leaned in as if he hadn't heard me correctly, though the corners of his lips curled in a knowing smirk.

"I know Jessica, your wife," I repeated.

"How?"

"Long Island at Play," I said again. "We're friends on Frontbook. But I'm never on. Who has the time, right?" *Ha!* "But yeah, I know her. Very well. Well, not very well. We're friendly. We're always there at the same time. It's not that big of a deal."

"She never mentioned that." He was serious.

"Because she doesn't know."

He smirked. "She doesn't know she's friends with you?"

"No. She doesn't know that I know you. I mean, Todd, come on. What was I going to say? 'I used to date your husband?' I figured I should just keep my mouth shut for once."

As I said this, I had his full attention. For so long, he was my friend's good-looking older brother, who was aloof and unattainable. He had this way about him that made it seem like he was never that interested in anything or anyone, so when anyone did get his attention, it was the ultimate validation, as pathetic as that sounded and seemed now.

I fell for it then, though. When we ran into each other one night in the city six years ago, it had seemed like fate. I was with Mark, my boyfriend of two years at the time, but I broke up with him to be with Todd. It seemed like we were headed in the right direction at first, until our dinners and nights out together became more and more infrequent and his declarations about how busy he was and how he didn't like to define relationships became more and more frequent.

One morning, I told him my parents were coming into the city to go to lunch and asked if he wanted to meet them, and that was when he ended it. I'd left in a ball of fury, breaking his UPenn mug in the process.

So mature.

Not long after, I'd reconciled with Mark, which was easier than it should have been. He'd welcomed me back with open arms. I'd felt then like I didn't deserve Mark and was lucky he would even have me back.

I asked the bartender for water. "And honestly, is date even the right word for what we were? It would be more like 'Your husband and I used to... I don't know what. I fell in love quickly, and then he ripped my heart out.' But at least I got a book out of it, and all he got was a broken mug."

I gulped my water. I realized I'd never ordered food. I was drinking on a few oysters, a basically empty stomach. As I was about to reach for the menu, he squeezed my hand. "I'm sorry I hurt you, Jada."

I stared at his hand on mine. "It's okay." I pulled my hand away.

He ordered another round.

I shook my head and changed the subject. "Social media can be so deceiving."

"How so?" he asked.

"It just looks like everyone is so happy. It's a big fucking façade. It never seems like anyone has a fight, or feels drained from work, or from commuting, or taking care of their kids, or doesn't love their spouse anymore. And maybe never did."

He nibbled on his cocktail straw as he readjusted himself on the leather barstool, never taking his eyes off me.

"I have another confession," I said. "I check Frontbook every day, every hour. And I check Jessica's in particular—often—because I want to see how you're doing and how you look. I never really stopped thinking about you."

He released the straw and studied me.

It's all out there now. I pulled the curtain back, and I'm still the same old pathetic, pining Jada, just older.

"I have a confession too," he said.

I sat up.

"I know that you know my wife. She mentioned a kind of foul-mouthed but funny mother at LI Play. That's how she described you—foulmouthed but funny—and I asked her name. There aren't a lot of Jadas in the world."

My mouth fell open.

"And there's only one Jada who could fit that description. You're one of a kind."

I know I'm drunk, but I have to commit this to memory. One of a kind. That's better than piece of work. And this whole time, he knew? I have to digest this when I'm sober.

"There's more," he said.

"If you tell me you know my husband, I'll vomit."

"No, not that, but I'm on Frontbook too. I don't use my name, just an abbreviation of first and middle name, and my profile picture is a Giants helmet."

"You have a fake account?"

"Well, it's me, but yeah, I guess so. And I can see your pictures when you allow friends of friends to see them. I've seen you and your husband and your son. I think about you too, Jada. A lot. I'm sorry I ever hurt you. I'm sorry you're not happy. You're still beautiful."

My throat constricted. Tears welled up. *Do not cry, you pathetic loser!* I tried to breathe, but no air was coming in. *You're acting like a teenager! You're a wife and mother. Get it together. Oh, fuck it.*

I leaned in to kiss him. *When was the last time Mark and I looked at each other? Really looked at each other? I can't remember.*

I jerked my head back before our lips could touch.

Mark.

The combined motion of leaning in then jerking back made me dizzy, and before I could steady myself, my butt slid off the stool and landed firmly on the floor.

That's going to hurt tomorrow.

Todd knelt down to help me up. "Let's get out of here."

He paid the bill, and we went back to his room.

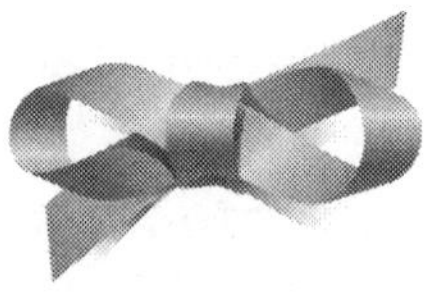

Chapter 6

After he shut the door behind us, he leaned in for the kiss he was denied earlier.

He was denied yet again. "Stop!" I grabbed the wall for balance as I concentrated on not feeling dizzy.

Not now. Not this way. On a business trip while our spouses are home with our children? No. If there is even a remote chance that we can be together—and a coincidence like this makes me think all of those bullshit memes on social media about coincidences and the universe might be right after all—we have to do it the right way. This is the wrong way.

"Let's talk more," I said.

He seemed amused by that as he plopped down on the bed and propped himself up on a hotel pillow. "What would you like to talk about?"

"Do you have water?" I asked.

He popped back up, rushed to the mini bar, and grabbed water, soda, pretzels, chips, chocolate, and gummy bears. He poured them onto the bed, and I busted open the pretzels.

"Did you read the most recent book about Mary Pinchot Meyer?" I asked through a mouthful of pretzels.

"The CIA guy's wife? No, but I've seen enough shows and read enough articles to believe she was murdered. What do you think?"

"I think so too. And what ever happened to her diary?" I attempted to open the cap on a bottle of water.

"I think her brother-in-law burned it," he said as he took the bottle from me and twisted the cap off.

"This is the best conversation I've had in a long time," I said.

"Me too."

"What kind of losers go back to a hotel room and stay fully dressed, talking about history?"

"Who are you calling a loser? And I didn't want to stay dressed."

I slapped his arm and reached for the chips.

"You and Mark don't stay up all night discussing conspiracy theories?" he asked.

"He has no interest. Science is his thing. He always wants to go to planetariums." I rolled onto my back and faced the ceiling. "You know, when we were dating, I used to wake up and immediately check to see if you texted me. Even before I opened my eyes, I'd think, 'I hope I have a text from Todd.' God, I sound so pathetic. And am I really saying all of this out loud?" I touched my lips. "I am really shit-bonkers drunk."

"It's cute."

"No, it's not. But I liked you. I always liked you. I always thought you were cute. Michelle's brother."

"I always thought you were hot."

"When we finally got together, I risked so much to be with you—breaking up with Mark and all. I had perfect, wonderful Mark, who my family adored, and why would I ever give him up? But I couldn't believe it was finally, really happening with you. Holy shit, what is coming out of my mouth?"

"Don't stop. I like it."

"Of course you do!"

"Keep going."

"No. It's your turn. Considering you ended it, I'm guessing you weren't eagerly anticipating texts from me, but tell me something good, something you remember about our brief but, I like to think, intense time together." I faced him. He was fiddling with a chocolate bar wrapper. "Make it really fucking good."

"Okay. Um. Let's see."

"You have to think that hard?"

"You liked chocolate. And whenever we would go out to dinner, on the way home, you'd stop at a bodega and get a dark chocolate bar. And then we'd get back to my apartment, and you'd break off one piece of it, and that's all you'd eat. You would put the rest in my refrigerator. I had a bunch of partially eaten varieties of dark-chocolate bars in my fridge. After it ended—"

"You ended it."

"Yes. I stand corrected. Well, after that, I kept them for a long time. It took me a long time to throw them out. I don't know why. But here." He handed the opened chocolate bar to me. "It's milk chocolate. Sorry."

I took it. "Thanks, but that's what you think of? Chocolate? I want a compliment! I was fishing for a compliment, you idiot. Oh, how sad—you held on to my chocolate bars. No, you didn't. You worked ninety hours a week. You barely opened your fridge. You probably forgot them in there for six months."

"Probably."

We both laughed.

"No, seriously," he said. "They were hard to throw out. And whenever I'm in a store, and I see a dark chocolate bar, I think of you."

"Oh, please." I tore off a piece of the chocolate bar and chewed. "Well, you better."

"And my heart hurts a little."

"Too far. But nice try."

"I also missed your perfume."

"Lovely."

"I know. Nice of me, right?"

"No. That's the name of it."

"Oh. Yeah, I remember. A very polite-sounding name for a very blunt girl."

"I can be blunt, but I'm not a girl."

"Woman."

"I just hate beating around the bush."

"That's putting it mildly. But it's part of your charm." He put his arm behind my neck, and I relaxed into it. "And that's what I really missed."

We eventually fell asleep but were luckily woken by a screaming child running down the hallway. In our drunken geek-out over JFK assassination history, neither of us remembered to set our alarms. We didn't look at our phones at all.

A few hours later, as the sun shot like a laser through an opening in the blinds, and it sounded like the screaming child in the hallway had a megaphone in front of the door, I bolted upright and winced in pain at the sharp jabs behind both eyes. I shook Todd. "Do you have Tylenol?"

"Yeah." He walked to the bathroom, still in his suit pants, his white T-shirt stretching across his muscular chest. "Here you go."

"What time is it?"

He lifted the alarm clock on the bedside table to show me. It read 7:09.

"Fuck." I had to get out of there and get dressed fast to be at the office by eight o'clock in San Francisco traffic. I swallowed the pills and slowly lifted myself off the bed. "Will you make your flight?"

He nodded.

"So you're in Dallas until Friday? Jessica mentioned you were traveling all week."

"Did she?"

There was a new kind of pang, right in the chest. It was a guilty pang at the thought of what Jessica was doing right then. Innocent, unknowing Jessica was probably emptying the dishwasher while I was waking up in a hotel room with her husband.

"Did the Tylenol go down wrong? Why are you holding your chest?"

"I'm fine. Are you going to take your JFK nerd coworker to see the X?" I asked, referring to the X in Dealey Plaza, where JFK was shot.

"If we have time. I'll send you a photo."

"Okay, well, text me when you land." As I put my shoes back on, a wave of anxiety rushed through me. First, I felt a jab of pain in my eyes, then a pang of guilt, and now a rush of anxiety. *I might start missing my boring life.*

"I'll text you before I land." He kissed my forehead. "Until we meet again?"

What are we going to do now? How are we going to see each other at home? Are we going to see each other at home? "Will we meet again?" I asked.

"Yes."

"What are we going to do?"

"We'll figure it out."

I nodded before walking out the door.

• • ❧ • •

THE REST OF THE MORNING was torture. I sat in depositions for hours, trying not to check my phone and trying to guzzle enough water to relieve my pounding head and cotton mouth. I also wondered what I was doing there since I wasn't conducting a single deposition.

"Optics," Dan replied when I eventually asked him that exact question via text.

Fine by me.

During breaks, I called Joyce and Ethan and checked my phone, waiting for a text from Todd, like the old days.

As the deposition proceeded, I relived the past few hours like it was a dream I didn't want to forget. My daydreaming was interrupted by a nightmare, however, when Lionel arrived. Sweaty and huffing, he marched into the deposition room and demanded to know where the printer was.

"I can show you," Kaya said.

He didn't acknowledge her as he set up his laptop and, evidently, printed something. "Can you bring me that?"

I read Kaya's mind. *Was he talking to her? Yes, he was. And he expected her to fetch whatever it was he'd just printed.*

I sprang up. I might as well make myself useful and spare sweet Kaya from Lionel as best I could. "I'll get it. How are you, Lionel?"

He squinted in my direction. "Jada. You know where the printer is? Getting the lay of the land here, are you?"

I walked out of the room, not needing to bite my tongue. I was in too good of a mood as I thought about Todd and all that we'd talked about the night before.

I spent the rest of the next few days doing more of the same—protecting Kaya from Lionel, sitting through more depositions, calling Joyce and Ethan during breaks, and texting with Todd. Ethan seemed unfazed by the fact that I was not there, which made me wonder if he was more adaptable than I thought. *Would he be able to split his time between his father and me? Would he like Todd?*

I typed a text to Todd from my laptop as I sat in the war room with the others past ten p.m.

Jada: *How is Dallas?*

Todd: *It'd be better if you were here. No one else seemed to appreciate it when we passed Parkland Hospital.*

Jada: *You poor history nerd, all by yourself.*

Todd: *Stuck with finance assholes. Come save me.*

I sent a smile emoji.

Todd: *It was nice to spend the night with you.*

Jada: *You too.*

I shifted in my chair. *Spend the night? Wow.* That was what we did, technically.

Todd: *Too bad you made us keep our clothes on.*

Lionel caught me smiling. I bit my lip.

"Enjoying this case, Jada?"

"Warehouse leases light up my life, Lionel."

"They should. We pay you enough."

I typed one last text before closing the texting window on my laptop: *Sorry. I have to get back to work.*

Todd: *Too far with that comment? You're really a good girl, Jada. I always knew that about you.*

Jada: *I'm not a girl. And not that good.*

Todd: *I know that too.*

He ended that text with a wink emoji.

Jada: *Okay, I really have to go. We will figure this out?*

Todd: *Yes. And then we'll get naked.*

Jada: *When it's actually appropriate. Bye.*

Todd: *Yes, ma'am.*

I slammed my laptop shut.

Kaya stared. "Everything okay?" she whispered.

I shook my head. "It's nothing." I mouthed back and lifted the screen up to get back to work.

By Friday, I had mixed feelings about going home. I missed my son, but the thought of getting back and facing Mark and what was ahead filled me with dread. Before the trip, I'd wanted Mark and me to go our separate ways. I just hadn't had the courage to pull the plug. Now I knew I had to do it. Ending up with Todd was the ultimate incentive, but actually going through with it—hurting Mark, Jessica, and dear God, Ethan too, and Todd's kids—was in no uncertain terms, terrifying.

We'll figure it out.

Todd and I had texted nonstop from Tuesday through Thursday. His last text on Thursday read: *We are going to make this happen. We'll figure it out. There has to be a reason we ran into each other, right?*

So I wasn't terribly concerned when I didn't hear from him on Friday morning.

I texted him from the car to the airport: *Back to LI, I go. Bracing myself.* I added a sad emoji and a plane emoji.

Silence from him.

Hmm. Maybe he's in meetings. I know what that's like.

On the flight home, the guy next to me hogged the armrest, and I let him have it. I actually let him hog it. And I even let someone cut in line at the Hudson News. I felt like a new person—lighter, happier, and hopeful. *Change is ahead. I will do this.*

• • ❧ • •

ON FRIDAY NIGHT, I tiptoed through the front door of my dark house and rested my suitcase down before taking off my shoes on the cold marble foyer. Every light was off.

I unzipped the top of my suitcase to take out my bag of toiletries and held on to the curved railing as I headed upstairs. I knew Ethan would already be asleep, but I opened the door to peek at him and then snuck over to put my face close to his.

I was hoping Mark was asleep. I couldn't face him at that point, though I knew I would have to eventually. I was just hoping to put it off at least for a little while. I had to get settled back in, get my bearings, and figure it out with Todd. *One thing at a time.*

Mark was in bed, watching some docuseries called *The Story of Our Planet.*

"Hey," I said as I walked directly to the bathroom attached to our bedroom.

"Hey!" He perked up. "Was there a lot of traffic?"

"Yeah."

"Which car service did you use?"

"I took an Uber." I put my night cream back in the cabinet.

"Oh, because we don't use Advantage anymore. Supposedly, there was a mix-up, and they refused to pick up Keith Carrington"—one of the partners at Mark's firm—"from JFK two weeks ago, and now the firm took them off of our approved vendor list. I was going to tell you they stink and not to use them."

"They stink?" You're an adult. You can say, "They suck." And more importantly, I just flew home from San Francisco on a five-hour flight on a Friday night after a long week. I'm exhausted. And you're talking to me about car-service companies? I think I prefer the Mark who is in the middle of working on something and doesn't want to have a serious conversation about the state of our marriage.

"I took an Uber," I repeated then grabbed a T-shirt and pajama bottoms from the dresser in the corner next to the coffee table and chaise lounge, which did nothing but take up space. "Listen, I'm exhausted." I pointed at the TV. "Are you watching this?"

He yawned. "I'm going to sleep."

I hit the power button on the remote and went to the bathroom to brush my teeth. When I got into bed, Mark's eyes were shut. I reached for my phone.

"What's the plan tomorrow?" he asked as he rolled over.

I startled. "Uh. Can you take Ethan to the park? I have to unpack and do a million other things." *And figure out exactly how to eventually tell you I want a divorce.*

"I have a couple of calls throughout the weekend. But I might be able to. You might have to take him to LI at Play at some point. He keeps talking about it." He yawned and turned the other way.

I am going nowhere near LI at Play.

"Okay. Good night." I unlocked my phone—still nothing from Todd.

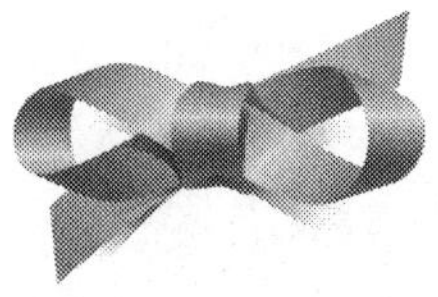

Chapter 7

Gina swirled a lo mein noodle with her fork and leaned in. "So, do you think it was a conspiracy?" she mocked in a high-pitched whisper. "Do you think he acted alone?"

I rolled my eyes and bit into my greasy egg roll.

"Holy shit!" Gina cackled, leaning back in her chair, her knees lifting up as she howled. "What a couple of geeks! I mean, honestly." She shook her head and went back to twirling her noodle. "Fucking dorks."

"Shut up. Please."

"No wonder Grandma and Grandpa quit."

"I wasn't cool enough for them?" I asked.

"No. I'm kidding," Gina said. "They didn't quit. It doesn't work that way. But I can see why they needed me. After we knew he'd be there, it was obvious that it was about to get complicated. I mean, not complicated like 'tracking Oswald to Mexico' complicated, but you know."

"Would you shut up?" I glanced up from my egg roll. "Wait, you knew he'd be there? How?"

"We can see things. Like flies on a wall. We could see that the guy you still think about was going on a business trip to San Francisco and that your case was going to have depositions there the same week. And—'God help us all' as Grandma and Grandpa would say—we could then see you'd be staying at the same hotel. Of all the gin joints."

She was wearing one of her white T-shirts. It showed a drawing of a melting ice cream cone with little paper-doll-like children holding hands as they surrounded it.

"How do you know I think about him?"

"We can see that too."

"You can read minds?" I asked.

"No. We can read hearts."

"Why don't I feel that guilty? I mean, I could barely look at Mark when I got home, and I can't even think about Jessica without feeling ill, but I feel like I should feel worse."

"Mmm." Gina swayed her head back and forth as if she were trying to figure out how to phrase what she was going to say next. She stared out toward Queens Boulevard. Light from the streetlamps surrounded her in a sort of golden glow.

The streetlights in that part of town cast shadows on the sidewalks. Gina and I used to try to jump over them, and whoever got caught in a shadow was the loser. We used to go to this restaurant, Hunan Palace, a lot with our families when we were kids.

She was taking too long to respond. I placed my egg roll down. "I know Mark is a good man. But I almost feel like if Mark and Jessica could put themselves in our shoes, they would understand."

She smirked. "They would understand?"

"Well, they wouldn't say, 'Go ahead and be together,' but they would understand it wasn't out of malice. It was out of something else—I don't know—something that has been missing for so long that got found."

That was bad poetry. But it was true.

"That's what everyone thinks in these situations. 'You'd understand if you were me, if you knew how I felt.'"

A server appeared with a pitcher of Coke filled to the brim with ice.

"I know it's wrong. I tried to talk to Mark, to have a real conversation, before I left for California. It didn't go well. It was so out of our norm, he thought I was acting weird. Now we're back to the way it was. Just hollow. Just nothing. There's just nothing there." I poured Coke into my glass then pumped the straw through the ice and took a sip. "Have you heard him eat celery?"

Gina cocked her head. The look on her face said, "Are you kidding me?"

"What? I have an affliction. There's a name for it. It's called misophonia. A hatred of specific sounds."

"I think you have Markophonia. And who eats celery quietly?"

"It's not a matter of quiet. There's a specific cadence to each bite."

Gina nodded slowly, in mock understanding. "Speaking of quiet, you did what I said. I saw."

"It helped."

"You're welcome."

"It helped me see that I wanted a divorce even before running into Todd." I sipped my drink. "I know that no matter how Mark chews his celery and no matter how much I cringe at everything else he does—how he pinches his eyebrow, everything—he's not a bad guy. But are we supposed to go on like this for another fifty years?"

Gina picked up a crunchy noodle, dipped it in duck sauce, and leaned forward as she bit and chewed deliberately. *Chomp. Chomp-chomp-chomp. Chomp.* "You wanna punch me?"

"No." I laughed. "I think this is the thing. I can't believe I'm going to say this, but I don't love Mark." I gauged her reaction, but there was no judgment. "Not every bad marriage is bad because the couple fights," I continued. "Some could be bad because the couple barely speaks, like us. It was wrong from the start. And it just got worse. And then I spent the night with another guy. Nothing happened, but still."

"Nothing happened, all right. You can say that again. But you wanted it to happen." Gina's eyes met mine. "At the end of the day, it's not a matter of right or wrong. The question is, what will you learn from your walk down this road?"

"What will I learn? Spare me. And hand me a rib while you're at it."

She lifted the plate of ribs toward me. "Spare you the truth? I will do no such thing."

"Yeah, well, here's a truth: I just want to be happy. I don't care what I learn."

"Yes, you do. That's why you're here."

"Where? At Hunan Palace?"

"Living. On earth. You're going through life to learn your lessons."

"I am?"

"Yeah, it's kind of the purpose of this whole thing." She cut wide circles in the air with her hands.

"Ugh. Please. I have bigger fish to fry than this esoteric bullshit. I need to get out of this marriage in a way that will cause the least amount of harm to Mark and Ethan. And Jessica and her kids too if, you know, it works out with Todd."

"This esoteric bullshit will help you figure all of that out," Gina said.

"What have they done to you here? Were you always like this? Talking about the purpose of life?"

Gina cackled again. "You could say I have a new perspective."

I took another sip of my icy Coke. "How come we never hung out in the city?"

"You were too busy with your fancy lawyer friends," she teased as she bit into a spare rib.

"I'm sorry."

"I'm kidding. I wasn't calling you to hang out either. I had cooler friends."

"Ha. True."

Gina leaned in. "What happened to JFK's mistress's diary?" She was back to her mocking whisper. "Do you think it was burned?"

"Shut up!" Then something occurred to me. "Hey, you must know the truth. Now that you're here, you must know! Tell me. Was it a conspiracy? While we're at it, did aliens land at Roswell? What really happened to that nurse who mysteriously died after seeing one of the alien bodies?"

"Ha! It doesn't work like that."

"Pffft. Figures. So if you don't get handed a file with all the big secrets revealed, then can you use your 'fly on the wall' powers? Read over someone's shoulder at the CIA in your invisibility cloak? Did Oswald act alone?"

"What I mean is, I don't care. I mean, I care, on a soul level. I care that someone passed and that his family grieved, but my focus is you and my family. I care about your journey and what you learn."

"My *journey*? They've turned you into a greeting card."

"Two people died that day."

"When?"

"November 22, 1963. Well, a lot more than two people died that day, but I mean related to this event."

"You mean the police officer? JD Tippit?"

"Yes. And do you think when both souls crossed over, they had a bigger party for the president? Of course not. No one is famous here. No one is more important than anyone else. All that matters is the *journey* they were on and what they learned, how much their souls evolved."

"So Marilyn Monroe wasn't greeted by throngs of fans?"

"Marilyn Monroe was greeted by the people who cared about her and her journey, by her spirit guides and her loved ones who'd gone before her."

"That begs another question, dear cousin. Couldn't they help her get her shit together like you're helping me?"

"Her mistakes were part of her journey. They had to happen. They were part of her lessons, part of what made her soul evolve, which is the whole point of coming to earth. And that's what I'm supposed to help you learn—there are no mistakes."

"So I'm not making a mistake with Todd?"

"There are no mistakes, only lessons. Remember?"

"That wasn't the response I was looking for. I wanted to hear, 'Not a mistake. You're finding your happily ever after with him now after all.'"

I studied her face for some validation of my hope, but she was back to her lo mein and sucking up a single noodle. "Eat!" she finally yelled.

"When you don't sound like the Dalai Lama, you sound like Grandma."

"You should have seen your face when you saw him."

"Todd?"

"No, the fucking Duke of York. Yes, Todd."

"I can imagine. At least I have you to talk about it with. Even if I won't remember this when I'm awake."

"But you'll feel something when you wake up. Gut feelings are messages from this side. Pay attention when you're awake." She smiled. "So you don't think Veronica would at least appreciate the coincidence?"

"She thinks he's a piece of shit. So, no. And anyway, even though we do text sometimes and have lunch, I couldn't share this with her. We text about things like the JFK assassination—go ahead, laugh—and some interesting parenting articles, but we're not really connected in the way we used to be. One of those parenting articles was about how lonely motherhood can be. It's true. It's like friends just seem to float away. I don't know. And I certainly can't confide in any of the mommy group ladies for obvious reasons. Besides, we're not that close to begin with."

"Danielle seems cool."

"She is."

"Reach out to her. Get your head out of your own ass for once."

"Is that my next assignment?"

"Yes. Remove head from ass. Check. Hang out with a new friend. Check."

"Yes, teacher."

"It's okay to have different friends at different times in your life."

"Is it okay to have none? I can't even talk to my sister. I wish I could, but you understand."

Gina nodded.

"Your sister is like my sister," I said. "No desire to leave Queens. Husbands they met in high school. Two cute kids. Always posting about reality shows."

"Don't forget their Quality Shopping Network products."

"Oh my God. The duster sweaters. Orly has one in every color. I just saw Andrea with one on in a picture." I squeezed out another packet of duck sauce for the rest of my egg roll. "Why are they happy with the simple things, and you and I always wanted more?"

"We're different people. We all have different things to learn. Some of them can be learned by going out and seeing the world, and others can be learned by not doing that."

"So who's more evolved, as you would say?"

She smirked. "It's not a race, Jada. I guess it's like a scavenger hunt with different prizes for each participant."

"So they started at home base in their scavenger hunt and thought, 'Hmm, not so bad here,' and just squatted down. And we were like, 'Off to wander. Later!'"

"Nothing wrong with either one. Everyone who participates in the scavenger hunt gets a prize: they evolve in some way just by living."

"So everyone gets a participation trophy. Those are bullshit."

"In competitive sports, maybe. But again, this is not a competition," Gina explained.

I bit into the other half of my egg roll and spoke with food in my mouth. My mother would have called me a "gavone" for doing such a thing, but this was a different plane, where there were no calories and no judgment. "I think the Gina I knew would have said 'Todd's hot. You should have had sex with him.' But this version of you is all 'This is affecting the evolution of your soul and blah blah blah.'"

She guffawed and spit out a piece of spare rib, which made me laugh, which then made her laugh even more. If we were outside, jumping over streetlight shadows, I would have pushed her in one and yelled, "You lose." Then I would have run up the street, and we would have cackled like we used to.

"So why didn't you sleep with him? Or even kiss him? I mean, I know you tried and ended up on the floor of the restaurant, which was real sexy by the way. But later, why didn't you go for it?"

"I didn't want to cross that line, and I think, deep down, it felt like it should be more than that. Not just sex. I mean, what are the chances I'd run into him for just one night? It's got to mean something, right?" I looked her in the eye. "It's got to mean that we should try this. We should try for our happy ending. Right?"

"Every ending is happy." She wiped her hands on one of the hot towels that suddenly appeared.

"Oh, come the fuck on, Gina! No, they're not. Your ending wasn't happy. What happened to you was not a happy fucking ending! And what it's done to us, to your mom, to your family."

"We'll talk about that another time." Gina lit a cigarette and blew the smoke toward the window. "What I mean is, no matter what happens, you'll learn."

I wanted to scream at her, "Enough with the learning and the lessons! Everything happens for a reason, and sometimes the reason is that you learn something is bullshit!" But I'd said all that already, and she hadn't stopped.

So I thought about how to prove her wrong as I picked up a fortune cookie. "You know, it was a mistake to marry Mark. What the hell did I learn from that? Yes, I have a beautiful child. But what did I learn?"

"You'll see."

"Whatever. Now I have a chance to do what I should have done and be with the person I should have been with. If I do, I'll be happy. If I don't, I'll just continue to be stuck. There are only two options. I don't see it any other way."

"Of course you don't."

I cracked open the fortune cookie. "This should be interesting." I pulled out the little slip of paper. It was blank. I threw it onto the table. "Wonderful. I have no future."

"Of course you do. Pick that back up." She jutted her chin toward my fortune atop the pile of ribs. She pulled a pen from behind her ear that wasn't there before and held it out to me.

"Let me guess. I have to write my own future. I have to find my own happiness, whatever the situation. Like the memes on social media tell us. Ugh." I grabbed the pen and washed down my disappointment with my ice-cold soda.

"Okay, here goes." I read aloud as I wrote in tiny letters on my blank fortune. "You will learn nothing and just be happy."

"In bed."

"Huh?"

"You're supposed to add 'in bed' to fortunes," Gina said.

"Oh yeah. Ha! Well, I hope so."

Gina held her cigarette between her teeth and grabbed the pen. She crossed out "Learn nothing and just." Then on the other side, she wrote, "And you will learn."

She removed the cigarette and declared, "You will be happy. And you will learn."

"In bed? I hope so. It's been so long. I almost forgot how to do it."

We fell into a hard fit of cackling again until she smashed her cigarette in the old-fashioned glass ashtray and hopped up. "Let's go."

I watched as she hurried out of the restaurant and zigzagged across the street, her arms spread out as if she were about to fly away. I followed her, and we jumped over the streetlight shadows together. Neither one of us, it seemed, felt the urge to push the other in a shadow and run off.

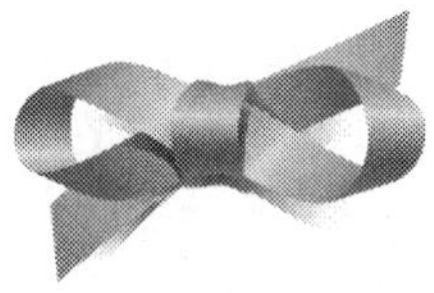

Chapter 8

With one eye half-opened, I grabbed my phone. It read 5:03. I pried the other eye open to confirm what else I saw... or didn't see. Nothing from Todd.

I checked my email. I had nothing but a few annoying weekend work emails and one from my sister with two lines. "Hey, how was Cali? Did you go on one of those trolleys?"

Is she for real? It wasn't a vacation. It was for work. Though I did want to go on one of those, but I never got a chance.

I wished there was someone I could talk to. *Just not Mark.* I knew that conversation had to happen but not yet, not until I found the right words and the right time. Until then, I would do my best to avoid him. I had a feeling that would be easy. *He probably won't even notice.*

I scrolled through Frontbook. There were Syd and Veronica twirling their girls on the dance floor at some cousin's wedding.

I replied to Orly. "It was for work, so it was uneventful. How was Mom's doctor visit?"

I went back to Frontbook. No updates from Jessica, which was a little unusual. I was now, more than ever, grasping for any peeks into Todd's world. But at the same time, if I saw a "Going to Long Island at Play all day" update, I would stay far away. I couldn't look her in the face.

Then I saw that Danielle had asked for lunch recommendations in the city because she was taking the Tree kids to a matinee on Monday of something Ethan wasn't interested in. I said a quiet prayer that *Buddy the Bulldozer* never made it to Broadway.

Get your head out of your butt. Reach out, lonely girl.

My fingers took control before I could stop them, and I sent a message to Danielle.

Jada: *I don't work far from the theater. I'd love to meet you for lunch.*

I immediately had message regret. *She would have her kids with her. Why would she want me to join them for lunch? And she was asking for recommendations, not company.*

"Vroom!" Ethan was up and "vrooming" his trucks and, from what I could tell, jumping on the bed.

As I turned to get out of bed, Danielle replied. She even sounded excited. She had already received a recommendation for a "kids' bar" where each place setting had a tablet propped up in front of it. It sounded like a germ fest and a prime example of what not to teach kids to do while dining. But it also sounded like the perfect place for adults to catch up, undistracted. And so I had a date for Monday, a friend date.

The cold, hard marble floor of our hallway felt like ice on my bare feet. I held my ear to Ethan's door before opening it to hear him happily vroom around a bit more.

"Mommy!" he shouted and ran to me. I knelt down and picked him up. His big brown curls smelled like his delicious baby shampoo.

I brought him to the bathroom, and then we played with his trucks on the floor for a little while. Afterward, we went downstairs so I could have coffee.

"What do you want for breakfast?" I asked when Ethan was settled in front of the TV, watching *Buddy the Bulldozer.* I sipped my coffee and checked my phone.

Mark appeared in the doorway of the TV room. "How 'bout slapjacks?"

Slapjacks? Has he gotten cornier in the past few years, or is it me?

"Slapjacks!" Ethan yelled.

They headed to the kitchen to make pancakes—and a mess—while I leaned against the window to see rain pelting the pool and the umbrella over the table swaying violently.

"Ethan, it doesn't look like we're going to swim today. The park is out too. I guess it's a pajamas and *Buddy* kind of day."

"Or you could take him to LI at Play," Mark said.

I bit my lower lip, still facing the yard.

"Yes!" Ethan screamed. "LI at Play. LI at Play."

Mark chimed in with the chant. "LI at Play. LI at Play."

Fuck. I better nip this. I spun around. "No! In this weather, it will be a zoo. More than the usual zoo that it is. Not today. And I'm exhausted from traveling."

Ethan instantly burst into tears.

"He's been in this house with Joyce all week," Mark said as he hoisted Ethan into his arms. "And it rained every day, so they couldn't go in the pool or to the park. I think he's got cabin fever."

"Well, maybe we'll go to the mall." It was a lame suggestion, but my mind was fried. "We'll get one of those hot pretzels."

"LI at Play." Ethan sobbed into Mark's shoulder.

"Do you want to take him?" I suggested. "Just for an hour?" Mark had never taken Ethan there before. It was more of my activity with Ethan, but there was no reason Mark couldn't take him.

"I've actually got three conference calls today and have to prep for each one. We've got a filing on Monday." He handed Ethan to me. "If you go for just an hour, that'll satisfy him, no?"

I received a whimpering Ethan in my arms. "We'll go after you eat, but we are not staying long. Do you hear me?" Like that meant anything to a kid.

Ethan ate his pancakes and watched *Buddy the Bulldozer* while I showered. *Maybe if I hang out in the trampoline room, I can avoid seeing Jessica.* Mommy group just got more complicated.

• • ❧ • •

JESSICA WAS NOWHERE in sight. While I was as curious as ever to gather any information about her and Todd, I also didn't want to get too close. I didn't want to feel even more guilty about what we were possibly about to do and about all that I now knew. *Still, where could he be? How could I have not heard from him? Is he still traveling for work? Did something come up?* I had tried to find his imposter Frontbook account, but it was as private as he'd described. *Nothing to glean there.*

Danielle was also absent, unfortunately. But there sat Melody. *Crap.* I tried to make a beeline for the trampoline room, but she spotted me.

"Jada!" She sat up straight.

I waved and headed over.

"How've you been?" Melody asked as I sat down.

"Good. I'm a little tired. I was away all week for work."

She smiled widely and leaned in. "Have you heard from Jessica?" she asked in a concerned voice.

My heart skipped. "No, why?"

"We texted and messaged on social media all week, but I haven't been able to reach her since yesterday, and we're supposed to meet tonight to put together the gift bags for the boys' swim class. We're doing this fundraiser—I think we sent you the email—and we're doing these aquatic-themed goodie bags. We both bought stuff for it, and we were supposed to put them together tonight, but I haven't heard from her. It's weird because she usually responds right away."

My heart was racing. "Maybe she just got busy."

"I wonder if I should just show up at her house with my goodie supplies."

"No. I wouldn't do that. You know how it is. We get busy. Her husband just got home from a business trip, and—"

"He did?"

Fuck. "Yeah. She mentioned last week that he was going away all week and how hard it is when he travels."

"I know he was away last week. Yeah, he must have just gotten home."

Melody stared directly into my eyes for a beat too long. *Does she suspect something? How could that be? I must be getting paranoid.*

I turned away, pretending to search for Ethan among the crawlers and climbers. I spotted him and waved.

"Yeah, they're probably having family time with Todd," Melody said.

The sound of his name made my heart jump. I waved wider and faster for Ethan.

Before I could escape this painful conversation, Jessica was sitting next to me.

I gasped. Her hair was tied back, and her face looked redder than usual. I wasn't sure if I was imagining things or if her eyes were actually puffy. *I'm probably just studying her extra close today. Well, as close as I can study someone while being afraid to make eye contact.*

"Hi." I could have sworn I caught a slight croak. She even sounded tired. She didn't offer an apology for sneaking up next to me.

I turned back to searching for Ethan. "We're going to have to go soon," I said. "I told him just a little while, but I should have known better."

Oh dear God, what if Todd confessed? What if she knows everything? What if she's planning to be coy to test me? Or trap me? And Melody knows too, and she was fucking with me ever so slightly. I have to get out of here.

Jessica moved to sit next to Melody.

"Hi, Jess. Listen, did you get multicolored Swedish Fish or all red?" Melody asked like she was asking her doctor exactly how many milligrams of meds she was supposed to take.

"Uh, all red," Jessica croaked. *That was a definite crack of the voice. Maybe she has a cold.*

"Do you think we should return them?" Melody asked. "You know, and get the multicolored because the boys' swim trunks and caps are green. Maybe to add a bit of green, we should get the multicolored? I'll return them, no problem. I'll do it."

Is Melody fucking serious?

Jessica seemed to be thinking the same thing as me. "I don't think we have to worry about having green Swedish Fish to match their swim trunks. And we should probably get them done tonight because we don't have much more time."

"I'll go real quick!" Melody said. "It won't take long. You bought them at the party-supply place?"

Before Melody could move the conversation to making sure their jellybeans were color-coordinated, Ethan ran over and announced that he had to poop.

Saved by the shitter!

"Okay! Can you hold it until we get home? We'll go right now."

"No. It's coming out."

Shit.

I carried him to the bathroom. He went quickly, but the cleanup took a while. By the time we finished, Melody had left to replace the Swedish Fish, and Jessica was sitting there alone. She smiled in our direction.

But I couldn't bear to be in her presence. "We have to go." I shook my head and tried to appear like the harried mother I felt like.

"No!" Ethan wrestled away from me and ran off.

"I just got back from a business trip." All of a sudden, the collar of my shirt felt like it was shrinking as I spoke. I tugged at it, trying to make it seem like an unconscious habit as I babbled on. "And I have to do laundry, food shop, get my nails done. You know how it is. Unpack! I still haven't unpacked. Can you believe it?"

"Is everything okay?" Jessica asked.

"Yes!" *Weird question. Does she mean something by that?* "Well, on top of everything else, Ethan just shit his pants, and I feel like I smell like it. So, I need a shower."

Real smooth, Jada.

"Ha. I've been there." Jessica smiled through her tired eyes.

I marched over to Ethan, who had a death grip on a monkey bar. I managed to pry his hands free and only withstood one karate chop to the head.

"Jada!" Jessica marched toward me. She was determined. She even stopped Ethan in his tracks. He stopped whining about leaving and was suddenly fixated on her.

"Did you leave this?" She held my phone. I must have left it on the seat when I rushed Ethan to the bathroom.

"Thank you so much! I'm addicted to this thing. That would have been bad."

Her bloodshot eyes met mine. I could see I had several text messages.

No! What if one is from her husband? Did she see it? Why didn't I ever change that stupid setting so someone can't read messages when my phone is locked? Shit!

I said goodbye and speed-walked with Ethan to the car, wrangled him into his car seat, jumped in the driver's seat, and reached for my phone. I had four text messages. One was from Orly, asking if we could have a family dinner tomorrow. Another from her was asking if it could be at my house because her dining room was still being painted and my parents' grill was broken. One was from Mark, asking if I could pick up milk. *What is it with him and running out of milk?* And the last was an invitation to the "summer soiree" from the gym I'd joined four years ago and hadn't been to in about three years and eleven months.

Nothing from Todd.

• • ❧ • •

MARK HAD JUST FINISHED one of his calls when we got back to the house. As I pulled into the garage, I called him to help with Ethan.

"He has to go to the bathroom. And be forewarned, we had a little incident earlier. Can you take him in? I have to return a work email."

I didn't have a work email, not that an urgent work email was unheard of on a Saturday afternoon, but I had other business to attend to.

"Hey, kiddo," Mark said as he came into the garage in his white T-shirt. He could win a "Who wore it better?" T-shirt contest with Todd, but that would never change who I desired more.

Mark unbuckled Ethan and maneuvered him out of his car seat.

I unlocked my phone and waited for the door to shut behind them before I tapped Todd's name to call him.

It rang and beeped. And rang and beeped. He was obviously on the other line with someone.

When it finally went to voice mail, I said, "Hi. It's Jada. Obviously. Um, just calling to see if you got home okay. I'm at home tonight—not doing anything, really—so call me. I can get away to talk anytime. Bye."

I needed to talk to Mark eventually. I'd made my decision, and he needed to hear it. We needed to discuss it. But I could only handle one stressful situation at a time. At the moment, all I could handle was finding out where Todd had disappeared to. I needed confirmation that we were on the same page, that our chance meeting meant something, and we were going to see where it took us. We needed to figure things out.

I spent the rest of the day and night alternating between tending to Ethan in front of the TV and begging him to eat his fish sticks, take a bath, put his pajamas on, and brush his teeth. Then I read him a book, named his toes, and finally watched him drift off to sleep. And at every turn, I checked my phone.

Nothing.

It was my turn to get ready for bed. I flossed, brushed my teeth, shellacked my face in antiaging cream, and put on my moisturizing undereye masks. I waited fifteen minutes like it said on the package then removed them. And of course I checked my phone.

Nothing.

• • ~ • •

"CRAP!" ETHAN YELLED as he jumped from the top stair of the pool into the shallow end with his swimmies on.

"What did you just say?"

The day after our short LI at Play visit, I promised Ethan we would spend all day in the pool if the weather was good. As if God wanted to be sure I made it up to Ethan, it was sunny all day.

When I saw my phone light up with a text message, I almost slipped and cracked my skull as I ran up the concrete steps of our shallow end to check it before Mark happened to walk by and glance at my phone, not that he ever did that.

I scratched my knee in the process of making it to my phone. But it was only Orly.

Where the hell is Todd? Did he not get my message? I sound like a lovesick teenager. Of course he got my message. But why hasn't he called back or even texted? He better have a damn good reason.

"Crap!" Ethan repeated.

"No, no, no," I said. "That's a Mommy word. Remember Mommy words?"

"What'd you say?" Mark was chomping on celery and reading his iPad.

"Nothing," I called back as I read Orly's text.

She wanted to have a family dinner with our parents later that evening, even though I'd already told her I just got back from traveling for work and didn't want anyone coming over. *Why should that stop her from asking again? She can be so obtuse.*

I replied: *Did you get my text yesterday? We can't today.*

Orly: *Maybe one night this week.*

She must have lost her mind. We never did a family dinner during the week.

Jada: *During a workweek is never good for me. Next weekend?*

Orly: *Okay. Sorry you're so busy. Too bad you can't get a job closer to home.*

I rolled my eyes and plopped onto the lounge chair.

As I watched Ethan splash around and Mark tap on his iPad, the gravity of what had happened only days prior jolted me. I'd woken up in a hotel room with someone who wasn't my husband. I had confided in Todd things I'd never confided in anyone. I had completely detached from my real life and fallen into this new reality, this new hope that something was going to change. And I was excited about it. I felt guilty, of course. I couldn't look at Mark or Jessica, and I was a nervous wreck about how this would all play out. But once everything was settled, it would be a new life, a whole new existence.

It was the kind of excitement I felt when changing jobs or moving to a new place—the feeling of possibility in the air. Things were going to be different and better. That feeling of just existing, of just going through the motions of life, was going to be lifted. I was going to be happy. *Happy for real.* Mark would move on. Todd and I would finally be together. And hopefully, our kids would all be okay, maybe even better for it. I hoped.

Mark stood up to start the grill for lunch. I watched him lift the cover and spray something.

Why do I feel so numb toward him? He must feel the same way toward me. Does it not bother him that we haven't had a real conversa-

tion since before Ethan was born? I tried. Once. But then again, did we ever have real conversations? How did we end up together in the first place? And how did it get this far?

I tried to turn my mind off and get quiet.

"Catch!" Ethan yelled one second before a ball bounced off my head. I retrieved it and threw it back.

Then I picked up my phone and swiped it to take a picture. "Smile," I called to him.

He showed me a toothy grin. His brown curls were matted to his head, and his swimmies were attached to his side. I posted it with the caption "Another peaceful day in the pool" with a sun emoji.

Someday, the things I post on social media will actually be true. If only Todd would get back to me, we could get the show on the road to this new life. Where is he?

A few minutes later, I checked to see if my picture had racked up any likes yet and saw that I had a text message from Todd. *"Can you talk tomorrow?"*

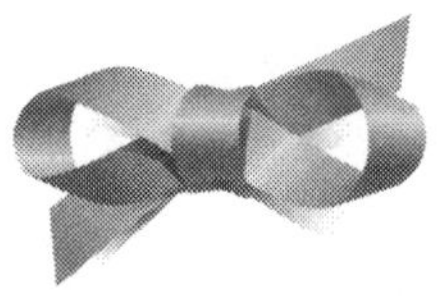

Chapter 9

I barely slept. *One line. A question. Can I talk tomorrow? So straightforward. So unemotional. What could it mean? And when can I stop feeling like a teenager and fast-forward to a happy life together? This is ridiculous.*

In the morning, Joyce arrived at six on the dot as usual and asked, "Did you get a chance to review my mother's lease?"

Crap!

"Joyce, I am so sorry. It's been nuts around here. I reviewed it briefly, and it looks to be a standard residential lease, but let me have a go at it again today. I am so sorry," I pleaded as Mark and I ran out the door.

Joyce waved her hand as if to say it was no big deal, but I knew it was, or she wouldn't have asked. I felt awful.

Instead of reading magazines and checking my phone during the commute, I committed myself to Joyce's mom's lease, and I was right. I found nothing out of the ordinary. I sat back and considered what her recourse could be. The more I thought about it, the angrier I got at her landlord. *Who the hell lets an old woman roast in this summer heat? We will get this AC fixed. It's the least I can do. What would we do without Joyce?*

When I got to work, Dan and Karen still hadn't arrived. I checked social media on my desktop. I saw nothing noteworthy except that my cousin Gina's friend Cori asked for hotel recommendations in Cabo for her honeymoon. *Going on a honeymoon. Another thing Gina will never get to do.*

I finally logged into my work email. When the name of my least favorite client, Lionel, popped up in my inbox, I knew it was going to be one of those weeks.

Re: Hannon v. Fortified—Hannon deposition

Did anyone go through this depo and highlight the factual statements? Who took the depo?

This was the shit that really pissed me off. The answers to both of his questions were in the email he was replying to. And his tone was unacceptable. I didn't care if he was an old dog. It was a new world, and he needed to learn how to conduct himself accordingly. I bit my fist and replied as I typically did to Lionel.

"As noted below, Matthew Wiler from Weston, Wiler, and Faust, our local counsel in San Francisco, took the deposition. Also, as you'll see in the email I sent you below, I attached the deposition with the factual statements highlighted PLUS a spreadsheet noting all of the statements that strengthen our position and all statements that may weaken our defense, along with corresponding page numbers for each. Did you not get this email? It says 'Sent.'"

I could just hear Dan. "Really, Jada? Just answer his questions."

I would respond, "No. He doesn't read emails and then asks questions when the answers are in front of him. He needs to learn."

And Dan would say, "Don't you know the saying about old dogs and new tricks?"

I believed I could train Lionel like I'd trained Dan. Dan used to be even more uptight than he was now. During my first year at the firm, we'd had to finish something on a tight deadline. Ten minutes before our meeting about it, I headed toward the bathroom.

"Where are you going?" Dan shouted from down the hall. "We have a meeting."

I stopped midstride, spun around, and said calmly, "My tampon is falling out. Literally. As we speak."

Dan turned white. The meeting wasn't for ten minutes, and Dan had to learn that he needed to allow his employees to use the restroom. And I would be the one to teach him.

When Dan and Karen arrived that morning, we met for our Monday meeting. Dan was eating a yogurt that was probably not his. He often treated the office refrigerator as his own personal food closet. I'd scolded him about it in the past, after he ate one of my cottage cheese containers. It had never happened again—at least not with my food.

I pointed to the yogurt. "That better be yours."

"It is."

"'It is' meaning you're a partner at the firm and therefore own the refrigerator and everything in it, or you brought it from home?"

"I brought it from home in my little lunch pail. Want some?"

"Ew, no."

I then briefed them on everything that had happened in San Francisco—work-wise, of course. Neither one of them brought up Lionel's email, and Lionel hadn't responded. *Ha! Another lesson learned. Class dismissed.*

I spent the rest of the morning going through emails and checking my phone for any word from Todd after I'd texted back, "*Yes. Call me anytime tomorrow.*" Still nothing.

I left to meet Danielle about fifteen minutes earlier than I needed to. I was anxious. I needed to engage with someone, anyone, to get my eyes off of my computer and my phone.

I opened the door of Tablet for Two to a cacophony of laughter and talking. *Shouldn't this place be like a library with no one talking to each other?* Luckily for the Tree kids, who were already in position, scrolling and eating french fries without taking their eyes off the screens, it was like a library. Danielle waved to me. As I approached, I admired her white-and-yellow sundress.

I hugged her. "You look adorable!" I realized we only ever saw each other in our "mom clothes," flexible weekend attire that could withstand any number of messes that happened before, after, or during a trip to LI at Play.

"Thanks! I'm so happy you messaged me. I knew you worked in the city, but I kind of didn't even think about it." She pushed back her bright-blond hair. "This is a pleasant surprise. How was San Francisco?"

"Good!" I tried to sound normal. "Just work stuff. The usual."

The server brought our Diet Cokes. I sipped and observed the utter silence of the Tree kids. They were transfixed. *Is this good for them?* I had to admit it was wonderful for me in that instance.

I turned back to Danielle. "I ran into my ex-boyfriend." *I can't hold it in any longer.* I told her what happened, careful not to reveal his identity. She was as transfixed as the Tree kids looking at the tablets.

"Can you believe that?" I asked when I finished.

She didn't answer right away.

I shifted in my seat.

"Believe it or not, I've been there myself," she said.

"You ran into your ex-boyfriend in San Francisco, talked about history and conspiracy theories all night?"

"We talked about art, not history." After a moment, she laughed. "Kidding. I mean, in a past relationship, I went even further. All the way. I was the cheater, not the cheated, and it was awful. It hurts in a way you can't explain because you're the wrongdoer. It's like this feeling—that knowledge that you could do that to someone you thought you loved—it eats you alive, from your stomach, from your core."

"What happened with your boyfriend?"

"We broke up."

"What happened with the other guy?"

"Nothing."

My stomach dropped.

"He wasn't ready for a relationship," she added.

"I've been there." I didn't bother explaining that was exactly what had happened with Todd the first time. "You never got back with your boyfriend?"

"No. He deserved to meet someone who was mature and respectful. I had a lot of growing up to do, and then I met my husband a couple of years later, when I was a different person, when the time was right. Timing is a funny thing."

"It sure is. I'm still wrapping my head around it all. I mean, what are the chances we would be in that very spot at the exact same time?"

"It's pretty crazy. What are you going to do?"

"I don't know. I know for certain that Mark and I are not sustainable."

"I'm sorry."

"And I hope it works out with the other guy, but I realize there's a lot of people's hearts on the line. It's scary, but maybe it will all work out. It could happen, right?"

"Happens every day. What's his name?"

My heart lurched. "Todd."

"What's his last name?"

I opened my mouth. *How will I get out of this? What do I say?*

"Don't answer!" Danielle sat up straight in her seat. "Oh my God. I sound like Melody. How nosy and awful!"

We laughed while I picked at my Caesar salad and asked Danielle about what was going on with her and her husband and family.

"My mom helps with the kids, but she's away this week with her boyfriend."

"Are your parents divorced?"

She shook her head. "My dad died ten years ago."

"I'm sorry."

"She never dated anyone, and I thought she never would, but she met this guy last year through a friend, and he's great. So yeah, my mom is in Paris with her boyfriend."

"Good for her!"

"Yeah. I miss my dad, though. I wonder what he must be thinking. She still has all of his fishing poles, and all of these pictures of him catching stuff, and the sign that says, 'Trip's Fishing Trips.' So corny."

"Oh, his name was Trip? He had a 'truh' name too."

"Yeah. They're all named after him in a way."

"I call them the 'Tree kids' in my head."

"You're not the only one. That's their collective nickname at school."

Maybe it was the Diet Coke racing through my veins, but I felt better, lighter, for having said it all out loud. I wished we could stay there all day, talking.

As we paid the bill, I noticed my phone light up in my bag. *Could it be? Of course he would call me now. Bad timing. And there goes the high I was on.*

"Well, try to enjoy the rest of your day," Danielle said. "I know it will all work out."

We hugged.

"I'm so glad we did this," I said.

"Me too. It's so much easier to talk when you're not trying to keep one eye on your kid climbing the walls."

"Ha! Or getting strangled."

She laughed. "I forgot about that!"

I exchanged goodbyes with the Tree kids then worked my way through the crowd and out the door. Like an addicted smoker, I checked my phone. I had a voice mail from Todd.

I needed to check the voice mail in the quiet of my office with the door shut.

I flew through the lobby, into the elevator, and finally, into my office, where I slammed the door. I dropped my bag and hit play on the voice mail.

"It's Todd. I got your voice mail and texts. Let's meet for a drink on Friday. Somewhere we can talk. Let me know if that's good for you. All right. Bye."

Somewhere we can talk? Is that good or bad? And I have to wait all week?

I leaned back in my chair, trying to absorb that new tidbit, when my office phone rang.

"Hey, Lionel called," Dan said. "He wants a summary of the status of the Zapora case."

"I sent him a summary. He needs to read his damn emails."

"Did you write anything in the subject line that would help him know what the email is about?"

"Are you kidding me? It probably said 'Zapora case summary.' I'm supposed to come up with something more mesmerizing so the dipshit can find it, read it, and not accidentally delete it?"

"What can we write next time that will make sure he reads it? Can we add 'Important' in the subject line? Do you think that would help?"

"I don't know what would help Lionel. Should I Google 'Charming ways to get your moron client to open an email'?"

He sighed. "No, but can you send it again?"

"I'll think about it."

We hung up, and five seconds later, I heard his little legs march swiftly toward my office. "Jada, come on!" He held out his arms as though asking me to throw him a bone.

"Fine. I won't forward it and write, 'See below, idiot.' I'll leave out the idiot part."

"Are you in an extra bad mood? Or is this just normal Jada? I can't tell anymore."

"I'm okay," I lied.

Dan's shoulders dropped, and he shuffled away.

At least I had a cool boss. I couldn't complain about Dan and Karen, although I did sometimes because that was what friends did—commiserated about work. But they let me get away with so much.

OK, to-do list. Reply to Lionel. Don't be petty. Try not to think about Todd. Help Joyce's mother.

Somewhere where we can talk? Is that what he said? I listened to his voice mail again.

Then I typed out a text: *How about Riverfall? Were you abducted by aliens? I hope they treated you well. Welcome back to earth. See you Friday.*

I needed to focus on something else. I replied to Lionel with as much reserve as I could muster. Then I pulled out Joyce's mother's lease and noted the name of the leasing company. After a few internet searches, I got a name and number and made the call.

"Hello. Is this Mr. Castilla?"

"Who's this?"

"Again, is this Mr. Castilla?"

"Yes. Who is this?" he demanded.

"My name is Jada Marlone. I'm calling on behalf of Martha Diaz. She's been having some issues with her air-conditioning, and—"

"I fixed it."

"Oh, because as I understand it—"

He hung up.

What the fuck? My blood was boiling hotter than Martha Diaz's rent-controlled apartment. *Not today, asshole!* And it only rose further when I called back and got Mr. Castilla's voice mail. "Mr. Castilla, it seems your phone broke in the middle of our conversation.

You're probably on your way to Verizon at this very moment. As soon as it gets back up and running, call me. Again, it's Jada Marlone on behalf of Martha Diaz. Thank you."

I hung up and tried again. That time, it only rang once and went straight to voice mail. *That's weird.*

I tried again and got the same thing. So I Googled, "Rang once and went to voice mail." The first result stated, "You've likely been blocked."

That fucker!

I searched furiously for an office number. I hadn't even realized my initial search had given me his cell phone number.

I called the office number of C&M Property Management, and a woman answered.

"Hello. This is the Department of Rentals and Leases. May I speak with Mr. Castilla?" *Department of Rentals and Leases? Good one, but will he fall for it?*

"Please hold."

"Castilla speaking."

"Mr. Castilla, hello. Jada Marlone here. Fix Martha Diaz's air-conditioning, or whatever department oversees landlords will be up your ass. Have you ever been audited? Oh, and perhaps all you have to do is *turn it on*. Flip the switch. The circuit. Whatever. I'm not an electrician, but we're not falling for this. She's not leaving anytime soon. So deal with it. You're not getting that rent-controlled apartment back in the near future. So turn it back on. Now."

I hung up. *Damn, that felt good.*

Then I called Joyce and relayed everything. "Whatever works at this point! We'll take it," she said.

I hope it works too.

After I hung up, I paused to be grateful for the AC in my office, in my car, on the train, and in my house. I rested my head on my cool desk.

“What the hell are you doing?” Dan was at my door.

“It’s nice and cold.”

“You’re a weirdo.” He walked away.

When I lifted my head, I had a reply from Todd.

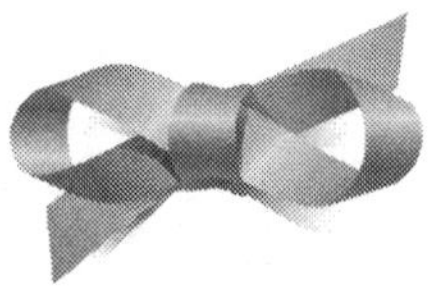

Chapter 10

Gina and I were at the same table in Bryant Park where I'd had lunch with Veronica before leaving for San Francisco. She was sitting on the small metal chair with her knees tucked up to her chin.

"Did you see us?" I asked. "When you passed, I mean. Were you able to see us, your family and friends, and how we reacted?"

"Of course." She lifted her chin off her knees. Her white T-shirt had little skulls forming the shape of a peace sign. "I saw it all then, and I still continue to see everyone."

I crinkled my nose and gave her a side-eye. "What do you see exactly?"

She didn't seem fazed. "When you're on this side, you're not interested in human-level things. I don't want to see my friends and family having sex, going to the bathroom, or human body-based things."

"I hope not!"

"You get a new perspective when you get here, a new 'knowing' when you've finished your life. You're here, and you still love all the people you loved—love doesn't die—so you want to be a part of guiding them on each of their *soul's journey*." I knew she said those last words in such a way to preempt mocking from me.

I still imitated her back. "*Our soul's journey*."

"So, yes, that's how it works. I saw." She put her chin back on her knees.

"I think about that day a lot," I said. "It still rips me apart if I think about it for too long. Hearing your mother's shriek. Seeing my mother screaming in a ball on our kitchen floor. I kind of just have to let the memory come and go, or I could really lose it." I coughed to clear the lump in my throat. "You had your whole life ahead of you. It's just so unfair."

"I know," Gina said. "It's impossible to explain to you why it happened. But know this at least—when we see our loved ones being happy, it makes us happy. We celebrate with you. If you had all thrown a big, fucking party with streamers and balloons and a stripper for my funeral, now that would have been the best, seeing everyone laughing and having fun. But no one ever does shit like that. It's too bad."

I shook my head. "You're nuts."

"Honestly, when I see my mom, sometimes when she's alone in our house and stares at my picture and cries, I scream 'Go out! Listen to music! Laugh! Please!' But I get it. I mean, I tell her that during visits I have with her, and I think..." She sighed. "I think we're getting there."

"She seems to be doing better," I said. In the years since Gina passed, Aunt Fran had been slowly going out more. I noticed a change from the first couple of years when she hadn't left the house, gone to anyone's wedding, except mine, or done anything except pretty much stay home in bed. She hadn't cleaned her house or cooked. My mom would visit and sit with her, straighten up, do the dishes, and help with laundry. She still helped like that, but now they did more together. They went out to lunch, dinner, the movies, and the beauty parlor, as they called it. "You really tell your mom to get out and do things? She's definitely been doing more."

"Hell yeah. Pretty much every one of our visits ends with me being like, 'Laugh! For the love of God, laugh!'"

"It's not that easy, Gina. She lost her child." If anything ever happened to Ethan, I didn't know how I would go on.

She glanced down. "I know."

"I still don't think any of us are over the shock. People talk about the stages of grief, but I don't think they're linear. I think you can go through all of them and still never get over the shock."

"I know," she repeated.

"A car accident. I still can't fucking believe it."

She untucked her knees. "Would you have rather I'd gotten cancer and died a slow death?"

"Yes."

"Gee, thanks." She offered me a cigarette. I declined.

"I would have gotten to say goodbye," I said.

"Death is not a goodbye," Gina said. "I'm still with you."

"No. You're really not, not in the way you should be. And we would have been prepared."

"Would you have been? Really?" She removed the unlit cigarette from her mouth and put it back in the pack. "I feel like having a chocolate milkshake. Let's go to Serendipity."

She stood and stretched her arms up. The peace sign of skulls on her shirt stretched to an oval. We walked out of the park and up Fifth Avenue, which was unusually quiet except for a few passing cars.

"So, in your invisibility cloak, what have you seen about Todd? The voice mail said 'Can you meet for a drink Friday night? Somewhere where we can talk.' Talk about us, right? He's being so damn cryptic."

"Ye-ah," she said with a sort of drawl.

"Ye-ah?" I realized I'd stopped walking. "What's going on?"

"Come on, keep walking."

"Tell me right now."

"Walk."

"No." *She knows something. I have to know what it is. Right now.*

"You really don't listen." She put her hands in her front pockets and rocked to her tiptoes for a second before saying, "Okay, don't freak the fuck out."

"Saying 'don't freak the fuck out' makes me freak the fuck out. So does your 'Ye-ah.' What the hell is going on?"

"You're not the first person Todd cheated on his wife with."

Ouch.

"We didn't have sex!" Even though that was the first thing that came out of my mouth, I knew it didn't matter. A million questions swirled in my mind.

"And there was someone he was with a few times about two months ago," she continued. "Someone he also met up with on a business trip."

That last part struck me particularly hard in the heart. *That's just his MO. Don't go thinking you're special.*

"And that's all I'm going to tell you right now."

"There's more? Can we sit down?" I pointed at a bus shelter a few steps away. As I sat, the sting of the cold metal through my pants caught me off guard. I stood up and sat back down again. "Does he love her? Is he going to choose her? Does she know who the lady in the red dress on the grassy knoll is? I bet she doesn't. I bet they couldn't talk all night."

Gina sat next to me. "I know you thought—were hoping—maybe there'd be a future with him. But, Jada, that's not why he came back into your life. I'm sorry. There was a different purpose."

"I don't want to hear about fucking purpose right now."

She put her arm around me.

"I can't believe it," I said.

"I can."

"Thanks."

We sat in silence a little longer, listening to the cars whiz by.

"Listen, there is something about him you're obviously missing with Mark. And that was the whole point."

"I already knew there was something missing with Mark. Did I have to run into Todd and get my hopes up?" I put my head in my hands.

"Listen." She stood up from the bench. "Todd's a piece of crap, yes. But it takes two. Whether you had sex or not, it was a betrayal. You wouldn't have gone back to his room if either of your spouses were watching. You have a lot of figuring out to do. But I can only get you so far in one day, in one visit. So get up! We're going for milkshakes."

I stayed seated. I didn't feel like eating anything or sipping a milkshake.

She leaned down. "I'm sorry."

We were surrounded in the bus shelter by an ad for whitening chewing gum. Gina's spiky black hair made it look like there was a porcupine kneeling in front of me. Any other time, I would have pointed that out to her, and we would have cackled so hard, we would've snorted.

But not now. I let my head fall back into my hands. *There goes hope. I should have known it was too good to be true.*

When I lifted my head, Gina was closer to the street, her legs in a wide stance as she stretched her torso from side to side, with a cigarette hanging from her mouth. *I thought she was sitting next to me, coming up with more words of comfort or wisdom, but she's over there, doing calisthenics.*

I rubbed my eyes. I could feel Gina move toward me. "All right, this is why I'm here instead of Grandma and Grandpa," she said under her breath. I anticipated a hug or stroke of my back. But I got a yank. She grabbed a chunk of my hair and yanked, hard, like she'd done when we were girls, sparring over Barbie. My head cranked sideways.

"Ouch!" I swatted her hand away, but she had a death grip.

"I'm not really hurting you. This isn't the physical world."

"Well, it feels like it's hurting. Let go!" I karate chopped her arm, and when that didn't work, I chopped her neck.

She let go and fell to the ground, giggling. "I'm sorry. I'm trying to change the mood. Jada, you are a piece of work." Her Converse sneakers touched the ground as she rocked back and forth.

"Don't call me that. And what the hell is wrong with you?" I touched my head where she pulled.

She stared at me like she was studying a painting. "You will fight for things. You will not let anyone get away with anything. My scrappy cousin. You may be a fancy lawyer, but you can get scrappy."

I was too confused to respond.

"Listen, I didn't want you to feel sorry for yourself for too long," she said.

"Well, I just found out. Can you give me a minute to mourn?"

"Wait 'til you hear the whole story."

"What?"

She lifted herself up and sat next to me on the metal bench.

"Tell me everything right now," I demanded while gathering my hair in a ponytail and inching away from her and her grabby hands.

"All I will say is, it wasn't the right thing to be hoping for, to be with him. Sometimes, we're given a glimmer of hope to make us realize what we were missing when we were too afraid to make a change."

I contemplated that. I didn't like it. *Why does the path to happiness have to be so complicated?*

"Listen, I want you to be happy," she said. "I want to help you. That's why I'm here."

"Thanks."

"Don't mention it." She stood and grabbed my arm to pull me off the bench.

"Don't pull my hair again," I said. "Fucking weirdo."

"Lighten up. It was a throwback to our Barbie days."

"When possession of a plastic doll would be our biggest problem, or so we thought."

"Exactly. Let's walk."

As we headed up Fifth Avenue, I surveyed the new status of things. "So I'm going to divorce my husband. I'm not going to end up with Todd. And I'll be a single mom."

"Is that so bad? Maybe you don't need a man. Maybe you'll find happiness in other things. In seeing Ethan grow up. Enjoying a piece of dark chocolate and a new JFK book at the end of the day. The little things."

"Watching the sun rise?" I mocked.

Gina turned abruptly to the right. I followed her gaze to see the big, fat yellow sun creeping up. We took it in.

I've never been a 'look at the sun, look at the moon' kind of person.

It was bright, and if we weren't on the other side, it would be strange to be walking for milkshakes after the sun just rose. But here, there was no time, and every restaurant was always open. We walked the rest of the way to Serendipity in silence.

We sat at a table outside and started with frozen hot chocolates. Then Gina had a chocolate milkshake, and I had a vanilla one. We got fries too. I dipped a french fry in my shake and chewed it slowly, taking a moment to enjoy the sweet and salty of it all.

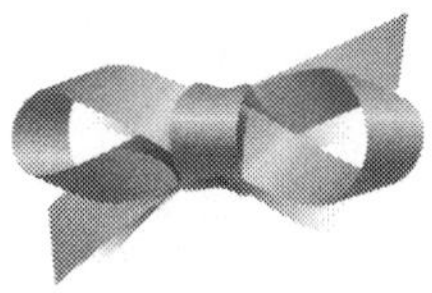

Chapter 11

I woke up with a heaviness in my chest. I attempted to shake it off or at least distract myself by hurrying around the house then hurrying to get to work. I emptied the dishwasher, folded the clothes in the dryer, threw more clothes in the washing machine, showered, blew out my hair, and put on my makeup, all before Joyce arrived.

I gathered my work tote bag and laptop when I heard her car pull up. Mark had already left for work that morning. There was an early conference call with the London office that he couldn't take from home for some reason that I didn't try too hard to understand. Joyce walked in and rested her leopard tote in the foyer. "Her air is back on! Can you believe it?" She raised her fists in triumph.

My mouth fell open. "That's great!" *Wow, that jerk listened to me. And I'm so happy for Joyce's mother. At least I did one thing right lately.*

"We can't thank you enough. My mother wants to bake you a cake."

"Please tell her not to do that," I said as I slid my laptop into my bag.

"What about cupcakes?"

"No, no. I was just happy to help."

"What can we give you? Please."

"Nonaddictive sleeping pills?" I hoisted my bag onto my shoulder.

"I have a cousin who knows a guy—"

"I was joking, Joyce!" I said as I reached for the doorknob." But there's one thing you can do for me. I might be a little late on Friday. Not too late, but hopefully, Mark won't be late too. Do you mind—"

"No problem."

I turned the doorknob halfway when I heard, "The sun!"

Ethan bounded down the stairs.

"It's still too early, hon," Joyce said. "We drew the sun, the stars, and the moon yesterday. Now he wants to witness exactly when it turns from night to day."

"Ah," I said. "That is something to see." I leaned down for a kiss. "And maybe later, we can watch the sunset, when it turns from day to night. Just you and me."

"And Daddy."

I shrugged. "If he's not working late again." I gave Ethan another kiss. "Enjoy watching the sun come up."

"You too," Joyce said.

I tried. When I was a block from the office, I stepped aside on the sidewalk to take in the changing sky, only to be bumped in the back by a young woman staring at her phone as she walked, an icy coffee drink in one hand.

"Sorry. I wasn't paying attention," the distracted girl mumbled as she continued walking.

"You should, especially when the sun is coming up. Get off your phone!" I hollered to her back. *Get off your phone? How rich coming from me.*

I continued on to the office, and by the time I arrived, the heaviness in my chest returned.

• • ❦ • •

LATER THAT WEEK, AS I rested my head on my cold desk in my air-conditioned office, I realized it was becoming a habit, a gratitude habit. My friend Veronica would be proud.

Orly had called earlier, but I didn't have the energy to call her back. Lionel had just pissed me off, but I'd taken a moment before replying and ultimately responded without any trace of snark to spare Dan a heart attack.

He entered my office slowly. "Are you having an affair?"

My head popped up. "What? No!"

"With your desk. You keep making out with it every time I walk in?"

"It's cold. It's refreshing."

"Do you feel okay? This desk thing. And then your professional reply to Lionel. Thank you for that by the way." He lowered his face to my desk. "It does feel nice."

"I'm fine. Just, you know, tired."

"You look it."

"Thanks." I pulled out the mirror I kept in my desk. I hoped I looked okay for later. "I can't work late tonight."

"You won't have to. It's Friday. Go have a drink. Then get yourself a good night's sleep, please."

I nodded. "That's the plan."

"Here. Bring your own glass." He lifted a #VeronicaSydYes wine glass off my desk.

I told Mark I was meeting Veronica for a drink and that I would be on a later train. I could have said I was working late, but I supposed it felt like the working late line was so cliché and the Veronica fib was kinder in some twisted way.

A few hours later, when I walked into Riverfall, a bar and restaurant within walking distance of Penn Station, it was empty. It wasn't as popular as it used to be when I was single and living in the city. The sun lit the front of the bar, but it became darker as I headed toward the back.

Todd was sitting at the end of the bar, drinking a clear, icy beverage in a short glass. He looked worse than I felt.

He stood up and hugged me awkwardly then pulled out a stool for me to sit.

"You look like shit," I said as I sat. My bag slid off the back of the chair and fell to the ground. I didn't take my eyes off of him as he reached down to lift it and place it back behind me.

"I feel it."

"What's going on?" I'd woken up every morning that week with what felt like a twenty-pound dumbbell on my chest. I knew something was wrong. I knew my happy ending with Todd was not likely. It wasn't just the lack of texting and calls. I knew it in my gut. I knew it on a cellular level. *But maybe I'm wrong. Maybe he wants to plan our future and find a way to do it without hurting our families,* I kept trying to convince myself.

"Can I order you a drink? Please?" he asked.

"I don't want a drink."

The bartender came over. "What can I get ya?"

"I'm good, thanks," I said, my eyes immediately going back to Todd.

"Can you bring over a dirty martini with olives? Do you have extra-large Spanish olives?" Todd asked the bartender. He cleared his throat and stirred his drink. "Listen, something happened."

I waited.

"A few months ago, I ran into an old friend from years ago." He finally made eye contact then stared at the floor again. "We hooked up, and"—he cleared his throat and swallowed—"she's pregnant."

I had to steady myself on the barstool. My whole body flushed with panic. "Pregnant?"

"I found out last Friday when I got home from Dallas," he continued. "She left me a message, and uh, she left Jessica a message too."

Is this really happening? I couldn't believe that only ten days ago we'd talked for hours, elated, with a promise that we would figure out our next steps. And no wonder Jessica had looked like she had last Saturday. *Poor Jessica. And I mean that in a whole new way now.*

"She's keeping it. She wants a baby. She's not married. I keep thinking, you know, if I'd run into you first—"

I felt something in my throat, a slight sensation, that nervous jolt before vomiting. I steadied myself on the chair. I swallowed slowly to make sure I wasn't about to heave. The bartender brought my drink. Another day, another time, not too long ago, I would have thrown it at him, leaving cracked glass on the floor like his UPenn mug. But I pushed it away, got up, slung my bag over my shoulder, and walked out.

• • ❧ • •

BY THE TIME I ARRIVED home, Joyce had already fed, bathed, and put Ethan to bed. Mark had worked late and had gotten home just an hour before me. He was watching *The Story of Our Planet* in bed. I mumbled that I was tired and needed to take a bath.

"How's Veronica?"

I had to steady myself as I peeled off my shoes and placed them in the closet. "Good."

"Good."

As I undressed, I heard the voice-over on TV. "It is nature's chain reaction. What is put out will come back."

I shut the bathroom door, started the bath, and poured in a capful of bubbles. I got in and leaned back as the water filled the tub around me.

I listened to the sound of the water.

I walked into this house, and my child was already sleeping. I spent no time with him today. *What kind of mother am I?*

I lied to my husband, among other things. *What kind of wife am I?*

I never got back to Orly. *What kind of sister am I? And daughter for that matter? What kind of person?*

I turned off the water.

How did I get here? And how do I get out of it? How do I fix it?

By the time I toweled off and grabbed my pajamas from the dresser, Mark had fallen asleep with the TV still on. I shut it off and crept down the hallway to Ethan's room.

I tried to open his bedroom door as quietly as possible, but he instantly popped up. "Mommy!"

"Shhh." I tiptoed toward his bed. "Go back to sleep." I stroked his curly brown hair as he put his head back on his *Buddy* pillow.

Ethan fell quickly back to sleep. I pulled the comforter up to his shoulders and tiptoed back down the hallway. I crawled into my side of the bed.

I left my phone downstairs in my bag in the foyer.

Chapter 12

Gina's white T-shirt had an image of a caterpillar with a fedora standing upright and dipping another caterpillar like it was the finale of a dramatic dance.

"The tango?" I asked.

She craned her neck to try to examine it. "I guess."

We were at Riverfall, sitting on the same stools where Todd and I had sat. "Do we always meet in the same place where I've recently been?"

"No." She sipped a clear cocktail. "You want to go somewhere else?"

"Yes, please. Anywhere."

"Italy? Paris? London?"

"We can do that?"

"We can do anything. There are no three-dimensional limits here. No time. No space. This is all yours." She opened her hands wide.

"Let's just walk." I got up from my stool, wanting to never see the inside of Riverfall again.

"Sure? It doesn't take any longer to get to Europe than anywhere else, you know. You understand how it works here, right?"

"I can't think right now, Gina. I just don't want to be here."

"Got it." Gina stood, still holding her drink as we walked out.

"You can't take that," I said.

"You really don't get it." She sipped as she strolled down the street. "I always liked Cellar Bar. It's dark and mysterious. Let's go there."

"Okay."

At the corner, Gina finished her beverage and threw it—glass and all—into a garbage can.

Instinctively, my mouth dropped.

"Jada!"

I held up my hand. "Never mind. I get it. A city maintenance worker is not going to find a glass in that garbage tomorrow. I get it."

"Good."

"I want a drink," I said.

"Me too. I'm parched."

Gina held the door open to Cellar Bar for me. We worked our way through the dimly lit lounge with its plush seating and flickering votive candles. We sat down in the back corner on a comfortable couch.

"I woke up knowing something was off," I said.

"That was your gut preparing you for what you already knew."

I nodded. A server came by, and Gina ordered two martinis for the both of us.

"I keep wondering how I got here." I leaned back. "But I know I have no one to blame but myself."

"No, no blaming." She leaned back too. "It was bound to happen. You never did things for the right reasons. You never listened to yourself, and to what you really wanted."

"How so?"

The server came by and placed our martinis on the round table before us. "Getting married. Becoming a mother. Was that what you really wanted? Even going away to school and law school. I mean, sure, you wanted to do those things, but you were also distinguishing yourself from your mother and sister, who you always felt collectively rejected you."

That stung. I cocked my head. "Damn." I thought about that for a moment. "I'm a highly educated, independent woman. I didn't get married and have a baby to make my mother happy or to compete with my baby sister." I reached for my martini a little too quickly, and some of it spilled on the floor.

"You can tell yourself that, but now you wonder why you want to leave your husband and why you don't feel like you think you should feel as a mother. It's because you weren't following your true path. You weren't living—aren't living—your authentic life."

"Oh God, you're talking like a meme again."

"You weren't true to yourself when you made those decisions," she continued. "And now you're suffering."

I tried to comprehend what she'd just put out there so I could respond coherently, but she continued before I could fully formulate a response.

"When you start realizing who you are and what you want, you will make choices and surround yourself with people and situations that don't cause inner conflict and outer turmoil."

"So I do have only myself to blame?"

"Stop focusing on that. You'll understand better after you see where we go next. Let's finish our drinks first."

"Okay," I said. "You're not going to pull my hair, are you?"

She spat out her martini. "No," she said as she wiped her mouth.

We finished our martinis then headed outside and down the street. When we turned the corner, I realized we were on my parents' block, a few yards from their house. *What is going on?*

I spun around, trying to figure out how we had arrived there, but Gina strode past me, her eyes on my parents' front door. "Remember? Any time, any place," she said.

My mother's old black Cadillac was in the driveway. She loved that car, with its red leather interior.

Gina made a left turn, and I knew she was headed to the backyard. My parents' above-ground pool and wraparound wooden deck had been the center of summer for me, my sister, my cousins, and all of our family and extended family. Everyone had come to the Santanellis' every weekend to swim and barbecue.

I thought about how Mark and I had essentially the same setup—a built-in pool and an even bigger house—but ours wasn't the same summer clubhouse for friends and family. Not at all.

Gina plopped down on a plastic lounge chair and was suddenly holding a bottle of Sweet Sun tanning oil SPF 2 and sniffed it. She squeezed out a dollop and handed it to me. This was the smell of our childhood summers—one-hundred-percent-artificial coconut.

"They still make this stuff?" I inhaled the aroma. "Oh, that smells delicious." I rubbed it all over my face and hands. It was hot and slippery, just like I remembered. And SPF 2? We didn't know better back then, and neither did our mothers.

"So what are we doing here?" I asked.

"Just watch."

Gina and I leaned back, lifting our arms overhead and wrapping our hands around the metal bar at the top of chairs like we used to do, and took in the scene.

I saw Orly as a little girl—about five years old—behind the sliding glass door, trying with all her might to pull it open and step out from our kitchen to the deck and pool. I was right behind her—about nine years old—and reaching past her. We pushed together on the count of three and finally emerged in our matching bathing suits—pink bikinis with white polka dots and ruffles by the hips. Our hair was wet and slicked back. We'd obviously been swimming already.

It was startling to see myself and Orly so young. On instinct, I sat up and waved.

"No one can see you," Gina explained. "Sit back. Relax. Enjoy the show."

Orly ran to the pool and put her toe in.

"No," the nine-year-old me yelled. "We just ate. You have to wait twenty minutes before swimming, or you'll get cramps." Little me put on sunglasses and pranced over to the other side of the pool.

"Hold on!" our mother yelled as she stepped out from behind the glass doors. She had big hair, big sunglasses, was snapping her gum, and wore a big, flowing gold cover-up over her gold bathing suit. "Hold on, Orly, honey. Don't swim right away. Ya just ate lunch. Wait a little. Here, float on the raft." She stood at the other end of the pool and pushed a big yellow inflatable raft toward Orly with her foot.

"I want to float on a raft too. Where's the other one?" I asked.

"I don't know what happened to it," my mother said before sitting down at the outdoor table by the large grill. She had a *Redbook* magazine in front of her as she a lit cigarette. "Check on the side over there. It might've gotten thrown over last weekend."

I leaned over the edge of our deck and surveyed the rest of our backyard, which wasn't much. The deck and pool consumed almost every bit of land.

"It's not there," I said.

"I don't know, then," my mother said, not taking her eyes off of her magazine.

Orly floated, eyes closed, hands behind her head, content and comfortable. I loved floating on the raft. I believed the sun's rays were attracted to water, and that was the way to get the best sun. I'd explained the whole theory to Orly, who seemed to understand. That was one of our top priorities over the summer: getting tan.

"What am I going to float on?"

"Jada, put your feet in and relax, please. You can swim in a few minutes."

"Not in a few minutes! In twenty minutes. It's only been two minutes. That's eighteen more minutes, and she gets to float the whole time?"

My mother inhaled deeply on her Virginia Slim.

"I'm not sitting here with my feet in like an old person," I continued. "In eight minutes, Orly should get off that raft and let me have it for ten minutes. Then we will both have had it for ten minutes. Fair is fair."

"Jada, just put your feet in and relax, like Mommy said," little Orly said.

"Shut up, Orly!" I snapped back. "That's what's fair. Right, Ma?"

My mother ignored me and called for my father. "Dominic! When ya going to the store?" I could tell it was a Friday because my father used to take Friday afternoons off in the summer. He owned his own small plumbing business, so he could do that. Still, his Fridays weren't for relaxing. My mother sent him food shopping for the weekend for when all of our cousins would come over. And she would make him clean the pool. I thought he liked it all, though, especially the pool stuff. He would tinker with the filter and analyze the tubes, like the plumber he was.

"Right, Ma?" I walked up to her. "Ma? Mom?"

I turned to Gina. "I am a piece of work."

"I prefer the term work in progress," she said without taking her eyes off the scene.

My father peeked his head out from the sliding glass door. He looked so handsome. His hair was dark, not gray like it was now, although we told him it was very distinguished now. He was wearing the big gold cross that my mother had given him for Christmas one year. He wore it every day, even to this day.

"I'm going in a few minutes. Did you check the downstairs freezer?"

"Yeah. We don't need burgers," my mother said, crushing her cigarette in the ashtray. "But get more hot dogs. For some reason, we're going through hot dogs this summer like it's nobody's business."

"Right, Ma?" It was like nine-year-old me was invisible.

"Jada, you want to come with me to the store?" my father asked.

"No," I said, still glaring at my mother, my hand on my hip. "I'll be relaxing on the raft in about five minutes."

"No, you won't!" Orly shouted from where she floated.

"Yes, I will," I shouted back.

"What happened to that blue raft, Dom? We can't find it. We only have the yellow one." My mother motioned to Orly.

"I don't know," my father said. "Did you look over the railing?"

"Yes," I said.

"Sure you don't want to come, Jada?"

"I want to be in the pool," I said. "It's summer! Why would I want to go to a boring grocery store?"

"Go." My mother waved the air. It wasn't clear who she was talking to. I assumed both my father and me.

My father left, but I didn't move.

"Oh boy. I know what's coming," I said to Gina.

"So do I," she said.

"It was stupid. It was just a raft. I should have let it go."

"That's not the point."

My mother flipped the page of her magazine. "What, Jada?"

"How many minutes ago did we finish lunch?"

She glanced up.

"About ten minutes ago, right?" I continued. "So tell Orly to get off that raft so I can float for the next ten minutes. Then twenty minutes will have passed, and we can both swim."

"Oh, Jada." My mother went back to her magazine. "You are unbelievable. Ya know that? Where did ya come from? Honest to God. Go play with a doll for ten minutes. Quit being silly."

"It's not fair!" I screamed. "I don't want to play with a doll. I want to get tan!"

"Jada, is Orly acting that way?"

"No, because she's getting what she wants!"

"Well, if the tables were turned, would she carry on like that?"

"Yes!" I practically shouted.

"I would not," Orly called from the pool.

That was it. I walked over to the pool, put my foot in the water and, with all my might, splashed a dry, sunning Orly on the raft. Five times.

She jolted up and screamed, "Jada!"

My mother yelled too. It was a chorus of the two of them yelling my name as I marched back into the house. I would have slammed the door if it was slammable, but it was the sliding door that was too heavy for us at that age. Yet I was angry enough to open and close it with no problem.

Gina and I stood there and watched my mother grab a towel from the side of the deck and hand it to Orly. My sister dried her stomach and legs and handed it back to my mother, who went back to her magazine and lit a new cigarette. Orly kept floating.

I spent the next hour in my room.

I turned to Gina. "I spent an hour in my room. I was only spiting myself and missing out on, what I believed then, was good sun time. I was a brat."

Gina laughed a little, still watching the scene before us—Orly floating and my mother smoking.

"Best friends, these two," I said. "Like water and water. I'm the oil. I don't mix with either."

"The suntan oil to their pool water." Gina adjusted herself on the chair and surveyed her bony arms, which glimmered from the Sweet Sun tanning oil. "You've been fighting for a long time. Fighting to be understood, fighting to get in there, to prove your worth."

I nodded but didn't have too much time to consider that. She popped up. "Let's go."

I stayed.

"What's the matter? Feel like you've seen enough?" she asked.

"Yeah."

"Too bad. There's more." She gave me her hand and pulled me up. Gina headed toward the house and opened the sliding door.

Orly and I were sitting at the kitchen table, doing our homework. We were about twelve and eight. I was reading something aloud as Orly listened.

"The hydrologic cycle is part of—oh, hold on. That's supposed to be 'of.' I wrote 'if.' When I read my essays out loud, it helps me catch mistakes."

"Me too," little Orly declared.

"My college roommate is going to think I'm crazy."

"Is she going to live here?" Orly asked.

"No. At college."

"You're not going to live here?"

"When I go to college? No way. You think I'm working this hard in seventh grade to go to Queens U and never leave the borough? I'm going somewhere prestigious."

Orly looked confused.

JoAnn came into the room to stir the pasta cooking on the stove. "Two more minutes," she said. "Clear the table."

"Jada's going to move for college. She's going to have a roommate," Orly said.

My mother stopped in her tracks. I could tell from her face that she thought this was a ridiculous conversation. It was a face she'd made often and still did. "Is that what she thinks? Move this stuff to the dining room table."

Now I was the one who looked confused.

"I never fit in with them," I said.

Gina nodded. "Let's go inhale some more artificial coconut and talk." We went back to the deck, where we reclined on the lounge chairs again and fixed our eyes on the clear blue sky.

"My mother always loved Mark."

"Part of the problem," Gina said.

"I didn't marry him for her."

"Not consciously."

I groaned.

"Remember introducing him to your family? You couldn't wait."

"My mother and Orly were so impressed with him. I loved it. It felt like I won. Like, 'See, you two, I'm not so odd. Someone extremely successful and good-looking thinks I'm amazing.' Wow, how twisted is that? But now when he laughs at every little thing my mother says, I pay for it." I lowered my gaze to the still water of the pool in front of me. "But he's a good guy. Do I have to tell him about Todd, even though we didn't have sex?"

"I was wondering when you were going to ask that." She rolled over to face me. "Let's back up. If you had pulled the trigger with Mark and moved forward with a divorce and *then* found out it wasn't going to happen with Todd, would you have thought 'Why did I even tell Mark? I broke up my marriage for nothing.'"

I shook my head.

"Of course not. You know better than to think that a marriage built on a shaky or virtually no foundation is better than nothing. You know it's not sustainable with Mark and, yes, you're possibly going to end up alone but—"

"I already feel alone."

"Exactly. One night with Todd made you realize, truly and deeply and in a way you never had before, that the brain is the sexiest organ. Not that Mark isn't smart. He's a genius. But the brain really is the essence of someone, and his brain and your brain don't want to stay up all night talking."

"We never did. But you couldn't have convinced me not to marry him. Not then."

"But you see now?"

"My eyes have been opened."

"So, do you have to tell Mark?" Gina rolled back over to face the sun. "Well, I've asked this before, but would you have gone back to Todd's room if Mark were standing right there?"

I knew the answer. *But how will I ever get the words out?*

Then I heard, "Shake 'em! I got maracas! You got maracas! Shake 'em. Shake 'em. Shake 'em!"

"What the..." I lifted myself up to see what the hell was going on.

Grandpa Tony and Grandma Rose were on the deck in a two-person conga line, coming toward us.

"What are they doing?"

"Dancing," Gina said.

"To the left. To the left!" Grandpa shouted.

"To the right. To the right!" Grandma sang.

"Shake 'em. Shake 'em. Shake 'em!" they yelled in unison.

"Oh my... God," I said under my breath.

"Where are you two crazy kids coming from?" Gina asked.

Grandpa Tony took his hands off Grandma and did a little shaking move with his hips. "A welcome party. Our dear friend Louise Lucci always loved to dance." He took two steps backward as Grandma took two steps forward, and then he twirled her.

Grandma untwirled and sat on the edge of my lounge chair. "So, how's it going here?"

"Not as much fun as you're having," I said.

"Well, that's how it goes." She patted my leg. "This is the hard part, dear."

"Seeing flashbacks?"

"No, life. Going through it. Learning the lessons."

"So I hear."

Grandpa Tony sat on the edge of Gina's chair and leaned toward me. "But your soul will be better for it."

I motioned to Gina. "He sounds like you."

This visit is leaving me with a lot to digest, and not in the eating way, which is so much more fun.

Grandma and Grandpa stood. "Come on!"

Gina grabbed my hand and pulled me off the lounge chair. Then she and my grandmother sandwiched me in a conga line with Grandpa leading.

"Hold my hips," Grandma called back to me.

We congaed away, and when we reached the edge of the deck, my grandmother leaned back as Gina leaned forward. It was a conga hug. I rested my head on my grandmother's shoulder, and Gina rested hers on mine.

"You may not like where you're being led, but you'll appreciate it once you get there," Grandma whispered. "In the meantime, dance." She jutted her butt backward, which made me bump into Gina and made us both laugh. Then Grandma grabbed Gina's hands, tightening our conga hug.

Chapter 13

On Saturday, my family all arrived at the same time. My mother carried a pastry box. She brought pastry every time she came over, as if it were always a holiday or special occasion, even though all we would be doing was barbecuing. Orly carried a watermelon.

"You carried a watermelon," I said.

"Huh?" Paul asked.

I took the watermelon from Orly.

"Nothing," she said. "*Dirty Dancing*."

"Oh," Paul grunted and walked toward the backyard with the girls.

As I held the big, round watermelon in front of me, a memory came to me. We had been at Aunt Fran's for Easter, one of the few times she'd gotten out of bed for so many hours at once in that first year since Gina passed. I was four months pregnant and supposedly my cousin Andrea had the magic touch. She could get any baby kicking.

"She's not far enough along," my mother said.

I glared at my mother. "Maybe she needs quiet."

But it didn't work. Andrea lifted her hand from my belly, clearly disappointed. "I'm sorry. Maybe we'll try again later."

I was disappointed too. "Yeah, maybe when some people leave the room."

We ate Easter dinner in the basement, where there was a second kitchen and a long table. As we were clearing the table, three hours and several courses later, something moved.

I stopped in my tracks, dishes in hand. "That was weird."

Andrea immediately put her hand on my stomach, and it happened again, stronger. Her face lit up. "I feel it."

"Let me feel." Orly stuck her hand on my belly. "I don't feel anything."

"Nothing, right?" my mother asked. "Probably *agida*."

"I felt it," I said.

"I felt it too." Andrea beamed. "It feels even more real now, right?"

"Yeah." I smiled back but only to hide the wave of terror that washed over me. *It's really real.* From that moment on, that terror had never left me. Sometimes, it rose to the surface faster and more intense. Other times, it lay dormant, but it was always there, always simmering. That other person was here, and I was responsible for his whole life.

His life is in my hands. I rested the watermelon on my kitchen table. Through the glass enclosure of my kitchen, I could see Ethan punch his arm through his swimmie as Mark held it out. I knew I had to talk to Mark, though it never seemed like the right time. *When is there ever a right time to hurt someone? And what will it do to Ethan? I'm responsible for him. For all of this.*

My mother plopped the pastry box down. My nieces, with their bathing suits on under their summer dresses, which they instantly tore off, ran outside and jumped right in the pool. My mom and Orly unloaded the bag Paul had carried in. They'd brought containers of potato salad, macaroni salad, olives, and pickles. All I'd done was make sure the burgers and hot dogs were defrosted. I should have gone to the market for the fresh stuff, but I had other things on my mind.

"Thanks for the pastry and all of these fixings," I said. "And the watermelon. We have Coke, Diet Coke, and your Sprite in the cooler outside."

"I don't know if I want to drink that stuff anymore," my mother said. "Because of the, you know..."

"Why? The what?" I asked.

"Did you move your serving spoons?" My mother was going through my kitchen drawers. "Oh, here they are. Never mind."

I made myself useful in my own kitchen and grabbed the plates and napkins from the cabinet next to where my mother was standing.

"We'll talk more when we sit down, but the good news is it hasn't spread."

I stood still. "What?"

"It hasn't spread. Ya know, that's the thing ya really gotta be concerned about. Spreading, ya know? To other organs, that kind of thing. So that's good."

"What are you talking about?"

My mother looked up from scooping out a container of pasta salad then over to Orly, who was now kneeling by the refrigerator, moving things around to fit the watermelon.

"She doesn't know yet, Ma." Orly zeroed in on the "Ma."

My mother seemed confused. "I thought ya said ya called her."

"She didn't pick up."

"What the hell is going on? Please!" I pleaded.

My mother sighed and put her hands on her hips. "I have uterine cancer. It's stage two. But it hasn't spread. So they're just gonna take it all outta me. What do I need a uterus and ovaries and all that friggin' crap for at my age? Take it. Who the hell needs it? Louise Lucci, Darlene's mother, had the same thing. Got it all taken out. Lived another I don't know how many years. God bless her. She just passed."

Orly shoved the watermelon in the refrigerator and came toward me. "Mommy wanted me to tell you. I called you after she spoke to the doctor, but you didn't pick up. I didn't want to text it."

"I'm sorry I didn't pick up."

"I guess I should have called Mark and told him to have you call me because it's important."

"It's okay." I pulled at the collar of my shirt. My heart was in my throat.

"What the hell's wrong with your neck?" my mother barked. "I'm gonna be fine!"

I wanted to scream at her to stop yelling, but nothing came out.

After a few more moments, a million questions popped in my head. *Did you get a second opinion? When is the surgery? What was the doctor's exact prognosis? How do you feel now? How's Daddy? Did you tell Aunt Fran? Who else knows? Where did your doctor go to school?*

While Orly took the plates and utensils outside, my mother answered most of my questions. "What do we need a second opinion for? I'll be fine. I feel fine. Daddy's fine. Of course Aunt Fran knows. Ya know, thank God I had my kids when I did. You should never wait to have the second one. You never know."

"Well, I just want you to be okay," I said. "Your mom died young. Your dad died young. Cancer." I realized I'd whispered the C word after I said it.

"I've already outlived them by twenty years, Jada." She cut the conversation at that and grabbed the salads and pickles, managing to carry everything Orly hadn't taken out. I, per usual, felt useless and ran to the glass doors to open them.

"Where's my bag, Paul?" Orly called out before finding it in a corner and retrieving a bottle of Sweet Sun tanning oil.

"What are you doing?" I asked. "That's got no coverage!"

"I mix it with this other SPF spray I have. Where is it? It's in here somewhere." She glanced in her bag. "Isabella? Arianna? Get out of the pool for one second. Come here."

"How high SPF?"

"I don't know—twenty something. I'll find it in a minute. Arianna, hold out your arm." My sister slathered my nieces in tanning oil. "Doesn't this smell great?"

I inhaled the familiar scent. "I can't believe they still make this stuff."

"I don't like the sprays with the SPF. They don't smell good."

I rolled my eyes. *Yes, because that's what's important.* I sniffed it again. *It really does smell delicious.*

My mother walked over. "Orly, I think I put my sunglasses in your bag. Ooh, doesn't that smell good? Give me some."

"No!" I screamed. "You already have one kind of cancer."

"Huh?" Isabella asked, confused.

My mother and Orly froze.

I guess the children have not been told.

I turned to Isabella's sweet but puzzled face. "Nothing. Want a raft? Or a tube? We have one that looks like a doughnut with frosting."

"Where?" Isabella and Arianna asked at the same time.

While I retrieved the doughnut tube, I also found our SPF 70 spray. "Psst. Isabella. Arianna." I called for them to come to me by the side of our house. "Close your eyes and don't breathe in." They closed their eyes, and I sprayed them from head to toe. "Here. Put this in your mother's bag."

Later, the kids devoured their cheeseburgers and hot dogs and went back to swimming—after waiting twenty minutes, all on their own rafts. As the adults ate, my mother mentioned her life-threatening disease to Mark as if it were any other banal news, like deciding to buy a new car. "So we found out I have cancer. Uterine. Stage two. But—"

"I know. Paul just told me. If you need anything—I know you pick the girls up from school every day—if you need us to pay for or arrange childcare or aftercare or whatever it is, please let us know if we can help in any way. My coworker Alana's father had a great radiologist."

That throat thing attacked me again. I swallowed a mouthful of potato salad, and it hurt going down. *Why does Mark have to be so kind right now? And Alana's father had cancer?*

"Oh, Mark, you're a doll. We'll work it out. And my doctor, is he fantastic or what, Dom?" My mother turned to my father.

"He's very good," my father mumbled with food in his mouth.

"He went to high school with my friend Elaine's son. Did I tell you that?"

"That's great, but can he cure cancer?" I asked.

My mother shrugged. "He's very good. Trust me, Jada. Ya know, don't you think Italian hot dogs are so much better than these?" My mother held up her hot dog. "What are these? They're not very good. We shoulda made sausage and peppers."

"I'll make sausage and peppers tomorrow," my father said.

"I bought those hot dogs from the gourmet butcher who delivers," I said. "They're not good?"

"They're terrible," my mother said as she took another bite.

"Well, stop eating it. We'll, I don't know, feed it to the birds."

"Feed it to the birds? You probably paid a fortune for these. You're a piece of work, Jada."

"Jada would tell the birds off if they didn't like them," Mark said. My mother laughed.

Shut up, Mark. "We have burgers too. You want a burger?" I asked.

"Nah." She continued eating. "I'm not wasting."

We spent the rest of the day watching the kids swim in the pool. In between "Ma, look at this!" and "Ma, watch!" and helping them dry off so they could run into the house to use the bathroom, I wanted to know more about my mother's treatment plan, but she didn't want to talk about it. So we talked about everything and nothing.

"Have you tried those new dryer sheets I told you about? They made my new pajamas soft in one dry. You have to get them," my mother informed us.

"Was there traffic on the LIE?" I asked.

"Did you hear Arlene and Don are moving to Florida?" Orly asked.

"Can you hand me that pitcher of water?" Mark asked.

As I handed it to him, I was transported to our first date.

"I'm just going to have water," Mark had said as I ordered an extra-dirty martini with extra-large Spanish olives. "I'm not drinking. I'm training for a fifty-mile bike ride around the planetarium in upstate New York. Then we sleep over, under the stars, kind of."

"That sounds fun," I said. *Not really.* "Do you think you'll ever move out of the city?"

"I don't know." He tore off a piece of bread and offered it to me. I declined then watched him, with perfect care, pour the extra virgin olive oil onto his bread dish along with a delicate sprinkling of parmesan cheese, salt, and pepper.

"When I get married," I said, "I want to move to Long Island. I want a pool." Risky conversation for a first date, but this was a test, and he passed.

He didn't flinch at the Long Island part. It was true. I wanted a pool, and I wanted to be close enough to my family to see them if I wanted or needed to but far enough away that they couldn't just pop in.

"That sounds nice." He dipped his bread. He made it look delicious as he chewed. He was so good-looking that he could make anything look tasty.

I leaned in. "You wouldn't mind Long Island? The LIE and the traffic?"

He shrugged. "What are the other options? Jersey? Westchester? There's traffic everywhere. My family is in Albany, so it's all the same to me."

Too easy.

A guy who was perfect on paper, seemingly perfect in person and willing to live wherever I wanted one day made me feel like I'd won the lottery. What more could I ask for? A lot, it turned out, starting with a deeper connection. If I only knew then what I knew now, I could have spared everyone a lot of pain with what was to come. But I guessed that was the point of life. I had to learn it.

"Snap out of it!" I heard my mother bark. "He wants an ice pop."

Suddenly, Ethan's hot, sticky hand was on my shoulder. "Do we have any more of those ice pops with white stuff on the inside?"

"Let me check." I stood and asked if any of the adults would like an ice pop.

"Ice pop? We brought pastry," my mother said. "Bring out the pastry. It's on the counter."

I went inside, opened the freezer, stuck my head in, and waited a few moments before returning with pops for Ethan and my nieces. I forgot about the cannoli.

"Where's the pastry?" my mother yelled.

I pivoted and retrieved it from the kitchen. That was when I heard Orly mention the memorial.

"Is Aunt Fran having Gina's memorial this year at her house or at the restaurant again?" Orly asked my mother. "Cordillo's?"

Every year, on the Sunday after the anniversary of my cousin Gina's death, there was a memorial. All of my aunt and uncle's friends and family would go to mass with them around noon, and then we would either go back to their house or to a restaurant. It would always turn out surprisingly upbeat. The mention of her name at mass would prompt some hand-reaching across the pews, but no one ever broke down. The meal afterward was always delicious, always loud, and always filled with laughter. Every year, I looked around and wondered if I was the only one who thought it seemed incongruous. We were remembering the worst thing to happen to our family, and it always felt like just another christening or communion.

"Cordillo's," my mother responded to Orly.

No one mentioned the cancer again, but when they were carrying the leftovers out the door, my mother said, "Orly will eat these leftovers during the week. She loves that pasta salad. You didn't want it, right?"

I shook my head.

"Why do you look so upset? I'll be fine."

"I'm just tired," I mumbled. "I'm fine."

As soon as they turned off the street and were out of my line of sight, I shut the door and scooped up Ethan. "Bath time!"

"It's still day," he said.

"No. It's closer to night than you think. Let's go."

Bath, pajamas, brush teeth, book, toes, bed.

But after I went through our nighttime checklist, he was still bonkers. I put on some loud, squeaking, repetitive cartoon while Mark and I cleaned up the kitchen.

"I need to take a shower unless you want to go first," I said as he lifted and tied the garbage bag.

"No. Go shower. I'll stay with Ethan."

I thought it was strange that he hadn't said anything about my mom. Maybe he knew I had to process it alone first. Maybe he knew me better than I thought.

When I got upstairs, I peeled off my sticky, sweaty cotton dress and got in the shower. It would have been the time to have a cry—a big cry with loud, guttural wails—but nothing came.

I got out of the shower, wrapped myself in a towel, and sat on the vanity bench in our bedroom with my head down, listening to my breath. I didn't realize how long I'd been there until Mark knocked on the door.

"Jada? You okay?"

"Yeah." I got up and opened the door. "Do you want to shower? I'll put Ethan to bed."

"Already done. Went out like a light."

"Oh. Okay." I walked toward him, my towel tucked under my armpits. As he took off his shirt to throw it in the hamper, I opened my mouth to speak, and a nonsensical sound emerged.

"You want to talk about your mom?" he asked.

I shook my head.

"I didn't think so. It sounds like she'll be fine." He grabbed a sleep shirt from the dresser.

"I cheated," I blurted out. "Well, sort of."

His eyes widened. "What?"

"When I was in San Francisco, when I was there for work, with a guy I used to date in the city. It wasn't planned. I ran into him, and I spent the night with him. We did not have sex! We didn't even kiss! He's married too. I just feel I should tell you this out of respect. I will never speak to him again. It was a mistake. But I had to tell you. You had to know. You have to know how I'm feeling."

Mark stared at me, straight in the eye, with an expression like he'd suddenly noticed something about me he'd never noticed before. Not something good or bad, just different. "You were with him last night, weren't you?"

"No! Oh God, no! Well, technically yes, but it was just... just to say we're not going to do this."

"I know you didn't meet up with Veronica. She wasn't even in the city yesterday according to her social media." He said that with a nod and smile like he'd finally caught me.

Fucking Frontbook. "Yes, I did meet up with him. But it's not what you think. It was a quick meeting at a bar, and that ended it. Not that it was ever something, really."

He put on the shirt he was holding and left the room.

There was so much more I had to say and explain. Todd was just the tip of the iceberg, a symptom. I had to get to the root of it, say what needed to be said.

But at the sound of the door clicking shut, my knees buckled. And then the wails came out of me, hard and unrelenting, as I crumbled to the floor.

Is this all really happening? I didn't need to pinch myself to make sure it was real. I felt it with every thought, every stab of pain, guilt, and regret.

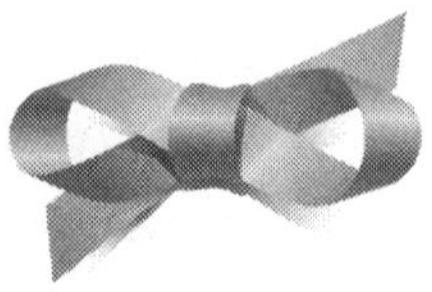

Chapter 14

"Another round?" Gina asked.

I nodded.

"Vanilla with chocolate chip?"

I nodded again.

It was cold inside Scoop Me Up Ice Cream Shop, like the freezer section of the supermarket, where I would shiver while my mother shopped for groceries. I remembered pleading with her to get out of the freezer section as she examined a carton of ice cream with a cigarette dangling from her mouth and saying, "Rub your hands together. Maybe they'll catch fire." I rubbed my arms while a server appeared and set our bowls in front of us then cleared away our empty ones.

We were sitting at one of the wrought iron table and chair sets that were lined up a few feet from the row of red-upholstered swivel stools along the soda fountain counter. Next to the counter was a display case full of cakes and pastries all adorned in some way with Scoop Me Up's signature red-and-white candy striper logo.

Gina was wearing a black T-shirt that read, "Better Off Dead." A skull wearing a Santa hat replaced the letter O in "Off."

We finished our ice cream in silence then guzzled glasses of ice-cold water that had suddenly appeared.

"Is my mother going to be okay?"

"I can tell you she's going to be okay." She leaned back. "No matter what happens."

"You're the grim reaper. Where's your hood? Do you ever deliver good news?"

"Listen, whether she lives many more years or passes and joins me here sooner rather than later by your definition of time, she'll go on. She'll be okay." She spun a little ball of the paper wrapper from her straw, stuck it in the bottom of her straw, and blew it in my direction. "But you don't want to hear that."

"No, I don't want to hear that. What if she dies and I never have any chance of ever feeling close to her?"

"Sometimes certain relationships aren't meant to be easy while on earth. Then one person passes, and you can actually have a better relationship than when they were alive."

"I prefer a better relationship while alive."

"Of course you do."

"What can I do, though? I can't insist on helping her. She'll just say Orly is there to help." I glanced toward the window. It was snowing, that pretty initial dusting when everything seemed peaceful and quiet. "It's summer. What's going on?"

"It's summer where you are."

"Oh, right." I shrugged. "What's going on with my throat? What the hell was that?"

"Ah, good question." She leaned in. "For that, I can provide an answer you will understand. You see, Jada, my dear cousin, you felt nothing for a long time. You were always acerbic. Kind of a bitch, some might say. At times, that's for sure."

"I'm supposed to like where this is going?"

"So, there you were, Jada Ann Santanelli Marlone, one of the bitchiest girls on the island of Manhattan. 'Fuck this. Fuck that. Fuck you. I'll fix that person. Lionel? I'll set his stupid ass straight. I will teach him a lesson. My boss? I've got him wrapped around my finger. Nobody's going to tell me what to do. Line cutters? Going down.'"

"I get it. Where is this going?"

"You are spirited. You always have been. But spirited and having a full spirit are two different things. Your spirit, your soul, which is on this journey, was on a path that was not true to... well, your spirit, your soul."

"Now I'm lost. I understood the bitch part."

"Okay. Let me lay it out this way. You've always felt that your mother favored Orly. Right?"

I nodded.

"And you've always been trying to get your mother's respect, whether you consciously acknowledge it or not. Trust me on that. You tried to prove your small-minded mother and sister wrong and get them to see you differently. You went away to school. You became a lawyer. You lived in the city. But they still didn't get you. They became as close as ever, and instead of being proud of your success and adventures, you just baffled them even more. But then you married Mark. You had a baby. Those were things they could relate to you about. But did anything change? No. They've never made you feel the way you want them to make you feel, but that's the thing."

"What's the thing?" *This recap is depressing.*

"The lesson. It's not how others make you feel. That should never be your motivation, consciously or subconsciously. Fuck that. Follow your path. Do what you want. It's about how you feel about you."

"What does any of this have to do with the heart attack I had in my throat?"

"You felt nothing for a long time because you were on the wrong path. But now that you're being set in the right direction in alignment with your spirit, you're feeling things. And when you've been numb for so long and then do an about-face, you'll catch the wind in your breath."

"How am I going in the right direction? I betrayed my husband. I feel like an alien in my own family. I'm a... I don't know what kind of mother I am."

"Todd was the right direction."

"What!"

"You're not supposed to marry him! But you ignored your gut for so long. You went down a path that wasn't true to you. You married this guy who looked good and impressed your family, and you posted all this fake shit on social media. And then you got stuck and were afraid to change, afraid to do anything to reset the course. When you're finally following your gut, you'll be on the path, the direction that will lead you to the most growth. You needed a jolt, something that would make you finally change instead of staying stagnant as you were."

"He was the jolt I needed?"

"Todd is not what will make or break your marriage, but he jolted you to face what needs to be faced. You're a big talker, telling Grandma and Grandpa you want a divorce, but you were taking no action."

"I knew before I ran into Todd in San Francisco that Mark and I couldn't go on like that. I was going to do something."

"Were you?"

"I had finally admitted it to myself and tried to talk to him."

"Would you have actually taken any action?"

I scraped the last bits of melted ice cream from the bowl in front of me. "Well, the course has been reset, all right. Change is in the air. I'm catching it right in my windpipe."

"It'll stop when you're sailing in the right direction. That's how you'll know. You won't have these mini panic attacks. That's what they are, technically, I suppose."

More ice cream appeared, and I dug in. I scooped up a wad that was the perfect temperature—starting to melt but still firm—and had the perfect amount of chocolate chips. I savored it then sipped my ice water.

"Will Mark forgive me?" I asked. He had never returned to bed before I'd fallen asleep.

"Is that all you want? To be forgiven?"

"We have to finish the rest of the conversation. We can't go on like this. But just seeing him stung by the news I did share... I can't stand to see him hurt." I touched my wedding band, an eternity band of channel diamonds in a platinum setting. It was always loose when I was cold.

"I know."

"And what about Ethan?" I asked. "Is he going to be okay? I don't know what kind of mother I am. Am I screwing him up? I mean, this is horrible, but sometimes I just want to put him to bed to shut him up." I lifted my head to the ceiling for a moment. "Sometimes I think this is so hard. Why is this so hard? It's like I'll never be free again. Even when he's eighteen and goes to college, I still won't feel free. It's this invisible prison for the rest of my life." I gripped my temples and squeezed my eyes shut.

"Brain freeze?"

I shook my head. "Is that the worst thing you've ever heard a mother say?"

"It's my fault," Gina said, barely audible. It sounded like she didn't want to say it but was resigned to it.

"What?" I opened my eyes.

"The reason you feel that way. I mean, it's not really my fault, but—" She popped up from the chair. "Let's go."

The bell on the door of the old-fashioned ice cream shop rang as we left. I followed Gina down the street. She turned right, and we were suddenly on my street on Long Island.

"What happened to the driveway?" I asked.

"What do you mean?" Gina did not break stride as she walked up the driveway, past the garage, and toward the front door.

"It's just not right." I looked back. "We had paving stones put in last year. What happened?"

"Oh." She pressed down on the heavy gold handle of my front door. "This is before that."

I wasn't positive about what we were about to see, but I was somehow certain I wasn't going to like it.

"Come on," Gina called.

As I walked in, I spotted the big cardboard Elmo holding up one finger and a sign above the dining room archway that read, "Happy First Birthday, Ethan." Pre–*Buddy the Bulldozer.*

I saw my parents, Mark's parents, my sister, my brother-in-law, and my nieces, as well as Mark's sister, brother-in-law, and nieces. They were all chatting in the living room and eating lasagna on Elmo plates. Mark was organizing the gifts in the corner. All of our nieces looked so young. *Amazing how much kids change in only a couple of years.*

As I turned around, I saw a one-year-old Ethan, toddling along, unsure on his feet, but eager to move forward. Then he wobbled and fell.

I gasped in delight as I knelt to his eye level. "Look at him at one! Oh my God." Then my heart thumped. "Oh. Now I know why we're here," I said as I stood. "I've blocked it so well."

"Not that well. Consciously, yeah. But not subconsciously."

"Is it really going to help me to relive this? And how is this your fault?"

"We'll talk about it."

I watched myself walking behind Ethan, hunched over, picking him back up.

"What a little potato head," Gina said.

I marveled. "He has grown into his head."

"But that hair," Gina noted. "Ethan would not be Ethan without his big brown curls."

"I know." I couldn't take my eyes off him.

"Let's sit." Gina propped herself up on the bar we'd set up in the corner. It didn't seem so sturdy, and I would never dare try to sit on it with my legs dangling in real life. But this was the other side, so I jumped right up after her.

Gina shimmied her hips back and forth on the bar, getting comfortable.

My eyes went back to Ethan. I saw myself follow him a few more steps from the kitchen before picking him up from behind. "Ma, take him," I called out. "I want to put the cookies out, and then we'll do the cake."

My mother hurried up from the couch. She'd been sitting next to my aunt, and they'd been watching my nieces sing and dance.

Aunt Fran was admiring politely and throwing in a few claps and "God bless 'ems." Gina must have been on her mind at all of these family parties.

My mother knelt down and held out her arms. "Come on. Walk to me."

Ethan stared, frozen in place.

My mother looked over at the coffee table and eyed a marshmallow Elmo wrapped in plastic and tied with ribbon. "Hand that to me, Fran."

Aunt Fran obeyed, dutifully peeling the plastic wrapper off.

"You want this?" My mother held up the candy, tearing off a bit.

He lifted his left leg as if it weighed more than him and then his right until he was barreling toward the bright red sweet.

"I thought so," she said.

Ethan, with no teeth, opened his mouth wide for the marshmallow piece then tried to swallow it whole. He wobbled back and forth, already unsure on his feet, and now unable to breathe. His brow furrowed, and his eyes narrowed on my mother to help him.

I hadn't seen it from this angle, how it happened, his facial expressions. I was in the kitchen when it happened.

"It's stuck! I think it's stuck!" My mother's voice had a sharp panic I'd never heard from her before.

I watched myself run to the living room as my mother's left hand clutched the curls at the back of Ethan's head and her right index finger poked inside his mouth.

Choking. One of the hazards. One of the statistics. No. No. No.

I lunged toward them and flipped Ethan upside down. I remembered exactly what had been going through my head: *Flip? Right? That's what they say to do? I should know. I'm the parent. Is this right? Is this what I'm supposed to be doing? Out. Out, whatever it is.*

My son's little feet inside his brand-new miniature Asics sneakers grated my chin.

"Ouuuuuut!" I remembered feeling the word come up from my gut. "Out."

When I heard him cry, I could have cried from relief if I weren't still in shock over what was happening. My brain told my body, *It's okay. He can't cry if he can't breathe. He's breathing.* I lowered him to the floor. The room was silent.

"He's all right," Aunt Fran kept repeating. "He's all right."

I hugged my crying baby. Eventually, that wave of relief washed over me, mixed occasionally with the sting of terror. *What would I have done if anything happened to you?*

I wanted to hug little Ethan again right at that moment as I watched this from the bar in the corner with Gina.

Our guests resumed talking, and I quickly learned my mother had given him a marshmallow. I immediately chastised her. "You gave a one-year-old a marshmallow?"

She became defensive. "The girls"—meaning my nieces—"have been eating chips since before they had teeth."

I was too relieved in that moment to yell, "Of course they did!" or to even fight with her at all.

I wanted to go upstairs to his room and rock him until everyone downstairs left. But he wiggled away, and everything went on as usual—the cake, the candles, the singing of "Happy Birthday," and the opening of gifts.

But of course, it felt anything but ordinary. It had stuck with me.

Later on, I'd tried to talk to Mark about it. "Do you know how quickly he could have lost oxygen? Over a marshmallow. A fucking marshmallow. It could be anything. It could be like that." I snapped my fingers. "In a second. My poor aunt Fran. How does she go on? She doesn't really. And I don't blame her. At least she was here today. I guess that's good."

He had only nodded and said, "I know, Jada. I know." He'd been taking out the garbage when the whole thing happened.

I tried never to think about that memory. I glared at Gina. "Thanks a lot for the reminder."

She stared straight ahead. "No one actually likes to be vulnerable, completely helpless to what could be. But that's exactly what you choose when you choose to have a child. There is nothing you can do about the fact that now he's walking around on earth with all of these potential threats to him at any moment. And there's not a damn thing you can do about it."

"Every parent knows that. You're stating the obvious. Thanks again."

"You kind of knew it deep down before the marshmallow incident. Then it hit you. You could be like my mother. You could be Aunt Fran. Anything can happen at the drop of a hat. A marshmallow. A car colliding with a tree."

"Okay. I get it."

"It's fear. And it's okay. It would be weird if you didn't have a little bit of it. But it's also why Ethan doesn't go to preschool. It's why you don't go to the beach, not just because you don't want to sit on the Garden State Parkway. It's why you can't relax when he's in the pool. It's the real reason why he's never stayed over with your parents or in-laws for even a night. You have to try to overcome some of it for

Ethan. Enjoy him. Live in the here and now. It's the best thing you can do for him and for you."

"Why does it seem like some moms are loving every minute of this? Motherhood is not how it looks on social media." I held onto the bar with both hands by my thighs.

"Pffft, ya think? Don't worry how other moms appear. You're all fucking lying on social media. You are the biggest fake of them all. But parenthood is not for you to love or like. It's not about that. It's for you to raise a human and to learn from that. Your favorite thing: learning. You and Ethan picked each other. You're in this together." She put her arm around me.

"He picked me? What was he thinking?"

"I see you being so sweet with him—another example of how your outward behavior doesn't match your inward thoughts and feelings."

"So I should tell my kid how afraid I am? How hard this is?"

"Of course not. It's just an example of how you sacrifice for him. He's changing you, and that's a good thing."

"Why do some moms look so relaxed?"

"Who cares? Stop worrying about how other people look!"

"No. Listen! Like the time at the beach. We went to the beach with Mark's cousins. They were sitting on their beach chairs, relaxed and drinking wine, while the kids played in the sand, a little too close to the shoreline for my liking. And they kept saying, 'Jada, sit, relax,' and I said, 'All it takes is one wave.' They thought I was joking. Was that wrong? That I didn't want my kid to get swept away?"

"There is no right or wrong, but try, a little, to stop waiting for the other shoe to drop. Stop waiting for something as small as a marshmallow or as big as the ocean to get him. Enjoy the now."

"Enjoy the now and watch my kid choke or float away?"

"She laughed. "No, of course not. What I'm saying is you would handle motherhood differently if I didn't suddenly die. I am your constant reminder that anything can happen at any moment. But, Jada, you can't go on like that. You have to stop, for your sake and Ethan's."

"I don't know how."

"You'll learn. Or unlearn. The seed is planted."

"But how? Give me specifics."

"Be in the now. Get off your phone. Have you ever actually played with Ethan? Have fun with him and allow yourself to enjoy it."

"You're like my dead therapist," I said. "Why don't you just send me to therapy in, you know, real life?"

"You would never go. You don't have the time, and you won't make the time. Believe me, if I thought you would go, I'd send you. I'd, I don't know, have you meet the right therapist for you through the mommy group or at the nail salon. But no, I know you, and I know what will work. We're doing it this way."

"How do you know this way is working?"

"I've seen it." Gina uncrossed her legs and hopped off the bar. "You might not remember this, but you are learning to listen to your gut. Something—me—told you to listen to the quiet, to admit to yourself what you really want. Something—me—told you to reach out to Danielle and help Joyce's mother. Get your head out of your own ass. Something—me—warned you about Todd and told you to talk to Mark, which, yes, we're still working on, but... Hello." She waved her hand above her head. "That's me, guiding you." She offered her hand to help me down.

"Thank you," I said and jumped down. "And I could really use a cigarette now."

"Oh yeah?" She skipped sideways out of my house, reaching for her pack of cigarettes and waving it in the air. "No calories, no carcinogens. Don't ya love it here?"

"Oh yeah, it's a real treat."

We sat on my front steps. She handed me a cigarette and lit it. "Enjoy it, cuz," she whispered.

And I did.

Chapter 15

"So, how's the house?" Mark's former coworker Jed asked as we waited for the train into the city. I wiped the sweat from my hairline with the back of my hand. It was early morning and already eighty degrees out.

"Good," Mark and I said at the same time.

Following my confession, Mark and I had not spoken. We were going on thirty-six hours without saying a single word to each other. We'd gone through our routine the following day—watching Ethan in the pool, feeding, bathing, and putting him to bed, then putting ourselves to bed—without any exchange between us. I hadn't tried because I was still trying to find the words for the next part of the conversation. Mark hadn't tried either. While I couldn't remember having a real conversation of any depth with my husband in the past couple of years, or ever, this was different, and not just because he was sleeping in the guest room.

When we arrived at the train station on the second morning of saying nothing, we stood in silence, staring down at our phones like everyone else around us, just like every other morning, until Mark glanced up and saw Jed. They used to work together, but Jed no longer worked in the city. He was only taking the train in that day for a meeting. Jed asked all of the usual catch-up questions: "How's your son?" "How's the house?" "How's work?"

Throughout the conversation, while we waited on the platform, Mark and I answered and asked questions in return in the same friendly way, but we never once looked at each other or engaged with each other at all.

While Mark was chatting with Jed as we boarded the train, I wanted to scream. *How are you acting so normal? Don't you want to talk? Don't you want to say anything?* But then again, I was acting the same way. I hadn't worked up the courage yet to continue the conversation. *It's the hardest conversation I will ever have, but it cannot be postponed any longer.*

"How did that settlement come about on the Crawford patent?" Jed asked Mark. "I read about it in the trade paper."

"Alana did a great job." Mark went on to explain.

As they continued talking about patent law, I zoned out. I stared out the window for the rest of the commute. As we stepped off the train, Mark was still chatting with Jed. After we made our way up the escalator and out the doors, I interrupted.

"Jed, it was great to see you. I just have to talk to Mark for a second before I head to my office."

Jed politely bid farewell, and I faced Mark. "What time do you think you'll be home tonight?"

"No idea."

"Well, after Ethan is in bed, we have to talk."

He sneered. "There's *more*?"

"No, there is not *more*. I think the next step, probably, is to go our separate ways, a divorce." I hadn't anticipated saying those words to him right outside Penn Station, but there it was.

"To be with your ex?"

"No!" As I said that, I was nailed in the shoulder by the backpack of a passerby.

"To be alone?" he asked.

"Yeah. I guess that's what will happen. But this marriage is not working and has not worked for a long time. It's the right thing to do. We both deserve to be with people who, I don't know, we want to be with. Or, yes, even be alone. We haven't had a real conversation in... maybe ever. It's not right. It's not normal."

"No relationship is normal."

"Well, it's not good."

He nodded. "Clearly."

"Lawyers say 'clearly' when it's actually not that clear," I said.

"Not always."

"Okay, fine. It's clear. I'm the bad guy. But it was bad between us before that."

"Hail to the chief!" A man in a full-length cheetah coat stumbled toward us. *Only in New York.*

"I'm sorry. This is not where we should be having this conversation. We'll talk later," I said.

"Bye." Mark walked away.

I couldn't concentrate the rest of the day. Every five minutes, I would find myself Googling "Uterine cancer stage II" and "How to talk to your child about divorce."

Dan caught me zoning out during a conference call. "So once those interrogatories are out the door, we can focus on that," Dan said during the call with Lionel.

"When are they going to be done?" Lionel asked.

"Jada, how are they coming along?" Dan asked.

I sat up. I was alone in my office on the call, but what I was actually doing was having an imaginary conversation with Mark in my head.

Listen, Ethan is our main priority. I pictured myself facing him. *Let's agree on how we should tell him.*

"How we should—" I said into the phone.

"How we should what?" Lionel yelled.

"Oh, um, sorry. I'm looking something up here. Can you repeat the question, Dan? My phone cut out."

My phone cut out? Good one. I'm not on a cell phone, so that makes zero sense, but whatever.

"How are the interrogatories coming?" he asked again slowly.

"Good. They're coming along."

"What were you asking me? How we should what?" Lionel insisted.

"I was talking to myself, Lionel. I do that," I said. "How we should... proceed with the condensed timeframe was the question I was asking. Your timeframe for me to finish the interrogatories has been quite condensed."

"Yeah, it has. ASAP is the answer," Lionel said.

"ASAP," Dan repeated.

They loved "ASAP" because they thought it meant "right now" and not "as soon as possible."

"I'll be able to finish them tomorrow or the day after," I said. "That's when it will be possible to have them completed because I only received them yesterday."

"Did you work on them all night?" Lionel asked.

"No. I had to put my son to bed," I replied. "I couldn't work on them all night."

"How old is your son?"

Where the hell is this going? "Almost four."

"So after he went to sleep, you could've worked on them then. No?"

I could hear Dan trying to interject. "Uh, well..." "Um, Lionel..."

I leaned in close to the speaker to answer the question. "No."

"All right, then. What about today?" Lionel asked.

I bit my fist. "I'll try."

"We have a saying in my house," he said. "No try. Do."

"Oh yeah? Well, we have a saying in my house—"

"Okay!" Dan finally found his voice. "Great call. We'll send everything over to you, Lionel. ASAP."

Dan knocked on my door moments later. "I don't want to know the saying you've got in your house and neither does the client. He's the client, Jada."

"And I'm an adult."

"What's your point?"

"He's a condescending asshole. 'No try. Do'? He can fuck off."

"He's the client," Dan repeated.

"I'm an adult," I repeated.

"Well, then, act like one. Please finish the interrogatories and send them to him. And if they're not done before you leave today, I'm going to have to put you on probation."

"Probation?"

"Yes, Jada. That's what we did with Lydia." Lydia was an old associate who used to leave for hours in the middle of the day to attend MBA school and thought no one would ever find out. They found out. She was fired.

"ASAP it is," I said.

"Thank you." He shut the door.

I did try to get to the interrogatories right away. But every few minutes, I went back to the open pages on my screen about uterine cancer. I was too overwhelmed to worry that I was doing all of this personal stuff on my work computer.

When I got home later that night, I found that Mark had arrived home before me. He'd already relieved Joyce and was doing a puzzle on the family room floor with Ethan. The television was on. There was a plate of chicken nuggets and a juice box by Ethan on the floor.

"Mommy! You're home." Ethan didn't get up.

"I'm home." I leaned down to kiss him on the head as he concentrated on putting in a puzzle piece. I turned around without saying a word to Mark and went upstairs to change out of my work clothes.

A couple of hours later, after Ethan had taken his bath, brushed his teeth, claimed to be hungry, and then fallen asleep, Mark came into our room to talk.

"I want to know details now. I want to know who this guy is and how this happened."

"Okay." My heart jackhammered in my chest all the way to my throat.

"Did you plan to meet him in San Francisco?" he asked. "Like ahead of time?"

"No! We just ran into each other at the hotel."

"He just happened to be in San Francisco the same time as you?"

"Yes."

"There was nothing behind my back beforehand?"

"No. I swear. Definitely not." I couldn't tell if he believed me or not. He was stone-faced.

"What about when you got back? Have you seen him since?"

"Well, just on Friday. And that was it."

He stared up at the ceiling, biting his bottom lip.

I inched closer. "What I mean is I met him briefly but just so he could explain that he got another woman pregnant. So he's a cheater. He's a bad guy. He's cheated with others. Obviously. And— "

"I don't care about his character. I'm not married to him. I care about you and what you do when I'm not with you. Cheating just once is enough."

"We did not have sex! We didn't even kiss!"

"I'm supposed to believe that?"

"Yes!"

"Jada, I'm not stupid. I know everything I do annoys you, but you can't think I'm stupid."

"I don't think you're stupid." I swallowed. "And everything you do doesn't annoy me." *I wouldn't believe me either.*

"So you're telling me what? What did you do, then?"

"We went back to his room and talked."

"You went back to his room?"

"Yes. But we just talked. I told you this only because I did something that looked and felt deceptive, and you have the right to know because we're married. But, Mark, we were broken before then. And we have been for a long time. The foundation of us was never that strong. Do we continue like this? Forever? Or do the brave thing?"

He lowered his head and raised his eyes to look at me, as if to really gauge my words. "You didn't sleep with him?"

"No! I haven't had sex in..." *He knows. A long time. Bad example, Jada.*

He sighed. "Well, my decision is made."

His decision? Okay. Let him phrase it however he wants.

"Jed and his wife still have their place in the city, and their renters moved out last month. So..."

Oh God. Okay, yes, I suppose this is how it happens, but that doesn't make it any easier.

"I'll probably stay there for a while until I find my own place."

That throat thing started again. I pulled at my collar. "Okay," I croaked.

He glanced down. When our eyes finally met, he shook his head and walked out of the room.

• • ❧ • •

ON SATURDAY, I GOT out of bed around seven a.m. after another restless night. Ethan was wide-awake, playing with his trucks on the floor of his room, oblivious to the structure crumbling around him.

"Good morning, buddy. Hey, guess what we're going to do today?"

"What?" He didn't take his eyes off of the miniature fire truck he was guiding along the edge of the circular rug in the middle of his room.

"We're going to play in the pool. We're going to play deep-sea diving. Me and you. We're going to search for hidden treasures." I hoped that sounded fun to him. I thought it sounded like something boys would think was fun.

He paused, probably unsure of what deep-sea diving and hidden treasure meant, and then fiddled with something on the fire truck.

"Does that sound fun?"

"Yeah." He returned to zooming in circles.

"Okay. Let's go downstairs. What do you want for breakfast?"

"Cereal," he announced.

"Okay. Put your socks on."

"No socks." He made more circles with the fire truck.

"Okay. Come on."

He didn't get up from the floor. So I left him to his trucks to peek in on Mark in the guest bedroom, but he wasn't there, and the bed looked untouched. *Where did he sleep?* While the plan was for him to move into Jed's apartment, no definitive move date had been mentioned. After that conversation, we went about the rest of the week as usual. I went back to Ethan, who was still vrooming on the floor, and sent Mark a text as I stood against the doorframe. Jada: *Just want to see where you are. I will swim with Ethan today and then maybe go to the park.*

I checked social media then my email then social again. Then I checked my text messages again and reread my text to Mark.

Ethan stood up. "I'm hungry."

"Okay," I said, still studying my phone. "Come on."

He brought his fire truck with him, and as we were walking down the stairs, he vroomed it along the railing then left it on the third step from the bottom.

"Pick up that truck, Ethan," I said.

"No."

"Pick it up. You can't leave trucks on the stairs. Someone could trip on it and get hurt."

"No," he said, walking to the kitchen.

I picked up the truck and called his name again. He ignored me, so I grabbed his shoulder. "Do you see this?" I held up the truck then walked to the back door, opened it, and put the truck on the patio, just out of his view. "That is what happens when you don't listen to me."

That ignited a full-on screaming fit. He thrashed about on the floor, wailing, "Give it back!"

I rested my elbows on the counter and rubbed my eyes while he screamed. *How will this child ever cope with his father moving out and with other changes that are about to happen?*

A few minutes later, after promises to listen and put our toys away where they belong, I retrieved the truck and threw it in the toy basket at the bottom of the stairs while Ethan observed me. Satisfied that his toy was safely inside the house, he moved on to other things, like insisting on chicken nuggets for breakfast.

We settled on the couch as Ethan ate his nuggets. After one bite, he decided he wanted Mini-Wheats. I poured Mini-Wheats and milk. Then I made coffee and scrolled through my phone while Ethan watched cartoons and ate one Mini-Wheat at a time.

I'd still heard nothing from Mark. *Where did he sleep? And am I expected to have the "Daddy is moving out" conversation with Ethan alone?*

"Okay, time to swim," I declared. I retrieved my bathing suit that was hanging on a doorknob in the downstairs bathroom, changed, and brought Ethan's to him and helped him change. His eyes were still glued to the television. After I finally pried him away from the TV, we headed outside. It was a boiling-hot summer morning.

"How do we play?" Ethan asked as he kicked off from one side of the pool and floated to the center in his swimmies.

"What do you mean?"

"The game you said."

"Oh. Hidden treasure. Deep-sea diving." *Who the hell knows? I kind of made it up on the fly.*

"Okay, let's see. I looked around for something that would sink to the bottom. Here!" I spotted the three pennies my nieces had found on the ground, which were resting on the ledge by the grill. I brought them over and thought of Veronica, who believed her grandparents sent her pennies from heaven. *Cute, but I've never believed it.*

"Throw these in." I handed them to Ethan. "And I'll get them from the bottom. And you'll time me. I have to get them before you count to ten."

This lasted for about twenty minutes until I retrieved a penny just after the count of ten only to come to the top to see that Ethan had taken his swimmies off by himself and was beneath the water, his curly brown hair floating atop the shallow end, which wasn't shallow to him.

"What are you doing?" I cried while whisking him to the steps.

He caught his breath, cried, and sneezed all at the same time. Apparently, he wanted to find the pennies too. He was sick of being the "thrower," and he was sick of his swimmies.

My heart pounded as I brought him out of the pool and into the house to dry off and change into dry clothes. Ethan learned that day what it felt like to get water up his nose, and he sneezed three more times on the way to Long Island at Play.

• • ❧ • •

THE BEST THING ABOUT Long Island at Play was that the mothers didn't have to play. The worst thing about Long Island at Play now was the chance of running into Jessica. *I can't face her. What will we do? Not come here anymore? Ethan loves it. This must be what is meant by the phrase, "Don't shit where you sleep."*

We walked in, and Ethan immediately charged up a plastic slide. I had to chase after him to peel off the backpack he'd insisted on putting on after we'd gotten out of the car. He didn't look back, so

I made my way to the café to wash down my cheating heart, failing marriage, sick mother, and generally lonely existence with a strong coffee.

Danielle sat alone, staring at her phone.

"Jada." She smiled warmly. "I was going to text you to see if you were coming today, but then things got nuts. How are you?"

"Good!" I lied as I sat down.

"Yeah?" She stirred the milk in her coffee and studied me. It was like she knew that so much more had happened since we'd last talked and she was waiting for me to tell the truth.

"A lot has happened since I saw you."

Her eyes widened. "Get your coffee, and let's talk."

I did that and returned with a Rice Krispies treat too. I realized I'd been subsisting on nothing but coffee and Ethan's uneaten scraps for days. I tore a huge hunk off and shoved it in my mouth.

"Oooh." Danielle giggled. "Looks like you needed that."

"Haha," I said, which sounded like "Ho Ho" with my mouth full.

"Don't take this the wrong way," Danielle said, "but you look exhausted."

"I'm sure I look worse than that."

"Like, not regular mom exhausted, like really tired. Have you heard from the ex?"

"Mm-hmm." I tore off another chunk of my treat and washed it down with hot coffee.

"I wasn't going to tell you this because it's so gossipy and absurd and I know you have a lot on your plate, but I just want you to know that Melody is telling people that her husband saw you crying on the train last Friday night."

What the—

"It's so weird," Danielle continued. "I shouldn't even say anything. But he thought he saw you crying on the LIRR last week. Or was it this week? Whenever. On a Friday night."

"I've met her husband once. Is he sure it was me?" *It was definitely me.* After meeting Todd, I had let a few tears stream down my face as I stared out the window on the way home. I didn't think anyone had seen me. I hadn't been a blubbering mess, just a little tearstained.

"That's what I said. I was like, 'Not Jada. I can't picture it.' I just wanted you to know that she came in here, saying that. In case she asks you about it, you're prepared."

"Thanks. I'm not a crier but, wow, it figures the one time a few tears slip, Melody's gossiping little weasel husband sees me. They sound perfect for each other, by the way." I shook my head. "You don't even know all that's happened since I last saw you." I gave her the recap, starting with, "The ex got another woman pregnant."

Her mouth dropped open.

"Yeah. That's the kind of guy he is. I should have known better. I had this stupid hope that we would end up together, and if we did, I would never tell Mark I ran into him. Why hurt him with details of how we reconnected? But the truth is that hope was just a symptom of how broken Mark and I are, or were, or are, I guess. So I told Mark because I felt that I had to. And so, he left. He's moving out."

"I'm sorry."

"Oh, and my boss is fed up with me, but who can blame him? And that's actually the least of my problems right now since I also learned that my mother has cancer."

"Holy crap." She touched my arm. "I am so sorry. You weren't kidding. You had a lot to catch me up on."

"When it rains, it pours." I lifted my coffee but stopped when it reached my lips to add, "Those are the big things. But for good measure—you know, just to top it all off here with everything I've been feeling—I love my son, but being a mother is not what I expected. I'm not good at this. I almost killed him in the pool earlier. Long story. And I often think, will I ever feel free again? How horrible is that?

Oh, and I have no friends. I'm virtually friendless. I realized this recently. I have no one I can talk to about all of this. No one at all."

"You've got me. I mean, I know we're kind of new friends, but I'm a good listener."

"You are. Thank you. Really. So, yeah, that was me crying on the train. Ha!" It was a relief to be completely honest about everything.

Danielle tilted her head. "I've been there."

"I know. You mentioned."

"No, really," she said. "All of it. Well, a lot of it. My dad had cancer."

"Trip?"

"Trip. Oh, and the joys of motherhood? Welcome to my life. I have four of them, and at least once a day, I fantasize about running away."

I laughed.

"But the thing is I never went through it all at once."

"Yeah. The timing is impeccable."

"I won't say 'It'll get better,' because I hate when people automatically say that. I'm like 'Really? You know how it's all going to turn out?' But I'm a good listener, so if you need to talk, call me."

Before I could even say thank you and offer to return the favor, a familiar voice pierced the air behind me.

"Ladies!" It was Melody. She was the ultimate buzzkill. "What's up?" Melody dumped her huge pink Vera Bradley baby bag down on the chair next to me. "What's everybody drinking today?"

A cup of my train tears? We're drinking coffee, you nitwit. What else would we be drinking?

Danielle shrugged. "Just the usual."

"Cool!" Melody said as she turned to smile at me. I met her eyes and smiled back. While Melody walked to the counter to order her coffee, Danielle said, "Listen, call me whenever you want. I mean it. I know people say that, but I mean it."

"Thank you," I said, and I meant it.

• • ❧ • •

WHEN I GAVE ETHAN A heads-up that we were leaving in five minutes, he screamed, "No!" and resumed bouncing.

"Five minutes!" I called again then went back to the café just as Jessica arrived.

I almost tripped over a passing toddler but regained my balance. "Hey," I said as casually as possible. I sucked up the last sip of my coffee as Jessica rested her bags down. "I gave Ethan the 'five more minutes' alert. You know how that goes."

"Ha!" Danielle said. "You'll be here another hour."

"We actually have to go," I said, picking up Ethan's backpack and fishing for my keys in my bag.

"Was it something I said?" Jessica asked, which seemed like a joke, but she wasn't smiling.

Shit. Does she know? I couldn't look her in the eye. I had to leave before I screamed, "Nothing happened!" and then crashed to my knees and cried for forgiveness.

"Ha," I said as nonchalantly as possible. "No, no. It's just time to go." I turned to leave, trying to appear natural, like I wasn't hurrying to get out of there and away from Jessica and her possible suspicions.

"Wait!" Jessica said. "Can you sit for just five minutes? I have to ask you something."

My stomach flipped. "What's up?"

"Sit," Jessica said.

Be honest. Be kind. Ask for forgiveness. My God, is this really happening?

"What is it?" I asked as I sat, as I reached for my collar, ready for a heart attack in my throat.

"Ethan is almost four, right?"

"Right."

"Does he know how to swim?"

Where could this possibly be going? "Well, he still uses swimmies."

"And you have a pool? In your yard?"

"Yeah," I said slowly. *And he almost drowned this morning, and it was my fault, but she doesn't need to know that.*

"He should really know how to swim." Melody piped in.

"Thank you." I glared at Melody. "I plan to have a swim teacher come to our home, but I've been a *little* busy lately."

"They should start as early as possible," Melody replied.

"Would Ethan like to join our swim team?" Jessica asked. "Another swimmer quit, and we really need another boy his age. The best part is they teach them in an individualized, unique way. He'll be swimming on his own in no time and even be competing before you know it."

Your husband got another woman pregnant, and you're worried about having enough people on the swim team?

Still, I was relieved that this was what she wanted to talk about. "No," I said. "Thank you, but I'm sorry. I have so much on my plate right now, and there's just no way."

"Well, it's during the day for one more month, and your nanny can bring him," Jessica said. "Half the class is brought in by their nannies."

"No. My nanny doesn't take Ethan anywhere." *And definitely not to a swim class where she could turn around for one brief moment, and who knows what could happen?* I couldn't escape the picture in my head of Ethan's brown curls on the water's surface this morning. "But maybe next year. Yes, definitely. Next year." *Just not your swim team because I'll never be able to look at you again.*

"Well, we need someone this year!" Melody butted in.

I turned to Melody. "Too bad. Sorry."

"I understand," Jessica said.

Ugh, don't be nice. The next thing I knew I would be joining the swim team and racing four-year-olds myself, out of guilt. "We really have to go." I stood and waved to Jessica and Melody's disappointed faces and Danielle's smiling one.

As I entered the main playroom, I swiveled my head to find Ethan as quickly as possible and spotted him swinging like a monkey from a rope over a pool of plastic balls. I waved. "Come on, now."

He ignored me.

"Ethan Marlone. One more swing," I called.

He ignored me.

My eyes went toward the café. I could see through the glass window to Danielle, Melody, and Jessica still sitting at the table, talking. Then Jessica wiped her eyes, and Danielle put her hand on Jessica's arm.

She can't be crying about the swim team. She must be revealing the rest of her life to them, like I just did with Danielle. The confession café. Jessica, I am so sorry.

"Ma!" Ethan pulled my arm, and I gasped.

"You scared me, Ethan. Ready?"

"No. I want juice."

I reached in my bag and handed him a juice. He tore off the straw and handed it to me to unwrap and poke in the hole, which I did while steering him toward the exit.

When we got to the car, I strapped Ethan in then saw a text from Mark.

Mark: *I checked out the apartment. It's furnished. Dishes and sheets too. I stayed there last night. I'm going to bring another bag over there tomorrow night. But I'd like to spend all day tomorrow with Ethan alone if that's OK.*

I eased into the driver's seat.

Jada: *OK. How are we going to phrase this to Ethan? We should talk about it.*

"Hey, E, you're going to get Daddy all to yourself tomorrow. That'll be fun, yeah?"

"Yeah." Ethan was swinging his legs and staring out the window.

When we arrived home, Mark was in the family room, watching television and working on his laptop. We exchanged a muffled "Hey." He took over with Ethan from there, including dinner and changing episodes of *Buddy the Bulldozer*.

I retreated to our bedroom for an ugly cry, a full release right there on the floor of the bathroom, but nothing came out. I rested my head on the cold marble floor. *Will Ethan and I be okay all alone in this big house? Will Mark be okay?*

I finally grabbed the edge of the sink and lifted myself off the floor. I walked out to the bedroom to change into a pair of fresh pajamas.

I sat up on our bed. *Our beautiful bed in our big, beautiful bedroom with high ceilings and walk-in closets.* I was proud of this house because it was big and away from Queens. It was everything I'd imagined when I had dreamed of the money I would make as a lawyer. *This was supposed to be happiness, the place where I'd finally "arrived," but this is where I'd never been so unhappy.* Now what does happiness look like? I couldn't picture it.

• • ❧ • •

AFTER ETHAN'S BATH, I read to him, named his toes, then waited for him to fall asleep. When I went into the bedroom, I found Mark packing his suitcase.

"So the apartment is furnished?" I asked.

"Uh, yeah. All I have to bring is clothes and towels. They have dishes and a coffee maker. I might buy my own sheets, though." He stood and surveyed his packing so far. *All business, no emotion. Same old Mark.*

The idea of Mark having to go to Bed Bath & Beyond and order towels and sheets broke me a little. *You never thought you'd be there again. Me neither. I'm sorry.*

I wanted to scream, "We did not have sex! We didn't even kiss!" And not because I wanted him to stay, and not because Todd was even the cause, but because I was the reason for all this—him moving out, breaking up our family, changing Ethan's life forever. I was the one pulling the plug on the marriage. He would have probably just stayed in our coexistence forever, unfazed.

I knew he would miss the sounds of Ethan in that quiet apartment. Mark really had done nothing overtly wrong and shouldn't have to miss anything.

Not that much would change for me. I would wake up, get Ethan ready, commute to work, and probably utter the same number of words to Mark that I already did: next to nothing.

When did we stop talking? That's the real question. After Ethan was born? My pregnancy had probably been our most connected time. Every night, we would go through the developments of the day—"He is the size of a plum now"—and we would research strollers and discuss the pros and cons of each one.

"Do you want to take anything in your nightstand?" I asked as I opened each drawer, trying to make myself useful.

"I'll get that stuff later."

Before the pregnancy, what did we talk about? While dating, what did we talk about? What the hell have we ever had in common? I couldn't remember.

Does he even realize this? Does he think he tries and I shut him down? What about when I tried?

That was partly true, but in my defense, he would bring up the inanest topics. "What car service did you use?" "Do you know what the hydrologic cycle is?" "Guess what PSI our water pressure is at in the new house. You won't believe it." I later learned that meant pounds per square inch. "Guess what they're estimating as the new time frame for life on Mars."

Who gives a shit? How's this for a time frame? Between now and forever, I'll never give a shit about life on Mars. Or the hydrologic cycle. Or anything you think is interesting.

"Maybe you should bring some of Ethan's clothes or pajamas so he has them there."

He didn't look up from rolling his T-shirts and lining them up. "Okay."

How did we ever end up together?

We'd met a couple of years after law school at a Fordham alumni event that Veronica and I had decided to go to for the free booze. It was at a fancy Park Avenue law firm, and the only alcohol they served was red or white wine, so we had several glasses each then gorged on cheese and crackers.

It was over the cheese cubes that I met Mark. I reached for a piece of Gouda at the exact moment he did, and we bumped toothpicks.

"Sorry!" I'd said, waving for him to go ahead. But Mark, ever the gentleman, insisted I pick my cheese first, so I did.

"Are you a young attorney hoping to connect with a mentor who will advise you in your budding career?" I was drunk, and that was word-for-word from the invitation.

"Ha. Uh, no. I'm a young attorney, but I didn't attend the event. And I didn't go to Fordham. I work for this firm and needed a break."

"So you just came for the food and beverage? Us too." I pointed at Veronica, who was catching up with some know-it-all we'd gone to law school with, who I'd managed to ignore this whole time, but Veronica was too friendly.

"Yeah." He smiled. "I worked until midnight last night and then barely ate anything today, so I'm hurting."

And that was when I noticed. *Holy shit, he's fucking adorable.*

Mark had black hair and dimples on both cheeks. He was in really good shape then and still was, thanks to his love of working out. Back then, he would often "relax" by watching TV while pedaling furiously on his stationary bike. I preferred to watch TV while scrolling furiously through my phone on the couch.

"I'm Jada."

"I'm Mark. Jada? That's an exotic name."

"Not really. I'm named after my dad's mom, who doesn't speak English and gives me leftover chocolate-covered almonds from weddings for my birthday."

He laughed. *This cutie thinks I'm funny?*

I smiled. "I'll tell you all about it over dinner one of these days."

And that was how it had begun. It had never gotten much more exciting after that. At the time, I'd been okay with that. Mark was someone I could take home to my family, and they couldn't not be impressed. *See, Mom and Orly, I've clearly been waiting for perfection, so you can shut up now about when I'll ever meet someone.*

I'd shut them up, all right. *Big deal. Look at us now.*

Mark stuffed in one last shirt and zipped up the suitcase. "Okay, I'm going to take this downstairs."

"I hope the water pressure in the apartment is a good, um, PIS. No. P... Uh, I hope it's a good PSI."

"Huh?"

Forget it. "Never mind. Do you have everything?"

"Yeah. I think so."

I changed and got into bed, but I couldn't sleep. At one point, I tiptoed downstairs to the refrigerator, where I found Mark's Tupperware container of celery sticks and threw them in the garbage.

I went back upstairs, settled into bed, and opened Frontbook. *Cori is having a wedding cake tasting. Ugh.* I opened my Notes app and made a list:

#1 Ethan—ask for advice on how to handle this with him.

#2 Mother—review treatment plan and demand to speak to her doctor.

#3 Mark—check on him.

#4 Work—grow up and grow patience. Work in progress.

#5 Mommy group—find another one?

#6 Hang out with Danielle away from LI at Play.

#7 Break social media addiction. Work in progress.

I finally fell asleep with my phone on my chest.

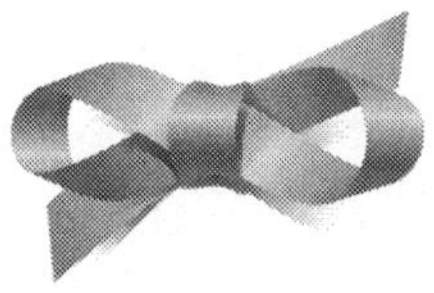

Chapter 16

"Your memorial is in a few days. Does it bother you that we commemorate your passing by eating eggplant parm at Cordillo's?" I asked.

Gina fixed her eyes on mine. "Are you kidding me? No way does it bother me."

We were at Cordillo's, in the catering hall, with its wood-paneled walls and framed posters of coastal Italian towns. There were a lot of images of mountains by turquoise seas dotted with yellow, pink, and blue buildings with narrow windows.

"You died, and it was the worst thing that could ever happen to our family, and now we get together like it's a christening every year around the anniversary. And we barely talk about you the rest of the year. At least I don't."

"I know." She was in her usual black jeans and T-shirt. This time it had an image of an angel with large outstretched wings, balancing like a ballerina above the planet earth. "Listen, you don't have to talk about me. You don't have to remember me. Only do it if it helps you. I'm okay over here. But if it helps the living to talk about those of us on the other side, do it. Talk. Remember. Party. Laugh."

"I want to, but I find it hard."

"I know. People like your friend Veronica are afraid to bring me up."

"Why?"

"She's open about how she believes her dead grandparents are guiding her and using their energy to send her pennies. You're open about how you don't believe in that, in signs. It's not your thing."

Veronica had known Gina in life—not well since I hadn't hung out with Gina a lot, even though we'd both lived in the city, but Veronica had known her the way someone knew their best friend's family. "So that's why she doesn't talk to me about you?"

"Well, she's sensitive to the fact that it's one thing to lose your grandparents, but to lose a young family member in, as you see it, such a tragic way—"

"It was tragic."

"I know. She doesn't want to dismiss your pain. She knows you would say, 'I don't want her to send me a damn penny. I want her to be here on earth, with us, alive.'"

"She's right." I cut into a piece of eggplant parm and watched the gooey mozzarella split apart. I savored the perfect amount of cheese, gravy, and breaded eggplant. "I see so many more status updates from Cori Colter as her wedding approaches. God, it really pisses me off. It just reminds me you're not doing those things. And I'll never forget, right after it happened, seeing her family making comments on social media like 'The angels answered our prayers. What a miracle that Cori survived.' What about our family? What about our miracle? Why didn't we get a miracle?"

Gina rested her fork and lifted her arms to the table. "Listen, I can't explain to you why I had to die when I did and why Cori had to live. You wouldn't understand because you're still living. We're not on the same plane right now. I wouldn't even try. I can say that my lessons were learned, my evolution was over, and hers wasn't."

"You're right. I don't understand. Why did your evolution have to be over?"

"It was. And it happened as it was supposed to happen. I know that's not what you want to hear, and I know it hurt all of you."

"Hurt? Decimated."

"When I see any of you sad or crying, I cry with you. Not because I'm sad to be here but because you can't understand. You're still living. You don't understand why I had to go, and that's where the pain is. And I hate to see any of you in pain, especially my mother. If you want to do something for me, make my mother laugh. Even if it's just remembering old times that'll make her laugh, then do that. Go through old photos with her if you have to. I love to see her laugh. When you guys are happy, I am so happy. Like cigarettes and gin and live music happy!

"Oh, well, as long as you're happy." I rolled my eyes as I tore off a large chunk of bread from the basket. "It's not easy, Gina. It's not the same without you. Not that we hung out all that much, but I knew you were around and okay."

"I'm still around and okay." Her diamond nose ring glinted as her nostrils flared while she tried to make her point.

I held up my finger as I chewed. I didn't want her to move on to another topic because I had something to say about this. I swallowed, and the crusty bread worked its way down my throat. "Stop it! It's not the same. Your mother lost a child. There is nothing worse."

"I know. I didn't say it should be easy. I'm just saying how it is. When you laugh, I laugh. And I like to laugh. So less crying, more laughing."

"Fine. But why would Cori friend me? Isn't that tacky? I don't understand why she was never punished."

Gina leaned in. "Because I was the one driving."

I stopped midchew. "I thought—"

"There was a lot of misinformation at first. The car was mangled. We were both flung from it. But it was eventually figured out."

"Oh."

Cori wasn't the one driving? I wonder if my aunt and uncle ever bothered to correct this info to the rest of the family. It wasn't ever conveyed to me.

I swirled a piece of bread in circles in the marinara sauce. "Honestly, it helped to be aggravated by Cori, as strange as that sounds," I said. "It was a source to which I could direct my anger."

"Well, I guess you're going to have to let that anger go." Gina shrugged. "What do you think of that?"

I shook my head. "I don't know what I think of that. It'll require some rewiring of the brain cells that are inclined to immediately think, 'Ugh, Cori. I blame Cori.' I know I should have been happy for her anyway for getting on with her life and for good things happening for her. Her happiness should never have been a reminder of our loss. That was never the right way to view her. But I suppose it's only natural, right?"

"It is natural. Don't beat yourself up. But focus on not holding onto that. It's so heavy to be carrying that around."

"I'll try."

"No try. Do." We laughed. "What a relief. You can finally let it go. You can release that energy that's not serving you."

I grabbed an imaginary ball from my chest and tossed it away. "Poof."

Gina swung an imaginary bat at it. "Cool. Now we can go." She pushed her plate away. "Dessert time."

As we headed to our old favorite place, Scoop Me Up, a man around our parents' age in a "Rather Be Fishing" T-shirt smiled in our direction.

"Hi, Trip," Gina said.

He tipped his fishing hat as he continued on.

Trip?

Gina nodded, as if she'd read my mind. "Such a sweet man."

We made our way to the counter to order one of our old favorites—soft-serve vanilla in a wafer cone with rainbow sprinkles. We sat on the bench by the door.

"Things are so fucked up." I licked my vanilla ice cream, which was swirled so high, I was afraid it might tip over.

"You can say that again," Gina said. "You had to go through this, though. All of it."

"Okay, now that's fucked up." I lowered my cone and glared at her. "I don't want to hear any shit about what I had to learn from all of this. What I want is to hear is that my son will be okay and my mom will be okay and Mark will be okay."

She didn't answer. She just sat there, eating her ice cream.

"Okay, so what the hell am I supposed to learn?" I asked.

"Ha! That's for you to find out."

"How am I supposed to find out? And by the way, it hurts." I switched my ice cream to the other hand and glared out the window. "Like hell."

"I know. Growth always hurts. It's like you were a size six shoe and now you're a seven, but you're still in your old heels. Don't worry. We're going shoe shopping. Theoretically speaking. Hang in there. It hurts, but at least you have shoes."

Anticipating what Gina would say next, I added, "I know I'm lucky. I'm healthy. I live in a country where I'm free. My child is healthy. I have it easy at the end of the day. Well, for the most part. I'm going through some shit, but I know, in the grand scheme of things, my kid is okay, so all is okay."

"Yes, but what's also okay is to feel your pain. You're right that it's good to have perspective, but pain is pain. It hurts. It's okay to feel it. Just don't direct it at others, like Cori."

"I'm feeling it, all right. I can't sleep. I can't concentrate. I go into work looking like an electrocuted raccoon," I said.

"Just don't start eating out of the garbage can. But yeah, you're going through shit. Feel it. Feel it through."

As I spun my cone and licked, creating a perfect, smooth sphere of vanilla deliciousness, a familiar voice filled the air.

"There they are. Miss America and Mrs. America."

"Two beauties. Gah bless."

I turned around to see Grandpa Tony and Grandma Rose. Grandpa was wearing a tux, and Grandma had on a blue dress and a mink stole.

"Hi, Grandma. Hi, Grandpa. Where are your maracas?" I asked.

"No maracas today, but did we go to a party. Let me tell ya," Grandpa said.

We scooted over to make room for them on the bench.

"We just came from a wedding," Grandma said. "What an affair."

"Pastry after pastry after pastry," Grandpa added. "Cannoli, sfogliatelle, pizzelle. And the cookies, the pignoli. Then they had this whole gelato area—what do ya call it—like a station, a gelato station. And then they passed out zeppole."

"Oh, was it beautiful or what?" Grandma exclaimed. "It was something else."

"What do you mean you were at a wedding?" I asked. "You're dead."

My grandparents cracked up at that.

"Don't you think we were at your wedding?" Gina asked.

"I can't imagine you had any fun. There was a sadness in the air," I said, thinking about that day. Gina had died three months earlier. We'd still gone ahead with the whole thing at Aunt Fran's insistence. We'd set up a corner table with Gina's picture and had leaves and candles spread around it. It had felt morbid as fuck to me. I'd assumed that feeling had everything to do with Gina, but maybe there'd been some cold feet involved too. The whole day and night were a blur, actually. I just remember feeling sad but smiling for photos anyway, kind of like I'd been doing on Frontbook for years.

"Our souls are no longer in human bodies," Grandpa said. "Makes it pretty easy to be anywhere." He winked.

"We were there when Ethan was born too," Grandma said. "All of it. We have the best seat in the house, as Grandpa always says."

"Are ya done with your ice cream? Now have a tartufo. One for you, Gina?" Grandpa asked.

"After eating ice cream?" I wondered aloud.

"Why not? That's why they call it heaven," he said.

Grandma and Grandpa walked over to survey the glass case of pastries.

"Isn't it weird how I feel so close to them, and yet I've never known them?" I turned to Gina.

"It always makes me smile when you say, 'I never knew my grandparents on my mom's side,' when the truth is they've been guiding you your whole life," Gina said. "You know them better than anyone. You just don't realize it when you're awake."

I did always stop on their photo at my parents' house. My mother had a photo of them standing in front of an old car. Grandpa was wearing a hat, and Grandma had on the stole she was wearing now. The photo was on a table in the living room. Whenever I was there, I studied it. I liked the patina of it and had always wondered about the looks on their faces. They'd looked so serious, not like everyone smiling from ear to ear in every photo on social media. *Were my grandparents sad in that photo? Or just serious? Or just honest?*

Grandma and Grandpa returned with four tartufo, each on a plate.

I set my ice cream cone aside.

"One for you, one for me," Grandpa said as he handed them out.

Grandma sat and handed out the forks. She observed me crack the chocolate shell of my tartufo and said, "Atta girl, breaking through." She flashed me a smile. "That's how you do it."

I bit down into the shell of chocolate and cold ice cream. I winced at the initial sting of cold ice cream and then worked my mouth around the hard shell at the same time. What followed, as the delicious combo settled in my mouth, was divine.

Breakthrough, then a sting, then the good stuff. That's how you do it.

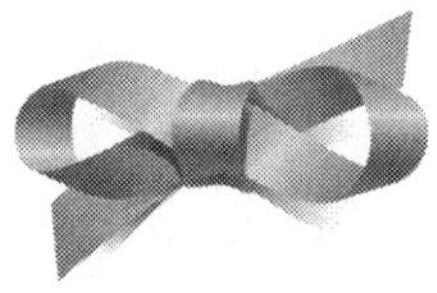

Chapter 17

Mark picked Ethan up at 8 a.m. He looked well rested and freshly showered.

"How's the apartment?"

"Good."

"Do you need help with anything?"

His lip curled in anger. "How could you help me, Jada?"

Whoa. "I don't know, Mark." I spat the words. "I'm trying to make this as easy as possible for you." *Can we go back to barely speaking to each other? I think I liked that better.*

"How kind."

"Can we just focus on how we're going to explain this all to Ethan? He woke up this morning asking where you were. I told him you stayed in the city, and he didn't ask anything else."

"We'll say Daddy is living in the city now because of work."

"But that's not the truth, and we have to be honest with him."

"Honesty? That's your big concern? Then we'll say Mommy wants a divorce."

"And you don't?" I held my arms out in disbelief.

He shrugged.

I imitated his shrug. "On the fence? Mark, there is nothing here between us. You would have been just fine going through life like that? I want more. I want a connection. I know we had something once, but not enough to sustain a lifetime together. It's over. It's been over for a long time."

"We should have had this conversation before San Francisco."

"I tried!"

He shrugged again.

"Stop shrugging!"

"Sorry. Does that annoy you? Everything I do annoys you. Let me get Ethan and get out of here before I do something else that irritates you."

Mark walked to the television room, and I heard Ethan full of delight. "Daddy!"

They came back toward the foyer. I kissed Ethan's head before they headed out the front door. "Have fun with Daddy today." He kissed my cheek and bounded down the front steps.

I tapped Mark and whispered, "Tell him Mommy and Daddy are going to live separately now, but we still love him."

He nodded. I didn't want to watch them drive away but thought it would be wrong to skulk back inside. I waved and grinned as widely as I could. *See? Mommy is all right, so you can be all right. Everything is all right.*

Ethan waved back.

What to do with a wide-open day ahead of me? I didn't have the energy to go to the gym. I didn't feel like going shopping, though I did need new shoes. I didn't feel like doing anything. Instead, I did something I hadn't done in a long time—I called my mother.

"Jada? What's wrong?"

I leaned against the kitchen counter. "Nothing. How are you feeling?"

"Good."

"Good."

"What's going on?" She sounded suspicious.

"Nothing. What's going on there?" I walked to the living room and plopped on the couch.

"Orly's coming over to eat because Paul took the girls to a daddy-daughter picnic."

I hugged one of the many beige pillows on our large sofa. "Oh, nice."

"Do you feel okay?" she asked.

"Me? I feel fine. I'm just worried about you."

"Why? I'll be all right. Why don't ya come eat?"

My initial instinct had always been to make up some excuse why I couldn't spend time with my family, but this time, I said, "Okay."

• • ❧ • •

THEY WEREN'T EXPECTING me until noon, but I arrived at their house at ten a.m.

My dad answered the door, looking perplexed. "Hi. You're early. Did Mommy tell you to come early?"

"No." I walked through the front door.

"Where are Mark and Ethan?" He watched me walk through the living room.

"Oh, um, Mark has some work calls. And Ethan wanted to swim today, so Mark's going to swim with him between calls." *I will tell them the truth eventually. One thing at a time.*

"He could have swam here."

"He likes his own pool."

I sifted through the newspaper on the kitchen table.

"All right." He grabbed the odd-looking metal pipe contraption that was on the counter and went back to his plumbing work in the basement.

I picked up the Real Estate and Business sections and stepped outside, where my mother was drinking coffee, reading the paper, and smoking.

"What are you doing?" I screamed.

Her mouth gaped open, and she caught her cigarette before it fell from her mouth. "What the hell is wrong with you?" she snapped.

"You scared the crap out of me, screaming like that. And I don't have lung cancer."

"Still!"

"Jada, you almost gave me a heart attack!" She shook her head, adjusted her paper, and sipped her coffee. "What are you doing here so early? Where's Ethan and Mark?"

I sat down across from her on one of the white outdoor chairs with plastic cushions. I gave her the work-swim excuse then grabbed the mostly finished cigarette in the ashtray and crushed it out.

"Well, Orly's not getting here until noon. You should go swimming."

Just my parents and me. When was the last time that happened?

"I didn't bring my bathing suit. Listen, I want to speak to your doctor."

"Why didn't you bring your bathing suit?"

"I don't know. What is your doctor's name?"

"Will you stop it?"

"Does your doctor know you're smoking?"

"Oh, Jada, you could use a cigarette. Want one?"

"Very funny." I sat back and got comfortable, unfolding the newspaper in front of me.

I sat there with my mother, drinking coffee and reading the paper, mostly in silence, until Orly arrived. She came in wearing a T-shirt image of an angel with large outstretched wings, balancing like a ballerina above the planet earth.

The shock of seeing Orly in that shirt must have shown on my face.

"What?" she asked.

"It's just, I don't know." I swallowed. It was an odd, familiar feeling that I didn't understand, like I had just seen that shirt recently or something.

"Does it not fit right?"

"No, it's so not you, I guess. That's what it is."

"Well, it's not mine. It's Gina's. Aunt Fran insisted I take a bunch of her T-shirts. She gave you a bunch too. Didn't she?"

"I don't remember what I did with them. It looks cute on you. I was just shocked to see it."

"Jada! What do you mean you don't know what you did with them?" my mother scolded.

"I mean, I know they're in my closet somewhere. I've just never worn any."

"You should," my mother said. "It'd make her happy."

I didn't know if she meant Gina or Aunt Fran, but I didn't ask.

"I had them in the corner of my closet forever, and I finally went through them." Orly held out the shirt as she glanced down at it. "I'm surprised any of them fit me. She was so tiny."

"Yeah," I said. "She didn't get the big-boob gene like the rest of us."

"All right, come on now! Let's eat." My mother shooed us out of the kitchen toward the deck.

My mother cleared the table, then Orly and I set it with her red ceramic dishes and matching salad bowls.

Sunday dinner always included "macaroni," which is what we called all pasta, "gravy," which was marinara sauce, and gravy meat, which was either meatballs or sausage, always homemade by my father. When the four of us sat down for dinner in the middle of the day—which was how we always did it on Sundays—my father said, "Just like old times."

I cut a meatball with my fork and inhaled the delicious aroma. "When's the next doctor's appointment?"

"Tuesday," Orly answered. She sprinkled grated cheese on her macaroni.

"Are you going?" I asked.

"Of course," she said.

I nodded. "Are you going, Dad?"

"I gotta work," he said. "They'll let us know everything. Don't worry so much, Jada."

"I can leave work for a few hours," I said. "Or even take off. When is it? In the city, right?"

"No, not that doctor," my mother said. "This one's here, on Queens Boulevard. The surgeon. You don't have to be there."

"Yes, I do. What if he or she says something either of you don't understand?"

"It's a he, and we're not idiots," Orly said.

"I didn't mean it that way. I mean three heads are better than one... or two. I can take the train from work. What hospital?"

"Don't worry about it, Jada." My mother twirled her linguini. "Please. What you can do for me is not be there. You're giving me *agida*, and I don't need you there, questioning this doctor and making it uncomfortable. He's got the highest ratings everywhere. We looked on the computer."

"What's his name?"

"Dr. Omar."

Note to self: Research him when I get home.

"Ma, can you watch Ari tomorrow?" Orly asked. "I have to take Isabella to the other Isabella's birthday party."

"Of course."

"Are there a lot of Isabellas in the class?" I asked.

"Only one other one."

This reminded me of a conversation we'd had while I was pregnant with Ethan. We were out to dinner with my parents, Orly, Paul, my nieces, and Mark, and the issue of baby names came up.

"You named me after Daddy's mother, right?" I'd asked my mother. Even though I'd heard this story before, Mark hadn't.

"Sort of. I wanted to name you Roseann or something after my mother, but I figured Fran might have a girl too, and so I let her have it. That's why Gina was Gina Rose. And Daddy loves his mother so much. Grandma Giada. Oh, how I hated that name, but I compromised. I said it'll be spelled J-a-d-a and pronounced Jay-da. I think of it as the American version of that name. Compromise. That's what it's all about."

"Well, Grandma still pronounces it 'Giada,'" I said. I thought of my dad's parents, who we rarely saw and who spoke very little English. They lived in New Jersey with my aunt, and we never learned enough Italian to have complete conversations with them, so it was always a little awkward. They would give us biscotti and stroke our hair and call me 'Giada, Giada, bella Giada.' They were cute. I was happy to be named after my grandmother, and I liked having a unique name.

"Who's Orly named after?" Mark asked.

"My grandmother who I never met," my mother said. "Her name was Ornella. I always liked that name. I thought it was different. But of course, Jada couldn't pronounce it, and we've been calling her Orly ever since."

"And I like it," Orly said. "If you called me Ornella, I might be like 'Who?'"

"So, what are you thinking for baby names?" my father asked.

"We like Ethan," I replied.

"What?" My mother stopped eating. "No, no, no." She shook her head.

"What's wrong with it?"

Orly was also making a disgusted face. "It just sounds, I don't know, like a lawyer's name."

"Well, both of his parents are lawyers, so that's fitting," I said.

"It's not Italian," my mother said.

"It's just so formal," Orly said.

Are they kidding me? "What do you want me to name him? Rocco? Mario? Paulie?" I turned to my brother-in-law. "Sorry, Paul."

He shrugged and kept eating.

"Jada picked it," Mark said.

I snapped my neck toward him. "And we agreed on it."

"As long as you like it," Orly said.

Oh, now you say that. Like it will erase the fact that we now know you don't like our son's name.

"I guess." My mother shrugged. "Ethan Marlone. It just doesn't go."

"We think it goes perfectly," I said.

Mark and I had actually talked about changing the name after that dinner. *Did it not go with our last name?* But I'd woken up the next day with the conviction that Mark and I liked it, and that was all that mattered.

I shook the memory off. "Is there anything for dessert?" I asked my father. "I'm craving a sweet."

"I brought cannoli," Orly said.

"Oh, good." I stood and brought my dish inside to the kitchen sink. I spotted the pastry box and brought it outside.

I devoured my cannoli while my mother and Orly talked about people I didn't know. Someone named Alicia, who was trying to have a baby, and Felicia, who still hadn't closed on her house. "What do you think the problem is? The inspection?"

After dessert, Orly and I helped clear the table, wiped the counters, and took the garbage out.

"Want to take a cannoli home for Mark?" my father asked as I grabbed my car keys.

"Nah." I kissed everyone goodbye and hugged my mother a little longer. "Let me know if I should meet you at the doctor's appointment."

"Not necessary," my mother said.

"Let me know what he says at least."

"They will," my father said.

It was too early to go back to an empty house, so I drove to our local park, where I sat in my car, checking my phone.

I researched Dr. Omar. My mom and sister had been right—he had excellent credentials.

Then I checked Frontbook. There was an update from Gina's friend Cori. She'd gone for her final wedding dress fitting with her mom and sister. I wondered what kind of wedding dress Gina would have gotten. *Probably something with a skull pattern that would horrify Aunt Fran and my mother.* Gina was one of a kind. *Cori looks pretty, though.* She was standing outside the bridal shop, holding up a long white garment bag. The caption read, "Said yes to the dress." That was corny, but I tapped Like.

Congratulations, Cori.

I was dying to text Mark to see how his day with Ethan was going, but I felt like it wouldn't be received well, considering the tension between us that morning. When there was nothing left to see on social media, I headed home, where I poured myself a lemonade with a little vodka, grabbed my *Vanity Fair* magazine, and sat by the pool.

As I flipped the magazine pages, I remembered being so excited to have some alone time without having to keep an eye on Ethan when I'd gone to San Francisco, but now I didn't know what to do with myself.

When Mark and Ethan came home, Ethan ran up to kiss me hello and tell me all about what they did all day—video games, miniature golf, McDonald's.

Mark and I made conversation about the traffic and weather, but it was obviously for Ethan's sake. Luckily, he was in a lighter mood than he had been that morning.

We went through the motions, and then after Ethan went to bed, Mark walked into our bedroom with a duffel bag. He loaded it up with more of his T-shirts, jeans, and workout clothes. "All right, I'll probably come back next weekend to see Ethan and get more clothes, and you know, some more things."

"What did you say to him?" I asked.

"Exactly what you suggested, that Mommy and Daddy are going to live separately now, but we still love him."

"Thank you. What was his reaction?"

"Honestly, I don't think it registered."

We stood in silence for a moment. I stepped toward him and put my arms around his neck. He hugged me back. It was oddly familiar and, at the same time, foreign, comforting, and yet uncomfortable.

"I'm sorry this is so hard, but we're doing the right thing," I said.

"Are we?"

"What? Do you think we should have gone to counseling?"

"I think you should have never gone to San Francisco."

"If you think that, then you're not understanding."

"I understand very clearly."

"Okay. Goodbye."

"Goodbye."

And he walked out.

• • ❧ • •

THE NEXT DAY, JOYCE arrived at her usual time. "Is Mark sick?"

"No. He's staying in the city this week for work." *I can't get into it right now. I hope she'll understand the fib when I eventually explain the truth.*

I drove to the train station alone, parked alone, bought my pass alone, and stood on the platform alone. As I stood there, I checked social media, my email, People.com, and NYPost.com, never daring to glance up and, God forbid, see Jed.

When I arrived at the office, the first thing that greeted me was an email from Lionel with the subject line "Where is the Bennett filing?" The message read, "Was this filed? I don't have a copy."

I don't want to risk being on probation. I have to handle this with care. Step away. Breathe.

I inhaled deeply, tried to let it out slowly, then typed out my reply. "I believe you are asking about the response to interrogatories. Yes, it was filed, and yes, you have a copy. Please check your Inbox folders." *He is infuriating.* I bit my fist and returned to typing. "Otherwise, I am going to have to bill you for the time it takes me to check my Sent folder. Have a wonderful rest of the day."

Moments later, Dan was standing in my doorway.

"What? I said, 'Have a wonderful day.'" I reached for the pile of mail on the corner of my desk.

"You can't send emails like that to the client. If he wants us to resend him something, we have to just do it!"

I looked up from the mail. "I'm sorry." I pushed my hair back. "I really am."

"Jada, what's going on? You're always a nutbag, but you're, I don't know, extra nutbaggy lately. Am I right?"

I nodded.

"I don't need you to tell me your personal business, but whatever it is, if you need time off to get things situated so you can better do your job—"

"Mark and I are breaking up. And my mother has cancer."

It suddenly occurred to me that the only people who now knew that were Danielle from mommy group and Dan, my boss—not Veronica, and my family knew nothing about Mark. These two non-friends, in technical terms, knew my deepest, darkest agonies at the moment.

Dan's jaw dropped. "Oh my God. I'm sorry. I can't hug you. That would be an HR violation. Shit. Listen, take the rest of the day off. Take the week. Whatever you need."

I shook my head. "I made it through last week. I can keep going. I don't have a choice."

"Wow. Is your mom going to be okay? And Mark, is he going to be okay?"

I smiled at his effort but shook my head.

"All right, we don't have to get into it," he said.

"It helps a lot that I just let it out. At least you know now. I'm sorry, Dan. I oscillate. One moment wanting to do right by you because you're a cool boss, and other times getting overwhelmed with rage by Lionel."

"Listen, take it out on me. But can you go easy on the client? For me?"

I nodded. "I will. I've been trying. I slipped."

"All right, skip the morning meeting. It's okay."

"I'll be there. But thanks."

For the rest of the week, I spent most of my days hiding in my office. I didn't need to leave for lunch because I couldn't eat anything. I didn't go to my mother's doctor's appointment because everyone insisted it wasn't necessary. I had to finish something by noon on that day for Lionel anyway.

I asked Joyce to feed Ethan dinner, bathe him, and put his pajamas on before I got home on nights I had to work late. He seemed to be completely unfazed by Mark not being around and Joyce doing more. It unnerved me, though. I feared when it finally hit him, it wouldn't be good. But for the moment, he was fine. I heard from Mark around seven each night when he called for Ethan. But there were no other calls, emails, or texts from him.

And that was how it went. That time was the sad calm before the storm.

• • ❧ • •

ON THE SUNDAY OF GINA'S memorial, I had to come up with another excuse for Mark and Ethan's absence. "It's one of Mark's partner's son's birthdays. They had to go."

"They couldn't skip a birthday party for this?" my mother asked. "Isn't this more important?"

"It's the managing partner," I said defensively. "I wanted them to at least make it to the church, but their party starts too early," I added for believability. The truth was I was fine being there alone with my family. I had to get used to it anyway. This was our new normal—Mark having Ethan on weekends.

"I guess he has to do what he has to do," Orly said. "They don't understand about family at law firms, I guess."

I ignored her and pried open the heavy church door. *I know I have to tell them what's going on, but it never feels like the right time, and my cousin's memorial certainly isn't the right place.*

The annual memorial was held at Holy Trinity, our church in Queens where all of us—me, Orly, Gina, and Andrea, Gina's sister—were baptized, made our communions, and were confirmed. It was where we'd had Gina's funeral five years ago. It was also where Orly and Andrea had gotten married. I'd married Mark at the hotel in Manhattan where our reception was held.

My mother had been horrified at the time. "How can you not get married in a church?"

"We're doing it our way," I'd said. "And I'm a New York City bride. I have to do what feels right for me. Getting married in Queens is so not me. And besides, I'm paying, so if that's how I—we—want to do it, that's how we'll do it." Mark had agreed that the city suited us, but deep down, I didn't think he'd really cared.

A few years later, when we'd baptized Ethan at Holy Trinity, it felt like an apology to my mother for having had the wedding I wanted. I realized how messed up that sounded, but it was the truth, and I believed that was how she'd taken it.

The memorial was a regular mass. Then Father Bertoli—who did the baptizing, confirming, marrying, and burying—made the same speech he made every year. He talked about how he remembered the day Gina was born, and he remembered the day she died. He said no one should ever remember those two days in a person's life, that it was completely unnatural, but we knew Jesus was holding her in His arms.

I looked up as if to wink at Gina, who I imagined was not being held by Jesus but tapping her feet to music I'd never heard, smoking and cursing, like I always remembered her.

"Every year, around this time," Father Bertoli continued, "I call Gina Rose's parents, Fran and Eddie." He motioned toward a sniffling Aunt Fran. Uncle Eddie put his arm around her. "And we always say we can't believe it's been one, two, now five years. But it's not the amount of time she was here. It's the impact she had. And Gina Rose left her mark."

I hated platitudes like that. *Come on, Father Bertoli, you're better than that. Gina would have thought the same thing, I think.*

But what could he say? I wish he would just be honest one year and say, "She was too young. It was too sudden, too shocking, and you'll never get over it for the rest of your lives. Nothing I say will make it better. Now, go eat."

I wondered if anyone could read my mind. I surveyed everyone around me and caught my cousin Andrea's eye. She gave me a sad smile, which I returned and then let my head fall. My phone sat in my lap. My screensaver of Ethan with chocolate all over his mouth lit up as I checked the time. His smiling eyes were crinkly with sugary delight.

Poor Aunt Fran. How does she go on?

My throat pulsed hard and fast. I reached for my collar and shut my eyes.

"Ya swallow your gum?" My mother's loud voice reverberated.

Everyone turned in our direction.

I shook my head and placed my hands on my lap. Apparently, like scaring someone to get rid of their hiccups, mortifying me made my throat thing disappear.

After the service, we went next door and ate. While I ate and chatted with Andrea, I watched her kids and my nieces run across the restaurant, chasing some electronic car. They giggled loudly, and I wished Ethan were there.

When I finished my coffee and cake, I started kissing everyone goodbye. Aunt Fran hugged me and said, "I hope I see Mark and Ethan soon. Tell them I missed them."

"I will."

"Well, Ethan's birthday is coming up, so at least I'll see them then."

Oh, right, my child's birthday was in three weeks. *Mother of the year again.* And that meant I would have to plan a kid's party and a family party. *And Mark and I will have to fake it one last time in front of everyone we know and love.*

"Drive safe," Aunt Fran said.

I wondered how she was able to get through each day, let alone have a party every year. But this year, I pictured Gina thoroughly enjoying seeing everyone eating, talking, and laughing. She wouldn't want to see us sad, especially her mom. I was on the fence about showing her the shirt I was wearing, which was why I'd worn a jacket over it. But as we were saying goodbye, I unzipped my jacket. "Aunt Fran, look. It's Gina's."

She stepped back to get a better view. It was a black T-shirt with a dragonfly, butterfly, and ladybug sitting atop a martini glass, smoking cigarettes. Aunt Fran's smile grew wide.

"I thought I'd wear it today, but then I wasn't sure." I was going to say I'd recently found it, but I didn't want her to think I'd lost it. I didn't want her to know the truth either—that Gina's clothes were in a box in the closet of our guest room and I couldn't bear to go through it until recently.

"I'm so happy you wore it! She would love that you're wearing it."

We hugged longer than usual, and I felt happier than after any of Gina's other memorials.

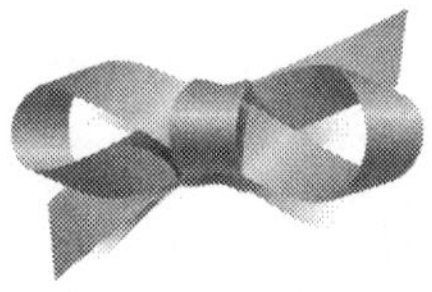

Chapter 18

"Didn't he have a *Buddy the Bulldozer* birthday party last year?" my mother asked while the nurse waited for her to swallow two pills.

"Yes. But who cares?" I replied, relieved that she was sitting up in the hospital bed and not attached to machines as I'd pictured her. "It's still one of his favorite things. And I still have the decorations, the plates, and the napkins. I know where to get the cake. I just have a lot going on. I can't plan a whole new kind of party right now. This is the best I can do."

"All right," she said. "If that's what you want to do."

"Yes. It is what I want to do. Ethan still loves *Buddy*! He'll probably have a *Buddy* wedding! So please... just, please!"

The nurse smirked as she took the pill holder and marked something on a chart.

I was yelling at my mother after she had gotten internal organs removed only a few days earlier. I had to make myself understood, even there, even in that situation.

Am I the worst daughter in the world or just the Western Hemisphere? I couldn't just let her win this one? I couldn't say, "You're right. I'll think of something else," even if I didn't plan to think of something else? I couldn't concede a little?

My mother had had surgery on a Monday. I'd requested the day off from work but wasn't able to get to the hospital again until three days later. Orly had been by her side around the clock but was now picking the girls up from a friend's house. My father had to take care of a client's toilet bowl that had overflowed, but he'd also been there pretty much nonstop. The surgery had gone well, and it looked like my mother would be released over the weekend. I would be able to be there when she got home because Ethan would be with Mark. I would have to come up with yet another excuse for where they were. I planned to tell my family what was going on, but I wanted to wait until after the surgery and after my mother felt better.

After the nurse left the room, I did the only generous thing I could think of. I changed the subject. "Do you know anyone who has been to Mexico recently?" I asked. I had been considering going away by myself, just for a weekend. The weekends were lonely in our big house, and I thought maybe I would go away by myself for a spa weekend sometime in the next few months.

"Aunt Fran. That's where she and Uncle Eddie went on their honeymoon. So, well, not recently. That was, what are we talking here, almost thirty-seven years? Oh my God, thirty-seven years..."

"I'm thinking of taking a vacation."

"You'll have to find a kid-friendly resort. A lot of them don't allow kids."

"I was going to go alone."

Her eyes grew wide. "Why alone?"

"I just need some time away."

"You can't travel alone to another country."

"Ethan will be fine. He'll be with Mark. He's with him every weekend anyway."

"Huh?"

Shit. "I mean, in Long Island, I do so much to care for Ethan during the week that Mark really shoulders the burden—bath, bedtime, all that stuff—on the weekends."

Nice save.

"Oh." She leaned to her right.

"Hand me my comb and that mirror." She pointed at a makeshift vanity set that had been erected by the window, complete with her magnifying mirror and makeup bag. "Why wouldn't you want to go away with your family?"

"When you were raising us, didn't you ever wish you had time to yourself?"

"No."

My mother looked tired, but her makeup was done, and her rings, bracelets, and earrings were all on. She even had her nails done. Her manicurist had stopped by the day before. That was who'd brought the third set of flowers, which was sitting on the windowsill, next to the one from my father and the one from Orly.

Am I the only one who remembered my mother hates flowers? "They die after a few days. What a waste of money," she would say. So, I'd brought her a cannoli from Carrolla's Bakery.

"I don't want that. I have no appetite," she'd said. "The pain meds make me nauseous."

"Well then, smell it later. It smells better than flowers," I'd replied, leaving it on the table next to her bed.

I stood up from the vinyl-covered guest chair to check my phone charging in the corner. "I have to go back to work."

"Why don't you have that party at that Long Island play place. Do they do parties? Ethan's always talking about that place. I bet he'd love that."

"I think they have a party room. But then you'd have to come from Queens." *And I've been relieved to not have to go to that place since Ethan is with Mark on the weekends now. I can't bear the thought of running into Jessica.*

"We'll be coming from Queens to your house anyway."

True. Why am I pushing back on this? Why do I push back on everything my mother suggests?

"That's actually a good idea. Then I won't have to worry about getting the house cleaned before and after, and I can combine friends and family and have only one party."

"See. Your mother had a good idea. I can't wait to see Ethan."

Ethan hasn't seen my parents since Mark moved. So now I would have to tell my family about Mark and me before the party in case Ethan mentioned "Daddy's place."

"I'll look into it." I reached for my phone and bag just as Aunt Fran walked through the door.

"Don't tell me you're going. What timing," Aunt Fran said as she rested her black-and-gold pocketbook and a pastry box on the chair.

"I have to go back to work," I explained. "But, oh! I almost forgot." I fished through my tote bag for a manila envelope buried at the bottom. "I found these," I said as I pulled out the envelope. "I thought they'd make you laugh."

For some reason, I'd woken up that morning with an urge to look at old pictures. Before Ethan had woken, I'd tiptoed to the ottoman in the television room, where I kept old photo albums.

It was filled with pictures from the days before kids had their picture taken multiple times a day. I peeled off the funniest ones—summers in our pool, trips to the shore, hanging out on the boardwalk, trips to Sesame Place and Hershey Park, and all the Halloween pictures. I'd been a cheerleader the same year Gina was a punk rocker. Orly and Andrea had gone as a pair of salt and pepper shakers.

I'd stuffed the photos in an envelope but hesitated before putting them in my bag. *What if they make her sad?* But something had told me to take them, so I did.

I handed the envelope to my aunt. "I have to go, but I'll leave these with you."

Aunt Fran took it and opened it. She stared curiously at the first picture on top then burst out laughing. "Jo, look!" She brought it over to my mother.

"Okay, talk to you later." I slipped out, hearing their laughter in the background. It was a beautiful sound, and I stopped for a minute to listen.

• • ❧ • •

AFTER MEETING WITH the manager of Long Island at Play, Gloria Fleishman—a wiry-haired, middle-aged, plump woman who could give my mother a "run fuh heh money" in the New York-accent department—Ethan's fourth birthday party was planned. I took my folder with my invoice and the *It's a Birthday at LI at Play* invitations, which I had no intention of mailing. Instead, I planned to send emails, social media messages, and texts to my family. I walked into the bouncing-ball room, which should have been called the "children bouncing off the wall" room. I spotted Ethan, who was in mid-bounce.

"Two minutes," I called. I'd planned to wait for him right by the bouncing balls so I wouldn't run the risk of seeing Jessica, but after I pried him away after ten minutes and turned to leave, I ran right into Danielle, Melody, and Jessica sitting along the wall on the way out.

Crap.

"Hi," I said as I rushed by them, holding Ethan's hand. "I'm in a hurry. One of those days."

"Did you just get here?" Melody asked.

I just said I'm in a rush, Melody, and I'm literally walking toward the door.

"Actually, I'm on my way out." I smiled.

"I'm having my party here!" Ethan announced and then wiggled free of my hand and ran for the ropes course.

Crap.

"When is it?" Jessica asked.

I moved closer toward them as I readjusted my bag on my shoulder and the party folder in my hand.

"Sunday, the eighteenth. Pizza and cake and all the bouncing off the walls he and my nieces can fit into three hours."

"Are we invited?" Melody asked.

Fucking Melody.

Before I could say "No, just family, sorry," I remembered I had to guarantee at least fifteen kids, and I wasn't even close. I was planning on paying the penalty, but maybe it wouldn't be so bad if there were so many other people there. Maybe Jessica would have something to do that day, but I would still get the Tree kids and Melody's kids to help lower the quota penalty.

"Yeah. I'll send you the invite on Frontbook."

"We never see you or Ethan anymore," Melody said.

"The party will be great," Danielle interjected. "We've been to one before. They do a good job here."

"Oh, good. It's going to be mostly family, so be forewarned—you're going to meet my mother." I turned to find Ethan but was called back.

"Can you sit for a minute?" Jessica asked. "We haven't seen you in so long."

Oh God. "Sure," I said. "I love your hair blown straight. It looks nice. Do you have somewhere to go tonight?"

"Ha, no. Thanks. We actually just got back from Florida. My husband gave me a bunch of spa treatments and salon packages, so on the last day, I thought I'd get a nice blowout."

Florida? With your husband?

"So now you know I haven't washed it in a day." She laughed.

So did Melody and Danielle.

I couldn't even fake it. "Did you bring the kids?"

"Yeah. But my husband also paid for our babysitter to come along, so we had a lot of time alone, a lot of time to do other things, especially at night." She looked directly at me.

Does she know something now? Did he confess? What about the other woman and her baby?

"That's so great," Melody piped in. "I have to remember that next time we go away. Bring the babysitter!"

"How long did you go for?" I asked.

"Four days, three nights. Not too long. Just enough time." Jessica sipped her latte as her eyes peered over her cup at me.

I see. Just enough time to forgive your spouse and fall in love with each other again. My husband, in the meantime, was in someone else's apartment in the city, and I was alone with Ethan in our house. *Wow, Todd got a reconciliation, and I got a separation.*

My breath caught in my throat. *That throat thing again. Fuck.*

No, I did the right thing. When I knew it wasn't going to work out with Todd, I could have just stayed with Mark, never saying a word. But I did the right thing. It wasn't sustainable. Still, right or wrong, I can't say this doesn't sting.

I tried to nonchalantly reach for my throat. I swallowed and sat up straight.

"Are you okay?" Melody asked.

Fucking Melody.

"Yeah," I said. "I'm fine. I... I..." I couldn't think of anything to say, so I told the truth. "Sometimes I get these, like, heart palpitations. I don't know what it is."

Intermittently, each of them said, "I get that," "Me too," and "Every once in a while."

I stood. "Well, it was good to see you guys. I have to go."

"Send us the party info," Danielle called.

"I will." I flung my bag over my shoulder and headed toward the ropes to grab Ethan.

"Don't forget!" Melody called.

Fucking Melody.

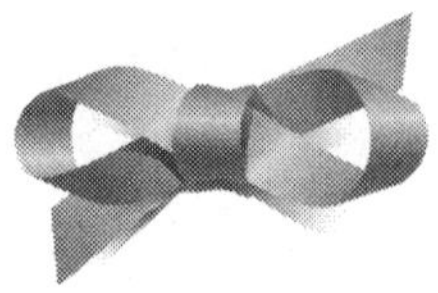

Chapter 19

Plates. *Check.*
Cups. *Check.*
Napkins. *Check.*
All branded with *Buddy the Bulldozer*.

I'd bought *Buddy the Bulldozer* key chains for the goody bags because four-year-olds really needed key chains. Chocolate balls wrapped in *Buddy* yellow, mini *Buddy* puzzles, plus other yellow-wrapped sugary treats would complete the bags.

On the morning of Ethan's fourth birthday party, after cleaning him up, feeding him, and dressing him, I had to finally plop him in front of the television so I could dig through the back of the closet in the guest room for the bag with the *Buddy* yellow utensils from last year's party. Then I needed to reply to some work emails.

Lionel had emailed me, asking what time that day he would get the responses to the Cooper interrogatories. I'd planned to work on the Cooper case on Sunday and had been given no indication that Lionel expected them sooner.

I wanted to reply, "What makes you think you're getting them today?" But I wouldn't have even gone that far in the past, and certainly not now since I was teetering on probation and had made a promise to Dan. I replied, "I'll try to finish ASAP and will send over tomorrow." I tossed my phone into my bag and threw my hands in the air.

Where was I? What else do kids do at birthday parties? Eat cake. My mother was picking that up on her way. *Drinks?* Kids drank juice, and I had that. Parents didn't usually drink at these parties, or at least I hadn't come across any that did, which always made me feel like I couldn't, which was a bummer. *What else?*

"Mommy!" Ethan called from the TV room. "I want cookies."

"But you're dressed," I answered as I packed the napkins, cups, and plates into a Bloomindale's bag.

"I want the chocolate ones with the chocolate on top."

"We don't have those." *Because Mommy hasn't food shopped in a decade.* "What about these?" I walked toward him in the TV room, holding a box of Oreos.

"No! I want the chocolate ones."

"These are chocolate." I opened the box and peeled out a few.

"I want the chocolate ones."

"We don't have them. Either eat these, or no cookies at all."

He grabbed three Oreos with his tiny hands.

"Hold on," I said as I grabbed the cookies and lifted his shirt off so he wouldn't wipe his chocolatey hands on his birthday outfit.

As he ate Oreos, shirtless in front of the TV, I ran back to the kitchen and tried to steal a few more minutes before he screamed for milk.

My phone buzzed.

Fucking Lionel probably.

It was a text from Todd: *So I hear you're going to be hanging out with my wife today.*

I held onto the island in the middle of the kitchen as I wrote back. I knew I should ignore him, but I couldn't help myself.

Jada: *I see you're still with your wife. How's that other woman carrying your child?*

Todd: *She lost the baby.*

Oh. I had to digest that a moment.

Jada: *I'm sorry.*

Todd: *My wife mentioned she had a birthday party for the kids today, for Jada's son.*

He added a smiley face emoticon.

Jada: *Does she know anything about us?*

Todd: *I didn't tell her.*

Jada: *I hope she doesn't know from finding out some other way. And if she's reading your texts, let her. Don't ever contact me again. We are not friends.*

I put my phone down.

Ethan was calling for me. "Can I have milk?"

I walked to the refrigerator to get the milk, when my phone buzzed. *Did Todd get hit in the head recently? What is he not understanding? No contact means from this point on.*

I poured the milk and delivered it to Ethan as the buzzing continued. *Is he calling me now?* I rushed back to the kitchen to see that it was Mark. I picked up as I continued gathering everything on my checklist into the Bloomingdale's bag.

"Hey," Mark said. "I'm around the corner in case you needed me to help you bring anything to the party."

That's awfully nice. "That would be great. Thank you." I still hadn't told my family what was going on and prayed Ethan didn't mention staying at Daddy's apartment. I planned to tell them after my mother was feeling better, but it never seemed like the right time. In the meantime, at least Mark seemed to be less angry toward me.

When Mark arrived, he was in a shirt I'd never seen before. *Trendy.*

"Is that new?"

"Yeah. I did some shopping recently."

"You look nice."

"Thanks. I thought I'd help you bring things over." He leaned against the kitchen island.

"I appreciate it," I said as I checked my list. *Wet wipes. Large garbage bags.*

"Hey, listen, can we talk first?" He moved closer to me. "Maybe outside?"

"Yeah. I'm just trying to gather everything and respond to work emails and keep him occupied. What's up?"

I followed Mark out the back door, where we could still see Ethan in the TV room.

"Listen, I hate to do this now, right before the party, but I was just going over some things with the accountant yesterday, and it looks like our property taxes are going to go up a lot. I think you'll agree that we should probably put the house on the market sooner rather than later. And to keep things moving along, I can be the one to file if you want. You know, for divorce. I've already spoken to a lawyer."

"A lawyer?"

"Yeah. I don't want it to get messy. I wasn't even going to hire a lawyer, but—"

"A real estate lawyer?"

"A divorce lawyer."

"Oh. Right. Of course." My knees buckled. Mark reached for my elbows. I sat down on the bench by a small patch that I'd always planned to turn into a vegetable garden but never did. "Divorce? Okay, yes. Sell the house? I wasn't ready for that one. I kind of just assumed Ethan and I would stay here. But, no, I guess I wasn't thinking clearly. Okay, let me digest this."

"You know, Jada, since moving out, I've felt differently. Better. I didn't realize I'd been walking on eggshells all this time."

"Is that right? Was I so hard to live with? Okay, you know what?" I turned to him. "Yes, this is the path we're going down, but can we talk about this later when we're not on our way to our child's birthday party with everyone we know? Like a real conversation, possibly? Later?"

"Sure." Mark went into the TV room. "Hey, bud, where's your shirt? Excited for your big bash?"

Big bash? Can the divorce filing cite irreconcilable corniness?

When I returned to the kitchen, I had a new email from Lionel that read, "Tomorrow is not going to cut it, Jada. I need it TODAY."

"This." Ethan was at my side. "This."

"This what?" I yelled.

He held up a straw. "I took a juice from that bag."

I tore the plastic back, shoved the straw in the juice box, and gave it back to him. *You couldn't ask your father to do that?*

I tried to calm down before replying to Lionel. *Stop, Jada. Take a second. Breathe. In. Out.*

Oh, fuck that!

I typed out an email reply on my phone. "Not going to happen, Lionel. We're not saving lives here. You will get it tomorrow. And didn't anyone ever teach you in the one hundred years you've been alive not to use CAPITAL LETTERS in business correspondence? It's rude."

I threw my phone into my bag, shut off the television, and told Ethan to put his shirt and shoes on before I counted to twenty. I told him he could finish his juice in the car. "Hurry!" I barked. Mark gave me a side-eye and picked up the bag of party supplies as we walked out the door.

• • ❧ • •

WHEN WE ARRIVED AT Long Island at Play, everyone was already there—my parents, Orly and Paul, my nieces, Mark's parents, who'd driven down from Albany, Mark's sister and her kids, Aunt Fran, Uncle Eddie, cousin Andrea and her husband and kids, and my aunts, uncles, and cousins on my father's side. My grandparents had not come because it was too much to ask them to travel from New Jersey to Long Island.

I kissed everyone hello as Ethan ran up to the presents piled in the corner. Before I could utter, "Hold on. We'll open those later," my mother took the Bloomingdale's bag from Mark's hand.

She was thinner, weaker, and paler than ever, but she was still herself.

"Ma, what are you doing?"

"Are the plates in this bag?" she asked. "We'll be serving the food soon," she announced to the crowd of mingling friends and family. "You only have the room for a certain amount of time. Let's get the show on the road. Orly, lift the top off that salad."

Everyone lined up on one side of the room, still chatting and snacking, while I tried to get a picture of the birthday boy in front of his presents.

Jessica, Melody, and Danielle were lining up for food as their children ran between their legs.

I remembered their kids' parties. Ethan hadn't been invited to any of them because we hadn't gotten that close yet, but from what I'd seen on social media, they'd each had themed parties complete with visits from their favorite characters. Jessica even had a *Little Mermaid* party at an indoor pool at a local Hilton because it was winter, and Ariel swam, chatted with the kids, ate cake, and sang "Happy Birthday" without ever getting out of the pool.

No characters would be making surprise visits at this party. Buddy was not going to bulldoze through the door to the kids' screaming delight. *Nope. Not this party. Maybe next year, Ethan.*

"Is everything out? Did we go through all the bags? Do we have drinks?" I asked Orly and my mother.

"The soda is over there." My mother pointed at the corner where drinks were set up. Cups and ice were in another corner.

"Who brought the ice?" *Because I definitely didn't think of that.*

"I did," Orly said as she bit down on a piece of pepperoni. "Don't let me forget my ice bucket."

"Thank you for bringing so much stuff. I've been a little preoccupied."

"We knew you'd never remember these things," she said.

"Uh, okay. I need a *drink* drink," I said under my breath.

I didn't think anyone heard me, but Orly said, "Daddy brought wine."

"White?" my dad asked.

"Anything," I said.

"Someone brought vodka?" Orly asked as she surveyed the drink area. I whipped around as she held up a bottle of Grey Goose. "That's what this is, right?"

"Is there club soda?" I asked.

There was.

"I brought that," Danielle said. "I never go to a kid's party without a gift for the parents."

"That's so sweet," I said as I started mixing myself a much-needed cocktail. This probably went against the contract I'd signed with Gloria, the party planner. *But she'll never find out.* I took a long sip.

By the time we had eaten and worked our way over to the trampoline portion of the party, I was feeling pretty good, and I had successfully avoided Jessica for the most part other than a brief hello. I was glad Danielle was there. It was good to see her. Then there was Melody. *Ugh. Look at her. Does she ever shut the hell up? Where's your gossipy little husband today? Having tea with Page Six?*

I jumped at the touch on my shoulder, though it was gentle. "Are you done, dear?"

Aunt Fran held a large trash bag as she collected everyone's plates and cups.

"Thanks, Aunt Fran. You're the best."

"Go watch Ethan bounce. Don't miss it. I'll clean up the plates and stuff."

I headed toward the trampoline room but first stopped for another drink. I mixed and poured and mixed and poured until it was the perfect mix of vodka and soda. Then I walked into the trampoline room and realized I was the last one in.

I searched for someone I felt like talking to. Danielle was in a huddle with Jessica and Melody, so she was out.

Where's my dad? Not that he talks much, but he's better than nothing. Oh, there he is, on picture-taking duty right behind the trampoline coach and Mark. Who are some of these other people?

The trampoline room was supposed to be reserved for one hour exclusively for Ethan's party. I guessed we had party crashers. *Whatever.*

I imagined myself screaming, "Welcome, party crashers! Now find your mothers and beat it! You know how much I paid for this party?" I started laughing to myself.

My uncle Eddie must have thought I was amused by the trampoline-jumping kids. "Aren't they cute?" he asked.

"Yes." I gulped my drink. "They are."

"Wanna get up there?"

"Ha. No. I'm good." I watched as Uncle Eddie was snapping photos of Andrea's kids jumping up and down.

Should I be taking photos? Crap. Well, I'll take pictures when it's Ethan's turn. I finally feel relaxed. One more drink, and I'll be good. I walked into the other room and almost made it to the drink table without incident until I tripped over something.

Fuck.

I caught my balance, glared down at the offending object—a kid's sneaker—and kicked it to the corner. I made my last drink and went back to the trampoline room. It was finally Ethan's turn. I grabbed my phone and turned on the video mode.

As I recorded him, I became a bit queasy. *Perhaps I should look at him instead of through the phone. It might be affecting my equilibrium.* When it was time to chant his name as he jumped, we all cheered together. "Eth-an. Eth-an. Eth-an."

What's after this? Cake, and then we're out of here.

"Eth-an! Eth-an! Eth-an!"

I held my phone with one hand and sipped with the other.

"Eth-an! Eth-an! Eth-an!"

"Ouch!" I turned around. Orly had scratched the back of my ankle with her shoe.

"Sorry," she uttered, her eyes glued to Ethan as she held her phone up.

You seem really sorry. When is this damn bouncing over? It's making me nauseous. I feel like I'm on a boat.

"Eth-an! Eth-an! Eth-an!"

I stopped recording and shouted, "Okay!" I walked over to the trampoline master. "Okay, thank you. That's enough." I quickly turned away from the master's bewildered face and back toward the guests. "Cake time!" I turned to Ethan and shouted, "Come on! Don't you want cake?"

The "Eth-an! Eth-an! Eth-an!" finally came to a halt.

"Cake!" I spilled a little of my beverage as I threw my arms out in front of me. "Cake!" I enunciated to Ethan.

"I want cake!" he exclaimed after he read my lips.

I noticed a side glance between Orly and my cousin Andrea but didn't think much of it.

"Good!" I searched for my mother then realized she was right in front of me. "Where's the cake, Ma?"

"I asked someone to put it in a freezer," she said.

"Let's get Gloria to get that out."

Mark made his way to the trampoline to help Ethan down.

"Back to the other room for cake," I bellowed, making a herding motion.

My mother tilted her head as she glared at me.

"What?" I demanded.

She shook her head. "He wasn't done jumping."

"I'm sure people want to go home. And we have the room for less than an hour now. How much longer could it have gone on?" I waited for an answer to appease my guilt.

"All right," she conceded. "And then he's got to open gifts too."

"We'll open them at home."

"You can't do that!"

"What are you talking about?"

"Everyone came all this way. Let them see him open their gift."

"It's a four-year-old's birthday party, not a bridal shower. All these kids want to do is bounce around. We'll open them at home, and then I'll send thank-you cards."

"No. You have to have him open his gifts, Jada." She pointed her finger at the floor. "That would be so rude."

"Well then, it's a good thing I got him off the trampoline. Right? Let's go."

After Gloria brought the cake out and we sang "Happy Birthday," it was gift time.

Ethan, Mark, and I stood at the front of the room, where the gifts were piled high. Ethan insisted on ripping the wrapping paper off of each one. While he did that, I opened the card, read it, and said thank you to whoever it was from.

Then we oohed and aahed over each gift before moving on to the next one while my mother stuffed the discarded wrapping paper into a garbage bag and Mark stacked the gifts in the corner.

As Ethan was ripping open the wrapping paper on the second to last gift, I turned sharply to my left to grab it from him and felt a bit bobbleheaded.

Uh-oh.

There was a gurgling, not in my belly, but in my throat. If I could slip away to the bathroom to let it all out, no one would be the wiser.

I handed Ethan's final gift to my father and whispered that I had to go to the bathroom. I announced, as clearly as I could say the words, "Thank you, everyone! Thank you so much! Don't forget your goodie bags. They're in that corner over there."

As I headed toward the door, I tripped. Unfortunately, I didn't catch myself that time. I lost my balance, and my left knee crashed into the floor, but I didn't feel a thing. As my father helped me up, I surveyed the floor for the offending object.

"Another sneaker!" I picked it up and held it over my head. "Another fucking sneaker!"

I just yelled 'fuck' at my four-year-old's birthday party. Shit.

In my haze, I caught a glimpse of several faces.

Mark was flushed with horror. My mother was furious. Danielle pitied me. Jessica was confused, and Melody was full of morbid delight.

The yelling must have pushed the alcohol up. There was nothing else in my stomach. I realized in that moment that I hadn't eaten breakfast or lunch since I was saying hello to all our guests. I grabbed the garbage bag with the wrapping paper from my mother's hands and puked. I wished it was just one retch, but it was several prolonged retches.

Even though I was drunk and emotional, I didn't think I would have started crying if I hadn't caught Ethan's face. It was his look of concern—as though he were wondering if Mommy was okay—that made me unable to hold back the tears.

The room was silent other than Aunt Fran mumbling, "Get her a napkin. Where are the napkins?"

That should have been the worst part. But I felt the need to explain myself, and I made the mistake of opening my mouth.

"I'm so sorry. I'm... I'm so sorry, everyone. I'm not feeling well today," I said loudly, even though I could hear a pin drop.

What I did hear was a snort from Melody, which was the only thing more antagonizing than the sneaker.

"Did you just laugh?" I lasered in on her. "Go ahead and laugh! You're right. It's not that I'm not feeling well. I'm drunk. Okay? I'm drunk at my son's birthday party. Woo-hoo. Look at the drunk mother! Well, let me tell you something—" At that point, Orly touched my shoulder, but I shooed her away. "Listen, everyone, I'm truly sorry, but I have to be honest. I have to finally be honest."

I found Jessica, standing to the right of Melody, and pointed at her. "I spent the night with your husband. I know Todd. I knew Todd before you knew Todd, and I ran into him in San Francisco. We spent the night together. Then he told me he got that other woman pregnant."

Melody gasped. Danielle's eyes widened as if a light bulb went off. *Yes, he's the ex.* Jessica was stone-faced.

Mark was staring at me, as if he were concentrating on keeping his jaw in place. "And Mark left. He lives in the city now. He no longer lives in our house, in our big, beautiful house." I spread my arms wide as I said that. "That we're now selling. We're not together. We're getting divorced!"

His stony expression never changed. I couldn't bear to look at Ethan. *Does he know what divorce means? Oh shit, what have I just let out?*

My mother's mouth was hanging open.

"My mother has cancer. Does everyone know my mother has cancer?" I asked the horrified crowd. "Uterine," I continued. "And even though she acts like it's no big deal, it is a big deal. And even though she loves Orly more, I'm still sad. I'm your daughter, and I love you, and I'm sad." I stared at the floor as the tears flowed. "It's all too much. It's just been too damn much. And I'm sorry to anyone

I've hurt. I'm sorry." I whipped my head back to look in Jessica's direction. "But I want you to know we did *not* have sex! We didn't even k-k-ki—"

I couldn't get the last word out. That whipping motion made the room spin and led to another retch into the wrapping-paper bag.

Then I felt an arm around my shoulder. It was my father. "Why don't you go to the bathroom and wash your face?"

I nodded, grabbed a napkin from Aunt Fran, and blew my nose as I walked toward the bathroom. I turned back briefly. "Thank you for coming, everyone."

The only good thing was that, as I finally caught a glimpse of Ethan, he was no longer looking in my direction. He was preoccupied with a plastic tool set my cousin had given him.

"I want to open this one now," he said to Orly. "Can I open this one now, Aunt Oly?"

I stayed in the bathroom until everyone had left except for my mother, father, Orly, Mark, and Ethan.

No one said anything, not even my mother. Orly brought me water then drove my car home in silence. Mark came back to the house and stayed to bathe Ethan and put him to bed. He left with a simple, "We'll talk later."

I stayed in bed and tried to fall asleep, but I couldn't get certain faces out of my mind.

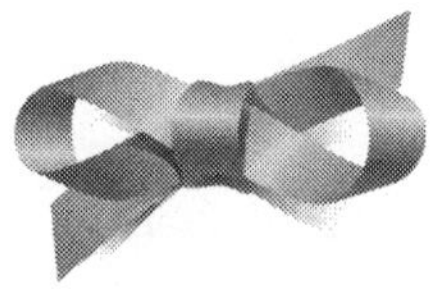

Chapter 20

"Was that real? Or am I dreaming? Was it a nightmare?" I asked.

"Ummm, that was real," Gina replied.

I adjusted my head on my pillow behind me. Gina lay next to me, wearing a black T-shirt with a dragonfly, butterfly, and ladybug sitting atop a martini glass, smoking cigarettes. "I've never felt so low," I whispered.

Gina sat up and crossed her legs. Her combat boots dug into my designer comforter.

"The sneaker." Gina's lip curled up. "That's when I lost it."

"Lost it how?"

Gina cackled so hard that tears fell. She stomped her black boot into my beige bed as she howled. "Sorry." She snorted.

"How nice to know when we're going through hard times, our loved ones on the other side are laughing at us. How comforting." I massaged my aching temples.

"That's not true at all."

"Well, you're cracking up over here."

"Just because it's you, Jada."

"It's not funny. I've hurt a lot of people."

"They're going to be okay. Yes, you shared some stuff that was pretty personal, revealed some private health information, but in the end, it'll be okay."

"My son?"

"Ethan was oblivious. And he's Ethan, remember? It means strong. That's why you liked that name."

"And I made a fool of myself. I can never show my face at Long Island at Play, or to anyone I know or am related to, for the rest of my life. Should I move to another state?"

"Well, you are selling the house."

"Not funny. Aren't you supposed to be helping me? You're not making me feel better." I shut my eyes. "I don't get it. I thought I was making progress. I wasn't thinking about Todd. I had the difficult conversation with Mark. I was appeasing my mother... at times. I was working on my Lionel trigger. But then, it all hit me at once."

"Progress is a lot of stops and starts." I could feel her rest her head on the pillow next to mine. "You still have a bit to learn."

I opened one eye. "When do I get my diploma?"

"Ha! When you die."

I closed my eye. "What a sobering thought."

"Well, you've got to be strong. Okay? Because it ain't over."

I opened my eyes.

"I don't think that last exchange with Lionel went over so well. You know, from what I can see," she said.

I shut my eyes. "Fuck."

"I know it's not what you want to hear."

"What can you tell me? Never mind. I don't want to hear it right now." *Fuck. On top of everything else.* "Is this really happening? Can't you do some voodoo mind trick and wipe everyone's memory? Lionel, Dan, everyone I know and love?"

"Nope. Sorry. Did you see Melody's face?" She started laughing again.

"Only when I caught her snicker."

"I'm talking about when you threw up in the wrapping paper bag. The first time. I guess you couldn't see her face because your head was down. Trust me—it was priceless."

"Trust me—I'm glad I didn't see."

"Let me tell ya, as Grandma and Grandpa would say, it was a Kodak moment."

That made me laugh a little, which was a temporary relief. "The whole thing is so awful. And how the hell am I going to fix it or make up for it, even a little?"

"You'll know what to do next," she said.

"Trust my instincts and all that crap?" I rubbed my eyes. "Can you give me some specifics of what I should do? Give me another assignment. I'll do whatever I have to do to make it right."

"Okay. Start with restraining yourself. And I mean restraining yourself for real. Not restraining when it's easy and you pat yourself on the back. Restraining when it's hard. When your emotions have gotten the best of you and you feel every reason to lash out, certain that you're in the right. You're not always in the right, Jada. Stop. Let it go. And watch yourself grow."

"Ugh, first of all, 'Let it go' is the most annoying, useless piece of advice, next to 'Enjoy the moment.' And I'm not a flower. You can't just water me with platitudes and watch me sprout."

"Yes, actually, I can. It's sinking into your subconscious whether you like it or not."

"You know, I like our visits better when we eat ice cream and talk about old times."

Gina reached over to Mark's nightstand. "How about some dark chocolate?" She opened the wrapper on my favorite kind and broke off a piece. "Remember the time my father stepped in dog shit at some fair? Our mothers tried to clean it off, but he had to sit in the passenger's seat the whole way home with his foot out the window." Gina handed me a chunk of chocolate.

I bit down. "My mother kept saying, 'Stepping in shit is good luck. Why didn't we win anything?'"

"And we couldn't stop laughing every time they said 'shit.' They kept trying to say crap and kept slipping."

"Those were good times," I said.

"When you're here, you realize everything—even the shit—were good times. When you're living, you take it all too seriously."

"I can guarantee you I will never look back on this day and think it was 'good times.'"

"As you evolve, you'll be able to look back at this time and understand why it happened, and as you learn to love yourself, you'll even be able to look back and not cringe."

"I doubt it."

"I promise you."

"Evolve. Grow. Love yourself," I mocked. "Every visit, I wonder who you are."

"Shut the fuck up and eat your chocolate."

I smiled. "Still Gina."

Chapter 21

I*s it possible to cringe so hard you crush an organ?*

I hadn't even opened my eyes, and I was already reliving every cringe-worthy moment of the previous day.

I grabbed the comforter and curled up. My temples throbbed with every heartbeat.

I kicked my leg out of the bed and slowly worked myself into a standing position. I didn't check the clock, use the bathroom, or drink any water until I checked on Ethan. He was still sleeping, soundly and snugly. The party had obviously knocked him out too. *Thank you, God.*

I treaded back to my bathroom, feeling the cold marble on my bare feet and willing to do anything to stop the throbbing.

I knelt down, put my cheek against the cool floor, and stayed there for a few minutes.

I did this to myself. This is where I deserve to be.

I took my time standing up, swallowed two ibuprofens then another one for good measure, ran a washcloth under the cold water, and went back to bed with the cool towel over my eyes.

I rested there until Ethan tottered through the door. "Why do you have that thing on your eyes? What is that?"

"A cold towel."

"Can I feel it?"

I handed it to him.

"It's cold." He handed it back.

"What do you want for breakfast?"

"Nothing. I want to watch TV."

"Okay," I said. "Why don't we hang here for a little bit? Come on, next to me."

"No."

"Get in bed with me, Ethan." I patted the pillow next to me.

"Nooo," he screeched.

A stabbing pain shot from my ears to my temples, increasing the throbbing beat. That behavior was unacceptable. But I would have to fix it another time. I was in too much pain at the moment, and I'd caused a scene and puked at my kid's birthday party, so I was giving us both a break today. "Okay." I lifted myself out of bed. "Want pancakes?" I asked as he ran out the door.

"Yes!"

Shit. When was the last time I made pancakes? I hope I still have the mix.

"We might have to go out for pancakes," I said as I grabbed my phone from the end table.

"To the diner?"

Ethan loved the diner. I hated it, especially their dirty silverware and gross coffee. Mark loved the coffee and their Western omelet.

"Sure." I followed him down the stairs. "First, you'll watch TV while Mommy has a cup of good coffee, and then we'll change and go."

"It's a plan!" he exclaimed. He got that phrase from Mark.

"It's a plan," I said under my breath as I walked into the television room. The plan was also that Mark and I were supposed to talk, but that had gotten derailed. I wondered if he would call to discuss things.

As Ethan plopped on the couch, I found *Buddy the Bulldozer* on the DVR then headed toward the kitchen.

"Not this one!" he announced.

I grabbed the remote and found another episode. Before I reached the kitchen, he informed me that he didn't want to watch that one either.

"You're watching that one, or we're not going to the diner."

"I want juice. I'm thirsty."

"What do you say?"

"Please."

After I retrieved a juice and poked the straw through the hole, which required as much concentration as performing brain surgery, I leaned over the cold kitchen counter and sipped my headache away. Then I finally bit the bullet and checked my phone.

The first thing I saw was a meeting request from Dan. The subject line was "Planning." It was scheduled for eight a.m. the next morning, and there was no other information. No one else was cc'd.

My heart sank. *I suppose I'm officially on probation. I will have to be a very good girl at work, and everywhere else for that matter.* I accepted the meeting request and moved on to social media.

Of course Orly had already posted photos from the party. I inspected each one and was relieved that there were none where I appeared visibly drunk.

Thank you, God. And Orly.

I continued to scroll, and that was when I came upon Jessica's latest update. "Don't ruin other people's happiness just because you can't find your own."

It was a meme, a photo of a cartoon pinup girl, hand on her hip, staring straight ahead with a snotty look on her face. I noticed the source in the bottom corner—a social media page called "I Hate Home-wreckers."

Adrenaline coursed through my whole body in waves of shame, and my throat started doing that thing.

I clicked Comment and wrote, "I'm sorry."

Then I deleted it.

Then I wrote "I didn't wreck my or your home all by myself, Jessica. Todd did his part too."

Stop. Let it go. Grow. Where did I hear that? Probably another meme.

I hesitated. Then I deleted it before hitting Enter. I couldn't say anything. There was nothing to say.

Suddenly, my phone pinged with a text message.

Todd: *I heard what happened. Working it out on my end. Hope you're OK. Don't check Frontbook, BTW.*

I downed another gulp of coffee before replying.

Jada: *I hope you work it out. I'm sorry. Again, please don't ever contact me again. Goodbye.*

"Ethan, let's go for pancakes!"

• • ❧ • •

AFTER THE DINER, I spent the rest of the day serving Ethan juice, chicken nuggets, grapes, and repeats of *Buddy the Bulldozer* while I finished my work for Lionel. Never had interrogatories been prepared in such a neat, orderly fashion. It was no easy task with a hangover, but I even color coded each interrogatory based on the corresponding substantive issue and provided a table of contents so Lionel's little pea brain could follow along. Dan would be happy.

I also checked my phone every time I stepped away from my laptop, anticipating texts, calls, or messages.

But there was nothing from anyone, not even Orly or my mom or Mark. *Maybe I should call Orly. Or maybe not.* I didn't know if I could handle hearing how pissed or embarrassed our parents were. Or my sister might throw in one of her Orly daggers like, "Has Ethan ever seen you like that before?" *No, Orly, this isn't a common occurrence!* So, I didn't call her, or anyone.

Once it was Ethan's bath time and bedtime, my headache was gone, but my heartache and mortification were still palpable. As far as Ethan was concerned, however, we'd had a good day.

"Did you have fun at your party?" I asked him.

"Uh-huh." He put his foot in a pajama leg while resting his hands on my shoulders.

"What was your favorite part?"

"The cake."

"What was your least favorite part?"

"The trampoline."

"Why?"

"It's boring. I like climbing and swinging and the balls and the rings."

Fifteen minutes after he fell asleep, I checked my phone one last time before falling into a restless sleep, waking every hour to check my phone and then passing back out again quickly. The only revelation was that when I checked to see if anyone had commented on Jessica's meme, I couldn't because she'd unfriended me. *I wish I could unfriend me.*

If only I could text Danielle, but I wasn't sure how she would respond or whose side she was on. I would love to talk to someone who wasn't actually there. I'd thought of calling Veronica, but I hadn't even invited her to the party. She hadn't invited me to her daughter's last birthday party, reasoning that it was small and mostly family and local friends, and she hadn't wanted to make me drive from Long Island to Jersey on a Saturday. So I'd reciprocated.

I had no one to rehash with, no one to confide in, and no one to talk to.

I woke up with the darkest circles and puffiest eyes I'd had in a long time. And I had no time to do my makeup tricks if I wanted to get to work in time for the eight a.m. meeting with Dan.

When Joyce arrived, Ethan had already been fed and was watching television. She seemed surprised. "He's up? How was the party? I saw your sister's photos. She tagged you."

"It was okay." I shrugged. "Well, it was fun. The kids had fun. I got sick. Long story. Anyway, I have to go. I have a meeting."

I kissed Ethan and ran out the door.

I noticed Dan's light was on when I arrived at the office. I peeked in, but he wasn't at his desk. *Maybe he's in the bathroom?* I made my way to my office, put my bags down, flipped on the light, turned on my computer, and checked my phone.

Dan walked by.

"Hey!" I called and waited, assuming he would turn around and lean against my door to catch up on the weekend, but he kept walking.

It was only then that I realized no one—not Lionel, not Dan, not Karen—had responded to my reply to Lionel on Saturday or to the email I'd sent yesterday with the work attached.

I checked the clock. It was 7:50. I went into Dan's office. "Hey," I said.

He seemed startled as he looked up from his desktop. "Hey," he said quietly.

I sat down. "How was your weekend?"

"Good." He sighed. "Listen, Tim McBride is joining us. He should be here in a few minutes."

Tim McBride was one of the managing partners. "What is this meeting about?"

Dan stopped typing and turned his chair to face me. "Jada, listen, I'm going to let Tim talk because he's the 'HR partner'"—he used air quotes around that phrase—"but I just want you to know..."

Ah. The HR partner. Of course. How could I have been so stupid?

I nodded along while he spoke, not necessarily hearing what he was saying yet fully understanding.

"If I need a recommendation in the future, can I ask you?" I cleared my throat. "Before you even answer, Dan, I know I'm a piece of work, but I always thought we had fun while getting our work done. But what I really want to say is, I'm sorry for any aggravation I've caused you."

"Don't apologize," he said. I noticed the edge of his mouth curl before adding, "Okay, you can apologize because you're a piece of work, Jada."

"Actually, I'm more of a work in progress."

"Sure. Whatever. We did have fun. And yeah, I will give future employers a warning." He smiled. "I mean, recommendation."

Before we could say anything else, Tim McBride arrived, did the deed, and I was no longer an employee of the law firm I had worked at since law school.

"Are you going to escort me out of the building?" I asked Tim as we all stood from our chairs.

"My secretary, Jean, will."

"Is Jean a black belt in karate in case I go berserk?"

Dan laughed. Tim swayed uncomfortably and put his hands in his pockets. "Please feel free to leave all personal items here, and we'll have them shipped to you."

"Thank you."

I knew I crossed the line sometimes. I knew I wasn't the ideal employee. But I always thought as long as I got my work done, I could help old dogs like Lionel change their ways in the process. I was the dipshit whisperer. I was teaching lessons, I thought.

But I wasn't changing anybody. I wasn't teaching anyone anything. I was only hurting myself, and I was finally paying for it all—at work, at home, everywhere.

I shook Dan's and Tim's hands.

Then I swung by Karen's office. She was on a conference call, so I mouthed, "I. Got. Fired."

"What?" she screamed. Then she frantically searched for the mute button.

"I'll call you. I guess you'll be getting all my cases, so call me if you have any questions."

She appeared speechless.

"Fired," I mouthed again and pointed to myself.

"I'm so upset," she said.

"You're too nice, Karen. I know there's a witch in there. Find her. Find your broomstick."

She stood to hug me, and there was suddenly a lump in my throat. I really needed a hug.

"Too nice." I pushed her away. "Get back to work."

I went back to my office and looked around for some personal stuff I needed to take. There wasn't much. Jean said she would ship my diploma and the rest of the papers for me to sign.

And that was it. I was on the train back to Long Island by 9:15 a.m.

Joyce was shocked when I walked through the door. Ethan was playing with Play-Doh while Joyce folded laundry.

"Hi! Are you okay?" She looked worried.

"Another long story. I'll explain everything later, but I have to make a few phone calls."

"Are you sure you're okay?"

"No, I'm not, but I'll explain everything in a bit."

I went upstairs, carrying my tote bag and my suit jacket. I shut the bedroom door behind me, dropped everything on the floor, and lay face down on the bed. I sniffed the fancy comforter and shut my eyes. I was too stunned to cry and too ashamed to laugh. I just lay there with my eyes closed, processing it all.

I didn't think it could get worse, but when I finally lifted myself up and checked my phone, I had an email from Mark. It read, "Hey, how are you feeling? I was going to call you yesterday but figured you might want to be left alone. I hate to bring this up again over email, but I wanted to let you know that I just spoke with the lawyer, and the filing will likely happen this week. We can talk about the house and everything later."

I let Joyce go home early and then did the whole bath-and-bedtime routine on autopilot.

After Ethan was asleep, I texted Mark.

Jada: *I was let go today. I received your email, and I know this throws a whole other complication into the mix. I'm sorry. I'll call you tomorrow to talk, if that's OK?*

He replied a minute later.

Mark: *Sorry to hear that. Call me when you are ready to talk.*

I then washed the dishes by hand and swept the kitchen floor. With each brush, I admired our beautiful kitchen floor. It was natural stone. I'd spent so much time picking it out before we moved in, and I hadn't given it a second thought since then.

When I was done, I went upstairs, washed my face, and reflexively set the alarm on my phone for 4:15 before realizing I had nowhere to be the next day. So I turned it off and went to bed.

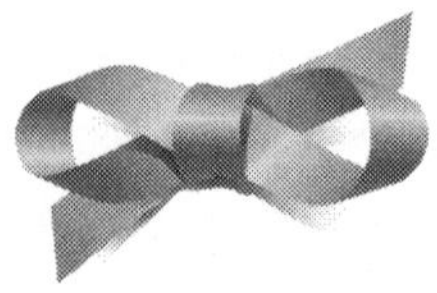

Chapter 22

The cold slush of lime and tequila filled my mouth as I let the sun hit my face.

"Where are we?" I asked without opening my eyes.

"Mexico," Gina answered and then paused to sip. "You deserve a vacation, even if it's in your dreams." She was sitting across from me on a lounge chair on the beach, wearing a black one-piece bathing suit that had a skull holding a long-stemmed rose in its mouth. The stem had a lot of leaves. She lifted her head toward the sun and shimmied her shoulders to the sound of a mariachi band in the distance.

"Thank you," I said as I held the icy margarita to my forehead. "Just when I didn't think it could get any worse. Bye, job." I waved with my other hand to no one in particular.

Gina lifted her glass in a toast. "Adios."

"Now what? Work was an anchor, at least. An anchor I should have appreciated more, like a lot of other things. What am I going to do now?"

"Say 'thank you.'"

"I did. Thank you for this trip." A server appeared to refill my margarita.

"I don't mean me." Gina sat up and pushed her hair back. "The thank-you will set you free."

"What the hell does that mean?"

"Thank every person and thing that you still have and thank every person and thing that has gotten you to this point, even the bad things."

"Even the bad things? 'Kay. Whatever that means." I turned away to think about that and take in the turquoise water and silky white beach. *Beautiful.* "Where are you?"

"Huh?"

"Where are you?" I asked again. "Like, you. Your body is here, but it's also, you know... there. Where is... you?"

"Oh. Well, the body that housed my soul when I was on earth as your favorite cousin, Gina, is buried in a cemetery in Queens. That, you know. And my soul is no longer in a human body. It's able to be here—on the other side—able to see you and everyone else I love and also able to hang with Grandma and Grandpa and all the ones who went before me and after me. I look this way to you because that's how you knew me. And I know we call this a 'dream,' but it's not a dream. It's a visit. It's real. You probably—almost definitely—won't remember it, but this is happening. This is real, and I'm guiding you, especially during this time. Because this time"—she took a deep breath—"this one's a doozy."

"A doozy? That's a word for it. I prefer shitshow." My hair stuck to the back of my neck. I pulled it into a high bun and readjusted my thighs, which were sticking to the chair.

"Me too. I've been hanging out with Grandma and Grandpa too much." She slipped on black flip-flops and a black T-shirt with a devil and angel playing hopscotch. "Let's get food."

We walked over to a café and dug into a pile of nachos that was waiting for us. The nachos were covered in cheese, beans, guacamole, and shreds of pork that melted in my mouth. I washed it down with an icy Coke and asked, "Am I supposed to thank Todd? Because I think it's best we never speak again."

She moved her sunglasses to the top of her head. "Agreed. When I tell you to say thank you, I don't mean in every case, literally. You can express gratitude to him and what it taught you without actually calling him and saying thank you. As for everyone else, it's one thing to say you're sorry to someone and to mean it. But to really think about that person and the good qualities they have that you genuinely appreciate, now that is evolution gold. You will learn so much more from that than from just saying sorry. But you should apologize too—don't get me wrong."

We digested the nachos, washed them down with another margarita, and headed back to the beach, to the two lounge chairs we were sitting on earlier under two palm trees.

"The thank-you will set you free," I repeated as the hot sand sank beneath me with each step. *Mark, Orly, my mother, father, Dan. I have to apologize and then thank these people?* "How will I know I'm doing it right, evolving or whatever? How will I know I'm on the right track?"

"Look for a sign." Gina leaned over and picked up a palm leaf from the ground.

"I don't believe in that."

"Of course you don't." She laughed as she waved the palm leaf in my direction.

"Have you ever heard of agenticity?" I asked. "It's the idea that it's human nature to want to assign meaning or significance to patterns when it's really just a coincidence. It doesn't mean anything. I would never say that to Veronica. It gives her comfort. But I don't buy any of it."

"Ha! And yet everyone has someone guiding them, ready to show them signs if they need it, but not everyone believes. Isn't it amazing?" Gina sat up and pushed her sunglasses back. The palm leaf hung from her hand between her legs as she glared at me. "I'm telling you to believe. I'm telling you these signs have meaning. I'm telling you what I know now that I'm here. I'm trying to help you. Agenticity? You're throwing out the term agenticity? Okay, fine. I'll have to work that much harder." She lifted the palm leaf and shook it furiously in my face.

I swatted it away.

She sat back. "Listen, you're going through a rough time. Understatement, if there ever was one. I know you feel like you're under a rock right now, crushed by guilt and shame and regret and confusion. But you'll feel it lift, I promise, and you'll feel yourself crawling out from under it. And I'll be there to let you know you've got this. How will you know I'm there for you?" She threw the palm leaf in my lap. "Look for the signs."

I picked it up and brushed off the sand. "Okay. Sure. And then what? How do I start to crawl out? Practically speaking. I guess I should look for a job."

Gina reached behind her and pulled out a cigarette. "What do you like about yourself?"

"Do you ever answer a question directly?"

"Pick one thing." She tapped the cigarette and popped it in her mouth.

I shrugged. "I don't know."

"Work with me here, Jada." She lit up and blew a stream of smoke in the opposite direction from me.

"I like my teeth. I like how each of them is shaped and that they're straight. The bottom ones too, thanks to my retainer."

She sat up. "Your favorite thing about yourself is your teeth?"

"Yeah." I nodded. "It's the first thing I thought of."

"Okaaay." She inhaled. "Wow. We still have more work to do than I thought."

"You asked!"

"All right. Now name something you like, really like, about yourself that is not physical."

"Well, I would have said that I liked how I didn't take shit from anybody, but that has since gotten me in trouble—Hi, Lionel—and it isn't the truth anyway."

"You don't like having a big mouth?"

"No."

"Aside from Lionel? Not even standing up to Joyce's mom's landlord or the straight ponytail bitches at the mommy group?"

"I don't know. People always say I'm so outspoken, and Veronica always says I'm so brave, but..."

"But what?"

"What people don't see is how I feel. Usually, after I let someone have it, I don't feel so great about it." I rolled a grain of sand in my left hand.

"Why?"

I flicked the sand away. "I don't know."

"Do you think you overreact?"

"Maybe."

"Maybe what you go nuts about is sometimes not worth it."

I lowered my sunglasses to glare at her. "Sometimes," I conceded.

"Like line cutters. Like, maybe you should just let them go." She met my eyes as she made her point.

"I know. Let it go. Grow."

"But other things, other people, not so much. You have a gift."

"The gift of going nuts?"

"You just have to use your powers for good."

"What is my power exactly?"

She blew out one last stream of smoke and smashed her cigarette in the sand. "Your inability to let anything you deem unfair or unjust go."

"You told me to let things go! How is that my power?"

"When it's something that perturbs you but 'correcting it'—in your view—serves no higher good, you have to let that shit go. But other things, certain people, they need you, Jada. Think of how great you felt helping Joyce's mom."

"So I should be a bitch for other people?"

"Bitch for hire."

"Bitch to the rescue."

"There you go. But you'll be helping people. You like helping people."

I cocked my head as I brushed sand off my chair with my foot. "Hearing that Joyce's mother's air-conditioning was fixed was an amazing feeling. I thought it was just a one-time thing, though."

"It doesn't have to be."

Gina picked up the palm leaf and covered my face with it until I swatted it away again. "You are so annoying."

"Bitch on call, reporting for duty," she announced. She shot the palm leaf high into the air like it was a sword in her hand. Then she swayed it back and forth to the beat of the mariachi music that was still playing.

Chapter 23

I bolted upright in bed and grabbed my phone. It was 5:07 a.m.

I dialed Mark as I glanced at his side of the bed. I ran my hand along our sheets and over the palm-print design of one throw pillow.

He picked up after one ring. "What's wrong?"

"Nothing." I sounded like I was gasping for air, which didn't help convince him.

"What is it? Is it Ethan? Is he okay?"

"He's fine. It's not Ethan. It's, um, I'm sorry. Sorry for calling you like this. Sorry for... Well, I'm sorry for everything."

"Okay. Uh, is that why you're calling?"

"Yes."

"Thank you for calling. I'm going to go back to sleep now."

"Oh, I'm sorry. I probably should have waited an hour, but I figured you were getting up soon."

"Actually, no. I don't have a commute anymore. I live in the city now, remember?"

"Right! Oh no, I'm so sorry, Mark."

"It's okay. Bye?"

"One more thing." I tugged at a loose string on the edge of what used to be Mark's pillowcase. "Thank you."

"For what?"

"For being a loving father and a decent man. For being a good person who would never hurt a fly. You have a tender soul, and it is a really admirable quality that isn't valued enough in society, and—"

"Are you drunk?"

"No! God, no. It's just, I realized we never had that really full, complete conversation. I just wanted to give you my own true, heartfelt apology. And I also wanted to say thank you. I am so grateful for all that you are and that you've been in my life. I wouldn't take any of it back." I wrapped the loose pillowcase string around my finger.

"You're not going to, I don't know, do anything?"

"No! I just wanted to say these things, and I couldn't wait. I forgot you don't have to catch a train anymore. Sorry." I yanked the string free and rolled it between my fingers.

"Well, thank you for the apology. And you're welcome."

"Okay, then. Have a good day. Sorry again to wake you up so early."

"Jada?"

I swallowed. "Yeah?" I braced myself for what he was about to say.

"It's okay. All of it."

Something about that caught me in the throat.

But before I could thank him for saying that, he said, "I haven't been faithful either."

My ears started to ring as if they couldn't believe what they were hearing. It was like the little invisible person who'd been punching me in the throat was now punching me in the ear. "What?"

"Alana," he said.

Alana. Of course.

"Have you slept together?"

"Only after I moved out."

"Wait, that's fairly recently," I said, trying to piece it all together.

"We've been in love for a long time. Well, over a year. But it was never physical. I promise you. But we've been talking for a while about how to handle this."

"How to leave me? And then I made it so convenient for you," I said almost to myself.

I had been beating myself up about Todd. I made a fool of myself in front of everyone in a drunken confessional. And Mark had Alana the whole time. "I thought you thought our stagnant marriage was normal. If I'd only known you'd been plotting how to get out." I kicked back the sheets and comforter.

"I did think it was normal. But then Alana and I would have these amazing conversations and talk late into the night, and I realized I didn't want to go home—I wanted to stay with her." I opened my mouth to respond, but no words came out.

"I'm sorry if I made you feel bad about bringing up divorce first," he said.

I found my voice. "Yeah, what the fuck?"

"I became defensive. Even though that's what I wanted too, it was still a rejection thing. I guess I've always kind of felt like you never thought I was cool enough for you, you never really liked me. You loved me maybe, at one time, but you never liked me. You thought I was a dork. And now you were rejecting me in the biggest way. It felt unfair. I should be rejecting you. Very immature, I know."

"It's not a competition."

"I know. And now you know everything," he said.

I flicked the pillow string that was still between my fingers to the floor. "Thank you."

After we hung up, I stayed in bed, thinking, trying to wrap my head around what I'd just learned and all that had happened. *Mark gets Alana. Todd will likely get to stay with Jessica. I get fired. And I get to have flashbacks of puking into a bag filled with wrapping paper.*

Awhile later, when the sounds of Ethan "vrooming" came through the baby monitor, I walked to his room. *But I also get Ethan.* I sat on his bed. "What should we do today?" *We've got all day, just you and your unemployed mother.*

He didn't look up from his trucks. "I don't know."

I called Joyce and let her know that we would be spending the day out of the house. Then I told her everything, including the fact that I wasn't sure when I would find another job or how long we would be in this house. That all meant I wasn't sure how long she would be working for us. I told her how sorry I was about that. It was a relief to let it all out but so hard to say the words to such a sweet lady who was the only person I trusted my child with.

"I see. I'm sorry to hear about all of this. Not just for me. I'm sorry for you too. You're good people."

"Are we?"

"Yes." She laughed. "What you did for my mother, that was so nice."

"That was nothing."

"It wasn't nothing. You helped her. You helped me. The stress that was putting on all of us was killing us slowly. We think he was turning the breaker off. We know it. But no more, thanks to you. All the neighbors are so grateful. It was going on for too long."

"I'm glad it worked out."

"She has another neighbor in another building who is going through something else now."

The old me would have said, "I don't know if I have time, Joyce," but I did have time. I had all the time in the world.

• • ❧ • •

"DISHWASHA!" ROBERTA was in her seventies with hair dyed jet black and a cane with a crystal-encrusted handle. "How can ya rent a place to a person with a dishwasha that doesn't work? But, ya know, hon, we're just gettin' stahted. Sit. What can I get ya?"

I sat down on her black couch, which she'd adorned with red pillows propped in each corner. "Water is fine. My mother has the same pillows."

"Aren't they beautiful pillows? Watah? I got soda. You don't want a soda?"

"Sure. I'll have a soda."

"Ah-right. Hold on." She disappeared into a pantry behind the kitchen and emerged with two cans of club soda in one hand against her chest, her cane in the other.

Over glasses of club soda and ice, I learned that Roberta was widowed. Her husband had died of a heart attack twenty years ago at age fifty-five. Her children were grown and had families, so she'd sold the house in Forest Hills to downsize.

"I mean, I didn't wanna be callin' my son every weekend. 'Can ya mow the lawn? Can ya do this? Can ya do that?' I thought a small apartment—ya know, it's just me—would be perfect. But, oh Madonna mia, what a nightmare this has been."

The dishwasher didn't work, there was black mold along the windowsills, and when the sink was turned on, water seeped out of the pipes.

"Tell me about your landlord." *Don't say Mr. Castilla. I think he's probably blocked my number. Let it be another dirtbag.*

"Oh! Forget it." Roberta clutched her chest with her long red fingernails. "For startahs, he's your age, a young man. But no time for me. No time to tawk when I call him. He'll say, 'Email me.' And I don't email. I don't wanna be asking my kids to email for me. So I call him, and I can't even get the words out before his secretary puts me through to his, you know, that recording thing. I leave a message, but then I never hear. He cashes my rent checks, though."

"We'll get him to respond," I reassured Roberta.

"Aren't you a doll?"

I pulled out my phone. "Do you mind if I take a few pictures?"

"Go to town, hon."

• • ❧ • •

ROBERTA WAS RIGHT. Her landlord did not answer phone calls and did not answer emails. And I left several. He was so elusive, like a scam artist who sells fake timeshares and then is untraceable.

So I dropped Ethan at my parents, telling them Joyce had to take the day off and I had to go to court in Queens. I still hadn't told them about being fired. I planned to tell them eventually, but we still hadn't talked about the party and all I'd revealed. *One bombshell at a time.*

Then I went to Roberta's landlord's office. It was on Queens Boulevard, above a nail salon and a taco place.

I rang the doorbell. No one answered. I knocked. No one answered. I opened the door. "Hello?"

The walls were wood-paneled, and the receptionist's desk was black lacquer. There was no one there.

"Hello?"

From the looks of Roberta's windowsills, I had a feeling I wasn't dealing with an upstanding citizen. He could be the type to accuse me of stealing something from his reception area, so I shut the door and waited outside in the tiny hallway with stained carpet.

I sat on the top step, scrolled through my phone, and let an hour pass. Still nothing. I pulled out a pen and a page from my yellow legal pad.

"Dear Mr. Nadine, My name is Jada Marlone, and I am Roberta Russo's attorney. I have left voice mails and emails about the things in her apartment that need to be fixed, but you have not responded. I have knocked and rang the doorbell, but it appears no one is available. I am downstairs at Tootie's Tacos. Please come find me when you return. I am in a gray suit. Thank you."

I knew he would probably not return any time soon and would ignore my note when he did. *But why leave his door open*? He must have just stepped out. Or maybe he was as careless about his office as he was about his tenants' apartments.

At least I have all day.

I set up shop at Tootie's and whipped out my laptop. *To work on what? I have nothing to work on. Should I apply for jobs? Lawyer jobs? Where? How? I haven't done this since law school. Is there a career services department for adults?*

I scrolled through some job websites then checked social media, *People* magazine, and *Vanity Fair,* keeping my eye out for William Nadine. I had a vague idea of what he might look like from the ill-lit photo on his website.

I waited. I ordered tacos. I waited some more. Then I had an idea.

What am I best at? Being a lawyer? I wasn't so bad. Standing up to people I feel have committed some wrong? Yes, and I'm trying to use it for good now. Internet stalking? Pro!

I went to Frontbook and found William Nadine in seconds, but his settings were private. I went to his friends list but couldn't see anything. I studied the profile picture of him with someone who appeared to be his wife. They were arm in arm, standing on what appeared to be a boat dock. The comments were all the usual, "You guys look great!" I Googled each of the commenters' names. None appeared to be a secretary or assistant.

So I examined his other cover photos. A generic sunset. A decorated Christmas tree. A boat in a dry dock. There was one comment on that one. "You're not going to be able to park that on Queens Boulevard." I searched the commenter's name. She was a legal assistant. It was worth a try.

I searched her name again and "phone." And just like that, I was calling Stacy Alina's cell phone. I got her voice mail.

"Hi, Stacy." I explained who I was and that I was looking for Mr. Nadine. I tried to sound friendly and vague enough for her to call back. After I left a message, I sat and waited some more.

Tootie's had a clean bathroom, and Gerald behind the counter kept an eye on my things when I stepped away. He refilled my Diet

Coke on the house throughout the day. But by the time it was dark, no one that looked like William or Stacy appeared to walk up the stairs to his office, and I was jittery from all the caffeine.

I was ready to give up. I used the bathroom one more time, and when I came out, Gerald was giddy. "The lady went inside."

"Who?"

"Next door. Where you're spying."

"Oh! Well, not spying but... never mind. No time to explain. Thank you, Gerald." I grabbed my things and ran out the door and up the steps. I had to grab the railing when I got to the top, just outside Mr. Nadine's office.

I knocked and stepped in. "Hello?"

Stacy was startled. Her black hair appeared blue in the cheap office lighting, and her big brown eyes were wide with fear. "Who the fuck are you?"

What a warm reception, but who can blame her?

I caught my breath. "Hi. I'm sorry to scare you. I'm Jada Marlone. I'm looking for William Nadine. I left a note. And a voice mail. And emails. And I left you a voice mail, I believe."

"Yeah, I got it. That's why I had to come all the way here from Brooklyn. I'm sending her file to Mr. Nadine."

"Great. Thank you. Please add a note from me that we're holding Ms. Russo's rent in escrow until the defects in my email are addressed. Do you want me to list them again?"

I waited for Stacy to grab a pen and a pad. I gave her all of the info and then said, "If all of the defects are not cleared by next Tuesday, I will be filing a complaint. If Mr. Nadine refuses to return phone calls or emails, the process server can just wait at Tootie's and drink Diet Coke all day. That's what I did."

Stacy stopped writing. "How the hell did you get my personal cell phone number?"

It's on the fucking internet. I shrugged and smiled. "I'm good like that."

There was a bowl filled with green apples next to the Reception sign. Without taking my eyes off of her, I picked one up, bit it, and walked out. When I got to the bottom of the stairs, I raced to the trash can on the corner to spit the apple bits out of my mouth. *Ick. Knowing this landlord, they're probably covered in dust and mold.*

I drove to my parents' house, and when I walked through the door, my mother quizzed me. "You had work to do until this hour? I fed Ethan. He's watching TV. What is going on?"

"Sorry I'm so late."

"You might as well sleep over at this point."

"That's okay." I stepped toward the TV room. "Ethan, we're going soon," I called to him and then turned back to my mother. "But first, I have to talk to you. Sit down." Then I called down to the basement. "Dad, can you come up here a minute?"

"You're making me nervous," my mother said. "My body can't handle any more. What? What is it? You're going to rehab?"

I sighed as my father walked into the room. "I barely ever drink, or I would have never gotten drunk like that after a few drinks. Listen, you know Mark moved out. He filed for divorce."

My mother clutched her chest and shut her eyes. *What did she expect?*

"And I got fired."

My mother dropped her head into her hands. My father nodded.

"I thought you recently got a promotion," my mother said with her head still in her hands.

"I did, but something happened. I'll tell you someday."

"Please don't."

"Anyway, we're going to have to sell the house for that reason, and because of the taxes, and Mark is paying rent in the city now. It's a lot, and I was wondering if we could stay here for a little while."

My mother lifted her head and opened her eyes. "With us?"

"Uh, yeah. You live here, don't you?"

"Of course you can stay here," my father said.

"Thank you. I'd like Ethan and me to be here, with you. Not forever, but just for some time. Maybe we'll be moving back into the city, maybe back to Long Island." *If we're going to move and be careful with money, why not be with family?* It wasn't like I had to pull Ethan out of a preschool he loved, though I knew he would miss Joyce. And he would miss Long Island at Play, but we could never return there anyway.

My mother glanced at my father as if making sure he was hearing this and then back at me. "I thought ya couldn't stand us."

"It's that obvious?"

She shrugged.

"Well, I..." I tried to find the words. "I love you. And I'm sorry. And thank you," I blurted out.

That was met with blank stares.

"I'm sorry if I've ever been anything but respectful to you. We have our differences of opinion and tastes, and I'm not always the most patient person—about some of the dumbest things sometimes, I know—but I'm sorry. And thank you. Thank you for everything. For raising me and putting a roof over my head, and uh, always cooking good food, and bringing meats and cheeses and pastry everywhere you go."

"You're thanking us for pastry?" my mother asked.

"You're welcome, Jada. You don't have to thank us," my father said. "You can stay in the guest room."

"I have all of Orly's stuffed animals in there. On both beds," my mother said. "All of those baby beanies."

"Beanie Babies," I corrected.

"Well, move them, Jo," my father said. "They're stuffed animals."

She shrugged one shoulder. "I guess I could put them in the other room."

I rolled my eyes. "Thanks."

"All right. I better get started on that," she said. "There are so many."

"I'll move them, Ma."

"No, no. They're not heavy. And I'm not dead yet."

"Thank you."

Chapter 24

Six weeks later, I looked over at Ethan, sleeping on his stomach in Orly's old bed. I knew it was her bed because the headboard was white lacquer. Mine was beige with leaf etchings on the corner.

"You're moving in with mom and dad? Aren't you going to miss your big house?" Orly had asked when I told her of my plan.

"Yes," I'd replied simply. But it turned out that I didn't end up missing our big house all that much, even as Ethan and I bunked together in my sister's old room.

My mother had converted my old room into a reading room, where she had bookcases packed with mostly cookbooks and a comfortable chaise lounge that she never used.

My mom had moved my bed into Orly's room and converted it into a guest room, consisting of the two mismatched twin beds, my old dresser, and up until recently, Orly's two hundred Beanie Babies, which were now in the reading room.

I glanced over at Ethan, who was still sleeping. He'd adjusted to the new environment easily. *A little too easily.* I had a recurring worry that it would all implode one day and that the effects of the divorce and the move would come out all at once. I tried to push that thought down. *Maybe kids are just resilient.*

Since that day when I'd stalked Roberta's landlord and asked my parents if I could move in, my mother had gone from insinuating, and sometimes downright asking, why I didn't want to have another child to now insinuating, and sometimes downright asking, why I didn't want to look for a traditional lawyer job.

Two days after the stake-out of William Nadine's office, Roberta's dishwasher was replaced, her windows were cleared of mold, and her pipes were fixed.

It was the most rewarding day's work I'd ever put in.

I had tried to explain that to my mother. "I would like to try something different, work-wise and life-wise. A new beginning."

"It's a career that you went to all that school for, not a damn dessert menu. Ya wanna try something different? Get the tiramisu."

My parents weren't the only ones who were concerned about me.

I propped a pillow behind my head and scrolled through old emails. I had to find an old lease for another one of Joyce's mother's friends who I was helping. That was when I reread the emails from a couple of weeks ago.

"Hi, Karen, so since I got canned, I haven't really had a chance to have a good, long goodbye with you. No time for that now, but I don't know if I ever thanked you."

I recalled the time I'd misplaced my phone and become hysterical. Karen had helped me look everywhere until we found it in the office refrigerator. It was the morning after Ethan had had a stomach bug, and I'd been up all night.

"I just want to say I really appreciated it when you covered for me if I had to stay home with Ethan for whatever reason. Thank you for being a good coworker. Whoever takes my place is lucky to work alongside you."

Ethan's footie pajamas were slightly twisted around his left ankle. He must have been tossing and turning. The comforter and top sheet were coiled and wedged between the bed and wall. I resisted the urge to untwist the pajama pant leg.

I went back to my phone and scrolled an inch to the next email.

"Hi, Dan. It's Jada, your favorite associate. I'm writing to say something I never had the chance to say to you on my last day, or ever. Thank you. I know I apologized, but I don't think I ever thanked you. Not once. Thank you for being a good supervisor and putting up with me. Thank you for everything you did for me."

Dan and Karen both replied right away, saying they missed me and that we had to get together for lunch sometime. We never did. Life got too busy. But it was easy to write them. It was easy to be gracious to people I liked. The challenge was extending that same courtesy to someone I didn't, to find something to appreciate about someone I found loathsome.

I readjusted myself on the bed and typed.

"Lionel, this is Jada Marlone. I'm writing to first, apologize for my last correspondence. It was disrespectful and unprofessional. This message is not at the prompting of Dan or anyone at the firm. In fact, they are not aware that I am emailing you. I am no longer with the firm, but I felt it was incumbent upon me to express how sorry I am. If you were my father or uncle or family member or even a friend, I wouldn't want someone to speak to you the way I did, and so again, I'm sorry. Thank you for your continued patronage of the firm. If you'd left them because of me, I would feel even more awful. So thank you, Lionel. I learned a great deal from the cases you brought to the firm. Thank you for that too, and good luck."

I clicked Send. I didn't expect Lionel to reply. But that was not my intention in sending it.

I checked the clock. It was 6:07 a.m. Ethan would be sleeping for at least another hour. We'd been up late with my parents, watching *The Wizard of Oz.*

A couple of hours later, while Ethan played with my nieces, I told my parents and sister I had to run a few errands. I drove to Long Island at Play.

I pulled into the parking lot for the last time and checked myself in the mirror. *Nothing in my teeth. Nothing on my face.* I hadn't been back since the party.

Am I really going to do this? Yes, because I have to.

I opened the doors to hear the cacophony of bouncing joy and inhaled the wafting scent of chicken fingers one last time. It was Saturday morning. Jessica always brought the kids on Saturdays.

I made my way around the padded wall, past the party room—the scene of the crime—toward the bouncing-ball den. And there they were. Danielle, Melody, and Jessica were seated on the mommy bench. I hadn't heard from any of them since the party.

Melody was the first to see me approaching. Her face filled with popcorn-eating delight at the possibility of impending drama. Danielle caught sight of me next, and her expression went from shock to a sympathetic smile. Then Jessica looked up from her phone.

"Hi." I focused on Jessica. "Can I speak to you alone?"

"What do you want?" She sounded like William Nadine's assistant. *What did I expect?*

"I'd like to speak with you alone if that's okay."

"It's not okay. What are you even doing here?"

Okay, we'll do it like this, in front of Danielle and Melody, and with you sitting and me standing.

"It's fine. There's something I also want to say to all of you anyway that I should have relayed sooner. I'm sorry. I'm sorry that you and your children had to see that. And it would be very easy for me to move away—which we did, back to my parents' in Queens—and never face any of you again, but that's the easy way out, and I want to be respectful."

"Ha!" Jessica said.

"You live with your parents now?" Melody asked with an incredulous smile.

"Yes. And thank you all for coming to Ethan's party. And thank you for always being cool and not being like the ponytail moms in puffy vests."

Danielle smiled.

"Despite everything—and I can't say it enough; I wish none of it happened, believe me—but I'm glad I met all of you. Honestly."

Jessica snorted.

"We're glad we met you too," Danielle said. "I hope everything works out for you."

Melody turned sharply toward Danielle.

"Thank you, Danielle," I said.

"Enjoy Queens," Melody said.

"And, Jessica, I am truly sorry for any pain I caused you. Not just at the party but even before that, even before you knew. It was all wrong, all of it, and I'm sorry."

"Is that it? Are you done?" she asked.

I didn't feel done. My apology didn't feel adequate. I wanted her to know I was sincere. "I hope that your family can heal. I really do."

"God works in mysterious ways." She smirked. "There will be no other baby. And *my family* is staying intact."

"I'm happy for you. I really am," I said.

Her eyes went back to her phone.

I turned to Melody and Danielle. "See you guys on Frontbook. Ha."

Danielle waved.

Melody sneered. "Byeee!"

"Byeee," I wanted to chirp back in mock imitation, right in her face, but I didn't. I let it go and walked away.

"Hold on!" Jessica called. She marched toward me. "I want to know something."

"Okay." I tried to sound willing. *Go ahead. I was in the wrong. I'll answer anything.*

"Why would you never mention, this whole time, that you knew my husband?"

"It was awkward. Would you have wanted to know that I used to date him?"

"Yes. *I* don't stand for secrets."

You might want to check your husband's text messages. "You're right. I should have let you know that I knew your husband. It was all so weird and coincidental and—"

"Like running into him in a hotel?"

"Yes. I'm sorry you found out the way you did. Believe me, not just because it was mortifying for me, but what an awful way for you to find out. I wish I could go back and take that away, and I wish I could go all the way back and change everything, but I guess it all happened the way it should."

"It all happened the way it should?"

I don't know where that came from.

Before I could even attempt to explain, she said, "Enjoy dating apps."

"Ha. I'm just focused on my son and my work. But thanks."

"Good. And good luck," she said coldly before turning away.

I couldn't blame her for not forgiving me. I hoped I would become a distant memory and that the sting of ever hearing my name again would fade. *Remember Jida? Joda? What the hell was her name? Remember her son's birthday party? Whatever happened to that piece of work?*

As I headed toward the exit, I spotted Ponytail Mom out of the corner of my eye. At least her child wouldn't be able to put his hands around my son's throat again. *This place is full of landmines.*

"Oh, hey!" she called.

Is she talking to me? I glanced to the side and saw that she was. *Oh, come on. What the hell could she want?*

She pranced toward me, with her slick hair and shiny puffy vest. "Did I hear you had a birthday party here? Because I was thinking of having my son's party here." She talked like she was trying to refrain from laughing. "How did it go?"

"Horribly. I drank too much and threw up."

She nodded slowly as if she already knew the answer but hadn't expected me to come clean so quickly.

"But the kids had fun," I added. "No one got choked." I smiled and left.

I couldn't let that one go. What can I say? I'm a work in progress.

After that, there was not a single loose end left in Long Island except for a massive house that we hoped someone would buy when the market improved.

• • ❧ • •

THE NEXT MORNING, I was just about to go through another lease from one of Joyce's mom's referrals when I heard, "Mommmyyyy."

I raced up the stairs to see Ethan sitting up in bed. "Shhh. No one's up yet. Why are you up so early?"

"I had a bad dream."

I picked him up and walked down to the kitchen. "What was it about?"

"You left and never came back, and I had to stay here forever."

"What a scary dream." I rocked him and kissed his head. "I spent eighteen years in this house, so I know."

He looked up at me with a horrified expression.

"I'm kidding. Is this place so bad? That was a joke. Okay? Don't repeat that."

"I want pancakes."

"Pancakes? Not cereal?"

"Pancakes."

"Okay." *I got work to do, kid. But fine. Pancakes, it is.*

"Can I watch *Buddy*?"

"No one is awake yet but us. Let's not turn the TV on."

"But—"

"Shhh." I nipped his impending wail in the bud. "We're going to play a game."

"What game?"

I went to the living room and opened the bottom drawer of a built-in bookshelf, where my mother kept the board games.

As I lifted Ethan onto the kitchen counter, I handed him UNO. "While I make the pancakes, you get the game ready. Okay? Here. Open it."

I was whipping the batter when Ethan asked, "Why is this one taped? And this one too?" He held up two cards that had tape holding them together.

"I don't know." *Yes, I do.* "Actually, it's a long story. I'll tell you over pancakes."

The truth was it was a short story, and I wasn't sure I wanted to tell my son.

I had been ten, and Orly had been six.

"You can't do that," I'd announced. My wet bathing suit stuck to my skin, and my wet hair left droplets on the outdoor table every time I leaned in to put a card down.

"I didn't do anything," Orly replied.

"You just put down a yellow four."

"I know, but—"

"Relax." My mother tipped her Virginia Slim into an ashtray and blew smoke away from us, but the wind carried it to our nostrils. "Whose turn is it?"

"It was Orly's, and she put down the yellow four and then took it back."

"No," Orly protested, putting down a yellow five.

I needed that yellow four. I seethed but kept playing... until she did it again.

Out of the corner of my eye, I watched as her arm reached out to drop down a card—the green six. I needed a six! Then she grabbed it back.

I glared at her.

"What?"

"You know you don't actually want us to see your cards, right? Green six. She has a green six, Ma." *That'll teach her.*

"Stop it. No, I don't!"

"I just saw it."

My mother flipped the page of her *Redbook* magazine. "Stop it, Jada. Go. It's your turn."

I put down a red six then took it back.

"No. No. You can't do that," my mother said, blowing smoke again.

"That's what she did. Twice!"

Orly was silent.

"Put that red card down," my mother said.

"No. Why? You need it?"

"Jada, watch that tone. Play right. Put the card down that you just put down."

"I'm just doing exactly what Orly did, but you didn't see."

"I saw. Now play right."

"Tell her to play right!" I demanded.

That was when I grabbed the three cards in Orly's hand and attempted to rip them in half all at once, but I didn't have that dexterity at ten years old, so I ripped them in half, one by one, as my mother and Orly watched, speechless, until my mother slapped my hand away and screamed, "Stop that!"

I could hear my mother screaming my name as I marched off to my room but not before turning back and yanking Orly's ponytail. "That'll teach you to play right."

Orly had screamed in surprise and possibly pain.

I suppose the ponytail yank was overkill. And it hurts, I know. I held my hand to my head, imagining the pain.

I was shaken from the memory as my mother appeared in the kitchen in her bathrobe and slippers. "What did you make?" she asked.

"Pancakes!" Ethan squealed.

"And you're playing a game? This early?"

"I didn't want to turn on the television," I said. "I didn't want to wake you and Daddy."

"We're going to play UNO," Ethan said.

"I see. Make sure your mother doesn't rip any of the cards in half."

"I won't." I flipped a pancake so hard, some of the batter splattered on Ethan's pajama leg. I wanted to say, "I didn't give birth to a cheater." But I let it go.

• • ❧ • •

LATER THAT MORNING, I went to work in my new "office," which was my parent's basement, and which I now shared with my father.

It was finished with a couch, coffee table, television, and two desks, plus the washer and dryer in the corner. With what I got paid now, which was virtually nothing as I tried to build a clientele, it was all I could afford office-wise: free. But hopefully, more clients would come my way, and more landlords would do the right thing after my pep talks. *Justice, Jada style. Bitch for hire.*

I dialed the number of the latest deadbeat.

Ring. Ring.

"Pick up, asshole." I tapped my pen against the desk, when someone coughed behind me.

"Oh, hi, Dad." *Where did he come from?* He was examining a piece of pipe with a magnifying glass. "Did you hear that?" *Hopefully my dad didn't hear me calling someone an asshole.*

"Hear what?" Benito Wolfe barked into the phone.

"Oh! Mr. Wolfe. How lovely to hear your voice. This is Jada Marlone again, Mrs. Hendricks's lawyer. How are you?"

"Yeah. Good. Why the call?"

"You must not have received my letter, or my email, or my voice mail. She hasn't received her security deposit back."

"Yeah. It's being processed."

"Excellent. How much longer will the processing take?"

"I can't tell you that."

"I'm assuming it will be for the full amount." I looked over at my father, who didn't seem to be listening. The pipes were far more interesting to him, I supposed. He ran a magnifying glass up and down the piece of metal he was holding.

"I can't tell you that," Mr. Wolfe said.

"What can you tell me?"

"It's being processed," he hissed.

"It's Thursday, right? One of the seven days I hate to be jerked around." I glanced in my father's direction. The metal was still more interesting. "Full amount in Mrs. Hendricks's mailbox by next week, or you will meet Renata."

"Get the—who?"

"Renata. From channel five. You know, *Renata Makes It Right.* Ever been on TV, Benito?"

"Fuck you!"

"Fuck you more!" I hollered.

"What the fuck do you want me to say? It's being processed."

"I'll believe that when it's in my client's hands. It's been eight months. Write the check. You were hoping she would die before you ever paid, weren't you? Well, sorry to tell you, but she's got a lot of life left in her, the old girl. She loves Zumba. Did you know that?" That wasn't entirely true. She told me the center brought in dancing teachers, but most residents stayed in their wheelchairs and moved their arms around. "She's a dancing fool, Benito! She's not going anywhere, and neither am I. Fair is fair."

I hung up.

"What's Zumba?" my father asked.

"Some kind of dance."

"Oh, good. I thought it was some kind of new pastry I hadn't heard about."

"What are you looking for on that thing?" I asked.

"Bubbles. Sometimes, when water flows over a pipe..." He went on to explain what could happen in full detail.

The man so rarely got a chance to talk that I tried to listen carefully.

"Interesting." I nodded. "Very cool."

"Not as interesting as Renata and Zumba."

"Whatever floats your boat."

I used to handle leases for large warehousing corporations. It was as interesting to me as bubbles on a pipe, but the money was good, and I could handle the people—or so I'd thought—but it wasn't fulfilling. I had never known what it meant when people said their work was fulfilling. But now I knew. Screaming at Benito Wolfe on behalf of Mrs. Hendricks filled my heart with something I'd never felt while reviewing a warehousing lease. I would do it for free... almost.

• • ❧ • •

"WHEN YOU GOT FIRED..." Orly spoke with her mouth full of chicken. My mother, father, Orly, Paul, my nieces, Ethan, and I sat around my parents' dining room table.

"Did they escort you out of the building? That's what they do at my office. If you get fired, a security guard literally walks the person out of the building."

Every time she said "fired," I cringed. But that was what had happened. I had to own it.

"No. One of the secretaries walked me out."

"Did you have photos up? Like what about framed photos of Ethan?"

"They'll probably sell them on the internet. His face could end up in a Target catalog on some other kid's body."

No one laughed.

"Seriously, you had to leave all that stuff?" Orly asked.

"A secretary mailed it to me a few days later."

"I just always wondered what happens to your stuff when you get fired."

"You have to get escorted out," my mother, who'd never worked in an office, chimed in. "They have to take precautions."

"Isabella, eat that right now," Orly said as she pointed to a chicken cutlet. "One more bite, and you can get up and play." She turned back to me. "Did Mark move out because of the affair?"

I glared at her. "I didn't have an affair."

"Well, whatever it was. You know, when you were in California."

"It's more complicated than that," I said calmly. *Can't she think of things in a more nuanced way? Is she capable of that?* I would love to scream, "It wasn't just because of Todd. And news flash: Mark has Alana! We had no connection for years. We were like robots. Is that happiness? Is that any way to live? Todds and Alanas were bound to get in the cracks that were already there."

But all Orly would say to that was, "So Mark was cheating on you too?"

I have to change the subject before I can no longer let things go. "I really like your T-shirt," I said.

"Thanks." Orly looked down. The shirt had a bear with a daisy behind his ear, sitting on the moon. "Another one of Gina's."

"I wore one of hers to bed the other night. I woke up remembering the weirdest thing. Remember the time Uncle Eddie stepped in dog shit at some carnival?"

"Yes! And Mommy kept saying 'shit,' and it made us laugh so hard."

"How about the time I ripped your UNO cards in half?"

That made Orly start to laugh hysterically, which made me laugh hysterically. My father seemed amused, while my mother shook her head.

"I can still picture Mommy's face as she held on to her Virginia Slim." She imitated my mother with her hand sticking out as if she were frozen mid-puff.

"What I wouldn't do for a Virginia Slim right now," my mother said.

"Don't even think about it," I said.

Orly wiped her eyes and exhaled. "Good times."

"They were," I said.

Should I thank Orly for being a good sister?

"Do you miss your big office and secretary? I can't believe you have to share with Daddy now."

Nah. Never mind.

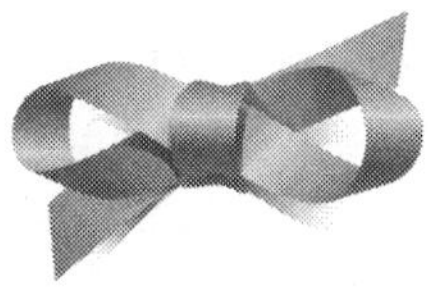

Chapter 25

Gina was in her usual uniform—black skinny jeans and a curious T-shirt. This time, it was a drawing of a naked lady covering her parts with big palm leaves, and the leaves were bedazzled.

"You wear bedazzled garments here? Remember our obsession with gluing rhinestones to everything?"

She smiled. "I wore it for you."

We were sitting on a bench on Prince Street in Soho, each holding a piping-hot cup of cocoa filled to the rim with marshmallows.

"When you yanked my hair, was it karma for the hair grab I gave Orly? You know, during the famous UNO cheating scandal?"

"What goes around gets yanked around."

"What is it with my mother and Orly?" I sucked up a marshmallow. "It's such work to connect with both of them."

"People think soul mates are the people you click with, but soul mates can also be the people who test you. They're the ones you learn the most from."

"My mother and my sister are my soul mates?"

"We have a lot of soul mates. It's not only a romantic thing."

"What am I learning from my mother? How to have an opinion on everything? She could teach a Learning Annex course on how to have a damn opinion about everything, even things she knows practically nothing about."

"You could be her teaching assistant."

"Ha ha."

"Let's walk." Gina tipped back the rest of her cocoa and stood. "If we could all see a movie trailer of each of our lives, we'd find it easier to love each other."

"Huh?"

"That's what it's like here. There's a whole new way of seeing each other on the other side. You can see everyone's soul. It's like you know everyone's story. And that's why it's easy to love without judgment from here. But where you are, you don't have that view. You don't get the full picture. And that's the test."

"I have no idea what you're trying to say."

"Come this way."

I sucked up one last marshmallow and followed her down the street.

• • ❧ • •

WE STOOD IN FRONT OF a narrow white two-family house on a street lined with identical houses and old Buicks in the driveway. *Where are we?*

We climbed the steep concrete staircase that led to the front door on the right. Gina didn't knock—she just opened the screen door and the door behind it and walked right in. I followed. *Whose house is this? She knows these people?*

We walked through the small living room with its plastic-covered brown sofa and chairs and a photo of the Virgin Mary above the fireplace.

When we got to the kitchen, I saw her. My mother. She couldn't have been more than ten years old. She was kneeling on a kitchen chair while she stirred something on the stove. Her hair was in pigtails. I froze.

"Come, sit," Gina said, pulling out one of the chairs at the green Formica table by the window at the back of the cramped kitchen.

As soon as I sat, I was face-to-face with Aunt Fran, who must have been about six years old. She was slouched at the other side of the table, watching my mother.

"Wow," I whispered. "It's so weird to see them like this."

"Yeah. They were cute."

Aunt Fran slid off the chair and flicked at something near her belly button as if pulling the elastic at the top of her underwear out of habit. My mother concentrated on stirring.

"How much longer?" Aunt Fran asked.

My young mother stopped stirring, lifted the wooden spoon out of the water, tapped it on the side of the pot, and rested it on the edge. She reached to her left and examined an egg timer. "Four minutes," she said in a little girl's high-pitched voice. She went back to stirring and wiping her hands on the apron tied around her waist. The apron was a Christmas-themed one with holly all over it.

It didn't look like it was Christmastime, though. There were no signs of it. No wreath. No tree. No stockings. But it was winter. I peeked at the barren trees through the kitchen window. Yet my mom and Aunt Fran were both in shorts and T-shirts.

"Get the forks, Frannie," my mother directed.

Aunt Fran opened a drawer and pulled out two forks and two spoons. "We need spoons to help us twirl," she announced.

My mother got down from the chair and dragged it to the other corner of the kitchen, letting its metal legs squeak across the linoleum floor. She jumped back up and opened a cabinet to take down two white bowls. "I don't need a spoon to twirl," she said, dragging the chair back over to the stove.

"Okay." Aunt Fran threw one of the spoons back into the drawer, mumbling, "I'm still little. I need a spoon to twirl my 'ronies."

The egg timer blared and scared all four of us.

"It's time!" My mother turned off the burner, jumped down from the chair, and grabbed a dish towel. Taking a deep breath, she wrapped the towel around the pot, covering the handles on each side.

How the hell is she going to carry that? I wanted to get up and help, but I knew that was not possible. We were just visitors. We were just observing.

As my mother lifted the heavy pot of boiling water, she took two quick steps to the chair Aunt Fran had pulled in front of the sink. She rested the boiling pot on the chair for a moment before lifting it again and pouring the contents into a colander in the sink.

I realized I was holding my breath as I watched her, not wanting my mother or Aunt Fran to get burned.

Aunt Fran seemed delighted as she pulled the chair back to the table. "We did it!" she yelled.

My mother was panting as she returned the empty pot to the stove. She wiped her brow with the dish towel. "Give me your bowl," she directed Aunt Fran, who dutifully brought both bowls over to the sink.

When they finally sat down to eat, I had to laugh at the four of us seated around the table. *Mother and daughter, and mother and daughter.*

Aunt Fran held a spoon in one hand and a fork in the other and attempted to twirl her linguini into a perfect bite, but it was too wet and kept falling off the fork.

My mother effortlessly did a perfect twirl with one hand, like an adult who'd been eating linguini for years. "Want a root beer?" she asked Aunt Fran as she chewed.

Aunt Fran didn't look up, still twirling, and mumbled, "Yeah."

My mother stood and opened the short, boxy white refrigerator. "There's only one left. We have to split it, okay?"

"Mmm, 'kay," Aunt Fran said, still twirling.

My mother, with the help of the kitchen chair again, retrieved two glasses and opened the root beer with a pop on the edge of the counter. "You're not eating anything," she said to Aunt Fran.

"It won't stay," Aunt Fran complained.

My mother used her own fork and cut Aunt Fran's linguini several times. "Eat it with a spoon, like soup."

Aunt Fran stared at the bowl as if trying to figure out how to eat it like soup when the back door flew open.

A dark-haired woman in a light-green wool dress and cat-eye glasses entered, carrying a paper bag in one hand and her car keys in the other, with her purse dangling from her wrist.

"Hi, Aunt Lu. Do you need help?" my mother asked, about to get out of her chair.

"No. Sit, eat," Aunt Lu said. "It's just gravy. I'll put it in the refrigerator. What are you..." She examined the bowls on the table.

Aunt Fran's big brown eyes were wide and attentive. "JoAnn made 'ronies."

"I see that. I see I was too late. No gravy? How do you have no gravy in the house?"

My mother shook her head, as if ashamed, and I wanted to jump to her defense. I wanted to scream at Aunt Lu, "She's ten years old and cooking for herself and her sister! Plain pasta isn't good enough?"

"Did you look in the icebox? Your father probably didn't defrost the batch I brought last week."

"I defrosted it," my mother said. "We finished it."

"Oh." Aunt Lu took a large plastic container out of the shopping bag and placed it in the freezer. "Why didn't you call me when you ran out?"

My mother shrugged.

"Well, keep eating. Don't let me interrupt you." Aunt Lu folded up the shopping bag as she examined her nieces, who looked at each other and then went back to their bowls. They finished their pasta in silence. My mother twirled, and my aunt Fran ate it like soup.

"When did their mom die?" I asked Gina.

"Two years before this," she said.

"Aunt Lu is their mother's sister? Grandma's sister?"

Gina nodded. We'd never met her. Not in life, and not on the other side.

Aunt Lu returned to the kitchen, holding a wicker laundry basket full of clothes. "JoAnn, I don't understand. These should be clean. You can't let it pile up like this. Ya hear?"

My mother nodded.

"I'm going to leave them by the tub. Okay?" Aunt Lu marched back out.

As my mother placed their dirty bowls and glasses in the sink, Aunt Lu walked back into the kitchen just as Aunt Fran pulled at her belly button region again.

"What are you doing? You did that before," Aunt Lu said. "Is your stomach bothering you?"

Aunt Fran shook her head.

"Why do you keep doing that?" Aunt Lu demanded.

Aunt Fran shrugged.

Aunt Lu, without hesitation, pulled down Aunt Fran's shorts while Aunt Fran looked pleadingly at my mother, who looked back as if to say, "I can't control Aunt Lu."

Aunt Lu tugged at the top elastic on Aunt Fran's little white underwear. "Oh, dear." She clucked. "When was the last time your father bought you new underwear?"

Aunt Fran shrugged again. Aunt Lu's eyes went to my mother, who was frozen. My heart hurt for her.

"All right, let me call Uncle Emil and tell him I'll be late," Aunt Lu lifted Aunt Fran's shorts back up. "Why don't you girls go get dressed—warm! Put boots on."

My mother and Aunt Fran ran out of the kitchen. Aunt Lu picked up the black rotary phone and dialed. "Hi. I'm at Tony's. I dropped the gravy off, but I have to take the girls to the store. I'll tell ya when I get home." Aunt Lu choked up. "If Rose could see this, she'd be turning over in her grave. All right, I gotta go. I'll be home later... Yeah... Yeah... Bye."

Aunt Lu placed the receiver down and exhaled as my mother and Aunt Fran walked into the kitchen. My mother was carrying a plastic bag that appeared heavy and handed it to Aunt Lu.

Aunt Lu looked puzzled. "What is this?"

"For our underwear," my mother said. "I need new ones too. If it's not enough, my father will pay you the rest. I will let him know how much."

Aunt Lu's shoulders dropped. "JoAnn, put this back, all right? Use it for something else. If it's that expensive, I'll talk about it with your father. Put this back. Let's get going."

My mother took the bag of change back and left the kitchen while Aunt Fran leaned against a cabinet, staring down.

"If Grandma Rose would have been turning over in her grave, why didn't she help from the other side?" I asked.

"Who do you think sent Aunt Lu?" Gina replied.

"Grandma sent the underwear police?"

"Yup. Grandma sent the panty police. She was also the gravy maker and delivery service."

"So how did she tell Aunt Lu to come here, to see this and do something?"

"They had meetings like this, like we have. Grandma asked her to help, and Aunt Lu did what she could, and Grandma appreciated it. Of course, Aunt Lu didn't know while she was awake that she was sent by Grandma Rose, but she had that gut feeling that she needed to help more, and she listened to it. Whenever she had the thought,

'Let me check on the girls today,' it wasn't out of nowhere. Everything comes from somewhere."

"I think I've seen enough for now," I said.

Gina put her hand on the back of my chair. "Want a root beer?"

I nodded.

• • ❦ • •

WE SIPPED OUR ROOT beers in silence for a while before I could articulate what I'd just witnessed. We were at a restaurant with a jukebox and a long row of comfortable booths.

"That was hard to see," I finally said.

"I know. But you had to."

"Why?"

"Follow these dots." Gina grabbed her straw and sipped from the malt glass filled with foamy root beer. "Your mother was basically a mother to her younger sister, my mother, and it wasn't easy, and she resented it at times. When your dad came along—your wonderful dad, love Uncle Dom—she jumped at the chance to get married and be taken care of after having to take care of herself and my mother for so long. So she got married and had a family of her own. Twenty-two years old. My mom was eighteen when she got married. They both couldn't wait to be part of a family again. Your mom, of course, had two girls, like her mother. And the older one—hear me out—is a lot like her. She knows that you can take care of yourself. So she coddled the younger one. But how did you see it? As favoritism. And what did that do to you? You've always sought her approval whether you consciously acknowledged it or not."

"You've mentioned that."

"You've been trying to prove your worth by doing your own thing, and when she and Orly didn't react the way you wanted—by admiring you for being a successful lawyer—you subconsciously tried to get them to approve of you on their terms. Remember how your mother pressured you to get married? At the time, you convinced yourself that Mark was the one. Did you marry him because you loved him or because, according to your mother, it was time to get married?"

"We've explored this idea already. I get it." I pumped the straw in my root beer.

"But now you get it a little more, I hope. You can understand her a little more. Marriage was security, based on her experience. She wanted that for her children. And little sisters need extra care, and big sisters are tough and self-sufficient. You've been doing a good job of letting things go. It's easier to do, though, when you know someone's story. This will only help."

"I'm still a work in progress, though."

"'Til the day you die. And that goes for everyone. But you are evolving." She lifted her root beer. "To the evolution of Jada."

I lifted my root beer tentatively. "Am I evolving?"

"Put it this way—one small step for Jada, one giant leap for her soul."

I clinked her glass to mine. "You have gotten so corny."

"Maybe that was always the real me. Maybe I was faking it. To Jada's evolution. And to corny. So fucking corny." She clinked her glass against mine with each word.

We sipped. "Oh, and hug her," Gina said. "Your mother may find it hard to take, but don't let it stop you."

"Okay." I suddenly saw my mother as someone who needed a hug instead of someone who couldn't stand them.

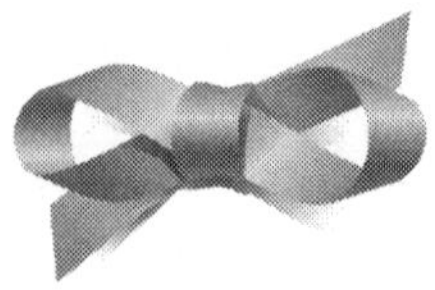

Chapter 26

As I was putting on my makeup, my mother appeared in the bathroom doorway.

"Let me take Ethan to school so you're not late," she said as I applied the last coat of lip gloss.

After Ethan had started preschool, both he and I cried every morning for the first month. Drop-off consisted of twenty minutes of saying our goodbyes, five minutes of waving, and five minutes of me trying not to interrogate Miss Lindsay about whatever I perceived to be a choking hazard. *Is that toy new? It comes with balls? Aren't those balls a little small?*

By the second month, Ethan cried for only ten minutes, but my emotional routine stayed the same. Now he was running into school, backpack bouncing behind him, leaving me, long forgotten, behind him. I practically had to beg him for a kiss goodbye now.

"Okay. Thank you," I said, carefully brushing a fleck of mascara from my cheek. "Don't forget—today is family picture day. I printed the one of me, Ethan, and Mark at his party at Long Island at Play, but I think I left it on the printer. Can you put it in his backpack?"

That photo showed the three of us smiling brightly by Ethan's *Buddy the Bulldozer* cake. *The calm before the shit storm.* No one studying that photo could have ever guessed what was brewing behind the scenes or what happened after the photo was taken.

Our custody arrangement stated that I had Ethan during the week and Mark had him every weekend. I wished it were every other weekend, but that was the arrangement that was best for Ethan. He wasn't shuffled anywhere during the week that might disrupt school or his sleep schedule. I wanted to include a photo of both myself and Mark because Ethan had started asking questions like, "Who is my new dad going to be? Is Alana my new mother?"

I had tried to instill a consistent message. "Mommy and Daddy are your parents, and we love you. Just because we don't live together anymore doesn't mean we're not a family."

In my towel, I sifted through all the clothes that didn't fit in the small closet along with Ethan's. There were hangers of pants, tops, and dresses all squeezed onto a clothes rack on wheels in the corner of the reading room.

What does one wear to sign divorce papers?

I settled on black pants and a charcoal-gray top. I knelt down to the shoebox that now stored all of my necklaces and grabbed my silver choker. As I clipped the back, I realized something. *My throat.* I touched it. That throat issue that made it feel like my own body was strangling me never happened anymore. *Thank God.*

Mark and I had agreed to meet at a Starbucks near Grand Central. The train from Queens was delayed. As I walked as fast as I could from the subway station, I thought of some of the things Veronica had said after I'd gotten back together with Mark before we got engaged—that I was doing it to please my mother and because I was afraid to be single. I remembered how shocked, horrified, and defensive I'd been. I still wouldn't change a thing. I knew now that it didn't matter what she or anyone might have said. It all had to happen the way it had happened, even if it meant I was now living with my parents and perfectly happy being single. I had my son to focus on and my new career direction. And I didn't care what anyone thought of that, including my mother.

Mark was seated at a table in the back, studying his phone, with the divorce papers in a neat pile in front of him.

"Well, hello there," I said as I approached and pulled out the chair across from him. "Sorry. The train was late."

"Hey," he said. "You wore your ring?"

Getting right to business.

We'd decided Mark would take our wedding bands and my engagement ring to a jeweler he knew next to Grand Central, and whatever we could get for them would go into Ethan's college fund.

"I had to scan the appraisal for your ring," he continued. "It was buried at the bottom of one of the boxes that are in my living room now. So I'll email you or text you as soon as I hear back."

"Okay, sounds good," I said as I pulled off my engagement ring and wedding band for the last time. I watched as he dropped them into a small manila envelope.

We could have signed the divorce papers electronically, but we'd had to meet up so I could give him the rings, so we'd done it all at once.

He tapped the papers in front of him. "I put tabs next to all the places for you to sign." He turned the papers around to face me and handed me his pen. He seemed nervous.

"I didn't get a chance to read the electronic version. I've been really busy with my new clients and Ethan and everything, but are there any changes?" I glanced up to see him pinching his eyebrow.

"There's one."

"Oh. Okay. Well, I'm about to sign, so I'm glad you're telling me now."

"I think you'll be happy with the change. You see, Alana is pregnant."

I opened my mouth, but no words came out. I had no reason to be shocked. *Why shouldn't she be pregnant?* "Congratulations," I said.

"And Alana thinks that, with the new baby, it'll be hard to have Ethan every *single* weekend."

"Is that what she thinks?" I asked sarcastically. Of course I was happy to not have to hand Ethan over every weekend, but I still took offense that he might be "too much" with a shiny new baby and all.

"So would an every-other-weekend arrangement work?"

"Sure. Of course. When is she due?"

We chatted about due dates and C-sections and Ethan as an older brother while I kept flipping and signing and initialing. "Any other changes? I'm trusting you here."

"You can trust me."

Is that a dig? I paused. I wanted to say, "Again, I'm sorry I hurt you, but as I recall, lucky for you, you had one foot out the door at the time anyway."

But I didn't. I just finished signing the papers then handed them to him.

He put them in his briefcase and tucked the pen in his jacket. "I'll drop these off at the courthouse. I'm sure you've got to get back home."

"Thank you," I said. "So I guess that's it."

He shrugged. "That's it."

"Too bad we're here and not at a bar. Feels like we should have a toast or do a shot. Something ceremonial. Something involving alcohol."

"I don't drink."

"Yes, I know. It was a joke, Mark."

"Oh. Ha." He stood.

"Well," I said as I extended my hand. "It was good being married to you. Thanks for Ethan."

He laughed, and we hugged. As people rushed in, waited in line to order their morning coffees, stared impatiently at their phones, we held each other in the corner. We hugged for the first time in a long time in the corner of Starbucks, divorce papers in tow.

As I headed to the train back to Queens, I grabbed my phone and tried to come up with a witty status update. How about, "Divorce papers signed. Ready to mingle"?

Nah. Not funny, and more importantly, not true. I was not ready to mingle.

I clicked out of Frontbook then held my finger over the little X on the app and deleted it.

• • ❧ • •

"SO, THEY'RE BACK TOGETHER?" a guy on the train asked.

Huh?

He sat several seats to my left and across the aisle, but there was no mistaking he was talking to me. He was pointing in my direction, smiling, and we were the only ones on the train.

"What?" I asked.

"They're back together?"

"Who?"

"Your magazine. Those two." He flicked his chin.

"Oh." I glanced at the cover of the magazine I was holding. It featured an actor and actress who had notoriously broken up a few months ago but were now reunited. "Yeah. Looks that way." I shrugged.

"That's nice," he said.

"I guess." *And I guess if you don't shut up, I will switch cars at the next stop.*

"My cousin went to high school with him. He said he was a good guy."

I glanced up again, lowering my magazine. *Should I tell this annoying guy in no uncertain terms that I just signed divorce papers, found out my son will have a half-sibling, and really just want to enjoy a quiet ride home, reading my trashy celebrity magazine? Maybe not. I'll let it go. I'll walk toward the door and switch cars at the next stop.*

Just as I was about to stand, I noticed something that pushed my butt back in the seat.

"Where'd they go to school?" I asked.

Chatty train guy over here is the furthest thing from an ogre. He had blue eyes and a chiseled chin. I'd never understood what was so great about a chiseled chin, until now.

"Somewhere in South Jersey." He got up and moved to the seat next to me. Mr. Chiseled Chin smelled good, too, like soap. "Supposedly, his dad is a teacher and still teaches at the high school. You never picture these stars with normal families."

"Yeah," was all I could say. *Would it be weird if I leaned over and sniffed him? Yes, it would. Do not sniff a man on the train. Act normal.*

"You live in Queens?" he asked.

"Yeah." *Shit! Think of something else to say!* "You?"

"No. I live in the city, but I have a client in Queens. I don't usually make house calls, but I do for her. She's in her seventies and lives alone. She's a sweet lady."

"You're a doctor?"

"Chiropractor."

"Nice. So you can straighten me out?"

"Back issues? Or daddy issues?"

I love him. "Mommy issues."

He chuckled. "Can't help you there. So, what were you doing in the city?"

"I just signed my divorce papers."

"Oh." He leaned back. "I'm sorry to hear that."

"Don't be. It was the right thing. It's all good."

"Good." He smiled. "I don't know Queens that well other than my client's neighborhood. Where's a good place for lunch?"

The train reached my stop at that moment.

"This is my stop." I stood, and so did he. I had to hurry off before the doors shut. "I can text you the names of a couple of places."

"Let me give you my number," he said as the doors beeped alerting us that they were about to close.

I grabbed my phone to put his number in my contacts, but the doors began to shut. I hopped onto the platform. He reached out his arm to stop them from shutting, and I got another whiff of his soapy scent.

He reached into his pocket, pulled out his card, and handed it to me.

I snatched it and waved as the doors shut and the train departed. Then I bounded up the steps of the station and squinted as the sun hit my eyes. I put on my sunglasses and examined his card.

Charles Loray, Chiropractor. Greenleaf Chiropractic. 188 Spring St., New York, NY 10012

• • ❧ • •

MY MOM, DAD, ETHAN, and I sat around the dinner table—our new normal.

"Ethan is a very good nurse," my mother said.

"He is?" I asked.

"While you and Daddy were working, Debbie from the hospital came. She laid out all of my pills and took my blood pressure. Ya know, the whole shebang. And as she's doing my pressure, Ethan lined all the pill bottles up, all in a nice row."

My mother still had a nurse come every month to check her blood counts. So far, every test indicated the cancer hadn't returned. She had gained weight and seemed pretty much back to normal.

"Good job, Ethan."

"He held my hand when she put the needle in my arm. Ya know, to take the blood? Right, Ethan?"

Ethan was preoccupied with his macaroni.

"Answer, Ethan." I nudged him. "You did that?"

"Uh-huh." He moved one noodle to the edge, and then another noodle, until three were lined up in a row along the edge of his dish. "Where do these come from?"

Oh, come on with this question. I thought we were past the "Where do things come from?" stage. I couldn't wait for him to read so I could say, "Google that shit, kid."

"The pasta factory," I said.

"How do they make it?"

I don't fucking know. "With a machine. We'll look up a video later."

"My mother used to make her own macaroni," my mom said. "With a little machine. I'd help her line them all up on the table, each little bow tie." My mother spoke to Ethan in a way I'd never heard her speak to anyone before—sweetly but sincerely.

"She had a machine?" he asked. "What did it look like?"

"It was metal, and it kind of had this crank that ya turned on the side. She would attach it to the edge of the table and put the pasta in one side, and out would come the bowtie on the other side."

"Bow tie?"

"The macaroni. Ya know, bowties? We had to pinch each one in the middle to give it that bow-tie shape."

"Then what?" Ethan asked.

"We cooked it."

"You cooked it or your mom?"

"Well, I was about your age, so my mom probably cooked it."

"Where is she now?"

"She's in heaven."

Ethan didn't know where to go with that, so he returned to the ziti lined up on his plate and shoved one into his mouth.

"She went to heaven when I was just a few of years older than you," my mother said.

I wanted to hug my mother, but she wasn't a hugger. "You were so young," I said. "I'm sorry that happened to you. So little."

"Oh, Jada." My mother swiped her hand in my direction. Any ounce of tenderness she'd just had for Ethan was not transferred to me. "It was so long ago."

"Still. It was your mother. She died, and you were just a little kid. That had to have some impact on your life."

"Sure." My mother took a bite of macaroni and shrugged. "It made me tough, and I made you tough."

Tough? In that moment, I saw her pain in a new way, like she'd been hiding it for most of her life under teased hair, red nails, and loud opinions, but there it was. She was a little girl who'd lost her mom and, a few years later, her dad.

I don't care if you're not a hugger. I will hug you. Hard! I stood up from the table and walked to my mother. I leaned down and put my arms around her.

"What the hell are you doing?" she asked. "What has gotten into you? Get off me."

I stayed there. "I'm sorry that happened to you."

"Jada, sit back down."

"No."

"I'm trying to eat!"

"Too bad."

"Jada!"

From the corner of my eye, I could see Ethan stand up and walk over. He put his arms around her too.

My father laughed. And then Ethan giggled, and I said, "Group hug!" That made Ethan laugh harder, which finally broke my mother. She relaxed her shoulders and laughed as she said, "Sit the hell back down, would ya? Have you lost your mind?"

Ethan fist-bumped my father on the way back to his chair, which I was glad about so he didn't feel left out.

My mother worked her fingers through her bouffant, which we had apparently messed up when hugging her. "What has gotten into you people? Eat your dinner."

I ate my dinner like my mother said.

"Ethan, want a spoon?" she asked him. "You can eat those 'ronies like soup."

Chapter 27

The next day, as I sat in my basement office, I texted the chiropractor to the cell phone number on his card.

Jada: *Hello, Dr. Loray. This is Jada, the trashy-magazine-reading woman you met on the train. It was really nice to meet you. I hope you made it to your appointment on time. Here are some great lunch places in Queens: Max's Deli, Wabi Sushi, Cordillo's.*

He replied an hour later.

Charlie: *Hi, Jada. Thanks for the recommendations. It was really nice to meet you too. If you're around this weekend, I'd love to meet up and talk about Hollywood breakups. And maybe baby bumps. I love baby bumps.*

Charlie: *P.S. I have a sister. She likes celebrity gossip. I don't actually know what a baby bump is. Maybe you can tell me in person, but I think if the kid has a bump on his head, the parents should love him anyway. Just my opinion.*

Charlie made me laugh! I had to share this news with someone. I sent a text to Veronica.

Jada: *After signing divorce papers in the city the other day, I met a cute chiropractor on the train, and we just texted!*

Except, I sent it to Charlie by accident. *Fuck!*

I froze. For two excruciating minutes, I contemplated what to write after that. *Blushing emoji and an oops?*

But then I received a text.

Charlie: *She's newly divorced, has dark hair and a great smile.*

That was immediately followed by another text.

Charlie: *Oops. Can't believe I did that.*

Jada: *Me neither.*

I tapped a finger on my phone for a moment, thinking. Then I typed out another text.

Jada: *She has a kid too.*

I figured I might as well tell him everything up front.

Charlie: *Cool.*

Cool, he was. And that was a good start.

I met Charlie at eight at a restaurant called Jake's. I took an Uber there since I could not endure the idea of Charlie picking me up and meeting my parents and Ethan.

Too awkward. Too early.

He drove from the city and texted me that he was waiting at the bar when my Uber pulled up. I stepped out, and my stomach flipped as I opened the large brass door and walked into Jake's. The clamor of music and chatter and glasses and dishes clinking rushed toward me when I stepped inside. But it all faded away the minute I spotted Charlie.

He stood and greeted me with a hug. "You look great." He was wearing a black sweater and jeans. I grinned. "Thank you. So do you." *Here I am—a lawyer, mother, grown woman—and I'm squirming inside like a teenager.*

"Do you want something warm to drink? They have hot apple cider, and it's spiked."

"Sounds perfect." I examined his chiseled chin as I tried to gracefully hoist myself up onto the barstool.

"So how long have you lived in Queens?"

I'd forgotten he had blue eyes.

"Too long. Ha. I live with my parents." I waited for his horrified reaction, but he didn't seem fazed. "The original plan was to be back in the city or back on Long Island by now, but a lot of my clients are in Queens, and my son loves—adores—his new preschool." *And with the rates I'm now getting paid, I will probably be living with them for a while.* "How long have you lived in the city?"

"Twelve years. I love my preschool too."

We both laughed. *What a weirdo. I like it.*

By dinner, I knew we were the same age, he had grown up in Pennsylvania, had never been married, had played baseball in college, loved the Yankees, and loved to ski.

And he thought aliens had landed in Roswell.

"Me too!" I shouted. The hot apple cider with alcohol was coursing through my bloodstream.

"I only have one other friend I talk about this stuff with," he said. "No one else is that interested."

"Same. I blame my one friend too. We're not the type to believe in conspiracies, but we like reading about them."

"I don't believe in them either, but it's fascinating to read about."

"Especially the anal probes," I said seriously.

He spat his beer out.

We talked for hours. I could have talked to Charlie all night. We talked so long that I lost track of time. Two couples had sat to our right and finished their meals. As the second couple stood to leave, I checked my phone for the first time all night. It was 11:11.

"Shit! I told my parents I'd be home by eleven."

"Ha. I better drive you home then, before you get grounded."

He paid the bill and, as we walked to his car, it felt warm out, and I hoped that meant I wasn't too drunk.

As he turned onto my street, I let out a quiet sigh of relief to see that the lights were out. *Whew. They're all asleep.*

"Thank you. Get home safe." I gave him a quick peck on the lips and could see his blue eyes light up, even in the dark.

"I'll text you when I get home," he said.

"Good." I walked up my parents' driveway, kicking the neighbors' leaves that were strewn across my parents' property. *My mother will have something to say about this tomorrow. I can already hear her. "The friggin' Meyersons."*

They'd been my parents' neighbors for over thirty years but hadn't spoken in twenty-five years, ever since Mrs. Meyerson refused to return my mother's lasagna dish, claiming it had cracked when she was cleaning it, and she'd had to throw it out. Yet she'd never offered to replace it.

I turned the key and gently shut the door behind me.

"How was it?" My mother was wide-awake in her bathrobe on the couch.

"Were you watching from the window?" I asked.

"No!" She adjusted the belt on her robe. "Nice car."

"Good night." I started up the stairs, trying to walk away from my mother quickly but trying to be quiet enough not to wake Ethan.

"I hope the front steps didn't look sloppy to your friend. The friggin' Meyersons used their damn leaf blower again, and I couldn't rake because I had to give Ethan his bath, and then it was dark out."

"Thank you. And it's okay. It's fall, Ma. There are supposed to be leaves everywhere."

I headed upstairs and quietly got ready for bed. Then I crawled into my old twin bed, next to my sister's old twin bed, where my son was sound asleep.

This was definitely not where I'd expected to be at this age, at this time in my life, but I was happier than I had ever been in Long Island, in our big house, working at the law firm in the city. I loved having dinner with my parents and Ethan every night. I loved seeing my nieces more often. I loved spending time with Orly, even though she grated on me, but we reminisced and laughed a lot about our childhood. I loved seeing Ethan go to preschool. I loved fighting landlords and helping people who really needed my help. And I knew I was happy because despite all that had gone wrong, I wasn't constantly wondering where it had all gone wrong.

Chapter 28

"You're right," Gina said.

"About what?" I asked.

We were at the restaurant I'd gone to with Charlie, at one of the tables by the window, splitting the mushroom-and-artichoke flatbread.

"There *are* supposed to be leaves everywhere."

"I know, right? It's fall."

"No! It's a sign. It's my sign. For you!"

"It is? I don't believe in that stuff."

"Ha! Yeah, well, you'd better start believing. Do you know how much energy I've been exuding, trying to get through to you? Look for the leaves."

"And I'm supposed to believe they're from you?"

"Yes! Signs that we're here. We're with you. You're on the right path!"

"You come down from heaven and plant them on the lawn?"

"No, smart-ass. I use my energy to make them appear in your path. And it's not always literal leaves. You didn't bother to notice the chiropractor's business name on his card? Greenleaf Chiropractic!"

I rolled my eyes.

"Right in front of your face, and you don't even notice. But at least you followed through with him." Gina took a big bite, and a mushroom fell onto her plate.

I felt a warm rush as I thought about Charlie. "I like him."

"I know." She smiled. "And you're right about not being where you expected but not wanting to change it either."

"You do read minds."

"No. Hearts." She was wearing a gray T-shirt that had an image of a heart with arms and legs. It was holding a cigarette and appeared to be tap dancing. "You're getting there, Jada. When you deleted Frontbook, I cheered."

"Can it be all good times from here now? I could use a little fun."

Gina was about to answer but couldn't finish.

"Take me out to the ball game!" Grandma and Grandpa strolled in, singing. He was wearing a big foam number-one finger on his hand, and she was wearing a baseball cap.

"Buy me some peanuts and Cracker Jack. I don't care if I never get back."

"Let me root, root, root for the home team!" Grandma inspected our flatbread. "Whatd'ya got here? Pizza?"

I observed how happy and carefree they seemed. *How could they be after dying young and leaving two little kids?*

"It's flatbread," I said.

"Looks like pizza to me, and don't mind if I do." Grandpa ripped off his foam finger and started to grab a slice.

I stopped his hand. "Underwear."

"What about it? I preferred boxers," he said.

"Where were you when your daughters needed you? They were cooking dinner for themselves and seemed neglected."

"Ah." He made himself comfortable next to me, sighing as if he'd been expecting this difficult conversation. "Well, where was I? Working to keep a roof over all of our heads. And I was sick too, though I didn't know it until the very end. Not that it's an excuse. I was doing the best I could, but you're right. I could have done better."

"You didn't see things from his perspective. You didn't see his story," Gina said.

"I saw two neglected kids," I said.

"It's amazing, Jada," my grandfather said. "You get here, and you get to review your life and all that ya learned, and you see how it all played out. You're not the same person you are when you're living."

"She is." I motioned to Gina. "Well, kind of."

"What I mean is, you're the same person but without all the stuff that weighed you down in life, without the heartaches, the mistakes, the misjudgments, the wrong beliefs about who you are. I was a widower, trying to make ends meet, and I made mistakes. Did I know my daughters' underwear didn't fit? Those were the things their mother handled. Did I make sure they had enough money for their weddings before I died? Both of my daughters? Yes. I worked around the clock for that. I had my priorities out of whack, and some things you don't see until you see them from here."

I nodded.

"You never thought you would like living with your parents, did you?" my grandmother asked.

"Like is a strong word." I chewed a bite of flatbread. "I'm kidding. I do feel a little closer to my mother, and I never thought I'd say that. It's not in the same way she and Orly are like best friends, all up in each other's business. But I do kind of like having my parents in my business in a way, helping with Ethan and waiting up for me when I went out with Charlie. It makes me feel less alone."

My grandfather patted my hand. "When you were living in that big house on Long Island, if I told you that one day, you're going to be back living with your parents in Queens, not working as a big, fancy lawyer in Manhattan, and that you're not going to hate it, you would have told me I was nuts."

"Bonkers," I agreed.

"And look at you now."

"Let's not get crazy. My mother and I aren't exactly best friends. And my sister still annoys the crap out of me."

"When you hugged your mother, we all cheered then too," Gina said.

Grandpa shot his foam finger into the air.

"So what's next?" I asked.

"No 'what's next?'" Grandma said. "How about 'Let me enjoy the right now.'"

"And it's not a competition," Grandpa added. "It's not whether you win or lose."

"It's how I play the game." I finished the corny line as a sort of peace offering.

"Yup." He picked up his foam finger and tapped me on the head. Then he pointed it sharply in the other direction and declared, "Pizzas for everyone! Extra mushroom."

When the new flatbreads were served, I grabbed a slice while it was still hot and gobbled it.

"Slow down, Jada," Grandpa said. "There's more where that came from, and we're not going anywhere."

I listened. I slowed down and enjoyed every bite.

Chapter 29

My mother died on a Wednesday morning. And it didn't happen in the way any of us expected. She didn't die from the cancer at all.

"Why wouldn't Mark come for Thanksgiving?" she had asked that morning as we stood in the kitchen.

I stirred my oatmeal. "Because we're divorced."

"He's still Ethan's father."

"I know, but he's going to his pregnant fiancée's for Thanksgiving, and I'm completely fine with that."

"Where does her family live?"

"Connecticut."

"And Ethan likes her?"

"Yes." *Does she like him? I don't know.* She wanted him around less, so that wasn't a good sign, but I was not about to reveal that Alana was the reason for the change in our custody arrangement. I didn't need my mother disparaging Alana to Ethan. That would add a whole other complication none of us needed.

"And she has red hair?"

Is she kidding me?

I glared at her. "Yes," I hissed. "She has red hair. Is that okay?"

She grabbed her left arm. "My arm. Oh, what is this? It feels—something doesn't feel right."

"What does it feel like?"

"Something's wrong," she said as she knelt to the floor.

"Ma, what is it?" I shot to the floor. "Here, sit. I'll get a chair."

She squeezed her arm and laid her head on the floor. "No." Then she closed her eyes.

"Ma! Ma!" I screamed over and over. She did not respond. I grabbed the house phone on the wall and dialed 911.

I'd never felt so alone in the world. And oddly, I'd never felt so young either. When I spoke to the 911 operator, I may have sounded like an adult. "Please send someone to 864 Berner Street immediately. My mother is having an emergency. She is fifty-nine years old. Uterine cancer survivor. But she just complained of an ache in her left arm and went to the floor. She didn't fall or hit her head, but she's not responding."

But inside, I was screaming, "It's my mommy! Please! Send someone!"

When the paramedics arrived, I briefed them again.

Help her! Do something! Please!

They did all they could.

Chapter 30

"She survived cancer and then died of sudden cardiac arrest. Un-fucking-believable." I shook my head as I stood at the back of the church, staring down the aisle at the coffin in front of the altar.

Charlie stood next to me, and Ethan was on my right. I hadn't intended to introduce Ethan to Charlie so soon, but we'd been spending a lot of time together, and they'd accidentally met when Charlie dropped me off one night and Ethan ran outside in his pajamas.

After that and after learning Alana was pregnant, Ethan was filled with confusion and questions. Each child had difficulties with divorce at different stages. Ethan had breezed through separation and moving to Queens, but now that new people were being introduced, he was struggling to figure it all out.

"So Charlie is my dad now. Now that Daddy will have a new baby, right?"

I'd tried to explain that wasn't how it worked. He seemed to understand but refused to spend the weekend with Mark. Perhaps not surprisingly, Mark had acquiesced a little too easily.

We walked down the aisle and sat near the front of the church. My father, sister, brother-in-law, and nieces were to my left. Aunt Fran, Andrea, and the rest of the family were a row behind us. Mark and Alana were sitting behind them.

"Where is Grandma?" Ethan asked.

"In heaven," I said.

"Who's in there?" He pointed at the coffin.

"Grandma."

He was understandably perplexed.

"I'll explain later. We have to be quiet now. They're going to start."

I glanced behind me to see if my father's family had made it on time from New Jersey, and I spotted Dan and Karen. *What are they doing here?*

As the mass started, I wondered how Dan and Karen would know of my mother's passing. *Why would they come? Do they want me to come back to the firm? What would I even say to that? And is this really what I'm thinking about at my mother's funeral?*

I turned to the other side. That was when I saw Danielle. *What is she doing here?* The last time I'd seen her, she was sitting with Melody and Jessica at Long Island at Play. But a few days later, she'd sent me a text saying that she hoped we could still be friends and keep in touch. I'd replied that I would like that very much. It was nice of her to come, especially by herself.

Who else is going to pop into my mother's funeral? I can't take much more. I just want to go home and go to sleep.

In accordance with my mother's wishes—since she'd believed at one point that she was dying of cancer, she'd given this some thought—we were not going to have a burial. We would just have a mass for her, and then we would have the repast—at Cordillo's, of course—but no burial. We were all fine with that, as that was what she wanted.

I remembered what she'd said after her surgery. "I do not want everyone standing in dirt and watching me go into the ground. Do I want people standing around, watching me go to the bathroom? No. Same thing. Give me some privacy."

"So you don't even want me, Daddy, and Jada there for the burial?" Orly had asked.

"No. No burial. It's so morbid."

"This conversation is morbid," I said.

"But the coffin will be at the mass?" Orly was still trying to get the logistics down. My mother and Orly were typically traditional about weddings and christenings and other family affairs. My mother bucking the trend had Orly in a tizzy.

"Sure. You can have my coffin at the mass. My coffin, which you, Orly, will probably pick out, and which you, Jada, will probably think is hideous, your favorite word."

"When was the last time you heard me use that word?" I asked.

"I don't know how old you were, but you used to say it all the time."

"Used to," I pointed out.

My mother imitated me. "You're going to wear that? That's hideous. You're hanging that on the wall? That's hideous."

She and Orly had laughed, and I'd smiled so as not to be a completely poor sport.

Now, as I sat in church, wishing I could hear my mother laugh again, I realized they were right. I used to use that word a lot. It was meant to show how different—and superior, in my mind at that time—I was to them, their little band of two that never left Queens.

But I'd changed. And not just because I was back in Queens.

Father Bertoli talked, and I was sure his eulogy was lovely, but I didn't hear any of it. When the mass was over, the two iced coffees I'd drunk to shake off the Tylenol PM I'd taken the night before kicked in, and I had to use the bathroom.

As people filed out, I worked my way through the crowd and toward the bathroom. I hurried down the steps and almost knocked over Dan and Karen.

"Hey," I said. "I saw you guys during the mass. I can't believe you would come."

"What? Of course we're here," Dan said.

"We're so sorry, Jada," Karen said.

"Wow. Thank you. It really means a lot. I've got to pee, but I want to talk. You'll come to the repast?"

"Yes. We miss you," Dan said.

"I miss you too." I said. "Actually, not really." Dan's head tilted like a confused dog. "But I miss busting your chops."

He laughed.

I faced Karen. "And I miss you being so nice that it was annoying. But I could never come back now."

"You're not invited back," Dan said.

"Gee, thanks. Well, you wouldn't even believe what I'm doing now anyway," I said as a few of my cousins on my father's side brushed past me and headed up the steps.

"We really miss you, though," Dan said. "And we're sorry."

"Well, thank you for coming. We'll talk more at Cordillo's. It's really good food." I started to walk away but turned back. "Hey, how did you know about my mom?"

"Frontbook," Karen said.

"I'm not on that anymore."

"You were tagged in someone's post with the obituary."

Tagged! Fucking Frontbook.

I finally made it downstairs and opened the door to the bathroom then almost bumped headfirst into Veronica.

I fell into her arms. "Oh my God. It is so good to see you."

"How are you?"

"Tired." I exhaled. "And I've got to pee."

She stepped to the side. "Go for it."

I headed toward the stall then turned around. "Hey. How do you know a sign is meant for you?"

She thought for a moment. "It's like falling in love. You just know."

"Well then, I'm screwed." I pushed through a stall door.

"Just ask. Ask, and you shall receive. You'll see," she called. "Want me to wait for you?"

"No," I said from the stall. "I'll see you at Cordillo's, right?"

"Of course." I quickly finished and headed upstairs to find my family when, at the top step, I ran into Todd.

"Oh my God. What the *hell* are you doing here?" I shouted.

He was stone-faced. "I saw the obituary on Frontbook. A friend of a friend of your sister's."

Fucking Frontbook.

"I wanted to pay my respects."

"Pay your respects?" *My old coworkers, maybe. Old and new friends, yes. But him? What the hell is he doing here?*

"I wanted to do something nice. I wanted to be respectful to you. I don't know."

"Then send a card."

"It's been awhile, but I still think about how it ended really ugly."

"You know what's ugly? This tie." I pointed at his paisley-and-leaf tie.

He glanced down. "It's for fall."

"It's ugly. Go home to your family."

"Jessica left."

"Aha." I shook my head.

"I really just wanted to say I'm sorry about your mom, and I'm sorry for everything. Are you holding up okay?"

"Yeah. I am." I held onto the stair railing.

He nodded. "Good. You know, when my mom died, I didn't cry for weeks. Maybe it was because I was young and distracted by things in college, but I know other people who experienced the same thing. I thought you might be the same way."

I actually hadn't cried. "Thank you for the info. Sorry about Jessica. I mean, good for her, but anyway, goodbye." I walked past him and then whipped around. "Listen, the repast, it's at a great restaurant." I stared at him. "But you're not stupid enough to show up, right?" I didn't want Charlie wondering who this guy was and then learning it was Todd, who I'd told him all about when we recapped past-relationship history. And I certainly didn't want him to think we were still in touch.

"You haven't changed, Jada."

"Actually, Todd, you have no idea. Goodbye."

"Goodbye," he said quietly.

I walked away.

"You look beautiful," he said.

I whipped around. "Oh, come on! Are you fucking kidding me?" I screamed in church.

The vestibule got quiet. I glanced around, and my eyes met Charlie's. He was standing with Mark, Alana, Ethan, my father, and Orly. Each one of them was wide-eyed.

There was my ex-husband, my ex-whatever, and my new boyfriend all staring back at me.

Charlie came over. "Is everything okay?" he asked.

"Yeah, well, you know my ex-husband." I motioned to Mark. "And now, here's my ex... whatever. You know, that big San Francisco mess I told you about. I don't know what he's doing here. He's an idiot."

"Hi. I'm the idiot." Todd stepped forward to shake Charlie's hand.

"Oh, ew." I reached out and chopped their handshake. "Stop that. Okay, listen. Let me give you a little update since I'm not on social media anymore. I'm really happy. I live at my parents' house in Queens. I share a bedroom with my son, and we both sleep in twin beds. I lost my job in the city, and now my clients are elderly, and I spend my days threatening their landlords, and I'm happy. Yes, my mother just died, but I'm happy. My child is healthy. My new boyfriend is... normal, in my eyes at least. Really, really happy."

I reached for Charlie's hand, and we walked out the door.

• • ❧ • •

AT CORDILLO'S, I SIPPED a Diet Coke—I didn't have much of an appetite—and chatted with Veronica and Danielle. I also spent most of my time trying to get Ethan to look in my direction and away from Charlie. I was asking him if he wanted to eat his pasta from the pasta factory with a spoon when Orly tapped my shoulder.

"Can I ask you something?" she asked.

"What's up?"

"Can we go in the hallway?"

"Sure." I excused myself from the table.

After we stepped into the hallway, between the kitchen and the dining area, Orly said, "Listen, the funeral director gave Daddy her rings—her engagement ring and her wedding band—and also the bracelet with the three diamonds."

I must have appeared as baffled as I was.

"You know, the one with the diamonds that are in a row."

"I know it. I just don't know why we're talking about this right now."

"Well, I figured you'd want one of those. Those were her nicest pieces of jewelry."

I squeezed the bridge of my nose. "Orly, this has been an insane day. Can we talk about this later? Why are you bringing this up now?"

"Because Daddy just got them, and he's holding them in his pocket, and he asked me. I'm being considerate."

"Considerate how?"

One of the servers carrying a tray of baked ziti scooted us to the near corner of the hallway.

"By not taking all three. We're sisters, remember?"

"Okay, well, listen, you can have all three. I don't care."

"I thought you would care now."

"Now that she's gone? I guess I'm just not as sentimental as you. Keep it all. I mean it."

"No. I mean, now that you're like the rest of us. You used to have your big diamond engagement ring, and now you're like, on our level. I thought you could use some jewelry. I thought you'd want one of these pieces."

Uh. Okay.

"Orly, I like being one of the 'regular people.'" I held my hand over my heart. "I'm happy. I don't need a big house or a big ring. And I don't need any of Mommy's jewelry. Keep it. You were her favorite. I could never compete."

"And you were the star. I could never compete."

Interesting.

"Well, now, according to you, I'm one of the 'regular people' so—"

"I'm just saying, your grades. All your success. I was never good enough. And you always made me feel it. And she always bragged about you."

"Who?"

"Mommy!" It came out in a shrill scream as she cried at the same time.

"She *did*?"

"Yes! To everyone."

Who knew? When? Where? To who? I couldn't ask now. Or maybe ever.

I touched her arm as she wiped her eyes. "Thank you," I said.

"For what?" Orly asked through a stuffy nose.

"For bringing supplies to Ethan's party."

She removed her hand from her eyes to get a better look at me. "What?"

"And for trying to help me, you know, when I got drunk. And for just always being a good sister. For even wanting us to go on vacation with you to the shore. That was really nice of you to even ask. It's nice that you want to spend time with me. Thank you."

"I love you."

"I love you too. I'm sorry if I ever made you feel like you weren't good enough. You're a great sister, and mother too. And you were Mommy's best friend. Thank you for that. She needed a friend. It's good to have friends." I hugged her.

And for the first time in our adult life, she cried on my shoulder, like friends do.

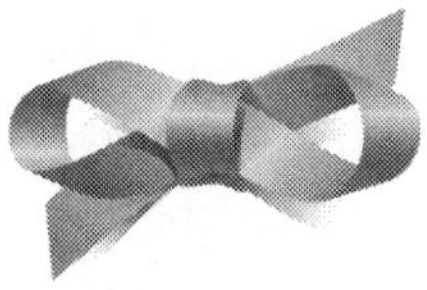

Chapter 31

"I can say it now because"—my mother paused to dunk a piece of fried calamari in marinara sauce—"you know."

"Know what?" I asked. It was so good to see her, healthy and full in her face. Her hair was done, her nails were done, and she was wearing all her jewelry. It was still her.

"You know, Jada. Oh, these are fantastic. Are you not eating?"

"What are you talking about?"

"She means she's here now," Gina responded, leaning back against the booth we were in. She wore a black T-shirt with a snake wrapped around a leaf. "She can say what she couldn't say before. She can say it more easily now."

We were at Basto's, an Italian restaurant in the city where we used to go on the rare occasions that my parents and Orly would come into the city to see me when I lived there.

"So say it," I said.

"Are you not eating?" My mother stuffed two calamari rings into her mouth.

"I'm not hungry."

"It doesn't count here, ya know."

I smiled. "I know."

"These are perfect." My mother held up a crispy golden ring up to the light.

I leaned in. "It doesn't seem like you're able to say whatever it is that's supposedly easier to say now."

She put the calamari ring down and reached across the table to grab my hand. "I love you."

I pulled my hand back. "Well, I love you too," I croaked.

She pulled my hand back in. "I love ya with all my heart and soul. And you never heard me say it because I wasn't able to. I just didn't understand ya, Jada. And you didn't understand me. And I'm sorry. But that was the thing. That was our thing. That's what we had to learn. I know that now. I'm sorry if I ever made ya feel unloved or if I favored your sister or anything like that. I did love you, and I still love you. I love you with everything that is in me, and it hasn't died."

"Thank you." I grabbed a calamari ring and chewed furiously. "You're right. These are delicious."

My mother stood up and scooted in next to me in the booth. She put her arm around me, and I touched her hand. "Do you want me to sing to you?" she asked.

"What the—who are you? Where's my mother? You look like her. You smell like her. Where's JoAnn?"

"It's still me," my mother explained. "But I know I never sang to you, ya know, when you were little."

"Oh God, no. You're going to bust out in 'Hush Little Baby.' Please don't. I like to eat and hear about how much you love me, but don't make me cringe. It'll ruin it."

Over eggplant parmigiana and chicken marsala, we talked about what was going on with Ethan, Mark, my dad, Orly, Paul, the girls, and Aunt Fran and her family. We discussed how everyone was handling her passing.

"Aunt Fran is a wreck." I shook my head, thinking of my sweet aunt crying over my mom.

"She'll be okay," my mother said.

"It's not easy," I said. "She lost her sister."

"Aunt JoAnn," Gina piped in. "Now that you're here, wouldn't you agree that when you look at your loved ones who are still living, nothing makes you happier than to see them happy?"

"Yes!" my mother shouted.

Grandpa Tony walked through the door. "Is the calamari that good?" Grandma Rose was behind him, carrying a cake box.

We hugged and kissed, and when I turned around, our dishes had been cleared. Grandma Rose rested the cake box on the table.

"You forgive him?" I asked my mother while motioning to my grandfather.

"Yes," she said. "I do. Like you and me, sometimes people can have a better relationship with someone after they've passed than they did in life. You'll see. You may not remember these meetings, but your thoughts of me will change."

Grandma Rose tapped the cake box. "Open it."

"Why me?" I asked. "Shouldn't Mommy open it? I'm assuming it's a 'Welcome to the Other Side' cake."

"We did that already." Grandma Rose waved her hand. "Whatta ya thinkin'? This is the first time we saw our daughter here? No. You open it, Jada Ann."

I lifted the box cover. It was a white cake with shiny, thick frosting and sugary pink roses with big leaves. Gina reached past me and swiped up a pink rose with her index finger. "Remember these cakes from that bakery on Queens Boulevard? We used to fight over who got the rose."

"Nothing changes," my mother said. "The two of them, still busting each other's chops."

I met Gina's eyes. "Thank you for everything."

"I was starting to think you forgot to thank me." She sat back and reached for another rose. "Kidding. You don't have to thank me. But I did teach you well. Not teach, guided. I've been guiding you well."

"Very well. Thank you."

"Here." My mother swiped up one of the roses and put it on my plate. "A pink rose with pretty green leaves."

"Pretty leaves, yes." I smiled at Gina. "All right, the leaves. I get it now."

"Better believe it," my mother said.

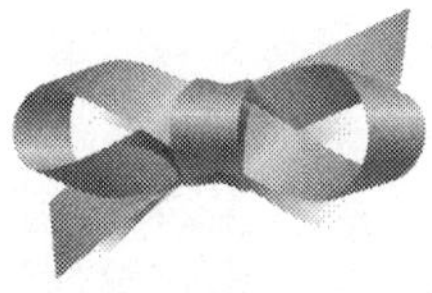

Chapter 32

By the following Saturday—almost ten days since my mother had passed—I still hadn't cried. It didn't happen until I was in the checkout line at Target and sensed a hand on my back.

I'd woken up early and had had the whole morning to myself since Ethan was at Mark's and my dad was at a client's. I didn't feel like going to the gym, so I went to Target to buy athletic gear to wear everywhere but the gym.

After an hour and a half of meditative strolling through the aisles, I had picked up one pair of Lycra pants, multivitamins, and breadcrumbs. I was going to make chicken cutlets. Even though our house was still filled with gift baskets with crackers, cookies, apples, and pears, we still had to eat regular food. And my father, our usual chef, hadn't been feeling up to cooking. I would try to fill the void.

I finally got in line to check out when I found myself swaying back and forth. It's a motherhood habit. Even when I wasn't holding my child, I swayed. I caught myself this time and wondered when I would break the habit. That was when I felt the hand on me, the long nails, the pat at the top of my back, by my neck. *Ma?* I jerked around.

"Sorry, dear. Your tag was sticking out, and I tucked it." The woman was in her sixties, with coiffed, dyed hair and long, fake red fingernails. "I don't know why I did that. I'm not a crazy person. I usually keep my hands to myself."

"Oh." I reached for the back of my shirt. "It's okay. Thank you." I turned back. I didn't know how long we stood there before the tears came. It couldn't have been more than a few seconds.

I didn't cry when the doctor said they'd tried everything. Or when my dad broke down when we first saw her in the coffin. Or when Orly, or Ethan, or Aunt Fran cried.

Did I really think that was my mother behind me? For a split second, maybe I did, even though my mother hadn't been the tender kind. She hadn't been the kind to give an extra pat after tucking in my tag. She would have given a hard pat and said, "How long were ya walking around like that? Like a ragamuffin." Still, for some reason, for one second, while wide-awake in the middle of Target, I was fooled into believing it was her, that she was still there, and that for some reason, she was tender now.

And then I was crushed when I came back to reality. And that was what it took to make me cry—one second and one stranger. I reached for tissues in my bag, but I was fresh out. *Friggin' figures.* I wiped my face with the back of my hand.

"Are you okay?" the lady asked.

"Yeah," I croaked out.

"I don't know what's gotten into me today. I usually mind my own business," she said.

"It's okay. My mom died ten days ago, and..." I couldn't finish the rest of the sentence.

"Oh, dear," she said as she pulled me into a hug.

That was when I really lost it. I cried into this woman's navy-blue blouse. When I lifted my head, I was speechless. "I am so sorry. Oh my God. I am so sorry." I waved my hand over her now soaking shoulder like I had an invisible blow dryer in my hand.

"I have to go to the cleaners today anyway," she said.

"Let me pay for it."

"Don't be silly. I am so sorry about your mother, dear."

A roll of paper towels seemed to fall from the sky onto the conveyer belt. I glanced behind me and saw a smiling cashier.

I thanked her, and as I wiped my face, I noticed the paper towels had leaves on them. *Could it be? Maybe?* I paid for my items, apologized to the lady behind me again, thanked the cashier, and bolted.

I got in the car and rolled down the windows to let the fall air cool my red face all the way home.

• • ❧ • •

THE NEXT DAY, CHARLIE and I took Ethan to the movies. We saw a matinee of an animated film starring dancing vegetables.

"Did you like it?" Charlie asked as we held each of Ethan's hands while leaving the movie.

"Yeah." Ethan said.

"I liked the broccoli that slipped on a turnip during the tango," Charlie said. "He was funny."

"Yeah," Ethan agreed. "I liked the broccoli."

"What about the carrot who uncovered the biased judges in the dance competition? She was my favorite," I added.

"No. I liked the broccoli," Ethan repeated.

After going for ice cream, we headed back to my parents' house. I found myself concerned about leaving my father alone. *Is he lonely?*

I'd asked earlier if he wanted to go to the movies with us.

"A movie about vegetables? Nah. I have my own vegetables. I still have zucchini from the farmer's market I have to fry up."

"Okay. What else are you going to do besides fry zucchini?"

"Don't worry about me, Jada. I have things to do around the house. I have work to do."

"You have pipes to inspect?"

"I have pipes to inspect. Yes. Go."

As we pulled up, I noticed the front lawn was strewn with leaves.

"Uh-oh," Charlie said. "Meyerson strikes again?"

"Looks like it." *I wonder if my mother has forgiven the Meyersons now that she's on the other side.*

"I like leaves," Ethan declared. "I want to play with them."

"No, Ethan. They're dirty."

"We'll wash them," he said.

Charlie parked the car, and I got Ethan out. As soon as he was free, he ran to the leaves. He jumped in them, threw them, and made angels in them like they were snow. Soon, Charlie followed suit, picking them up and throwing them.

There was a time when I would have gone over to the Meyersons' with a bag of leaves and dumped them on their lawn. That seemed like an unnecessary use of my energy now. I walked over to Ethan and Charlie. I kicked some leaves, threw some up in the air, and even lay down in them.

I looked up at the clear fall sky and thought, "Thank you." Something told me they could read my heart.

Acknowledgements

To Howie, as I stated on this page in my first book, to put it simply, thank you, my muse, my love, my everything.

To my mother, this one is for you. Thank you for always encouraging me to go for it, whatever it was, and believing I could get it. And thank you for being nothing like Jada's mother.

To my family, immediate and extended, blood-related and through marriage, and those not technically related but I still call my aunts, uncles and cousins, and my friends, too, especially GJ, thank you for rooting for me like you do. You are the best cheerleaders.

To everyone at Red Adept Publishing, especially Lynn McNamee, thank you for your skill, competence, organization and support. I know that I—and my stories—could not be in better hands. To Alyssa Hall, the best editor in the world, I am so grateful I won the lottery and was able to work with you twice. To Streetlight Graphics, thank you for another beautiful cover.

To Sarah Kovan, thank you for the most perfect hashtag.

To the person reading this right now, I am so grateful that you picked up this book, and I hope you enjoyed it. If you have a personal story about receiving signs from the other side, please feel free to reach out to me on social media. I am always open to discovering new stories, and I love hearing from readers.

Also by Fern Ronay

Better Believe It

Watch for more at https://fernronay.com/.

About the Author

Fern Ronay was born and raised in Belleville, New Jersey. She is a lawyer and CPA as well as a writer, reporter, and blogger. After six years in Manhattan and six years in Chicago, she now lives in sunny Los Angeles with her husband.

In addition to writing novels, Fern authors the blog *Stop and Blog the Roses* and is a co-host on AfterBuzzTV. When she is not writing, reporting, or blogging, Fern can be found eating something, reading something, or running.

Read more at https://fernronay.com/.

About the Publisher

Dear Reader,

We hope you enjoyed this book. Please consider leaving a review on your favorite book site.

Visit https://RedAdeptPublishing.com to see our entire catalogue.

Don't forget to subscribe to our monthly newsletter to be notified of future releases and special sales.

Made in the USA
San Bernardino, CA
18 January 2020